Manchester Eng Chetham Society

Remains Historical and Literary Connected with the Palatine Counties of Lancaster and Chester

Vol. 64 Part 2

SALZWASSER
VERLAG

Manchester Eng Chetham Society

Remains Historical and Literary Connected with the Palatine Counties of Lancaster and Chester

Vol. 64 Part 2

Reprint of the original, first published in 1865.

1st Edition 2022 | ISBN: 978-3-75258-945-0

Verlag (Publisher): Salzwasser Verlag GmbH, Zeilweg 44, 60439 Frankfurt, Deutschland
Vertretungsberechtigt (Authorized to represent): E. Roepke, Zeilweg 44, 60439 Frankfurt, Deutschland
Druck (Print): Books on Demand GmbH, In de Tarpen 42, 22848 Norderstedt, Deutschland

REMAINS

HISTORICAL & LITERARY

CONNECTED WITH THE PALATINE COUNTIES OF

LANCASTER AND CHESTER.

PUBLISHED BY

THE CHETHAM SOCIETY.

VOL. LXIV.

M.DCCC.LXV.

PREFACE TO PART II.

In concluding this Work, which has extended beyond the limits I had originally proposed, I may venture to express a hope that the notes and extracts which I have added to diversify the monotony of a long enumeration of Tracts may not be found uninteresting, and, still more, that nothing may have crept in, through any inadvertence of mine, which is calculated to give reasonable cause of offence to any reader, whatever his faith may be. My object has been, in addition to what bibliographical information I was able to collect, to afford the best references in my power on the various subjects treated of in this series of Tracts, and to exhibit as shortly as was consistent with clearness, and generally in their own words, the conclusions and opinions of the ablest and best informed writers on the main points, and particularly those of an historical nature, which were mooted in the memorable controversy in the reign of King James the Second.

It will be seen that chapters xl. and xli., containing the lists of the controversialists on both sides, have been much enlarged. Instead of a biography of each author, which the remaining space did not allow, I have given references, as far as practicable, to the single lives or collections in which an account of the particular writer may be found. I have also supplied a tabular index to the Tracts in the two editions of Gibson's *Preservative*, which will, I think, facilitate the search of those who consult it in connection with the present publication.

Dodd's *Certamen Utriusque Ecclesiæ*, first printed in 1724, 4to, is a brief but useful list, compiled by the Roman Catholic historian, whose real name was Hugh Tootle, of the authors on both sides, with the principal work of each, from the period of the Reformation to the end of the reign of James the Second. It is very scarce, and has sold, when it has occurred, at a high price, and has not been reprinted except in Sir Walter Scott's edition of the *Somers' Tracts* (vol. xiii.). Through the kindness and liberality of LEWIS LOYD, Esq., to whom I made known my desire to add this Tract to my concluding volume, and who has favoured the CHETHAM SOCIETY with a donation of ten pounds for that purpose, I am enabled to accomplish this object. The reprint will be found as nearly a facsimile as possible. The short historical sketch at the bottom of each page it was considered unadvisable to omit, but I scarcely need say that it will hardly be accepted as a correct or impartial summary of the portion of English history to which it refers.

Dr. TODD, my learned coadjutor in the first Part, was, unfortunately, too much engaged in various literary publications to afford me the same co-operation as that he had so kindly supplied in the preceding pages. Another contributor however, whose valuable aid has already been acknowledged, has continued to take the same unremitting interest in the publication; and these sheets, as they have gone through the press, have been submitted to his critical revision. The PRESIDENT of the CHETHAM SOCIETY is the friend here referred to, who has assisted me with his advice and varied information, and whose literary attainments are too well known for me to dilate upon. I have also, in this second part, pointed out my obligations to some other correspondents for useful information and suggestions, for which I feel it a pleasurable duty to return to them, severally, sincere thanks.

T. J.

CONTENTS OF PART II.

DODD'S *CERTAMEN UTRIUSQUE ECCLESIÆ.*

A

CATALOGUE OF THE DISCOURSES

WRITTEN

For *and* Against *Popery in the time of* James II.

PART II.

CHAP. XIX.

Of the Discourses written of St. Peter and the Pope's supremacy.

223. ✠ A Sermon of St. Peter, preach'd before Her Majesty the Queen Dowager in her chapel at Somerset House, on the twenty-ninth of June, 1686, being St. Peter and St. Paul's Day. By Thomas Godden, D.D., Preacher in Ordinary to Her Majesty.* Published by Her Majestie's command. C. L.
pp. 42, 4to Lond. (Henry Hills) 1686

See [State, p. 26] Contin. p. 31, where the author, Abp. Wake, says: "Dr. Godden began the contest as to this matter." For an account of Godden, see No. 85, p. 126, in part i. and a note to the Life of Bp. Patrick in the Biogr. Brit. For the arguments in favour of St. Peter's residence at Rome, consult Card. Perron, book ii. chap. iv.; and for those against it, Spanheim de ficta Profectione Apostoli in urbem Romam. Opp. ii. pp. 331-388.

224. A Sermon preached upon St. Peter's Day, 1686. Printed at the desire of some that heard it, with some enlargements. By a Divine of the Church of England [Simon Patrick, D.D.] Anon. pp. 73, 4to Lond. (R. Chiswell) 1687

See [State, p. 20, Contin. p. 32] Cat. No. 126.

"I will not say any thing more of these two discourses than this, That whoso please to read them, will find what is to be urged from that famous text, Thou art Peter, &c., on either side; and when they compare them together, may judge as they shall find the evidence of Truth to incline them." (Wake.) This tract is in the Author's Works, vol. vi. 609-58, edited by the Rev. Alexander Taylor, M.A., Oxford 1858. See also by the same, Nos. 377, 378.

The various interpretations which have been given to the term Rock, *Πέτρα*, by the primitive Fathers, who in this as in other matters were very variable, some of them assigning two meanings in their works — (but in this sermon, p. 36, Patrick maintains that the ancient Doctors used only a diversity of speech, not of opinion; see also Burnet's Exposition of the XXXIX Articles, Art. XIX) — will be found, together with references to authorities, in Gieseler's Ecclesiastical History, vol. i. pp. 265, 441, and vol. iii. p. 159 (where are also exhibited the interpolations introduced by the champions of the Apostolic Throne; cf. James's Treatise on Corruption of Scripture, &c., 1688, p. 113, Bp. Bedell's Letter to Waddesworth, ch. vi., Taylor's Liberty of Prophecying, Eden's edit., vol. viii. p. 6); and in Palmer on the Church, vol. ii. pp. 484, 5. The inconsistency above referred to, originating in that economy of speech with which the Fathers, *ἀλλοπρόσαλλοι* monitu temporis, accommodated their addresses to the present audience, afforded a dangerous example, inasmuch as it terminated in equivocations and mental reservations. *Decipit exemplar vitiis imitabile.* Hor. i. ep. xix. v. 17.

C. L. 225. The Catholic Balance: or a Discourse determining the Controversies concerning I. The tradition of Catholic Doctrines; II. The primacy of St. Peter and the Bishop of Rome; III. The subjection and authority of the Church in a Christian state, according to the suffrages of the primest antiquity. Written with most impartial sincerity at the request of a private gentleman [by Samuel Hill, Rector of Killmington in Somersetshire and Archdeacon of Wells].

pp. 136, pref. v. 4to Lond. 1687

See Cat. No. 127; Contin. p. 32; Ath. Oxon., vol. ii. col. 1000.

The list of Hill's publications, as given by Wood, is imperfect. The Bodleian Library Catalogue gives an extended list. Of one of them, A Vindication of the primitive Fathers against Burnet, 1695, 8vo, Mr. Crossley has a long MS. Defence prepared for the press by Hill, but never published, with a copy of the Vindication, revised for a second edition, with considerable additions. He zealously defended the Fathers; see Allix's Animadversions on Mr. Hill's Vindication of the primitive Fathers against the Right Reverend Gilbert Burnet, Bishop of Sarum.

In the second article he explains the passage in Irenæus, upon which the Romanists very much build their appeals. The following is extracted from the Memoirs of Scipio de Ricci, Bishop of Prato and Pistoia, Reformer of Catholicism in Tuscany under the reign of Leopold, translated and edited by Thomas Roscoe, 1829. The passage which occurs in a memorial drawn up by Ricci, and read in the Assembly of Florence, is here inserted as a *summary of the article:* "During the first ages of the Church no instance occurs of any general and perpetual reservation by the councils in favour of the Pope, nor of any limitation of the power of the Bishops prescribed by the Popes themselves. What now remains of the applications which were made to Rome at that time are, in fact, any thing but reservations or limitations. The practice of the Church then was to communicate to the See of Rome the most difficult and important cases which occurred: to inform her of the fortunate or unfortunate state of the Churches which were spread abroad in different parts of the world, and to request her to interest herself in regard to them. The Church of Rome communicated in the same manner her affairs to the other Churches, particularly to those which were most celebrated and most respectable...... The communications to the Church of Rome were naturally of more frequent occurrence than to any other, from its being, without exception, the most important and respectable. That circumstance, however, does not by any means prove a right of reservation on her part, which in fact is contradicted by what actually took place on such occasions; the most authentic of the ancient decretals being only simple advices or exhortations." (Vol. i. p. 229.)

In the conclusion of the Catholic Balance, Hill lays down rules by which the liberty and rights of both the spiritual and secular state may be determined so that neither *exorbitate.* Compare his Municipium

Ecclesiasticum in answer to Dr. Wake on Ecclesiastical Synods, 1697, and The Rights and Liberties of the Christian Church asserted with a Justification of Municipium Ecclesiasticum, Lond. 1701; and A Thorough Examination of the false Principles and fallacious Arguments against the Christian Priesthood and Religion in a late pernicious Book ironically entitled The Rights of the Christian Church, 8vo, Lond. 1708. See Swift's Works, edited by Scott, vol. viii. p. 108 sqq. and 168. "Dr. William Wotton . . . . Samuel Hill, Conyers-Place, and finally Mr. Oldisworth, entered also into the controversy, which was maintained with equal zeal on both sides, until it was swallowed up in the more furious and universal disputes occasioned by Sacheverell's sermon. Among these [champions in defence of the establishment] the most remarkable was the learned Dr. Hicks of Oxford, who published two treatises, Of the Dignity of the Christian Priesthood, and Of the Dignity of the Episcopal Order, and several other pieces in answer to Tindal's Rights of the Christian Church." The fourth edition (in Library of Anglo-Catholic Theology) contains very copious notes by the Editor and includes the Supplement of 1715, copies of which are very rare. See also Spinosa Revived with a Preliminary Discourse by Dr. George Hickes, Lond. 1709, and his posthumous publication on the Constitution of the Catholic Church and the nature and consequences of Schism, 1716, which was the immediate occasion of Hoadley's Preservative against the Principles and Practices of the Nonjurors being written.

En passant, I may remark that a full account of the *Bangorian Controversy*, so called from Dr. Hoadly, who, when Bishop of Bangor, published a Sermon upon these words, My kingdom is not of this world, 1717, has yet to be written. Refer to Hoadly's Works, vol. iii. pp. 379-401, and vol. i. p 689; his Life prefixed to his Works, from the Supplement to the Biogr. Brit. with large additions; Tindal's Contin. vol. v. p 536, 8vo edit. xix. 133 sqq.; Oldmixon's History of England, vol. i. p. 651; A Review of the most considerable Writers in the great Controversy with the Bishop of Bangor, by Dean Pratt, 8vo, Lond. 1719; Cardwell's Synodalia, vol. ii. p. 832. "Both the Preservative and Sermon were censured, as tending I. To subvert all government and discipline in the Church of Christ, and to reduce his kingdom to a state of anarchy and confusion; and II. To impugn and impeach the regal supremacy in causes ecclesiastical, and the authority of the legislature to inforce obedience in matters of religion by civil sanctions. . . . . . The tracts published on this occasion, on both sides, are said to be about seventy." (Tindal.) Pamphlets included, I find them to amount to one hundred and fifty-six. The account given in Hoadly's Works is a reprint of that published by Heron, of Merton College, Oxford 1716. The most distinguished members of Convocation and adversaries of Hoadly were Dr. Snape, Dr. Sherlock, Dr. Cannon, Dr. Hare, Dr. Potter, Dr. Wake and Dr. Stebbing. Among the opponents of the Nonjurors were Bp. Kennet and Bp. Fleetwood.

To return to Samuel Hill, and the *Catholic Balance.* Compare A Journey into the Country; being a Dialogue between an English Protestant Physitian and an English Papist, wherein the proper state of the Popish controversy is discoursed. With reference (only) to the Government of England in Church and State. In some answer to Peter Walsh, and pursuant to the Directions of a Person of honor. Lond. 1675. "Peaceable Mr. Walsh" in the fifteenth and sixteenth of the Controversial Letters, 1679, replies to Bellarmine "concerning the pretended Temporal Authority of Popes over the whole Earth, and the True Sovereign of Kings within their own respective Kingdoms;" and refutes the 28th and 29th chapter of his first Book de Clericis (Opp. 1620, vol. i. t. ii. pp. 323-332), in which a distinction is made between directive and coactive obligation. "The truth is, 'tis all contradiction from first to last. [That] Secular princes are not lawful superiors, and yet kings of the clergy, is contradiction: [that] they have kingly, that is, supreme power, and yet the ecclesiastical is to be obeyed in case of contrary commands, is contradiction: [that] they are kings in respect of those who are not subjects, nor formally parts of the commonwealth, is contradiction," &c., p. 56. The Roman Catholic doctors Bellarmine, Suarez, Gotti, &c. distinguish the human right of the civil power from the divine right of the ecclesiastical, and declare that as God conferred power directly upon Moses over the Jews, and upon those who sat in Moses' chair, so Christ has conferred it upon the supreme Pontiff over the whole Church. The Christian fathers entertained widely different sentiments, as may be seen in the 33rd and 34th chapters of Tertullian's Apology; cf. Reeves's Note, and Bellarmine's Responsio ad cap. iv. Optatus Milevitanus (quoted by Goodman in his Sermon on Matt. xvi. 18, 1677) writes: "Respublica non est in Ecclesia, sed Ecclesia in Republica." (Opp. 1700, lib. iii. 52.)

The character of Donatus drawn by this writer, who lived in the fourth century, is to the life a description of the Pope and Popery. "Extulit cor suum, ut nullum hominem sibi comparandum arbitraretur; et tumore mentis suæ altior sibi visus est esse; quia quidquid est supra homines, jam quasi Deus est. Deinde cum episcopi Deo debeant famulari, tantum sibi de episcopis suis exegit, ut eum non minori metu omnes venerarentur, quam Deum: hoc est, quod sibi Deus visus est . . . . . . Deinde cum ante ipsius superbiam omnes qui in Christo crediderant, Christiani vocarentur, ausus est populum cum Deo dividere; ut qui illum secuti sunt, jam non Christiani vocarentur, sed Donatistæ." This Donatus was Bishop of Carthage. Walsh undertakes to produce authority of a higher form than that of Bellarmine, beginning with St. Paul, Rom. xiii., "Let every soul be subject to the higher powers," and subjoining the interpretations of Theodoret, Theophylact and St. Chrysostom. He then cites Popes themselves acknowledging their submission to emperors; Gelasius to the emperor Anastasius; Anastasius to the same emperor; Pelagius to Childebert, king of France. "St. Gregory the Great speaks with a submission which offends Baronius, and makes him strain his wits to find a scurvy way to colour the business. But no varnish will ly. That he was subject to the emperour's command; that he did what he ought in obeying the emperour on the one side, and speaking for God on the other; that power from heaven is given to the piety of his lords, as he calls emperours, over all men, over priests as well as soldiers, &c., have a blunt ill-natur'd clearness, which no art can practice upon." (pp. 53-4.) Of Anastasius II. Milman observes: "How deep and lasting was the tradition of detestation against this meek renegade to papal authority, may be supposed by its survival for at least nine centuries. Dante beholds in hell the unhappy Anastasius condemned for ever for his leniency to the heresy of Constantinople." His Epistolæ will be found in Labbe, vol. iv. 1275-83. "The letter of Gelasius to Euphemius of Constantinople is a model of that haughty humility which became the ordinary language of the Roman Bishops. In his letter to the emperor Anastasius he asserts boldly for the first time, in these strong and discriminating terms, the supremacy of the clergy in all religious matters. 'There are two powers which rule the world, the imperial and the pontifical. You are the sovereign of the human race, but you bow your neck to those who preside over things divine. The priesthood is the greater of the two powers: it has to render an account in the last day for the acts of kings.'" (Milman.) His Epistolæ et Decreta will be found in Labbe, vol. iv. 1054-1260.

"Is it possible that Bellarmine should in earnest persuade himself the Apostles meant only in general, that every one should obey whom he ought to obey, the laity their secular, the clergy their ecclesiastical superiour? Are not the superiours, or higher powers, whom all are commanded to obey, expressly named by St. Peter, kings and dukes, or governours, sent to punish evil doers; and by St. Paul, magistrates who bear the sword? Can he think this command is comply'd with by obedience to ecclesiastical superiors? Are they kings? Do they bear the sword? Are they the ministers of God to wrath and vengeance? What better proof would he have that kings are lawful superiours even of the clergy, than St. Paul gives, viz., that their powers are ordained by God, whom to resist is to acquire damnation?" Walsh, Controversial Letters, p. 54; also Historia Operis a Reginaldo Polo adversus Henr. VIII. in Schelhorn. Amoen. Eccl. i. 83, &c.; Abbot de Suprema Potestate Regia contra R. Bellarmine et F. Suarez, 4to, 1619; Andrewes, Responsio &c., 1610; Cardwell's Synodalia; Gen. Dict. art. Hayward; Coleridge on the Constitution of the Church and State according to the idea of each; Hey's Lectures (on the 37th Article).

"On the other hand as sovereign princes cannot prescribe what laws they please, contrary to the laws of nature and of God, so they can not impose what religion they please, contrary to what He has enjoined." Lord Clarendon on Religion and Polity; cf. Comber's Discourse of Excommunication; Leslie's Case of the Regale; Beveridge on the Articles (37th), and his Thesaurus Theologicus (Works x. 547-54); Thorndike on the right of the Church in a Christian State, ch. iv. "Bishop Warburton says, that no particular scheme or mode of religion is under the care of the magistrate, till he has compacted for the purpose. Alliance, p. 41. Certainly no form of establishment is properly within his province till adopted by the state. The state is bounden by obligations to God to accept of that form which it conceives to be most consistent with the promotion of truth, and the maintenance of religion; but the civil magistrate can have no arbitrary right to impose his own system. Charles the First could not have been blamed for proposing and recommending the establishment of episcopacy to Scotland, if he had confined himself to the experiment of its being approved by the nation. He offended as much against religion as policy, when he persisted in his endeavours to establish it in opposition to the determined sentiments of his subjects in that country. However the sovereign may hesitate at accepting the guardianship of a system which he individually disapproves, he certainly must maintain a delegated trust upon the principles to which he is pledged; a rule by departure from which James the Second justly lost his kingdom, and by the observance of which the king of England governs Scotland and Canada." Grey's Bampton Lectures, 1796, p. 96. On the violation of trust, or of the *Coronation Oath* here referred to, see A Letter of several French Ministers, &c., *ut supra* (part i. p. 101); Blackstone's Commentaries, ch. vi. and the authorities cited in Amos's edit. of Fortescue de Laudibus Legum Angliæ, p. 126.

> "Let not your King and Parliament in one,
> Much less apart, mistake themselves for that
> Which is most worthy to be thought upon,
> Nor think they are essentially the State:
> Let them not fancy that th' authority
> And privileges upon them bestown,
> Conferr'd are to set up a majesty,
> A power or a glory of their own!
> But let them know 'twas for a deeper life
> Which they but represent —
> That there's on earth a yet auguster thing,
> Veil'd tho' it be, than Parliament and King."

This passage is from George Wither's Vox Pacifica, and is quoted by Coleridge in his treatise on the Constitution of Church and State, who remarks: "The reader will be pleased to observe that in the passage here cited, the 'State' is used in the largest sense, and as synonymous with the realm, or entire body politic, including Church and State in the narrower and special sense of the latter term." (Ch. xi.) See also, Some Observations upon the Ecclesiastical Jurisdiction of the Kings of England, with an Appendix in answer to a late Book intitled, The King's Visitatorial Power asserted (see part i. p. 87), 8vo, Lond. 1689; The Constitution of the Catholic Church and the nature and consequences of Schism, by Geo. Hickes, D.D., 1716; The Life of Abp. Sharp, to which are added select original Papers in three Appendixes, Lond. 1825; Appendix Second,

No. xiv. In order to ascertain what the conditions were on which conscientious men among our predecessors consented to parliamentary interference in matters spiritual, consult the 8th book of Hooker's Ecclesiastical Polity, cf. 35 Eliz. A.D. 1592, and Gibson's Summary of Temporal Laws against Separation (Codex Juris Ecclesiastici Anglicani, vol. i. p. 492); The History of the Troubles and Tryal of Abp. Laud, p. 301 sqq.; "Our State has no right to make the King Archbishop of Canterbury; or to change the Doctrines; it might ally itself to a new Church;" Hey's Lectures, book iii. ch. xiv. sqq.; Bramhall's Works, 1845, see General Index, s. v. Kings of England; and Bishop Sanderson, Episcopacy not prejudicial to Regal Power, Works, vol. i. Oxford 1854.

226. A modest Enquiry whether St. Peter were ever at Rome and Bishop of that church. Wherein I. The argument of Cardinal Bellarmine and others for the affirmative are considered. II. Some considerations taken notice of that render the negative highly probable. [By Henry Care.] C. L.

pp. 116, 4to. Lond. 1687

See Cat. No. 33, Contin. p. 32 [and p. 76, part i.] An abstract of this tract is given by the author himself in his *Weekly Pacquets of Advice from Rome*. See Notes and Queries, 1st ser. vol. iii. p. 264.

Cf. Tho. Ittigii Animadversiones ad Censuram Facultatis Theologicæ Parisiensis latam in Sorbona A. 1683 de Propositione: Ad solam sedem Apostolicam divino immutabili privilegio spectat de controversiis fidei judicare. Intelligitur autem sedis Apostolicæ nomine non alia quam Romana, cui qui præsidet Episcopus se Petri in cathedra Romana successorem gloriatur. At Petrum Romæ unquam fuisse multi sunt qui cum Ulrico Veleno negent non modo ex Lutheranis et Calvinianis, verum etiam ex ipsis Pontificiis, e quibus jam nominasse sufficiat Aventinum et Marsilium Patavinum, qui in Defensione Pacis Petrum Romæ, nedum ejus urbis episcopum fuisse e S. Scriptura probari posse negat, et contrarium potius e sacris literis demonstrari posse satis aperte judicat, quamvis eum Chr. Lupus non aperte sententiam dixisse, sed sputa et lapides a fideli populo timentem tantum mussitasse referat. pag. B. The treatise of Velenus in which he endeavours to prove that St. Peter never was at Rome will be found in Goldastus de

Monarchia S. R. Imperii. See a most interesting analysis of the famous work of Marsilio of Padua in Milman's L. C. v. 297-99. "The Bishop of Rome can in no sense be called the successor of St. Peter, first, because no apostle was appointed by the divine law over any peculiar people or land; secondly, because he was at Antioch before Rome. Paul, it is known, was at Rome two years. He, if any one, having taught the Romans, was Bishop of Rome: it cannot be shown from the Scriptures that St. Peter was Bishop of Rome, or that he was ever at Rome. It is incredible that if he were at Rome before St. Paul, he should not be mentioned either by St. Paul or by St. Luke in the Acts. It is curious to find this argument so well put in the fourteenth century." I here subjoin an account of the work above referred to, which was written by the late Dr. Bliss and inserted in his copy of the book.

"*Pacquets of Advice from Rome.* Care's portion. The most perfect copy of this curious Periodical I have yet seen is that in the hands of Mr. Godwin. It contains volumes 1, 2, 3 and 4, corresponding exactly with those in my set. *Volume* 5, *Number* 1, *Friday Aug. 25th,* 1682. *The Introduction and scope of this Fifth Volume. The means of facilitating the Reformation. 'Tis now almost Four years since I have labour'd in this poor work. Lond. Printed by A. Maxwell for the Author,* 1682. So the work continues to No. 11, November 3, when it was printed for the assigns of the author Henry Care, and may be had at his House in the Great Old Bailey, 1682. No. 13, November 17, is simply printed for the Author Henry Care in the Great Old Bailey, 1682-4. No. 14, November 24, is printed by J. Astwood, for the Author Henry Care in the Great Old Bailey, 1682. It so continues to No. 47, July 13, 1683, pp. 376, which is Care's last number; this was printed by J. Astwood, for H. Care, and entered according to order. At this time Care fell sick, after which he wrote no more, although he lived till August 8th 1688, when he died.

"The following from Mr. Godwin's copy. 'His character: He was a person of a good literature, slow in speech, but of a quick and satyricall pen. Whatever was written by him was thought considerable for the advantage of his party: and whomsoever he attackt he was sure to vex, and worry as bad as the Tartars do the Poles. In a word, he lived and died both loved and hated.'

"*Pacquets of Advice from Rome.* Salmon's, vol. v. In 1682 a difference took place between Care and Langley Curtis, the original publisher, when Care, as we have seen, continued his work on his own account, till he was taken ill in 1683. But at the commencement of the quarrel, Curtis, not willing to give up a profitable speculation, employed W. Salmon, a well known and multifarious writer, to publish a continuation of the Pacquets, which he did from Friday August 25, 1682, to Friday May 4, 1683, which professes to be the fifth volume of the original work, and ends on p. 296. To this is prefixed a general title, a preface and an index, in all two sheets. Langley Curtis, probably having the stock in trade in his own hands, added his own fifth volume to all the remaining copies, and accordingly Care's fifth volume is rarely met with."

227. Sure and honest means for the conversion of all heretics: and wholesome advice and expedients for the reformation of the Church. Writ by one of the Communion of the Church of Rome, and translated from the French printed at Cologn. [With a Preface (anon.) by William Wake, M.A. Pref. pp. viii. Author's Pref. xiv]. pp. 120, 4to Lond. 1688 C. L.

See Cat. No. 129; Contin. p. 33; Ath. Oxon., vol. ii. col. 1060.

"I should think," writes Dr. Fisher (Notes and Queries, 3rd ser. vol iii. p. 396), "the following work to be found in Barbier (vol. ii. p. 430) is that which Archbishop Wake translated: 12,224. Moyens (les) justes et efficaces pour ramener dans le Sein de l'Eglise Catholique ceux qui en sont séparez [par Vigne, Ministre de Grenoble, devenu ensuite Catholique]. Cologne, P. Martean, 1684, 12mo." The project of the French author, who was truly a member of the Church of Rome, however dissatisfied with it in many of its pretences, will be found in p. ii. of the translator's preface. The translation of this tract probably emanated from the archbishop's desire to unite the two Churches of England and France. See Mosheim's History, App. iii. [Maclaine's Translation], the Biogr. Britann. art. (Wake.) Cf. the conclusion of Bramhall's Just Vindication of the Church of England, "How far the Protestant and Roman Churches are reconcileable;" and A Paper concerning the differences concerning the chief Points of Religion &c. by Dr. John Cosins, in the Appendix to Hickes's Several Letters.

The author denounces the pretension of the Papacy to temporal power and sovereignty directly, or as the pretended consequence of spiritual dominion, p. 48; and, as furnishing occasion to this, even the retention of the primacy in honour over all other bishops, after Rome had ceased to be the metropolis of Christendom, is noticed as a subject of regret, p. 46. 2. The boast of papal infallibility, p. 4. 3. The derivation of the Episcopal power from the Papal, and the dependence of Bishops on the Pope, p. 27. 4. The right of exercising authority in other dioceses besides that of Rome, p. 29. 5. The privilege of receiving appeals; with the power of subjecting all churches in all parts to the ecclesiastical discipline of the Church of Rome, pp. 31, 32. 6. The Pope's pretended superiority to an Ecumenical Council, p. 30.

Wake, in his Discourse on the Holy Eucharist, mentions, among those who disbelieved Transubstantiation, the author of *Moyens surs et honnêtes*, "whom we dare not affirm to be the same who published a treatise of Transubstantiation, which the fifth tome of the French Bibliothèque speaks of, p. 455." (*The Young Student's Library*, p. 134.)

C. L. 228. Dialogues between Philerene and Philalethe, a lover of peace and a lover of truth concerning the Pope's supremacy. [Part I.] Pref. pp. ii. 40, 4to Lond. 1688

See Cat. No. 130; Contin. p. 33. [Dr. Gee, Cat. No. 130, says that this tract is "published by Ignotus," meaning, I suppose, that he did not know who published it. J. H. T.]

"Dato sed non concesso that St. Peter had a Primacy of Jurisdiction over all the general members of the Catholick Church; wherefore might not this have been a personal privilege and intransmissible to any successor, no less than the Gradus Mosaicus was to any other prophet?" Gourdon, (No. 241.)

C. L. 229. ✠ St. Peter's supremacy faithfully discuss'd according to Holy Scripture, and Greek and Latin Fathers. With a detection and confutation of the errors of Protestant Writers on this article. Together with a succinct handling of several other considerable points. [By Will. Clenche.] 4to Lond. 1686

[La Lettera Dedicatoria to Maria d'Este, Reina d'Inghilterra, in Italian, to which the author signs his name, p. xiii. Advertisement &c. and Contents, Pref. pp. viii., 203.] See Contin. p. 33. Macaulay has given a specimen of his style in Italian and English, vol. ii. p. 110.

230. A discourse of the Pope's Supremacy, Part I. An Answer to a treatise intituled, St. Peter's Supremacy faithfully discuss'd, according to Holy Scripture, and Greek and Latin Fathers. And to a Sermon of S. Peter, preached before her Majesty the Queen Dowager, on St. Peter and St. Paul's Day, by Thomas Godden, D.D. [By Nicholas Stratford, DD. pp. 126; Contents, pp. 2.] 4to Lond. 1688 C. L.

See No. 239 *infra;* Cat. No. 131; Contin. pp. 33, 34; Ath. Oxon. col. 1067. See No. 70 *supra*, and Worthington's Diary, vol. ii. p. 243. Our author notices also The Pope's Supremacy asserted, *ut infra*, No. 238.

"Three only but wretchedly abused Texts of the Gospel, viz. Ecce duo gladii, Luc. xxii. 38, and Quodcunque ligaveris &c. Math. xvi. 19, and Pasce oves meas, Joan. xxi. 17, must serve the turn, however, against the plain design of the whole Gospel itself, to drive directly by such positions at the proper scope of the Alcoran, and establish in the Church of Christ a worser tyranny than that of Mahometans and Mamelukes." Father Peter Walsh's History and Vindication of the Irish Remonstrance, p. ix. In the fourteenth century "the Bull *Unam sanctam* deliberately and fully defined the powers assumed by the Pope. It asserted the eternal unity of the Catholic Church under St. Peter and his successors. . . . . There are two swords, the spiritual and the temporal: our Lord said not of these two swords "it is too much," but "it is enough." Both are in the power of the Church; the one the spiritual, to be used *by* the Church, the other the material, *for* the Church. . . . . . . The spiritual instituted the temporal power, and judges whether that power is well exercised." Milman vol. v. p. 92. S. Bernard claims the two swords, the spiritual and the temporal for the Church (De Consideratione, lib. iv. c. iii.) and Innocent III., the persecutor of the Waldenses, very frequently avails himself of the incident here referred to in the Gospel narrative.

"And the world heard with awe this sanguine cry and impious nonsense." Milman, vol. iv. p. 119. Cf. Maimbourg, ch. xxviii.

On Math. xvi. 19, see Hammond *in loco*, Christ said to Peter (John xxi. 17), Feed my sheep, in general, not such or such a flock, from whence it has been inferred that the Pope, as successor to that Apostle, is to be acknowledged *the universal Pastor*. "Some told the Pope (Hildebrand) that the Emperor should not be so hastily anathematized; to whom he answered, Did Christ except Kings when he said to Peter, 'Feed my sheep?' When he gave him the power of binding and loosing he excepted none from his power. . . . . He that will see the many treatises that learned men then wrote for the power of Princes against the Papal tyranny and rebellion may find them in the voluminous collections of Michael Goldastus de Monarchia." Baxter's Church History, p. 353. "I have ever thought," says Coleridge, "that the derivation of the Papal monarchy from the thrice repeated command, *pasce oves*, the most brazen of all the Pope's bulls. It was because Peter had given too good proof that he was more disposed to draw the sword for Christ than to perform the humble duties of a shepherd, that our Lord here strongly though tenderly reminds him of his besetting temptation. The words are most manifestly a reproof and a warning, not a commission." Literary Remains, vol. iii. p. 266. Compare Stratford, pp. 99; Barrow on the Papal Supremacy, p. 586; Works, vol. viii. p. 151. *Monarchia Sancti Romani Imperii* is a collection of Tracts on Civil and Ecclesiastical Jurisdiction, 3 voll. fol. Hanov. et Franc. 1611–14.

C. L. 231. The necessity of Heresies asserted and explained in a Sermon ad Clerum [on 1 Cor. xi. 19], by the Author of the Catholic Balance [*ut supra* 225], and published as a consolatory letter to the Church of England in the days of her Controversie.

pp. 29, 4to Lond. 1688

For other publications by this learned and eloquent writer, Samuel Hill, besides those enumerated above, see Watt's Bibl. Britannica. On the subject of this tract compare Hooker's Ecclesiastical Polity, Book iii. § 8.

✠ Historical Collections out of several Grave Protestant Historians concerning the changes of Religion, and the strange confusions following from thence; in the reigns of King Henry the Eighth, Edward the Sixth, Queen Mary and Elizabeth. [By George Touchet.] 8vo 1674 C. L.

It is stated in the Preface that the chiefest matters of these Collections are gathered from Dr. Heylin's History of the Reformation. "Stillingfleet," observes Mendham, "in particular exposed the low political views of Heylin, which have as little to do with the substance or Christianity of the Reformation, as the shell with the kernel; indeed, hardly so much." "Whatsoever they have said, or can say, concerning Henry the Eighth, so far as it may reflect upon the Church of England, is cleared in my reply to R. C." See Bramhall's Replication to the Bishop of Chalcedon, ch. iii. sect. ii. pp. 99–101; ch. vi. sect. i. pp. 187–193. Compare Warner's Ecclesiastical History of England, vol. ii. pp. 227–32. "It can not be denied but that during the reign of that religious and godly young King (Edward VI.), without his knowledge as we verily hope and believe, or at most through the malicious suggestions and cunning insinuations of some that were about him, such sacrileges were acted, and that under the name of and pretence of Reformation as have cast a very foul blemish upon our very Religion, especially in the eyes of our adversaries, who have ever shewed themselves forward enough to impute the faults of the persons to the profession." Sanderson, *Episcopacy not Prejudicial to Regal Power*. Works, vol. v. p. 174.

The Papal Supremacy, a novel doctrine, or Considerations, &c. 1677 *ut supra*, No. IV. Reprinted in Gibson's Preservative, folio ed. vol. i. Tit. ii. p. 3. 8vo, vol. iii.

A Journey into the Country, being a Dialogue between an English Protestant Physitian and an English Papist, wherein the proper state of the Popish controversy is discoursed. With reference (only) to the Government of England. C. L.

Pref. pp. vi., 38, 4to Lond. 1675

In the first three pages and *ad finem* there is an allusion to the *Five Mile Act*. Walsh's political tracts are enumerated in part i. p. 4; to these may be added, Some few questions concerning the Oath of Allegiance propos'd by a catholic gentleman in a letter to a person of learning and honor (signed A. G.) 4to, n.p. 1661, and Lond. 1674.

A Letter to a Priest of the Roman Church, wherein the grounds of their pretended infallibility are called for and examined in some queries. 4to Lond. 1675

B. L. The Foundation of Popery shaken; or the Bishop of Rome's supremacy oppos'd in a Sermon on Matth. xvi. 18, 19. By Will. Cade. Pref. pp. iv., 31, 4to Lond. 1678

The Downfall of the pretended Divine Authoritie of the Hierarchie into the See of Rome. By V. N. N. 4to 1678

Compare the Memoirs of Scipio de Ricci, pp. 227–231. "Nothing is more common than to see absolute and unlimited power degenerating into excess and tyranny; and such was the case with the authority of the Popes. The extravagances of the despotism of the Court of Rome gave rise to murmurs and dissatisfaction. The power which they enjoyed was never a source of peace and tranquillity. The concordats of Germany and France [see Pradt, Les Quatre Concordats, 3 voll. 1818], the pragmatic sanctions [S. Ludovici, a Pinsonio], the liberties of the Gallican Church as they were called [voyez Pithoy ou Puy], are all of them to be considered as so many proofs of the opposition which was made to the attempts of the Court of Rome, and as so many bulwarks raised by the bishops and the people, with the view of preserving to themselves some portion of their primitive and indestructible rights.

"The Councils of Constance and Basle [Concil. Constant. A.D. 1415, ap. Labb. xii. pp. 19–23; Concil. Basil. A.D. 1431, *ibid.* pp. 477–8 et 619] wished to strike at the very root of the evil; that of Trent [Hist. Concil. Trident. lib. vii. et x.] attempted to restore to the bishops as much of their authority as the preponderance of the Court of Rome would admit. All these attempts have been unsuccessful; and Rome, by the creation of its numerous Congregations, has devised so many methods of multiplying its reservations, that they have become so numerous as scarcely to leave at the disposal of the bishops a shadow of the authority which originally formed an essential part of the episcopal character."

And, A Just Vindication of the Church of England from the unjust aspersion of Criminal Schism, wherein the Liberties and Privileges of National Churches, the Rights of Sovereign Magistrates, the Tyranny, Extortion and Schism of the Roman Court, with the grievances, complaints and opposition of all Princes and States of the Roman Communion of old, and at this very day are manifested to the View of the World. By Archbishop Bramhall. First printed at London in 1654, 8vo. (Works, Library of Anglo-Catholic Theology, vol. i.) See especially pp. 249, 250. John Bramhall, D.D., sometime Lord Archbishop of Armagh, Primate and Metropolitan of All Ireland, was descended from the Bramhalls of Bramhall Hall in Cheshire, related by intermarriage to the Keresfords of Keresford in Yorkshire. He supplies extracts from the tracts above referred to, *Traictez des Libertez de l'Eglise Gallicane*, commencing with a treatise of Pithou or Pithœus (for these see the Index s.v. Libertez.) For the Pragmatics of France see Encyclopædia Metropolitana, vol. xi. p. 716; for those of Spain see The Council of Trent &c., by Michael Geddes, 1714, pp. 41–43. For the History of Ecclesiastical Power during the Middle Ages, Hallam, Chap. vii.

Roma Ruit. The Pillars of Rome broken; wherein all the several pleas for the Pope's authority in England, with all the material defences of them as they have been urged by Romanists from the beginning of our Reformation to this day, are revised and answered. To which is subjoined, A Seasonable Alarm to all sorts of Englishmen against Popery, both from their oaths and their interests. By Fr. Fullwood, D.D., Archdeacon of Totnes in Devon. **C. L.**

Pref. pp. xxix., 292, 8vo Lond. 1679

See Wood's Athen. Oxon., Bliss, vol. iii. col. 299. "An eminent writer of his time." A new edition by Ch. Hardwick was published at Cambridge in 1847. "I have chosen not to dispute two great things, 1. That in the word (tu es Petrus et super hanc Petram) there is intended some respect peculiar to St. Peter's person ...... 2. That Tradition may be infallible or indefectible in the delivery of the *Essen-*

tials of Religion for aught we know. By the *Essentials* we mean no more but the Creed, the Lord's Prayer, the Decalogue and the two Sacraments. In this I have my second and my reason too; for then Rushworth's Dialogues and the new methods of Roman opposition need not trouble us." Epistle Dedicatory to Geo. [Morley] Lord Bishop of Winton. "No new opinion," says Rushworth, "can prevail in the Church of God without impeaching Tradition, the Rule of Faith; for that being once rejected, by the same right and principle they receive one errour they may admit any." Dialogues, enlarged by Tho. White, 1654, p. 166. This is admitted also by Sergeant: "Tradition is the testimony of the whole foregoing age of Christians to the next age of what had been deliver'd and explained to them . . . . hence 'tis manifest the last age of the world must have the same Faith that the first age of Christianity had." The Fourth Catholick Letter, p. 7. Cf. Part i. p. 131.

An impartial account of the Doctrines of the Church of Rome, viz. the Pope's supremacy, his infallibility, his power of indulgence, &c. pp. 17, fol. London 1679

C. 1. A Dissertation concerning the Government of the Ancient Church by Bishops, Metropolitans and Patriarchs. More particularly concerning the ancient power and jurisdiction of the Bishops of Rome, and the encroachments of that upon other Sees, especially the See of Constantinople. By William Cave. 8vo Lond. 1683

Cf. Archbishop Potter's Discourse of Church-Government, ch. iv. 1707, p. 205 sqq.; edited by Crosthwaite, 1839, p. 138. The jurisdiction of bishops was gradually more and more weakened till at length it was merged in the Papacy, and instead of a union of bishops (Barrow cites from Symmachus, notwithstanding that he styled himself Vicarius Petri, an acknowledgment of a universal episcopacy constituting one priesthood) there remained *no Bishop but the Pope.* See Pearson's Opp. Posthuma, vol. i. p. 274, Oxf. 1844; Leslie's Letter to the Bishop of Meaux. "The Abbe Guettée has recently published a large 8vo volume on this subject. It is entitled, La Papauté Schismatique, ou Rome dans ses rapports avec l'Eglise Orientale. It seems to be a learned and exhaustive work." (Christian Remembrancer, October, 1863, p. 331.)

"Some writers, namely Petrus de Marca, Archbishop of Paris, Christianus Lupus, Emmanuel Schelstratè, two eminent divines, the one of Louvain, the other of Antwerp, and Leo Allatius, have taken a great deal of pains to prove that these Ecclesiastical Dignities owe their origin to Christ, or the Apostles. But their arguments are unanswerably confuted by the learned Ellies du Pin; and besides it is evident from the entire conformity which the Ecclesiastical Government had, in most places, with the Political State of the Empire, as established by Constantine, that the Church in forming the Hierarchy I have described, adopted his plan; and consequently, that such Dignities are not of divine but of human Institution." Bower's History of the Popes, vol. i. p. 107. Cf. Bramhall's Just Vindication &c., p. 177, where he shews that Emperors have changed Patriarchs, in order to conform the ecclesiastical regiment to the political — "for this reason Cæsarea of old was a long time preferred before Hierusalem, and Alexandria before Antioch, and Rome before all others . . . . . and Constantinople was made of a mean city the seat of the Eastern Empire, and had as many dioceses and provinces subject to it as old Rome itself."

An Account of the Government of the Christian Church for the first six hundred years, particularly shewing I. The Apostolical practice of Diocesan and Metropolitical Episcopacy. II. The usurpation of Patriarchal and Papal authority. III. The war of two hundred years between the Bishops of Rome and Constantinople for universal Supremacy. By Sam. Parker, D.D. Bishop of Oxford. pp. 359, 8vo Lond. 1683 **C. L.**

At the Council of Constantinople A.D. 381, the Bishop of Constantinople was declared next in dignity to the Roman Prelate; in seventy years after he was made equal with him. Cf. Stillingfleet, Grounds of Faith and Defence of the Greek Church (works, vol. iv.); Patrick, No. 337; Abauzit's Letter to a Lady of Dijon in regard to the Doctrines of the Church of Rome. "In effect in these words of Jesus Christ, that the gates of Hell shall never prevail against his church, would every person clearly and distinctly see a promise made to the Romish Church rather than to the Greek Church, which, since the great schism, regards the Romish as a limb severed from her own body, and who alleges also the Succession of the Bishops from the Apostles, and particularly from Peter, the founder of the Church of Antioch, without speaking of œcumenical councils which were always held within her bosom, and whither the Latins themselves repaired to draw forth the truth?"—A Refutation of the Pope's Empire over the Church by Nestorius, translated out of Greek into Latin by Peter Allix, 1702. "In the first period of Christianity each Greek and Roman city, with its suburbicary territory, was under the government of certain magistrates appointed from its own body, who composed a council or senate, subject to one chief, styled Dictator or Defensor Civitatis; in superinduction upon which the Apostles, or at least the early Preachers of the Gospel, erected in every such district a Presbytery, with a President, Apostle, or Bishop or Angel of the Church, whose power reached over the whole diocese, which was often of very considerable extent, and commensurate with the civil jurisdiction. Titus, ch. i. ver. 5; Concil. Antioch. vol. ix. [*vide* Schelstrate, Antverpiæ, 1681]; Theodoret Epist. xlii. et cxiii. unjustly suspected; August. Epist, lxviii. ed. Frob. Greg. Naz.; [Salmasius de Regionibus et Ecclesiis Suburbicariis, 1621, 4to; Guizot on European Civilization.] The metropolitan bishopricks were established in the primacy of provincial towns, for central advantage and confederate government. On the new division under Constantine the Patriarchal supremacy arose in correspondence with the new constitution of the united provinces united under one Eparch, [Exarch,] Vicar or Prefect. See Bingham's Eccles. Antiq. Book ii. ch. 1; Petrus de Marca de Concord. Sacerd. et Imper. lib. vi. ch. 1. When new distributions of the provinces were made by succeeding Emperors, it was sometimes provided that the ecclesiastical allotments should not be affected as in the time of Justinian as to Armenia. Quæ ad sacerdotia spectant volumus in eadem manere forma. Nov. xxxi. ch. 2. See Maurice's Defence of Diocesan Episcopacy." (Gray's Bampton Lectures, 91-2; cf. Bower's Hist. of the Popes, vol. i. p, 106.)

"It does not seem at this day to comport with the greatness of the Roman Church to be content to be included within the ancient limits of the Suburbicary Regions. For not satisfied with a primacy of order, or with her ancient patriarchate (to whose jurisdiction the Britannick Churches were not of right subject) or with her other privileges, conferred upon her out of a respect to the imperial city; as if the spirit of the old Romans were infused into her, she proudly affects an empire over the whole body of Christians throughout the world." (Smith's Pacific Discourse, pp. 19, 20.) Cf. Bower's Hist. of the Popes, vol. i. pp. 108–10. Dr. O'Connor, the learned editor of ancient Irish Historians, says: "As Patriarch, the Pope's jurisdiction did not interfere with that of the Patriarchs of Milan or of Aquileia, so that they who have dubbed him patriarch of all the western world are quite ignorant of ecclesiastical history. De Marca clearly shews that the bishops of the Transalpine countries ordained their own metropolitans without any patriarchal interference, any authority or consent of Rome, and that this right is one of the fundamental articles of the liberties of the Gallican Church. From what has been thus clearly stated it follows that in his three qualities of bishop, metropolitan and patriarch, the Pope has no more to do with the Irish Church than the Bishop of Constantinople has, who is also a metropolitan and a patriarch." Columbanus, Letter iii. Cf. The British Magazine, vol. xi. p. 396. In Spanheim's Geographia Sacra et Ecclesiastica (Opp. 1), from which we learn how small a portion of the ancient Church fell to the lot of the Roman bishop, the various authorities are cited by whom was agitated the quæstio, What Provinces were Urbicariæ Regiones vel Ecclesiæ sub Vicario. On the Pope's claim to supremacy not only over all the Churches but over all the towns of Christendom, see Foxe's Martyrology, vol. ii. end of Book vi. Did the title *Episcopus Episcoporum* arise from his superiority to the Suburbicarian Bishops? But Baluze (see Routh's Reliquiæ, vol. ii. p. 153) observes that this designation was applied to other Bishops. Cf. Bingham, B. ii. ch. ii. § 8. "Cyprian liked not the swelling title of Bishop of Bishops." Bramhall's Answer to the Epistle of M. de la Milletiere; Works, vol. i. p. 61.

King Edward VI. Arguments against the Pope's Supremacy. Translated out of the original written with the King's own hand in French. To which are subjoined some Remarks upon his Life and Reign, in vindication of his memory from Dr. Heylin's severe and unjust censure. 12mo Lond. 1682

Republished and dedicated to King George III. by the Rev. J.

Duncan, 1811, and reprinted by the Roxburghe Club. The commencement, the conclusion and the dedication will be found in the second volume of Strype's Memorials, p. 434. On the subject, the Corruptions of the Catholic Church, see Sharon Turner's History of Edward VI. and his Authorities.

The following work may here be noticed, as it is rather a scarce book:

CL. *Essay upon the Government of the Church of England*, from the earliest to the present Times. Exhibiting the true causes of the Separation from Rome in the reign of Henry VIII. And the Review intended at the Revolution. With a Vindication of the Measures of Henry VIII., Edward VI. and Queen Elizabeth, from the calumnies of a Popish Writer [Dr. Charles Dodd, or Richard Tootle], published in the first and second volumes of an History entitled, The Church History of England from the year 1500 to the year 1688, chiefly with regard to the Catholicks. Being a compleat Account of the Divorce, Supremacy, Dissolution of Monasteries, and first attempts for a Reformation under King Henry VIII.; the unsettled state of the Reformation under Edward VI.; the interruption it met with from Queen Mary; with the last hand to it by Queen Elizabeth. And a Preface containing a Summary of the false Facts and Principles advanced by the Catholick Historian. By George Reynolds, [LL.D., Archdeacon of Lincoln.] Lond. 1743.

I am indebted to Hey's Lectures in Divinity for the following extracts: — "A great deal has been written on the subject (the Pope's Supremacy), but it is now less interesting than it was in the time of our Henry VIII. Historians tell us that Christianity was planted in our island so soon as the Apostolic age; though it is not known what persons first taught it to our ancestors. (Collier's Eccles. History, from Gildas, &c.; Comber's Advice, p. 111.) At the great Council of Nice in 325 it was understood that the British Christians were not brought under any foreign Patriarch or Metropolitan, but were an independent Church. (Can. 6 Dionys. Exig. referred to by Comber." [*Vide* Voelli et Justelli Canon, vol. i. p. 31. Comber's reference is erroneous; the 6th Canon does not mention the British Church. But see Part i. pp. 210-215; Notes and Queries, 2nd ser. vol. vii. p. 482 and *ante;* and Percival, The Roman Schism illustrated from Records of the Early Church, pp. 48-9, in which work extracts will be found from the Councils which bear upon the Pope's Supremacy. For other authorities see Bramhall's Just Vindication of the Church of England ch. v.]

"At that time (under Gregory the Great) it appears that the Bishop of Rome (who like other Bishops was sometimes called Papa, a respectful appellation) was subject to the Emperor, and considered the Emperor as governing sacred persons. See Bower's Lives of Popes, vol. ii. p. 500, where Gregory I. says that God gave the Emperor dominari sacerdotibus. Indeed the Emperors had always till the time of Gregory VII. in some degree conferred the Popedom; he was the last Pope whose election was confirmed by the Emperor. The early Christian Emperors had always ordered Councils, and presided at them; how much authority they exercised over the Church appears from a great many Roman laws now extant in the Corpus Juris Civilis. ["The Christian Emperor treats all mankind as his subjects in their religious as well as in their civil capacity. The Emperor's creed as well as his edicts are the universal law of the Empire. His code opens with the Imperial Creed on the Trinity, and the Imperial Anathema against Nestorius, Eutyches, Apollinaris. He recognises the authority of the four great councils. He even acknowledges the supremacy of the Roman Church, and commands all Churches to be united with her. . . . . . . But Justinian legislates for Rome as for the East." Milman.] Though the Popes, in the day of their greatness, assumed unbounded authority, yet in the early times of Christianity they had only that precedence which naturally arose from Rome being the seat of the Empire. [Cf. Townsend's Ecclesiastical and Civil History, vol. i. p. 496; and Geddes's *Essay on the Roman Pontificate, Heathen and Papal; shewing the Papal with all its Preheminences to have sprung from the Heathen. And that both of them do owe their Primacy solely to the Civil Primacy of the City of Rome.*] . . . . About the year 372 Valentinian published a law by which, in order to avoid going to profane tribunals, Bishops were obliged to refer their disputes to the see of Rome; this might be one reason why the papal pretensions kept rising till the Council of Chalcedon in 450. At this Council it was held that as there were two seats of Empire, the two Prelates who presided at them should be upon the same rank. This continued till 580, when Constantinople claimed universal church-supremacy. But Phocas, an emperor of flagitious character, being rather checked for his enormities by the Patriarch of Constantinople, and strongly flattered by the Pope, declared the latter the supreme Governor of the Catholic Church. In the ninth century the Eastern and Western Churches separated. [See Milman, vol. ii. p. 142 sqq.] The Pope became a secular Prince, by the Revolt of the Exarchate of Italy, in the contentions about Images, which must help the growth of his spiritual dominion." [The Bishop of Milan had previously exercised the power and authority of a Metropolitan over all the Bishops under the Exarch of Italy.]

"In England he gained an influence about the time of the Conquest by assisting the Conqueror, and from that time to the time of Henry VIII. it was a perpetual conflict between the see of Rome and the rational part of the English nation." (Hey, Book iv. Art. xxxvii.) Under Nicholas I. the popedom was advanced not only by his beneficently used usurpation of divine power, but by the promulgation of the false Decretals, which are supposed to have been drawn up by the same papal lawyer as Constantine's Donation. (See part i. p. 256.)

Under Gregory VII. (Hildebrand) the successor of Alexander II., who assisted the Conqueror, the temporal power of the Bishop of Rome was aggrandised by the right of investiture, the deposition of princes, the celibacy of the clergy, which after the strife of centuries was now enforced, and homage and fealty to be rendered to himself, which had hitherto been thought due to the respective princes. See his Epistle ad Hermannum Metens. Episc. pro justificando facto ex communicationis quam in Imperatorem fecerat, in Goldasti Replic., pp. 244–252; Bowden's Life of Gregory VII. vol. ii. pp. 139–144. "The anathema which in its theory at least and in its unmitigated language devoted its victim to eternal death, had hardly lost any of its terrors. Anathema became, without shaking the common dread of its effects, the ordinary weapon employed by the Pope in his quarrels; by Hildebrand it was fulminated with all the energy of his character." Milman. Under Innocent III. contemporary with King John were added Gratiæ Expectativæ, Reservations, Disposal of Benefices under the eight Papal months, Concurrent Jurisdiction. See Milman, vol. vi. p. 65 sqq. "A letter of Innocent to the Consuls of Milan declares it is sacrilege to doubt the decrees of a Pope; that though he is born of sinners, of a sinful race, yet since he fills the place of him that was without sin, he who despises him despises Christ. The cause of dispute was the excommunication of Passaguerra, against which the Milanese protested as unjust. [Innocentii III. Epistolæ, Baluzii, 210 sqq.]" Compare the high language of Innocent to John, King of England. Milman, vol. iv. p. 5, 6, and Lingard, vol. ii. pp. 306 and 326, who gives a long extract from one of his letters, "which shews more plainly than any speculations of modern writers the real ground on which the Popes assumed their pretended authority in temporal matters." Cf. Bowden's Life of Gregory VII. *ad finem*, and Milman's L. C. vol. iii. p. 101 sqq.

"Besides these (the articles of absolution and of transubstantiation) and other articles tending to the upholding of the Pope's authority, they had many fine points in their ecclesiastical polity conducing to the same end; of which I will mention only such as were established within the same time. For then it was the order came up of preaching friars, that wandered up and down, with power to preach in what congregation they pleased, and were sure enough to instil into the people nothing that might lessen the obedience to the Church of Rome; but on the contrary, whatsoever might give advantage to it against the civil power. Besides they privately insinuated themselves with men and women of weak judgment, confirming their adherence to the Pope, and urging them in the time of their sickness to be beneficial to it by contribution of money, or building religious houses, and pious works as necessary for the remission of sins." (Hobbes's Behemoth; Works, vol. vi. p. 183.) Cf. Staveley's *Romish Horseleech*, p. 102 sqq. These religious orders, established during the Crusades, A.D. 1097 et sqq., which were once twenty-three, were afterwards reduced to four: I. Augustinians; II. Carmelites; III. Dominicans; IV. Franciscans. See Matthew Paris, A.D. 1225, p. 909; Castello de Santo Domingo; Stevens, Mosheim, Dupin, (cent. xiii.); and Milman, Book xi. ch. ii. The Benedictines embracing the ramifications of the order, the Carthusians, Cistercians, &c., who were established in the sixth century, must be distinguished from the Friars, although they also became involved in civil affairs and the cabals of courts, and most eager to advance the authority and power of the Roman Pontiffs. But "among the Benedictines," says Eustace, "we find no inquisitors, no persecutors." (Tour through Italy, vol. ii. p. 540.) Cf. Mabillon, Marrier, Reynerus, Ziegelbauer.

"Under Boniface the Eighth the papal power was at its highest pitch of greatness. With all his ability and sagacity he was possessed even to infatuation of the conviction of the unlimited, irresistible power of the papacy. He determined once for all on the broadest, boldest and most uncontestable ground to bring to issue this inevitable question; to sever the property of the Church from all secular obligations; to declare himself the one exclusive trustee of all the lands, the goods, the properties, held throughout christendom by the clergy, by monastic bodies, even by the universities; and that without his consent no aid, benevolence, grant or subsidy, could be raised on their estates or possessions by any temporal sovereign in the world. Such is the full and distinct sense of the famous Bull ("Clericis Laicos") issued by Boniface at the commencement of the second year of his pontificate." Milman, vol. v. p. 44. See also an account of the Bull "Unam Sanctam," *ibid.* p. 91, 92. It asserted the eternal unity of the Catholic Church under St. Peter and his successors. But in this country, during the struggle of Philipp the Fair with Boniface, an opposition encountering the fundamental principles of the papal system first found vent. Gieseler, vol. iii. p. 188. Collier, vol. i. p. 497. It was in vain Boniface pretended a title to the realm of Scotland in his controversy with our King Edward I. (Matth. Westmon, in an. 1301.) "It is only right, however, to add that the pope asserted no claim to superiority which was not equally acknowledged and asserted by the Scottish government itself. See Fordun, vol. xi. pp. 51, 53, 54, 56, 57, 63." Tierney's note (Dodd's *Church History*, vol. i. p. 131.)

"In England the law in theory was against the see of Rome, and during the reigns of Henry II., Edward I. and III. and Richard II. several statutes were made, declaring the rights of England and enforcing them." Hey, *ut supra*, who refers to Blackstone [Book iv. ch. 33] for the statutes of the parliament at Clarendon or the Clarendon constitutions. See Matth. Paris, an. 1164, pp. 100–102, and Lord Lyttleton's Hist. of Henry II. vol. ii. Lingard's Hist. of England, chap. iii., who refers to two different copies of the Constitutions in Wilkins' Leg. Sax. pp. 321–324. "The lawful kings and parliaments of England were always essentially Protestant in feeling for a national church, though they adhered to the received doctrines of the Christianity of the day; and it was only the usurpers, John, Henry IV. &c. that went against this policy." Coleridge's Table Talk.

"But if any would see this argument on the King's Ecclesiastical Supremacy, as it more particularly regards the English Nation, deduced from a vast variety of our most authentic instruments and records, we must refer him to Mr. Prynne's voluminous collections on that head, in three volumes folio &c., of which we shall here next take a short survey." (*The British Librarian*, p. 10.) This is abundantly proved by Stavely in his Essay of the Supremacy of the King of England, and in Bramhall's Just Vindication in his Schism Guarded and in his Seventh Discourse, vol. v. p. 229 &c., where it is shewn that Saxon kings made ecclesiastical laws. See also England's Independency &c. and Twysden's Histor. Vindication, *ut supra*, part i. p. 205.

The Revision revised: or a Vindication of the Right Reverend Father in God, George Lord Bishop of Winton, against a late pamphlet, published by L. W. Permissu Superiorum, and entitled, A Revision of Dr. Morley's Judgment in matters of Religion; or An Answer to several Treatises of his, written on several occasions, concerning the Church of Rome, &c. [By Adam Littleton, D.D.?] 4to Lond. 1687

A list of his works is given in Wood's Athen. Oxon., and an account and character of him and his works in the second volume of Nichols' Literary Anecdotes; but in neither of them nor in Watt's Bibliotheca is this tract mentioned. Littleton's name was added in writing as the author in a copy recently in the possession of Dr. Herbert Evans. "You say this Second Age is yet to come, the Pope never having taken the title of Universal Bishop; and so I remember you say somewhere else (Revision, p. 14). It is strange that you alone should run counter to all your Fellows, that you should take from his Holiness that which they all give him, and that which entitles the Pope himself to an universal authority and jurisdiction, and that upon which his supremacy depends. For how can you pretend him to be the head of the Church, or Christ's vicar, what will become of the papal monarchy, if the Pope be not universal bishop and pastor? To go no further for proof, then [than] t'other day: in D. Stillingfleet's book called; The Rational Account, &c., there is one whole chapter from p. 422 to 450, where the title of universal bishop is canvassed betwixt the Doctor and his adversary T. C. whether it do of right belong to the Pope or Bishop of Rome, or whether he came fairly by it," *ad finem.*

C. L. An Historical Treatise of the Foundation and Prerogatives of the Church of Rome and of the Bishops. By Louis Maimbourg. Translated from the French by A. Lovel. 8vo Lond. 1686

See Notes and Queries, 2nd ser., vol. xi. p. 50.

Ebert states that the series of Mainbourgh's historical writings, in fourteen vols. 4to or twenty-eight vols. 12mo, is no longer sought after. Yet Bayle remarks: "I think he had a particular talent for history. His works are very agreeably written, contain many lively strokes and a great variety of occasional instruction. There are few historians who write better, and are more learned and exact than he, and who have the art of engaging the readers so much as he does."

Ch. xxvi. The distinction of the direct and indirect power. Ch. xxvii. A false distinction of Buchanan's refuted. It was upon an obligation of conscience, and not through weakness, the Christians obeyed infidel emperors and persecutors. The allegiance that subjects owe to their sovereigns is of Divine right, with which Popes cannot dispense.

The Ultramontane defenders of the *Pope's power over temporals*, included in the great collection of Rochaberti before mentioned (part i. p. 244), are enumerated in Struvii Bibliotheca Juridica, pp. 524-27. "Cardinal Bellarmine, in his book De Potestate Papæ in temporalibus, against Barclay's attack (De Romano Pontifice, lib. v.), cites the passages of twenty-one Italian writers, fourteen French, nineteen Spanish, nine German and seven English, between the era of St. Bernard and Sanders, who asserted the temporal powers of the Pope. The sentiment of the Cardinal Bishop, St. Bonaventure, one of the strongest, nearly corresponds with that of our English Carmelite, John Bacon, as to the Pope, but goes beyond it by ascribing the same powers even to priests. The saint's words are: "Jam vero possunt Sacerdotes et Pontifices ex causa amovere reges," &c. (Eccles. Hier. pars ii. c. i.) These earlier English friends of the popedom were: Alex. Hales the preceptor of Thomas Aquinas and Bonaventure, R. Holkot, J. Bacon, Thomas Walden ("Boniface, the missionary, and Grostete?") Sharon Turner's History of the reign of Edward VI., 4to, pp. 37-8. "All the great English schoolmen, Scotus Erigena, Duns Scotus, Ockham and others, those morning stars of the Reformation, were heart and soul opposed to Rome, and maintained the papacy to be Antichrist." (Coleridge's Table Talk, May 6th, 1833.) Cf. A Dialogue betwene a Knyght and a Clerke, concernynge the Power Spiritual and Temporal. Of this tract, by the famous William Occham, an abstract is given in Oldys's British Librarian, pp. 5-10. I have given an account of it in Bibliotheca Chethamensis, vol. iv. p. 434. An abstract is given of another of his works, Of the Authority of the Bishop of Rome, by Sleidan, De Statu Religionis, lib. ii. anno 1520. Turner has, like the papists, placed Grosseteste among the friends of the popedom! the Bishop who, as Brown in his Fasciculus rerum expetendarum observes (tom ii. p. 322), almost retorted excommunication for excommunication. See Chalmers's Biographical Dictionary for Life of Robert Grosseteste, by Samuel Pegge, LL.D., 1793, 4to, which, says Chalmers, "supersedes the necessity of any other references, except perhaps to Milner's Church History, who has ably analyzed the Bishop's character as a divine;" and the Archæologia, vol. xiii., where he is introduced as an Anglo-Norman poet. Dr. Pegge's work, one of his last and best, throws great light upon the history of the twelfth and thirteenth centuries. "Grosseteste was a Churchman of the highest hierarchical notions, and held the loftiest views of the power of the Pope; his earlier letters to the Pope are in the most submissive, almost adulatory, tone. The Canon Law is as eternal, immutable, universal, as the Law of God. The Pope has undoubted power to dispose of all benefices, but for the abuse of that power hell-fire is the doom. Vide Brown, tom. ii. p. 339;" Milman; who appears to have overlooked the Editor's remarks above referred to, *De novissima Epistolæ parte Editoris admonitio et censura*, pp. 322-23. Cf. Gieseler, vol. iii. p. 182, who mentions another English Bishop who at this time "made a more remarkable appearance," Sevalus, or Sewal de Bovill, Archbishop of York, who pursued a like course of action; he was excommunicated indeed by the Pope (Matth. Paris, p. 956, anno 1257), but "the dying man then thought upon the bold words of his old college friend, Grostete, and resolved to follow his example and acquaint the Pope with the evil he had done, protesting against the injustice," &c. (Raine's Lives of the Archbishops of York.) See also Bramhall's Just Vindication, pp. 182-83, and Dodd's Church Hist. of England. "In that great contest, which happened in this reign (Hen. III.) between the Church of England and the See of Rome, concerning papal provisions, and other matters of complaint, I meet with several bishops of remarkable learning and virtue that opposed the Pope; particularly Richard Wethershed, Archbishop of Canterbury. . . . . . . St. Edmund, Archbishop of Canterbury. . . . . . . Walter de Cantilupe, son of William, Lord Cantilupe, Bishop of Worcester," &c. Vol. i. pp. 126, 127.

Friendly and Seasonable Advice to the Roman Catholics of England. [By Thomas Comber, D.D.] Lond. 1685

In the fourth edition, 1686, the Author prefixed his name. See the Memoirs of the Life and Writings of Thomas Comber, pp. 78-81, where a general idea of the work is given, and the occasion which gave birth to it is mentioned. Cf. his Discourse of Excommunication, appended to his Companion to the Temple.

C. L. De Serie et Successione primorum Romæ Episcoporum Dissertationes duæ; prior de origine veritate et utilitate Successionis; et de incertitudine temporum quæ prioribus Romæ Episcopis, vel a Græcis, vel a Latinis, assignata sunt. Posterior de annis eorundem Episcoporum sigillatim. (H. Dodwelli Dissertatio de Pontificum Romanorum primæva successioue.) A. Jo. Pearsono, Cestr. Ep. 4to Lond. 1687

An article on this publication was given in Le Clerc, Bibl. Univ. vol. ix. p. 127. An analysis of these Dissertations will be found also in the Historical and Critical Dictionary, by Bernard and Birch. See cap. i.-viii. pp. 1-65. Pearson admits that St. Peter was the first bishop of Rome, in vol ii. pp. 338-41, ed. Oxon. 1844. "Mr. Bower, with some weak Protestants before him, almost pretends to deny that Peter ever was at Rome, p. 1, 2, 3, concerning which matter take my own former words, out of my three tracts, p. 53. 'Mr. Baratier proves in his first chapter most throughly, as Bishop Pearson had done before him, that St Peter was at Rome. This is so clear in Christian antiquity, that 'tis a shame for a Protestant to confess that any Protestant ever denied it.' I think St. John in the Revelation xi. 8, as the most and best copies have it, *where also their lord (Peter) was crucified*, has fully determined this point; and assured us that Peter was crucified at Rome, as all antiquity agrees also. This partial procedure demonstrates that tho' Mr. Bower has gotten clear of the prejudices of Popery, yet has he by no means gotten clear of the prejudices of some Protestants, as an impartial writer of history, which he strongly pretends to be, ought to do, and has in this case greatly hurt the Protestant cause instead of helping it. He might have denied his being bishop of Rome without disputing his being there." (Memoirs of the Life of Mr. Will. Whiston, p. 407.)

Lardner thinks that he did not come to Rome before the year 63 or perhaps 64, and obtained the crown of martyrdom in the year 64 or 65. Consequently he could not reside very long at Rome before his death. (Works, vol. vi. p. 543.) Cf. Greswell's Dissertations upon the Principles of a Harmony of the Gospels, vol. iv. pp. 257-8.

"As it is certain that there were bishops at Rome from the very beginning, it seems that the principal difficulty consists in discovering the first origin. St. Irenæus, who is followed by all antiquity, says that St. Peter and St. Paul founded the Church at Rome. Henry Valesius owns that St. Paul contributed to it by his labours there; but he cannot allow that he was bishop of that city. However, Epiphianius having observed that St. James was the first Bishop of Jerusalem, the most ancient of all the Churches, says that St. Peter and St. Paul were Bishops of Rome." (*Principibus geminis fidei sub principe Roma.* Venant. Fortun.) It is undoubted that St. Paul was at Rome; but with regard to St. Peter, there is not the least trace in Scripture. On the contrary, a great many able writers have denied that he ever went to Rome. Salmasius, who was an eminent advocate for this opinion, affirms [see his Apparatus ad Libros *de Primatu Papæ*] that St. Peter went from Antioch to Babylon, where there was a prodigious number of Jews; and that the name of Babylon, which was afterwards given to Rome, gave occasion to the notion that he was bishop of that city. But Bishop Pearson maintains that we ought not to oppose the voice of all antiquity; that the Fathers said St. Peter was at Rome before the mystical explication of Babylon was introduced; and that the city of Babylon, whither St. Peter went, was not situated in Assyria, but Egypt, whence that Apostle might easily go to Rome. The Bishop's principal design is to conclude that St. Peter having been the first Bishop of Rome, Episcopacy is of Apostolick institution. For this reason he vehemently opposes Salmasius, who asserts that the Apostles left no bishops behind them in the Churches which they had erected

(p. 382). He shews that this would be to accuse the primitive Church of having forged catalogues of bishops, and to have made use of frauds; which is overthrowing the truth of history, and the idea which we ought to have of the purity of those ages. (Hist. and Crit. Dictionary, *s. v.* Pearson.) On the identity of Babylon and Rome, one of the five arguments produced by Bellarmine, compare Care's Modest Enquiry, p. 15 sqq.; Sure and Honest Means, &c., p. 22.

The Pope's Third Breve threatening to excommunicate the Most Christian King, together with the French Clergie's Reply. 4to 1681

For this controversy respecting the Regale Rankin refers to Reboulet, Hist. du Regne de Lewis XIV. t. v.

C. 1. The Proceedings of the Parliament of Paris upon the Pope's Bull. 1688

"To give some colour to so scandalous an innovation (the destruction of the Franchises of Ambassadors of the Kings of France) the Pope refers to that famous Bull, stil'd in Cœna Domini." (See part i. p. 72, and D'Oyley's Life of Wharton in Life of Abp. Sancroft, Append. No. i. vol. ii. p. 125.) "True it is, that if this Decree, whereby the Popes declare themselves soveraign monarchs of the world, be legitimate, the majesty royal will then depend on their humour, all our Liberties will be abolish'd, the secular Judges will no longer have the power to try the possession of benefices, nor the civil and criminal causes of Ecclesiastical Persons, and we shall quickly see ourselves brought under the yoke of the Inquisition." (Page 11.) Consult Giannone's Civil History of the Kingdom of Naples, vol. ii. pp. 624-36. "When the Pope had a quarrel with any kingdom, was it usually with the king or the people? When it was necessary to oppose a firm front against tyranny and oppression, who stood forward more promptly or more firmly than the sovereign Pontiff? Does not Voltaire himself admit that the Popes restrained princes, *protected the people*," &c. (Quoted by M. de Maistre, book on the Pope.) It is very remarkable that the Bull, In Cœna Domini, which created so much alarm, contains in its fifth article an excommunication against "those who should levy new taxes upon their estates or should in-

crease those already existing beyond the bounds marked out by right." (Balmez, European Civilization; Protestantism and Catholicity compared, ch. lxi.) "In the 21st article," says Giannone, "all Princes are excommunicated who in their dominious lay on new tolls, taxes and customs, or augment the old, excepting in cases where they are allowed by, or by special license obtained from the Apostolic See; therefore, agreeable to this article, Martin Becan taught that a prince becomes a tyrant if he loads his subjects with unjust taxes, sells the offices of judges, makes laws for his own convenience, &c. . . . . And thus Christian princes must lay the secrets of their states and their necessities before the Pope, in order to obtain liberty to impose new taxes or augment the old." The Bull will be found in Toleti Summa de Instruct. Sacerdotum, lib. i. cap. 21; Cherubini Bullarium, t. i. See also Gibbins' reprint of the Roman Index Expurg., preface p. xiv. *The King of France ought to have been exempted.* "Can they forget that having been a long while persecuted, imprison'd, banish'd, one while by the Emperours of Constantinople, or by the Exarchs of Ravenna, and another while by the Kings of the Lombards: Pepin and Charlemagne not only freed them from that slavery, but they gave them out of pure liberality, what is now called the Patrimony of St. Peter." The Proceedings, *ut supra*, concerning the Franchises in the City of Rome, and the following Ordonnance of the 26th of December, 1687, pp. 37, 4to, Lond. 1688; p. 7. Cf. Milman, vol. ii. pp. 182-3; Mosheim, part ii. ch. ii.; and The Famous Bull in Cœna Domini, &c. C. L.
With a Preface containing some Reflections on the Bull, and Animadversions on the late Account of the Proceedings of the Parliament of Paris. pp. x–28, 4to. 1688.

Walsh, in his Hist. of the Irish Remonstrance (p. 647), states that when he endeavoured to prove that several great divines had opposed the deposing doctrine, Father Nettervil interrupted him, affirming that none had asserted to the contrary, but a schismatical historian and a poet, meaning Sigibertus Gemblacensis and Dantes Aligherius. (Quoted in a Defence of the Missionaries Arts, p. 94.) Sigibertus, who lived in the twelfth century, was a strong defender of the cause of the Emperors against the Popes; see Goldasti Replicatio, pp. 188-203: "Epistola nomine Ecclesiæ Leodiensis scripta contra Epistolam Paschalis II. Papæ Ecclesias Henrico Cæsari et Imperio fideles excommunicantis et devastantis." "To speak with the leave of all good men this only novelty, I will not saye Heresie, was not crept into the world before the daies of Hildebrand, that priests should teach the people that they owe no subjection to evill kings." (Sigebertus, quoted in the Epistle Congratulatory of Lysimachus Nicanor, &c. 4to Oxf. 1684.); and Crakanthorp, Of the Pope's Temporall Monarchy, *ut infra*.

That the oath of a Roman Catholic Bishop ascribes to the Pope spiritual power extending to temporal effects is admitted by Father Walsh in his Four Letters on several subjects; the fourth being an answer to Dr. Barlow's book entituled, Popery &c., 1686, and in his History of the Remonstrance; see Part i. p. 4, and No. 225, note. Baronius laboured to prove that every country in Europe, Scotland excepted, is a Province of the Pope's Royalties; see A Digest of the Evidence taken before Select Committees of the two Houses of Parliament appointed to inquire into the state of Ireland, 1824-5; by the Rev. W. Phelan and the Rev. M. O'Sullivan. "It appears," says Leibnitz, "that in consequence of the intimate connection between sacred and profane things, even over kings themselves, a certain authority was granted to the Roman pontiffs;" and he enumerates various instances of papal interference in the kingdoms of Hungary, Naples and Sicily; *De Jure Suprematus*, Opp. iv. cap. 21, quoted by Dr. Russell in his translation of Leibnitz' Systema Theologicum, with Introd. and Notes Lond. 1856. With Bellarmine he ascribes to the papal supremacy divine right as well as human expediency. Compare The Doctrines and Practices of the Church of Rome truly represented, by Edw. Stillingfleet, *ad finem*; Cardinal Perron's Reply to King James, book iv. ch. 39; and Barlow's Answer to a Catholic Englishman, *ut supra*, Part i. p. 59. Gregory the Seventh would have converted the sovereignty of Peter into an altogether secular empire; and he looked upon it as an insult to that sovereignty that a king of Hungary, who ought to have regarded himself a king dependent on St. Peter, should place himself in a relation of dependence on the German empire. Neander, vol. vii. p. 118; Milman, vol. iii. p. 27. The feudal oath taken to Boniface the Eighth by the king of Sardinia will be found in Mendham's St. Pius V., subjoined to which is, A Historic Deduction of the Episcopal Oath of Allegiance to the Pope, in the Church of Rome. "The oath of vassalage imposed upon all metropolitans by Gregory VII. served as an effectual assistance in the vindication, under all circumstances, of that idea of an episcopus universalis, whose vicars were the bishops." Gieseler, vol. iii. p. 168; who mentions four forms of the oath, one of which, that of the Patriarch of Aquileia in the eleventh century, he gives entire. For the oath taken by the English Bishops before the Reformation, see Collier's Church History, Part ii. book i. vol. ii. p. 68; Burnet's History of the Reformation, vol i. an. 1532. It is very remarkable that the new oath, as it is extant in the *Roman Pontifical*, set out by order of Pope Clement VIII., as well as that taken by the English Bishops, has changed these words, Regulas sanctorum patrum into Regalia Sancti Petri, *i.e.* the rules of the holy fathers into the royalties of St. Peter. See Barrow on the Pope's Supremacy, Introd. § xiv.

> Ah Constantine! to how much ill gave birth,
> Not thy conversion, but that plenteous dower
> Which the first wealthy Father gain'd from thee.
>
> Dante, *Hell.* Canto xix.

"He alludes to the pretended gift of the Lateran by Constantine to Sylvester, of which Dante himself seems to imply a doubt in his treatise De Monarchia: "Ergo scindere imperium, Imperatori non licet. Si ergo aliquæ dignitates per Constantinum essent alienatæ (ut dicunt) ab Imperio," &c. (lib. iii.) Therefore to make a rent in the empire exceeds the lawful power of the emperor himself. If then some dignities by Constantine were alienated (as they report) from the empire, &c. In another part of the same treatise he speaks of the alienation with less doubt indeed, but not with less disapprobation: "O felicem populum, O Ausoniam te gloriosam, si vel numquam infirmator imperii extitisset; vel numquam sua pia intentio ipsum fefellisset." O happy people! O glorious Italy! if either he who thus weakened thy empire had never been born, or had never suffered his pious intentions to mislead him. (Lib. ii. *ad finem.*) The gift is by Ariosto very humourously placed in the moon among the things lost or abused on earth. (Orl. Fur. ch. xxxiv. st. 80.) Milton has translated both this passage and that in the text. Prose Works, vol. i. p. 2, ed. 1753.

> Ah Constantine! how much ill was cause,
> Not thy conversion, but those rich domains
> That the first wealthy pope received of thee.

[The preceding verses are addressed to the condemned Pope Nicholas III. Cf. Gieseler, vol. iii. p. 181.]

Then pass'd he to a flow'ry mountain green,
Which once smelt sweet, now stinks as odiously;
This was that gift, if you the truth will have,
That Constantine to good Sylvester gave.
Carey's *Dante.*

"The Donation of Constantine is a senseless forgery; and so blaz'd by some of the learnedest of the Roman Church. Read it advisedly either in Gratian (Dist. 96 c.); Constantinus [folio, cxxxvi.]; or in the Decrees of Sylvester, with the Confession and Legend of Constantine's baptism, and say of your own judgment if any thing can be more fraudulent, more sottish." (Bishop Bedell's Letter to Waddesworth, ch. vi.) Cf. Geddes, The Grand Forgery display'd, whereby the Roman See was exalted and enrich'd, 1715; Chr. Lupus, Divinum ac Immobile S. Petri Apostolorum Principis circa omnium sub cœlo Fidelium ad Romanam ejus Cathedram Appellationes, 4to Moguntiæ, 1681; Bower's Hist. of the Popes, vol. i. p. 111; Milman's L. C., vol. i. p. 57. For a refutation of it see Laurentius Valla, Nicholas of Cusa, Antoninus Archbishop of Florence, &c., ap. Gratii Fasciculum. "To Sylvester Constantine did give, in full right, his palace of the Lateran, and with it the kingdom of Italy, to be judged by him; that Emperor's own words were: On which account we judge it to be congruous to translate our empire, and the authority of our kingdom into the eastern parts, and to place our imperial city, called after our own name, in the pleasant country of Byzantium, because it is not just that where the principality of the priests is, and where the Head of the Christian Religion is constituted by the Emperor of Heaven, an earthly emperor should have any power." (Geddes, p. 29.) See Petri Damiani Opp. t. iii. p. 55. "Marca the learned Archbishop of Paris [Lib. vi. ch. 6, Lib. iii. ch. 12] is of opinion that the writing, called Constantine's Donation, was forged by Pope Paul the First, or for his use, that he might have something wherewith to stop the mouth of the Eastern Emperors, who complained aloud of the injustice that had been done by K. Pepin's having given to the Roman See the Exarchate of Ravenna, with some other countries in Italy which belonged to their empire. But .... I take that counterfeit deed to be the work of Pope Stephen, who was both uncle and immediate predecessor to Paul the First." (Geddes, p. 23.) Muratori agrees with Marca about the time when and the end for which that Donation was forged. (Antiq. Ital. Medii Ævi, t. iii. pp. 28-9.) "Præter cœtera vide quæ pag. 637, Part ii. tom. ii. Rer. Ital. habet Farsense Chronicon *de hujusmodi Donationis usu sive abusu.*" The most learned treatise on this subject has yet to be mentioned,—The Defence of Constantine: with a Treatise of the Pope's Temporall Monarchie. Wherein, besides divers passages touching other Counsells, both Generall and Provinciall, the second Roman Synod, under Sylvester, is declared to be a mere Fiction and Forgery. By Richard Crakanthorp, Doctor of Divinity. 4to Lond. 1621. The formula or instrument is given in Arndii Antiq. Eccles., pp. 326-335; Banck de Tyrannide Papæ, pp. 62-75. For other editions and commentaries see Walchii Bibl. Theol., tom. iii., and Fabricii Bibl. Græca, vol. vi. p. 4, Lib. v. ch. 4. And compare Milman's L. C. on the donations of Pepin and Charlemagne, and the spiritual supremacy and feudal suzerainty asserted by Adrian I., vol. ii. p. 198. To return to Dante, Paradise, canto xx. line 50:

> The other following, with the laws and me
> To yield the shepherd room, pass'd o'er to Greece;
> From good intent, producing evil fruit:
> Now knoweth he how all the ill deriv'd
> From his well doing, doth not harm him aught;
> Though it hath brought destruction on the world.

"There is no passage in which Dante's opinion of the evil that had arisen from the mixture of the civil with the ecclesiastical power, is more unequivocally declared." (Carey.) Cf. Rossetti's *Antipapal Spirit which produced the Reformation.* "And this was a truth well known in England before this poet (Ariosto) was born, as our Chaucer's Plowman shall tell you by and by upon another occasion. By all these circumstances laid together, I do not see how it can be disputed what good this Emperor Constantine wrought to the Church, but rather whether ever any, though perhaps not wittingly, set open a door to more mischief in Christendom. There is just cause therefore that when the Prelats cry out, Let the Church be reform'd according to Constantine, it should sound to a judicious ear no otherwise, then if they should say, Make us rich, make us lofty, make us lawless; for if any under him were not so, thanks to those ancient remains of integrity, which were not yet quite worn out, and not to his government." (Milton *ut supra.*) Another English poet, John Longland, thus alludes to the working of the deed:

When Cōstatyn of curteisie
Holy Kirke dowed
With londes and ledes,
Lordshipes and rentes,
An aungel men herden
An heigh at Rome crye
Dos Ecclesiæ this day
Hath y-dronke venym,
And tho that han Petres power
Arn apoisoned alle.

The Vision of Piers Ploughman.

Milton, in an Apology for Smectymnuus, illustrates the truth that riches in the Church are the baits of pride and ambition by the same "voice from heaven," in the more elegant words of Gower.

B. M. Religion and Loyalty. The Second Part. Or, The History of the Concurrence of the Imperial and Ecclesiastical Jurisdiction, from the beginning of the reign of Jovian to the end of Justinian. By Samuel Parker, D.D., Archdeacon of Canterbury.

pp. 586, 8vo Lond. 1658

"I thought," writes Wake (*The Authority of Christian Princes over Ecclesiastical Synods*, 1697, 8vo), "it would be no small evidence of my good intentions towards the Church of England to shew that I pretended to nothing in behalf of our kings, but what the bishops and clergy, from the fourth century downwards, had readily allowed to their emperours; and what all other Christian princes continued to enjoy, till the Papal authority prevail'd over them, and deprived them of that supremacy in ecclesiastical matters which they originally had; and to which the Reformation has again so justly restored them." (Pref. p. iv.) "It was a famous saying of Constantine, the first Christian emperor to his bishops, that they indeed were *bishops in things within the Church*, but that he was appointed by God to be *bishop as to those without.*" (Euseb. de Vit. Const. lib. iv. c. xxiv.) Let us look into the several Collections of the Roman Laws; the Code of Theodosius (de feriis: de nuptiis: de fide Cath. de Hæreticis: de Episc. et Cleric. &c.); the Code and Novels of Justinian (lib. i. tit. 1-5, novell. vi. cxxxvii. cxxxi. &c.); the yet later Collection of Basilius, Leo and Constantine that followed after (Basilica, Fabroti, lib. i. tit. 3-5): how many constitutions shall we find in every one of these relating to ecclesiastical affairs. . . . . . . And when the empire began to be parcell'd out into several lesser states and kingdoms, we find their several princes still maintaining the same authority, as to all these things, that the emperors had done before: as from the capitularies of the French and German princes, the collections of the Spanish Councils, our own Antient Laws, (Leg. Ed. Conf. cap. xvii., Leg. Canut. cap. ii., Inæ Præfat. cap. ii., Leg. Edw. et Guthr. cap. iii., Alfred, cap. xxxix., &c.), and the histories which remain of the several other countries doth appear. (pp. xi. xii.) See also ch. iv., in which the state of the Convocation is historically deduced, 1. from the first conversion of the Saxons to the time of the Norman Conquest; 2. from the coming in of King William I. to the 23rd of K. Edward I.; 3. from the 23rd of Edward I. to the 25th of Henry VIII., when the parliament and clergy restored the crown to those rights which the usurpations of the court of Rome had before in great measure deprived it of; 4. from the 25th of Henry VIII. to our own times.

Collier has inserted in his Ecclesiastical History, vol. ii. pp. 89-92, a discourse which was written, 'tis most probable, in the reign of K. Charles II., and is intituled A Discourse concerning his Majesty's Supreme Power Ecclesiastical, establish'd by the Laws of this Kingdom, at the present time in their full force and vigour, in which the statutes in causes ecclesiastical from Henry VIII. to Charles I. are reviewed. Dodd, the Roman Catholic Historian, remarks:

"I will conclude this account of the supremacy with a word or two concerning a mistake of several Protestant lawyers, who pretend that King Henry VIII. did not assume unto himself any more ecclesiastical power than what had been claimed and practised by his predecessors, in former days, both under the British, Saxon, and Norman periods. The famous lawyer, Sir Edward Coke, undertakes to prove this point, in the fifth part of his *Reports*, and is seconded by Mr. Prynn, who in the years 1665 and 1666 published two folios, to which he prefixes the following title, *An Exact Chronological and Historical Demonstration of our British &c. King's Supreme Ecclesiastical Jurisdiction.* The arguments these authors make use of are distinctly answered by father Parsons in a work purposely written to discuss that point, and by Mr. Collier, who, in his Ecclesiastical History, undertakes to demonstrate the inconclusiveness of all the facts produced by Sir Edward

Coke, vol. ii. pp. 92–94; and concerning Mr. Prynn, Anthony Wood, speaking of his works, says: "In most of them he shews great industry but little judgment, especially in his large folios, against the Pope's usurpations." Athen. Oxon. vol. ii. p. 439. "The little judgment he and others shew upon this occasion appears from hence that they make all the controversies between the see of Rome and the Kings of England capital, and do not distinguish between civil and ecclesiastical jurisdiction, nor between ecclesiastical jurisdiction that belongs to faith, and ecclesiastical jurisdiction that regards discipline only," &c. Dodd's Church Hist. of England, part i. art. 3, *ad finem*. On the other side consult the authorities cited in p. 263 *supra*, and Stillingfleet, Of the Ecclesiastical Jurisdiction with respect to the Legal Supremacy, ch. ii.; The King's Supremacy by Common Law enquired into; Coke's Fifth Report, de Jure Regis Ecclesiastico, Examined, p. 772 sqq. "Though the Faith of Christ neither depends upon the Authority of Man, nor is subject to the power either of Synods, or Princes, as to what concerns the Truth of it: yet what that faith is which shall be allow'd to be profess'd, in every Community, by the Laws of it; and receive not only protection but encouragement from the Civil Power, must be left to the Prince to determine: and the definitions of Synods in favour of it will signify very little till what they have determin'd to be the right Faith be also allow'd by the Civil Magistrate to be publicly profess'd and taught, and be received into his favour, and under his Patronage, as such." Wake, *ut supra*, p. 79. "There is no one so great a Stranger to the History of the Holy Scriptures as not to know what Authority the Jewish Princes under the Law pretended to as to this matter." Ibid. p. 10. Cf. Ussher's Tractatus de Controversiis Pontificiis, ch. viii. §§ 4, 5. Burnet's Hist. of the Rights of Princes in the disposing of Ecclesiastical Benefices and Church-Lands: relating chiefly to the Pretensions of the Crown of France to the Regale, and the late Contests with the Court of Rome. 1682, p. 318 sqq. "This subject, the Government of the Highest Powers in Church-affairs, is admirably treated in A Letter of Hugo Grotius to the States Embassador in France, translated by Cl. Barksdale, Lond. 1675, 12mo. "Paul would not have appealed unto Nero had he believed no right of judging in a case of Religion belonged to him. Wherefore as Trajan civilly honest, Nero wicked, are nevertheless equal in the right of Government; so pious Constantine and impious Nero are equal in the right of judging, in aptitude and skill unequal." p. 37. "For a king to be so tyed up with the judgments of synods, that against his own conscience he ought to follow the synodical decrees, I cannot consent to this. And these matters are under dispute among us; but in Germany and other places the princes do openly exercise this right, not one of the pastors contradicting." Ibid. p. 47. Cf. Jurieu's *Historical Reflections on Councils*, prefixed to this History of the Council of Trent, 1684, p. ix.

The merits of Justinian, as "a wise and religious Emperor," are asserted by Crakanthorp, in Romes Seer Overseene, fol. 1631, ch. xxiii., entitled, How Baronius revileth both the Imperiall Edict of Justinian and Theodorus bishop of Cæsarea; and a refutation of the same. Dr. Reynold Pecock, "in his Repressour, speaking of the donation of Constantine, as a proof of the fiction of it, observes that many hundred years after the death of Pope Silvester, to whom this grant of Constantine's is supposed to have been made, the election of the Pope made at Rome, was sent to Constantinople to be confirmed or admitted of the Emperor." Lewis's Life, p. 117. Vide Lupi Decreta et Canones, pt. iii. p. 259.

Long were the task, through each degree to trace
God's Servants' Servant to his pride of place;
To note how, borne above his lowly birth
He reared his Crozier o'er the Lords of Earth;
To robes of Empire changed his Priestly gown,
And swelled the Mitre to the Triple Crown.

(Smedley's *Lux Renata*, p. 10.)

CHAP. XX.

Of the Discourses written of the Rule of Faith.

C. L. 232. ✠ Nubes Testium: or a Collection of the Primitive Fathers, giving testimony of the faith once deliver'd to the Saints. [Being a full discovery of the sentiments of the Ancient Fathers in the chief points of controversie at present under debate. With an Appendix containing the testimonies of many eminent Protestants, confessing the Fathers to have taught, profess'd and maintain'd these doctrins, of which they are here produc'd Abettors.]

D. Paul ad Hebr. 12.

Ideoque et nos tantam habentes impositam Nubem Testium, &c.

Serm. at the Visit. of Bish. of Norw. by S. Crispe, p. 6.

This will oblige us not to rest in our own private judgments for the sense of Scripture, but to take the concurrent sense of the Catholic Church in the first and purest ages of it, which may reasonably be presum'd the most authentick and credible witnesses of the Apostolical Faith and Practice, pp. Pref. &c. x, 210. 4to. Lond. 1686.

See Contin. p. 43. Ath. Oxon. vol. ii. coll. 1083.

We learn from Gee's Answer that the Nubes Testium is by the Author of the Papist Misrepresented and Represented. In his Introduction to the same work (No. 233) he remarks:—"One would have believed that a man who had presented the World with so large a Collection was very conversant in those Fathers he here makes use of; and for my part I should have had such an opinion of him, could he but have kept his own Councel a little better, and not have brag'd that the Latin of his Authorities was out of such editions as are most authentic. But when I came to examine things, I quickly perceived (to say no worse of it) that this Collector said more than he knew, since the present French Historian Natalis Alexandre, out of whom this whole Nubes Testium (excepting a very few passages) is wholly stole, does not acquaint his Reader that I can observe, what editions of the Fathers he makes use of; and reason good since I believe he saw very little more than our Compiler the Fathers themselves, but did very fairly take upon trust: And which is more F. Alexandre tells his Reader in his Preface to his first volume that he makes use of Christopherson's Translation of Eusebius's History, which the men of this age I am sure do not believe to be the most authentick; if our *Compiler* (for he that steals a whole book without mentioning whence he had it, deserves no better a title) of the Nubes Testium do, there is no help for it.

"It was by remembering this last passage in Natalis's Preface, and comparing it with our Compiler's brag about his editions of the Fathers being the most authentick, that I came to discover our Compiler's haunts, and found him to be the greatest Plagiary that has appeared (I believe) on the Stage in these times." p. 11. "There was," says Gee, "occasion for craft in the translation of this place (St. Basil's Homil. xix. upon the Forty Martyrs), however, I do not charge it upon the Jesuit (L. Sabran) who had it from the Compiler, nor the Compiler who had it from F. Alexandre, nor F. Alexandre himself, who had it from Bellarmine, or some other of their Writers, who all conspire in the same abuse of S. Basil's words. There is not a syllable for Invocation here," &c. *The Primitive Fathers no Papists*, p. 72.

Claget, in his Discourse concerning the Worship of the Blessed Virgin and the Saints (No. 326), admits that in the Fourth Age addresses were made to the Martyrs at *their respective Memories or Monuments*, pp. 76-95. Cf. Hey's Lectures, Bk. iv. art. xxii. § 5.

233. An Answer to the compiler of the Nubes Testium, wherein is shewn that Antiquity (in relation to the points of controversie set down by him) did not for the first five hundred years, believe, teach, or practise, as the Church of Rome doth at present believe, teach and practise. Together with a vindication of the Veteres Vindicati from the late weak and disingenuous attempts of the author of Transubstantiation Defended [132 *supra*]. By the author of the answer to Mr. Sclater of Putney; [viz. Edward Gee, M.A.] **C. L.**

pp. Introduction xii., 88, 4to. Lond. 1688

See Cat. No. 120, Contin. p. 44. Fasti Oxon. vol. ii. col. 222.

Of Gee an account is given in Part i. p. 153. He here challenges all the Romish Priests in England to shew him the canon of any Œcumenical Council in which the Bishop of Rome is constituted "Primate over the whole World, Head of the Catholic Church, and Father and Doctor of all Christians." (p. 20.) He asserts that "the Council of Florence, founding their definition for the Pope's supremacy upon the Acts and Canons of General Councils were notoriously guilty either of ignorance or forgery." (Ibid.) It may be added that about this there was a dispute, on which the Emperor threatened to break off the treaty, A.D. 1439. The Pope proposed "according to Scripture and the writings of the Saints." See Milman's Latin Christianity, vol. vi. p. 126. Gee adduces the testimony of Launoy in his Epistola ad Mich. Marollium [Cambr. edit. p. 174], that there is no canon in the code of the Universal Church (published by Justel), nor in the ancient code of the Church of Rome, that makes any mention of the Pope's supremacy.

Have not these writers forgotten the Novella of Valentinian III in causa Hilarii Episcopi Arelatensis, vide Leonis Opp. pp. 434–35, where we learn that at the avowed instance of Leo that Emperor enacted A.D. 445 that all bishops of the Western Empire should obey the Bishop of Rome, as Rector totius Ecclesiæ, possessing supreme authority by virtue of "Petri meritum, jura urbis, et synodum (Sardic)?" Cf. Lupus de Appellationibus, pp. 832–3. Bramhall, in his Replication to the Bishop of Chalcedon (Works, vol. ii. p. 226–7), has shewn that a similar testimony of Valentinian the Third, in his Letter to Theodosius, implies only "a principality of priesthood," not "a principality of power." The Letter will be found in Lupus *ut supra*, and in Labbe, Concil. t. iv. p. 52.

The epistles of Launoy were chiefly written against Bellarmine "to establish this important truth, *that the Pope has no power with regard to the Canons of Councils.*" Launoy is said to have obtained the victory. Vide Bellarmin. de Conciliis et Ecclesia cap. xii. Cujus sit congregare Concilia et c. 17 de Conciliorum autoritate (Opp. t. ii.); Launoii Epistol. lib. vi. Ep. iv. (Opp. t. v. par. ii. p. 252 &c. 1731). These letters were so much approved of in England that they were republished 1689, at Cambridge, by Dr. Saywell. They were also abridged and published in Germany by Reisures, with the title, Joan. Launoii Anti-Bellarminus. See also Ames's Bellarminus-

Enervatus; Reiseri Augustinus Vindicatus, de Eccl. c. xiii.; and Ranke's History of the Popes, ad ann. 1605–7. Barrow enumerates, (on the Supremacy, p. 19,) the royal prerogatives which by gradual usurpations the Popes came to claim; *e.g.* to be superior to the whole Church, and to its representative a general synod of bishops; to convocate general synods at his pleasure, all bishops being obliged to attend upon summons from him, &c.

234. ✠ A Letter from a Dissenter to the Divines of the Church of England, in order to an union. A single sheet, 4to 1687. [Without title, pp. 4. "London, printed and sold by Randal Taylor, near Stationers' Hall."]

See Contin. p. 44.

The author of the Nubes Testium resolved "under a new form to pickeer with the author, and see if he could prevent him by some cunning stratagem from being in a capacity of shewing him any such trick for the future."

235. A Vindication of the principles of the author of the answer to the compiler of the Nubes Testium from the charge of popery. In answer to a late pretended letter from a dissenter to the divines of the Church of England. By Edward Gee, M.A. pp. 36, 4to Lond. 1688 C. L.

See Cat. No. 125, Contin. p. 44.

"I have already hinted to the world in the advertisement at the end of my second Letter to Sabran the Jesuit [No. 321 *infra*] that I am very well satisfied, not onely that this *pretended* Letter came out of Henry Hill's press, but that it was the issue of the representer's (or *compiler's*, call him whether you will) malicious pen."

236. ✠ The Primitive Fathers no Protestants, or a Vindication of Nubes Testium from the cavils of the answerer. Published with allowance.

[pp. 48, including title]. 4to Lond. (Henry Hill) 1687

See Contin. p. 45.

[This is by the author of Nubes Testium.]

C. 1. 237. The Primitive Fathers no Papists, in answer to the Vindication of the Nubes Testium. To which is added an historical discourse concerning invocation of saints, in answer to the challenge of F. Sabran the Jesuit. Wherein is shewn that invocation of saints, was so far from being the practice, that it was expressly against the doctrine of the primitive fathers. [Anon.] By Edward Gee, M.A.

pp. 88, Pref. and Contents, vi.

See Cat. No. 146, Contin. p. 45.

"Of this (treating us scurrilously) we have had a great deal of late, and I have had my share from them ; I will not animadvert farther on it than to say that their late pamphlets against us are so abusive, as if they had been *written* as well as printed by the Ditch-side." (Pref.) "The antiquary of Putney [see No. 130 *supra*], and the maker of the Ecclesiastical Prospective-glass [see No. 109 *supra*], and the representer himself not only here but in his other pamphlets are very punctual in quoting the Protestant authors, whom they have no more read than the Alcoran in Arabic. But as soon as I saw Brerely's Protestant Apology, I quickly discovered that this was the armoury," &c. (p. 30.) The Protestant authors making concessions here referred to are Montagu and Sherlock.

238. ✠ The Pope's Supremacy Asserted from the considerations of some Protestants, and the practice of the Primitive Church; in a dialogue by a church divine and a seeker. In vindication of Nubes Testium. [By the Representer.] 4to 1688

See Contin. pp. 35, 45. This tract is omitted in Dodd's list of Gother's Works.

239. A discourse of the Pope's Supremacy, Part II., in answer to a discourse, intitled, The Pope's Supremacy Asserted from the considerations of some Protestants, and the practice of the Primitive Church, in vindication of Nubes Testium. By Nicholas Stratford, DD.

See Contin. pp. 33-4, and No. 230 *supra*. Query, whether ever published? J. H. T.

240. The Antiquity of the Protestant Religion; with an answer to Mr. Sclater's reasons and the collections made by the author of the pamphlet, entitled, Nubes Testium. In a Letter to a Person of Quality. Part I. [By Edward Pelling, DD.] pp. 59, 4to Lond. 1687 C. L.

See Cat. No. 128; Contin. p. 32; Ath. Oxon. vol. ii. col. 1083.

This author was a member of the university of Cambridge, vicar of Great St. Helens, London, 1674, rector of St. Martin's, London, 1678, canon of Westminster, 1683. Afterwards rector of Petworth, Sussex. For Part ii. see No. 341.

241. The Fall of Babylon; or Seasonable Reflections on the Novelties of Rome; with the rise, growth and final overthrow of Antichrist now at hand: occasioned by the preface to a treatise called Nubes Testium, or a Collection of Primitive Fathers giving Testimony to the Faith once delivered to the Saints. Written upon the first coming forth of the said treatise (but not permitted to be then made public); for the benefit of all who abominate the corruptions of the Great Whore, and would not be partakers of her sins or plagues. By B.[enjamin] W.[oodroffe], D.D. pp. xlii.–171. 4to Lond. 1690 C. L.

See Ath. Oxon. vol. ii. col. 1048. "He was nominated Dean of Christ Church by K. James II. upon the withdrawing thence of Mr. Joh. Massey."

This treatise is not mentioned by Watt. The author was principal of Gloucester Hall, now Worcester College. He had been chaplain to his royal highness James Duke of York, then high-admiral of England, with whom he was present in the same ship in the terrible fight of Southwell Bay betwixt the English and Dutch. Among his publications is, The great question to be considered by the King and Parliament, how far Religion is concerned in Policy or Civil Government, Lond. 1679, in 2 sht. in fol. Neither this nor the preceding tract is in the Bodleian Library Catalogue, which mentions another controversial writing of this author, viz. Examinis Examinantis Examen, sive Reformationis et Reformatorum defensio adversus calumnias F. F. Otrokocsi, in libro quem inscribit Examen Reformationis Lutheri &c., 4to, Oxon. 1700.

So now being priest he plainly did profess
To make a jest of Christ's three Offices:
The rather since his scattered jugglings were
United now in one both time and sphere.
From *Egypt* he took petty deities,
From *Greece* oracular infallibilities,
And from old Rome the liberty of pleasure,
By free dispensings of the Church's treasure.
Then in memorial of his ancient throne;
He did surname his palace, *Babylon.*

* * * * *
* * * * *

As new and old Rome did one empire twist,
So both together are one *Antichrist.*
(George Herbert, *The Church Militant.*)

Compare Gale's Court of the Gentiles, book ii. ch. ii.; Wordsworth's Lectures on the Apocalypse; and No. 244 *infra.*

The Rule of Faith; or an answer to the treatise of Mr. J. S.[ergeant], entitled, Sure-footing; (to which is appended a Reply to his Third Appendix, &c., by Edw. Stillingfleet, D.D.) By John Tillotson. 8vo Lond. 1688

It was published in 1666, reprinted 1676 (Works vol. i. 1696, pp. 675-779.) "I know Mr. S. is pleased to say that certainty and infallibility are all one. And he is the first man that I know of that ever said it. And yet, perhaps somebody may have been before him in it, for I remember Tully says, that there is nothing so foolish, but some philosopher or other has said it. I am sure Mr. S.'s own philosopher, Mr. Wh[ite], contradicts him in this most clearly in his preface to Rushworth's Dialogues, where, explicating the term moral certainty, he tells us that some understood by it such a certainty as makes the cause always work the same effect, though it take not away the absolute possibility of working other ways; and this, presently after, he tells us, ought absolutely to be reckoned in the degree of true certainty, and the authors mistaken in undervaluing it. So that, according to Mr. Wh. true certainty may consist with a possibility of the contrary, and consequently Mr. S. is mistaken in considering certainty and infallibility to be all one. Nay, I do not find any two of them agreeing among themselves about the notions of infallibility and certainty. Mr. Wh. says that what some call moral certainty is true certainty, though it do not take away a possibility of the contrary. Mr. S. asserts the direct contrary, that moral certainty is only probability, because it does not take away the possibility of the contrary. The Guide in Controversy differs from them both, and makes moral, certain, and infallible all one. I desire that they would agree these matters before they quarrel with us about them." (Vol. i., 1696, pref. pp. vi. vii.) Cf. Part i. p. 131. Elsewhere Tillotson has remarked: "Nothing has fallen out more unluckily than that there should be such differences among them about that (infallibility, where it is lodged) which they pretend to be the only means of ending all differences." (Vol. i., Serm. ii. on 1 Cor. iii. 15.)

Honesty the Best Preservative against Dangerous Mistakes in Religion. Three Sermons on John xvii. 17. By John Tillotson, D.D. (Works, 1712, vol. i. pp. 235-53.)

"Whereas it is pretended that the Scripture is but a dead rule which can end no controversy, without a living judge ready at hand to interpret and apply that rule upon emergent occasions; the same objection lies against them unless a General Council, which is their living judge, were always sitting. For the definitions of their Councils in writing are liable to the same and greater objections than the written rule of the Scriptures." (p. 250.) Cf. Dryden's Hind and Panther, and Scott's Note, p. 187 of vol. x.

A Letter to the Hon[ble] Robert Boyle, defending the Divine Authority of the Holy Scripture, and that that alone is the Rule of Faith, in answer to Father Simon's Critical History of the Old Testament. Written by C. M. du Veil, D.D. *B. L.*

Lond. 1683

A learned converted Jew, a native of Metz in Lorrain. See Supplement, ch. xlii. Conversions &c. This letter had been previously published in French, 8vo, Lond.

The Question of Faith, which resolved resolves all other Questions in Religion. This Question is, Who ought to be our Judge **C. L.**

in all these Differences. By James Munford [or Mumford.]
8vo Lond. 1686

See No. 261. According to Dodd it was first printed in 4to.

C. L. A full and clear Exposition of the Protestant Rule of Faith.
4to Lond. *n.d.*

C. L. Appendix to several Letters which passed between Dr. Geo. Hickes and a Popish Priest. Part. II. Mr. Chillingworth's Letter of the Infallibility of the Church of Rome, or of that Doctrine which teaches the Roman Church to be the Guide of Faith, taken from the printed copy in the Preface to a Book intituled, Certamen Religiosum, or a Dispute between a Papist and a Protestant, &c. Oxford, printed 1704

See also his (Chillingworth's) discourses against the infallibility of the Roman Church among his additional discourses.

Protestant Certainty; or a Short Treatise shewing how a Protestant may be well assured of the Articles of his Faith.
pp. 34, 4to Lond. 1689

A fair and methodical Discussion of the first and great Controversy between the Church of England and Church of Rome concerning the Infallible Guide. In three Discourses. Whereof the first is introductory, and states the Points, which are preliminary to this, and all the other Controversies between the two Churches. The second considers at large the Pretence of Modern Infallibility, and shews it to be groundless. The third by the help of the former briefly examines the Pretended Rational Account of the Roman Catholicks, concerning the Ecclesiastical Guide in Controversies of Religion; and detects its Artifices. [See chap. xviii.]
pp. xi.-132, 4to Lond. 1689

The third discourse is wanting in the copy from which the above description is taken. Query if published? See the controversial tracts occasioned by the publications of Dean Manby and Abp. King, mentioned in part i. p. 151.

On this head, embracing *this with the two following chapters*, the reader is referred to The Judgment of the Anglican Church (posterior to the Reformation) on the sufficiency of holy Scripture and the authority of the holy Catholic Church in matters of Faith; as contained in the authorized Formularies and illustrated by the writings of her elder Masters and Doctors [from 1556 to 1747]: with an introduction, notes and appendix by John Fuller Russell, S.C.L., Lond. 1838. Compare a Letter by the Rev. J. Irons, in the British Magazine, in answer to an article entitled The High Church Theory of Dogmatical Authority in the fifth number of the Dublin Review. "A reference to Laud's Conference with Fisher would be conclusive on this subject. And quotations to the point may be found ready collected in an Anglican Catena (Tracts for the Times, vol. iv.), which, by the way, beginning with Jewel, does not end with Brett or Waterland, but with Jebb and Van Mildert;" Replies to Essays and Reviews, vi.; Rationalism, by Rev. A. W. Haddon, B.D. On the particular subject of this Catena may be profitably consulted Laud, Thorndike, Patrick, Brett, Waterland, Allix.

"I subjoin only some of the principal evidences from the Reformers and eminent theologians of the English Church, who declare in express terms, that the Scriptures are the rule of faith to the reason of man. I find them to my hand in an anonymous publication." Townsend, Ecclesiastical and Civil History philosophically considered. vol. i. p. 45. . . . . "I pass over others which might be quoted from the writings of Stratford &c. contained in Bishop Gibson's Collection of Tracts. If, however, we do examine them, we shall find that not only the ancient Church but the Church of England also, as Dr. Hansard, Dean of Windsor, observes (Gibson, vol. i. title i. p. 217) follows (for) her rule the Holy Scriptures."

The Rule of Faith, which among Protestants is one and the same, the Apostles' Creed, (see Hickes's Letters, ch. iii.) is received by them *upon the authority of Scripture*. "The truth of the Christian religion and of the Scripture is presupposed to the being of a Church. And therefore cannot depend upon the authority of it." (Thorndike's Judgment of the Church of Rome, 1679; reprinted in Hickes's Letters, Append.) Among foreign divines, consult Episcopius, Gerhardus,

Musculus, Polanus, Riserus, Rivetus, Jurieu in answer to the Jansenists, to Maimbourg, and the Bishop of Meaux. Received by Papists ***upon the authority of the Church;*** see Canisius, Hosius, Stapletonus.

> By this you hear the ***different degrees***
> ***Of Catholique infallibilities.***
> The Prelates are ***infallible*** in preaching,
> The Doctors and the Pastors in their teaching;
> The Laity in finding what they sought;
> Children in holding what their Parents taught.
>
> (Turbervile's ***Poem on the Rule of Faith,*** appended to his Manual of Controversies.)

"I will but trouble him (the Popish priest) with one or two more questions occasion'd by the writings of a learned Father of great authority in the Latin Church, I mean Vincentius Lirinensis . . . . . He nor the Fathers who wrote before him ever so much as mention, much less direct to any living, infallible judge, but to Scripture expounded by antiquity, universality and consent; and therefore I desire the gentleman, upon reading that little book (*Commonitorium*) to tell me, if the Church knew of any living, infallible judge in his time, or if it did, how he came to be ignorant of it? Or if, as he writes in that book, Scripture expounded by Catholick tradition be a sure and certain rule whereby to determine all controversies, then how can there be any need of an infallible living judge?" (Hickes, pp. 11, 12.) Sed si doctrinis non creditur Sacerdotum, credatur oraculis Christi, credatur monitis Angelorum dicentium: Quia non est impossibile Deo omne verbum. *Credatur symbolo Apostolorum, quod Ecclesia Romana intemeratum semper custodit et servat.* (Ambrosii lib. x. epistola lxxxi., 1567, tom. iii.)

CHAP. XXI.

Of the Discourses written of Scripture Proofs.

242. A Treatise proving Scripture to be the Rule of Faith. Writ by Reginald Peacock, Bishop of Chichester, before the Reformation, about the year 1450. (Published with a Preface by Henry Wharton, M.A.) pp. xl.-41; Alphabetical Table of the more obsolete English words, 3 pp. 4to Lond. 1688 C. 1.

See Cat. No. 91; Contin. p. 39; Ath. Oxon. vol. ii. col. 875.

Ejusdem Hist. et Antiq Univ. Oxon. lib. i. pp. 220-23; eadem Narratio in Hemingford, vol. ii. pp. 480-89; cum Pecockii Abjuratione, pp. 490-502.

There is an analysis of this Treatise of Faith in the Life of the learned and right Reverend Reginald Pecock, S.T.B., Lord Bishop of St. Asaph and Chichester, in the reign of K. Henry VI., being a Sequel of the Life of Dr. John Wiclif, by John Lewis, Lond. 1744. His biographer has given an ample account of his writings, all of which remain in MS. except his Treatise of Faith. For the opinions which this pioneer of the Reformation was forced to recant, Wharton refers (p. 37) to Bale (Cent. viii. p. 594); Godwin de Præsul. Angliæ, p. 559; and Fox's Martyrol. vol. i. p. 928. "In the period in which Pecock lived, the dispute between the papists and Wicliffites ran high, concerning the superior antiquity of their respective tenets; as well as on various other points of doctrine. Wicliffe, as we have seen, was a powerful antagonist to popish superstition. Pecock, though a sincere advocate of popery, discovered on all occasions a wish to accommodate. . . . . . In particular he allowed that priests were fallible men, and consequently might be mistaken. But the *shibboleth* of a true churchman, in those times, was his insisting on the authority of the church, and the infallibility of its decisions. Hence those concessions, instead of being ratified by the catholics, excited their implacable rancour. For his attempt to reclaim dissenters, he was reproached for encouraging them," &c. Burnett's Specimens of English Prose

Writers, from the earliest times to the close of the Seventeenth Century; who furnishes extracts from his book, entitled The Repressour, vol. i. pp. 116-27. In the fourth part "the author goes on with the usual texts cited for the primacy, and seems in the whole of this argument to have been a thorough *Papist*." Waterland's Letters to the Rev. Mr. Lewis. (Works, vol. x. p. 268.)

After having given some extracts from the second part of his Dialogue, or Book of Faith, the same "very learned and judicious" divine (see Lewis's Pref. p. 7) remarks: "This is plain enough, and so we observe that it was with some distinction and qualification that this author allowed *Scripture* to be the *primary* or *only* rule of faith and manners. And to me it seems that Mr. Wharton has written rather too favourably of this author, as being more of a Protestant than he really was; though, all things considered, the steps he made towards it are worthy of much consideration." Waterland, *ut supra*, p. 225.

243. ✠ A Request to Protestants, to produce plain Scriptures directly authorizing these their tenets.

I. Scripture is clear, in all necessaries, to every sober enquirer. II. The secular Prince hath all spiritual jurisdiction and authority immediately, from and under God. III. Justification by faith alone (viz. a persuasion that we are justified) is a wholesome doctrine. IV. The substance of Bread and Wine remains after, what it was before, sacerdotal consecration. V. Our Lord's Presence in or with the eucharist is merely gracious and influential; and if more, only to the faithful. VI. Adoration of the Eucharist (*i.e.* of our Saviour under the species of Bread and Wine) is idolatry. VII. All Christians whenever they communicate, are oblig'd to receive in both kinds. VIII. Chastity deliberately vow'd may be, unoffensively, violated. IX. All Christian excellencies are commanded. X. Every soul, as soon as expired, is conveyed to Heaven or Hell. XI. Desiring the intercessions of the Blessed is more superstitious, and derogatory to our Lord's mediatorship, than entreating the prayers of holy men militant. XII. Honouring the Cross, the reliques and representations of our Lord and his Saints, with that degree of reverence as we do the Gospels (commonly kiss'd and sworn by) altar and other sacred utensils, is idolatry. XIII. The Pope is Antichrist. XIV. Every prayer, used in Divine

Offices, must be in a language vulgar and intelligible to every auditor. XV. A company of Christians, voluntarily separating from all Christian Societies, condemning their doctrines and rites, destitute also of any visible correspondence with them in the Eucharist, in any religious assemblies or solemn devotions, can notwithstanding this perverse, entire and manifest separation, be a mystical Member of Christ, in catholic unity, and a charitable part of the Catholic Church. XVI. The whole clergy of the Catholic Church may apostatize from fundamental truth and holiness; whilst part of a national Laity may preserve both, discover the Clergies defection, and depriving them, heap to themselves teachers of their own sending and instruction.

See Contin. p. 38. A single half sheet. Henry Hills. Lond. 1686.

244. An Answer to the Request to Protestants, to produce plain Scriptures directly Authorizing these tenets. [By William Sherlock, D.D.] pp. 18, 4to Lond. 1687 **C. L.**

See Cat. No. 92; Contin. p. 38; Tenet xiii; "*The Pope is Antichrist.* A[nswer]. This indeed has been affirmed by some Protestants, but is no Article of our Church, and therefore we are not bound to prove it, but when we have a mind to it. No man ever pretended that there is any such proposition in Scripture, as that the Pope of Rome is Antichrist; but some think that the Characters of Antichrist and the Man of Sin are much more applicable to him than the Universal Headship and Infallibility." p. xii. See Lowndes's British Librarian, col. 966-70.

"We must remember also the large and important treatise of Whitaker, De Romano Pontifice, whose works are very well worth being looked into by those who would know what can be said for and against the other principal points in controversy between Protestants and Papists, as well as against this primary pillar of the reformed faith. That the Hierarchy of the Church of Rome is the Little Horn of Daniel, the Man of Sin of St. Paul, and the Antichrist of St. John," &c. Bishop Watson's Tracts (vol. v. contents vi.), who recommends also Hurd's 7th Sermon at Warburton's Lectures. Compare The Fall of Babylon, No. 241 *supra*, and the Man of Sin, or A Discourse of Popery: wherein the numerous and monstrous Abominations in doctrine and practice of the Romish Church are by their own hands exposed to open light, that the very Blind may see them, and Antichrist in capital letters engraven on them; particularly in the infinite drove of their Adored, but Lying Wonders and Miracles. By no Roman, but a Reformed Catholick. Pref. pp. xix. Book i. pp. 46, ii. 248, iii. 142. 4to Lond. 1677.

"Perhaps nothing," remarks Dr. Todd, (Donnellan Lecture Discourses on the Prophecies relating to Antichrist) "can shew more forcibly the carelessness, if not the gross ignorance, of the class of writers who have laboured to establish the application of the Prophecies of Antichrist to the Papal communion than to find Bishop Hurd speaking of such a man as Norbert: 'He (St. Bernard) tells us in his 56th Epistle that he had heard *one Norbert*, a man of exemplary piety, say that Antichrist would be revealed in that age.'" Introd. Serm. vii. note [s]. See also Maitland's Enquiry into the Grounds on which the Prophetic Period of Daniel and of St. John has been supposed to consist of 1260 years, p. 54 sqq. "Surely, even if we should not consider the Papacy either as Antichrist or the little horn, we leave it more curses than its bitterest enemy could desire to see fulfilled. Surely it has blood enough to answer for, if we look only to its transactions since the twelfth century," p. 66. "The Ancients," observes the former writer, "reasoning from Daniel, xii. 11, supposed that the interval between the destruction of Antichrist, and the general Judgment . . . . would be forty-five days only." He quotes St. Jerome and Malvenda *De Antichristo* as thus expounding the passage, and remarks: "It deserves the serious consideration of the reader whether this exposition, which is in strict accordance with the letter of the prophecy, and was once almost universally received in the Church, is not, on the whole, more worthy of our adoption than the laboured and unsatisfying conjectures of our modern controversial commentators." Dr. Todd's Donnellan Lecture Discourses on the Apocalypse, p. 214.

"At first I was prejudiced against both Maitland and Todd, but a diligent perusal has satisfied me that they are both sincere and orthodox Christians, men of remarkably strong intellect, perspicuous writers, accurate and indefatigable in their researches, and accurate reasoners." Memoirs of Edward Copleston, D.D., Bishop of Llandaff, Lond. 1851, p. 172. Compare his Two Sermons, preached at Newport 1841, pp. 63-66; and Cuninghame's Strictures on the Rev. S. R.

Maitland's Four Pamphlets on Prophecy, &c., Lond. 1832. A list of Maitland's publications on this subject will be found in the British Librarian, col. 961. I cannot here pass by the striking conclusion of Warburton's fine Sermon, The Rise of Antichrist.

"One of the soberest as well as soundest Reasoners of this reasoning Age, who, free from the enthusiasm of party-zeal, carried with him to the study of Scripture all the philosophic light and precision, which he had learnt of his Masters, Locke and Newton (who themselves employed the richest of their stores in the sacred service) after having paid the closest attention to the predictions of the Apocalypse, hath, as the result of all, been bold enough to put the truth of Revealed Religion itself on the reality of that prophetic Spirit which here foretold *the desolation of Christ's Church and Kingdom by Antichrist;* and here foretell the restoration of both to their original Purity and Power. 'If' (says he) 'in the days of St. Paul and St. John, there was any footstep of such a sort of power as this in the world; or if there had been any such power in the world; or if there was then any appearance of probability, that could make it enter into the heart of man to imagine that there ever could be any such kind of power in the world, much less in the Temple or Church of God; and if there be not now such a power actually and conspicuously exercised in the world; and if any picture of this power, drawn after the event, can now describe it more plainly and exactly than it was originally described in the words of the Prophecy; then may it, with some degree of plausibility, be suggested that the Prophecies are nothing more than enthusiastic imaginations.'" Clarke's Evidences of Natural and Revealed Religion, 1725, p. 282. [In the fourth volume of Bishop Watson's Collection of Tracts.]

For an exposition of different views on the subject of Antichrist see the elaborate article in Smith's Dictionary of the Bible by the Rev. Fred. Meyrick, and the review of it by the Rev. J. E. Elliott, author of Horæ Apocalypticæ, in the Christian Observer, March, 1864.

245. ✠ Protestancy destitute of Scripture proofs.

pp. 11, 4to Lond. (Henry Hills) 1687 **C. L.**

See Contin. p. 38. This is an expansion of the Request, *ut supra*, in reply to Sherlock's Answer.

246. A short Summary of the principal controversies between the **C. L.**

Church of England and the Church of Rome. Being a vindication of several protestant doctrines in answer to a late pamphlet intituled, Protestancy destitute of Scripture proofs. [By William Sherlock D.D.]

pp. Contents viii.–150. 4to Lond. 1687

See Cat. No. 93; Contin. p. 38.

C. L. 247. The Lay Christian's obligation to read the Holy Scriptures. [By Nicholas Stratford, D.D.] pp. 38, 4to Lond. 1687

See Cat. No. 90; Contin. p. 39; Ath. Oxon. vol. ii. col. 1067. Compare the same author's tract, The People's right to read the Holy Scripture asserted in answer to the 6th, 7th, 8th, 9th, and 10th Chapters, of the Second Part of the Popish Representer. 4to Lond. 1687. Repr. 1688, 1689; and in the 5th vol. of Gibson's Preservative, folio ed. i. Tit. v. c. 3.

248. ✠ An Address presented to the Reverend and Learned Ministers of the Church of England, by one sincerely desirous of finding out the Truth, in behalf of himself and others equally concern'd, as well for their own as the general satisfaction.

4to Lond. 1688

See Contin. p. 38.

C. L. 249. An answer to the Address presented to the Ministers of the church of England. [By John Williams, M.A.]

pp. 31, 4to Lond. 1688

See Cat. No. 94. Contin. p. 39. Ath. Oxon. vol. ii. col. 1119.

"To have a Member of the Church of Rome (as our Author apparently is) personating an Arian and other Hereticks, and in the face of the World requiring Scripture-proof for those above-said Points of Catholic doctrine; to have this thrust upon us afresh after the unrefuted Answers given to the first Request, the Catholick Dialogue, and the Plea for a Socinian, is no good sign, whatever he pretends, of one sincerely desirous of finding out the Truth." Our author directs (p. 29) The Addresser to the following publications: The People's Right (*ut supra*, No. 70), A Discourse concerning a Guide, A Vindication of the Answer to some late Papers, p. 40 &c.; An Answer to a late Dialogue between a new Catholick Convert and a Protestant, to prove the Mystery of the Trinity &c.; The Doctrine of the Trinity and Transubstantiation compared &c. in two parts; An Answer to the Request to Protestants (*ut supra*, No. 244), With the Vindication of it (No. 246); An Answer to a Book entituled, Reason and Authority, p. 1, 2, &c.; The Difference between the Protestant and Socinian Methods, in answer to the Protestants Plea for a Socinian (No. 304 *infra*). Other Romanist Divines, *e.g.* Dr. Hawarden, in his Answer to Clarke and Whiston, 1729, have endeavoured to weaken the Scriptural proof of the doctrine of the Trinity. See Waterland, vol. v. p. 256.

"The very pious Mr. Nelson, in a Letter to a Popish Priest (No. 288 *infra*) has some reflections worth the inserting in this place.

'I am not ignorant that two of your great champions, Cardinal Perron and Petavius, to raise the authority of general councils, and to make the rule of their faith appear more plausible, have *aspersed* not only the holy Scriptures as uncapable, by reason of their obscurity, to prove the great and necessary point of our Saviour's Divinity, but have impeached also the Fathers of the first three centuries as tardy in the same point. Blessed God! that men should be so fond of human inventions, as to sacrifice to them those *pillars* of our faith which are alone proper and able to support it; I mean *Scripture* and primitive *antiquity*. But to do justice to the memory of so learned a man as Petavius, the Bishop of Meaux told me, discoursing with him once on this subject, that in the last edition he made of his works, he retracted this opinion; which I am willing to believe upon the authority of that great man &c. Dr. Hickes's Letters &c., p. 334. Compare Chillingworth, pref. sect. 16, 17, 18.'" (Waterland, The Importance of the Holy Trinity asserted &c.)

250. ✠ **A clear proof of the certainty and usefulness of the protestant rule of faith, Scripture, after the help of ministerial guides, finally interpreted by each mans private sense.**

4to 1688

See Contin., p. 38. ["This proof is drawn from the Answer to the Address" &c. (No. 249)].

C. L. 251. A vindication of the Answer to the Popish Address presented to the ministers of the church of England in reply to a pamphlet abusively intituled, A clear proof of the certainty and usefulness of the protestant rule of faith. [By John Williams, D.D.] pp. 41, 4to Lond. 1688

See Cat. No. 95; Contin. p. 39; Ath. Oxon. col. 1119. As in No. 243 we have sixteen Tenets of the Protestants requested to be authorized by plain Scriptures, we have here fifteen Queries propounded for the Romanist to resolve. pp. 37–39.

252. Omitted by Peck.

253. ✠ Pax vobis; or gospel and liberty, against antient and modern papists. By E—— G—— preacher of the word. The second edition, corrected and amended. 12mo 1687

See Contin. p. 56. In C. Dolman's Sale Catal. Suppl. list, 1845, is an earlier edition dedicated to the Right Hon. the Lord Halyfax, 12mo, 1679. Cf. Donne's Serm. lxxiii. on John xiv. 2.

254. Some dialogues between Mr. G—— and others; with reflections on a book called Pax vobis. By Thomas Linford, M.A. 8vo 1687

See Cat. No. 185; Contin. 58; Fasti Oxon. vol. ii. col. 202. "He had been lately the ingenious prevaricator of Cambridge, was afterwards rector of St. Edm. Lumbard-Street in London, D.D. chaplain in ordinary to their majesties King Will. III. and Queen Mary, author of three or more Sermons" &c. *ut infra.*

C. L. 255. The protestant and popish way of interpreting Scripture impartially compared; in answer to Pax vobis. By Robert Grove, D.D. Bishop of Chichester.

pp. Dedication ii.–83, 4to Lond. 1689

See Cat. No. 194; Contin. p. 58. In Gibson vol. vi. folio ed. i. tit. v. ch. iii. 1. A list of Dr. Grove's works is given by Watt. Compare Field of the Church, bk. iv. ch. xiii. &c. "We believe that the Holy Scriptures do comprehend all necessary supernatural truths (so much is confessed by Bellarmine, that 'all things which are necessary to be believed and to be done by all Christians, were preached to all by the Apostles, and were all written,'" lib. iv. *De Verbo Dei*, cap. xi.) (Bramhall, Answer to the Epistle of M. de la Milletiere; Works, vol. i. p. 49.)

256. ✠ **The catholic scripturist; or the plea of the Roman Catholics, shewing the Scriptures to hold the Roman faith in above forty of the chief controversies now under debate. By James Mumford, Priest of the Society of Jesus.** **C. L.**

pp. x.–324, 12mo L. 1686

See Contin. p. 56. "Nothing can be more unsatisfactory than Mr. Dodd's notice of this able writer (p. 321, vol. iii. Church Hist.) more especially after professing that he had F. Nathaniel Southwell's Bibliotheca Scriptorum, S. J., to refer to . . . . What will ever stamp his name as a controversialist, is 'The Question of Questions' under the assumed name of Optatus Ductor, 4to Gant. 1658. Reprinted, 12mo Lond. 1686-7, pp. 530 [with his name]; and the 'Catholike Scripturist,' Gant. 1662. A second edition appeared in London, 12mo 1686, pp. 432. A third was published by James Watson, Printer to his Majesty's Royal Family and Household, Holy-Rood House, Edinburgh, 8vo 1687, pp. 464. And we have seen a fourth edition of the 'Catholic Scripturist,' 12mo Lond. 1767, pp. 335. Dr. Oliver's Biogr. of the Jesuits. The title of the work here referred to is as follows: The Question of Questions, which rightly resolv'd resolves all our Questions in Religion. This Question is, Who ought to be our Judge in all these differences? This book answers this Question; and shews a most easy and safe way, how among so many Religions the most unlearn'd and learn'd may find the True."

257. A letter to a lady furnishing her with Scripture testimonies against the principal points and doctrines of popery. **C. L.**

pp. 83, 4to Lond. 1688

See Cat. 199; Contin. p. 59. Pp. 3–18 contain an Admonition to the Reader concerning the Authority and Use of the Holy Scriptures.

258. ✠ A letter to a Lady from William Darrell of the Society of Jesus; wherein he desires a conference with the gentleman who writ her a letter furnishing her with Scripture testimonies against the principal points and doctrines of popery. An half sheet folio.

See Contin. p. 60. "This is indeed a new way of answering Books, and becoming the busie assuming spirit of that Society. One would wonder after so little success as they have hitherto met with in these encounters, what should move this Reverend Father to come into the same list with Goodwin, Pulton, and a few others of the same character." See Oliver's Biography, p. 80. "He died at St. Omers 28th Feb. 1721 æt. 70. His pen was always ready, and he has left us the following monuments of his piety, zeal and talents; — I. The Vindication of St. Ignatius of Loyola, 4to Lond. 1688. II. Gentleman Instructed &c. [This is the popular work to which Dr. Hickes contributed a preface, and which went through several editions. — J. Crossley.] III. Theses Theologicæ, in quibus defenditur Collegii Leodii Doctrina, 4to Liege 1702. IV. On the Epistles and Gospels &c. V. The Case Reviewed, or an Answer to the Case stated by Dr. Charles Leslie (who had published his work in 1713). The Case reviewed certainly went through three editions. I think F. W. Darrell was the author of a Treatise on the Real Presence, in answer to the Author of the Case Stated, 12mo Lond. 1721, pp. 400. In Peck's Catalogue [No. 46] is a Letter ascribed to this Father on K. James's Letters of Indulgence &c. as also a Letter to a Lady &c. [No. 258]. I suspect that F. Darrell was the translator of Père Daniel's Discourses of Cleander and Eudoxus on the Provincial Letters, 12mo 1701 and 1704."

259. The Judgment of archbishop Cranmer concerning the people's right to, and discreet use of the holy scriptures. Published (with a preface) by Edward Gee, M.A. 4to 1689

See Cat. No. 201; Ath. Oxon. vol. ii. col. 222. Compare Cranmer's Pref. to the Bible, Oxf. 1833, vol. ii. p. 111. Miscellaneous Writings (Parker Soc.) p. 118; Strype's Life, Append. ch. iv. In the reign of Henry VIII. there was an act of parliament *prohibiting the reading of the Scriptures.* The Council of Trent's fourth Rule de

Libris Prohibitis including the Bible was approved and confirmed by Pius IV. See No. 98 *supra*. It is true that the condemnation of Quesnel's propositions (enforcing the reading of the Scriptures) appeared scandalous to the wisest and best of the Church of Rome; that a number of illustrious prelates in France appealed from the Constitution (Unigenitus). But it is not less certain that this is the bull of the great oracle of Rome, and that it is received not only in Italy and Spain, but also in a great part of France, Germany and several other states. Abauzit's Letter to a Lady of Dijon, p. 74. Cf. Bayle's Reflections occasioned by a Comet, p. 82.

The learned Bishop Kidder published in 1690 *Reflections on a French Testament printed at Bordeaux*, 1686, pretended to be translated out of the Latin into French by the Divines of Louvaine, 1690, 4to.

"Bordeaux Version of the New Testament. Memoir of a French Translation of the New Testament, in which the Mass and Purgatory are found in the Sacred Text; together with Bishop Kidder's Reflections on the same, accompanied by Notes by Henry Cotton, LLD. Archdeacon of Cashel. 1827. . . . . . . Bishop Kidder's 'Remarks' were published in 1690, but neither the bishop nor his editor seem to have been aware that in 1688 the watchful champion, Dr. Jurieu, had brought the imposture of the Bordeaux version before the public in his 'Pastoral Letters' (vol. ii. pp. 470–80) . . . . A notice of the book, 'Le Nouveau Testament' &c. occurs in the Rev. Joseph Mendham's 'Literary Policy of the Church of Rome, p. 357.' The Witnesses in Sackcloth, Bibliographical Appendix, pp. 175–78. Cf. Bibliotheca Sussexiana, vol. ii. p. 543, according to which four copies only are known of the edition 1686. The other copies are in the possession of the Duke of Devonshire, in the Library of the Dean and Chapter of Durham, and in the Archiepiscopal Library at Lambeth. A fifth copy I am enabled to add by the Catalogus Librorum Impressorum qui in Bibliotheca Collegii Sacrosanctæ et Individuæ Trinitatis, Reginæ Elizabethæ, juxta Dublin adservantur. Tom. i. folio 1864.

"The Douay translation of the Old Testament was published by the *English College* at Douay in 1609; and with the Rhemish translation of the New Testament, first printed in 1582, it forms the English Bible, which alone is used by the Romanists of this country. In 1805 a new edition of this English Bible, with notes by Bishop Chaloner, was printed at Edinburgh, in five volumes 8vo. Two more editions of this Bible are now printing; one at Manchester, the other at Dublin. But both of them, as I understand, are in *folio*, and therefore not very likely to be circulated among the common people." (Marsh's Comparative View, 1816.) In the Bibliographical Appendix above referred to, p. 173, is mentioned, The Holy Bible, revised and corrected according to the Clementine edition of the Scriptures, and approved of by the most Rev. Dr. Troy, R.C.A.D., folio, Dublin 1816.

"Martini's translation (the latest *Italian Version*) has been repeatedly printed without his notes, but these editions, conformably to the fourth rule of the Index of Prohibited Books, are not allowed to be sold at Rome. . . . . At Rome indeed the Bible is a strange and rare book. The only edition of it allowed to be sold is Martini's version in upwards of twenty volumes, which are filled with Popish commentaries. Of course none but the rich can purchase a copy of the Holy Scriptures. Very few of the common people know what we mean by the Bible." Horne's Introduction, vol. v. 1846. Cf. British Magazine, vol. xiv. p. 762 sqq.

A Collection of Texts of Scripture with short notes upon them, and some observations against the principal Popish errors. Being a Summary of the Doctrine of the Church, with a plain refutation by Scripture. 12mo Lond. 1686

C. L. This was afterwards altered and enlarged, and published in 1688 under the following title: The plausible arguments of a Popish Priest from Scripture [see No. 143] answered by an English Protestant, seasoned and useful for all Protestant families. [By Tho. Comber.] pp. 54, 8vo Lond. 1686.

C. L. Truth Triumphant: in a Dialogue between a Papist and a Quaker: wherein (I suppose) is made manifest that Quaking is the Off-Spring of Popery. The Second Edition. By Charles Earl of Derby. 4to Lond. 1671

Printed with The Protestant Religion, see Part i. p. 3. "Do not father upon our Church those opinions which she dislikes and abhors; Socinians, Quakers, &c. are yours, rather than ours, and join with you in abundance of your doctrines." Poole's Dialogue between a Popish Priest and an English Protestant; Divisions among Protestants, 1667, 12mo.

✠ A full and clear Exposition of the Protestant Rule of Faith with an excellent Dialogue laying forth the large extent of true excellent charity against the uncharitable Papists. [By Andrew Pulton.] pp. 20, 4to, *no place nor date*

The several ways of resolving Faith in the Roman and Reformed Churches &c. [*ut infra* No. 451.] Sm. 12mo, York 1677

The Truth and Certainty of the Protestant's Faith with a short and plain Account of the Doctrine of the Romish Church in its visible opposition to Scripture and the very being of Christianity. *No place*, 1678 *B. L.*

The Lively Oracles given to us, or the Christians birth-right and duty in the custody and use of the Holy Scripture; by the Author of the Whole Duty of Man. 8vo Oxford 1678

The Legacy of the Right Rev. Father in God Herbert [Croft] Lord Bishop of Hereford to his Diocese, or a short Determination of all Controversies we have with the Papists by God's Holy Word. pp. x., 73, Lond. 1679 C. L.

See Biogr. Britt. vol. iii. p. 1530, and Part i. p. 97.

A Supplement to the preceding Sermon, together with a Tract concerning the Holy Sacrament of the Lord's Supper, promised in the Preface. pp. 77–128, 4to 1679 C. L.

The Necessity of the Knowledge of the Holy Scriptures. A Sermon on Matth. xxiii. 13. By John Tillotson, D.D.

There are two things we charge them withall, and which they are not able to deny. Their performing the public service of God in an unknown Tongue; and depriving tbe people of the use of the Scriptures. . . . . Erasmus in his Annotations upon this Chapter (1 Cor. xiv. 19) breaks out (as well he might) into admiration of the practice of the Church of Rome in his time. 'Hac in re mirum quam mutata sit Ecclesiæ consuetudo.'" (Tillotson, vol. i. 1696, p. 346.)

✠ A Vindication of the Roman Catholics from the foul aspersions thrown upon them by J. Tillotson D.D. in a Sermon preached by him in Nov. 1687. With Allowance. Lond. 1688

Sound Advice to Roman Catholics; especially the residue of poor seduced and deluded Papists in England, who obstinately shut both eyes and ears against the clearest light of the Gospel of Christ and surest Evidences of Scripture and reason. By T. O. pp. 21, 4to 1689

The fundamentals of the Protestant religion defined according to the Scripture and judgment of the most learned and orthodox Divines in England. 8vo Lond. 1689

Cf. Sherlock's Preservative against Popery, No. 119.

CHAP. XXII.

Of the Discourses written of Tradition.

260. A Treatise of Traditions. Part I. Wherein it is proved, That we have Evidence sufficient from Tradition: I. That the Scriptures are the Word of God; II. That the Church of England owns the true Canon of the Books of the Old Testament; III. That the Copies of the Scripture have not been corrupted; IV. That the Romanists have no such evidence for their Traditions; V. That the Testimony of the present Church of Rome can be no sure evidence of Apostolical Tradition; VI. What Traditions may securely be relyed upon, and what not. Anon. [By Daniel Whitby, D.D.] pp. lxviii., 135, 4to Lond. 1688 **C. L.**

See Cat. No. 200; Ath. Oxon. vol. ii. col. 1071. Cf. The Council of Trent examin'd and disprov'd by Catholic Tradition, No. 97.

261. A Treatise of Traditions. Part II. Shewing the novelty of the pretended Traditions of the Church of Rome, as being: I. Not mentioned by the Ancients in their discourses of Traditions Apostolical, truly so called or so esteemed by them; Nor, II. In their avowed Rule, or Symbol of Faith; Nor, III. In the Instructions given to the Clergy, concerning all those things they were to teach the People; Nor, IV. In the Examination of a Bishop at his Ordination; Nor, V. In the Ancient Treatises designed to instruct Christians in all the Articles of their Faith; VI. From the Confessions of Romish Doctors. With an Answer to the Arguments of Mr. Mumford for Traditions; and a Demonstration that the Heathens made the same plea from Tradition as the Romanists do, and that the Answer of the Fathers to it doth fully **C. L.**

justify the Protestants. [Anon. By Dan. Whitby, D.D.]
Pref. pp. xliii., 167, 4to Lond. 1689

See Ath. Oxon. vol. ii. col. 1071; [Cat. No. 200.]

262. A Discourse about Tradition; shewing what is meant by it, and what Tradition is to be received, and what Tradition is to be rejected. [Anon. By Simon Patrick, D.D., Dean of Peterborough.] pp. 54, 4to Lond. 1683

C. L. See Cat. No. 5; Contin. p. 5 [second edition, pp. 37, published in 1685]; in Gibson, v. folio ed. i. tit. iv. In p. 31 he notices the doctrine of a Millenium, "which he (Papias) gathered, saith Eusebius, from some saying of the Apostles, wrong understood." For the character of Papias, see No. 226, p. 54. This tradition is rejected by the Romanists; see Clagett, No. 164.

"I conclude this with the direction which our Church gives to the preachers in the Book of Canons 1571 (in the title *Concionatores*) .... But though nothing may be taught as a piece of religion, which hath not the forenamed original, yet I must adde, that those things which have been universally believed, and not contrary to Scripture, though not written at all there, nor to be proved from thence, we do receive as pious opinions. For instance, the *perpetual virginity* of the mother of God our Saviour; which is so likely a thing, and so universally received, that I do not see why we should not look upon it as a genuine *apostolical tradition.*" Ed. 1685, p. 15. Cf. Pearson on the Creed. "When we say that the rejection of tradition distinguishes the Church of England from the Church of Rome, it must be obvious to every one who considers the subject, that no other tradition can be meant than the tradition which to the Church of Rome is a rule of *faith.*" (Marsh's View of the Churches, &c., p. 59.) Cf. Patrick, pp. 11-17.

"The explanations of tradition which have been given by Cardinal Bellarmine are contained in his treatise on the Word of God (De Verbo Dei). The three first books of his treatise relate to the written Word of God (Verbum Dei scriptum), as contained in the Old and New Testament. But the fourth book, which relates wholly to tradition, is entitled, Of the unwritten Word of God (De Verbo Dei non scripto), and declares therefore, by its very title, the quality of the tradition which is the subject of that book. In the second chapter of this work Bellarmine observes: . . . . . . 'such doctrines are called unwritten doctrines, in contradistinction to the written doctrines, or Scripture, not because such doctrines are no where written, but because they were not written by the authors themselves. They were written by the Greek and Latin Fathers.' A catalogue of the Fathers, who are supposed to be the principal recorders of the unwritten Word, is given by Cardinal Baronius in his Annales Ecclesiastici, tom. i. pp. 412-18. The first kind he calls Divine tradition; the second he calls Apostolical tradition. . . . . . . There is a third kind of tradition mentioned by Bellarmine, which relates merely to Church ceremonies, and is called therefore the tradition of the Church, or Ecclesiastical." (Marsh, p. 6, &c.)

One of the papers by Chillingworth (No. 441) is An Argument drawn from the communicating of Infants (as without which they could not be saved) against the Church's infallibility; and he also remarks, in his Answer to some Passages in Rushworth's Dialogues, that "the custom of administering the Eucharist to infants in short time grew universal, and in St. Austin's time passed currently for an apostolical tradition, and the Eucharist was thought as necessary for them as baptism. This custom the Church of Rome hath again cast out; and in so doing professed either her no regard to the traditions of the apostles, or that this was none of that number. This example is a proof sufficient that many things may get in by error into the Church, and by degrees obtain the esteem and place of apostolic tradition, which yet are not so." Mosheim observes, whilst objecting to the *occultation* of the Council of Trent, that the real doctrines of Rome are no where to be fairly got, no where authenticately stated. (Cent. xvi. sect. iii. ch. i. § 24.) "It has," as Lord Bacon said of the heathen religion, "no soul, that is, no certainty of faith or confession." Cf. Fulke on 1 Tim. vi. v. 20, and part i. p. 243.

263. An Historical Discourse concerning Tradition. [By John Williams, M.A.]

See Ath. Oxon. vol. ii. col. 1121, and Nos. 96 and 376.

[It is doubtful whether this was ever published, unless it be the same as No. 376.—H. J. T.]

SUPPLEMENT TO CHAPTERS XX., XXI., XXII.

✠ Methodus compendiosa perveniendi ad fidem, auctore J. Sargeant. 8vo Paris 1674

[See Dodd, vol. iii. p. 477, who gives the title in English. J. C.]

The Grand Presumption of the Roman Church, in equalling their Traditions to the Written Word; and their jealousy of themselves in refusing to admit the Holy Scriptures as the rule for the trial of their Religion. By Francis Gregory, D.D. 4to Lond. 1675

Compare Stillingfleet's Rational Account of the Protestant Religion (Works, vol. iv. p. 57 sqq.), and Waterland on the Use and Value of Ecclesiastical Antiquity (Works, vol. v. p. 270.)

Scripture and Tradition compared. By Bishop Stillingfleet. 4to Lond. 1688

(Works, vol. iii. p. 40. Also in Gibson, vol. v. p. 219.) Cf. Nos. 225, 232, 233, 265 (conclusion), 346, 376, 451, 455.

𝕮. 𝕷. The Plausible Arguments of a Romish Priest from Antiquity answered by the Author of the Answer to the Plausible Arguments from Scripture (in a Dialogue). pp. 50, 8vo Lond. 1687

This is a distinct work from No. 143, but is by the same author.

𝕮. 𝕷. The Protestant's Companion: Or, An impartial Survey and Comparison of the Protestant Religion, as by Law established; with the main Doctrines of Popery: wherein is shown, that Popery is contrary to Scripture, Primitive Fathers and Councils, and that proved from Holy Writ, the Writings of the ancient Fathers for several Hundred years, and the Confession of the most Learned Papists themselves. Whereby the Papists vain pretence to Antiquity, and their reproaching the Protestant Doctrines with Novelty, is wholly overthrown. By a true Son of the Protestant Church of England, as established by Law. pp. xvii., 45, Lond. 1685

In Gibson, vol. iii. 8vo edit. xvii. On Councils Basnage's work, Annales Politico-Ecclesiastici, is serviceable by correcting some errors into which Comber (No. 243) had fallen; also Spanheim's Historia Christiana, s.v. Concilia. (Opp. i.) Consult also Bray's Bibliotheca Parochialis, p. 353 sqq.

✠ **Of Faith necessary to Salvation and the Necessary Ground of Faith Salvifical; Whether this, alway, in every Man, must be Infallibility. Part II. Of Infallibility. Part III. Concerning the Obligation of not professing or acting against our Judgment, or Conscience. And whether the obedience of Non-contradiction only, or also of Assent, be due to the Decrees of Councils. Part IV. Concerning Obedience to Ecclesiastical Governors, and Tryal of Doctrines. Part V. Concerning Salvation possible to be had in a Schismatical Communion. And concerning the danger of living in, and the necessity of departing from a Known-Schismatical Communion. [By Obadiah Walker.] 4to Oxford 1688**

The Faith and Practice of a Church of England Man. [By W. Stanley, D.D., Dean of St. Asaph.] Printed for Walter Kettilby, at the Bishop's Head in St. Paul's Church-Yard. 8vo. Lond. 1688

William Stanley, D.D. (see p. 11), was born at Hinckley in Leicestershire, educated at a school at Ashley in Lancashire, and St. John's College, Cambridge. "He made that valuable Catalogus Librorum MSS. in Bibliotheca Coll. Corp. Christi in Cantabrigia, quos legavit Matthæus Parkerus Archiepiscopus Cantuariensis (fol. Lond. 1722), which he afterwards printed at his own expense, and which merits the acknowledgments of all lovers of antiquity, and especially of the history of this church and nation. . . . . . The doctor, when Dean of St. Asaph, was at the sole expence of that act of parliament which annexed prebends and sine-cures to the bishopricks of Bangor, Llandaff, St. David and St. Asaph, in order to relieve the widows and fatherless of the Welch clergy from the sore distress of paying mortuaries to the bishops upon the death of every incumbent within their respective dioceses and jurisdictions. . . . . . . An act of generosity and goodness in the dean that ought ever to be remembered with the utmost gratitude by the clergy of Wales. . . . . . . Dr. Stanley, considered as an author, published but few things, though probably he would have written more (as he began early to take a share with the London clergy in the popish controversy) had he not been prevented in going on with them by being sent over to Holland in the capacity of Chaplain to the Princess of Orange. However before he went abroad he was concerned with several learned divines in the scheme of printing an English Bible with a plain and practical commentary, but more especially levelled against the errors and corruptions of popery. His own province was to write that upon the minor prophets, a scheme that was superseded by the happy establishment of our church and nation at the revolution." (Masters's History of the College of Corpus Christi &c. in the University of Cambridge, Camb. 1753, 4to, pp. 173-6.) This memoir was reprinted, with additions, in Nichols's Leicestershire.

Previously to 1713 this tract passed through no less than seven editions, was reprinted in 1807, with an account of the author, was re-issued with notes in 1841 by the Rev. Kirby Trimmer, in 1848 by
C. L. the Rev. Robert Eden, and in 1854 at Manchester, with an introduction by George Frederick Mandley, Esq., entitled Tractarianism (so called by the Prejudiced and Misinformed) No Novelty; as exemplified in the Confessions of The Faith and Practice of a Church of England Man, of the ever memorable epoch 1688.

See also Nos. 198, 225, 376.

CHAP. XXIII.

Of the Discourses written of the Latin Service, or Prayer in an Unknown Tongue.

264. A Discourse concerning the Celebration of Divine Service in an Unknown Tongue. [By John Williams, M.A.] **C. L.**

pp. 56, 4to Lond. 1685

See Cat. No. 11; [State, p. 8]; Contin. 6; Ath. Oxon. vol. ii. col. 1121. In Gibson, folio ed. vol. ii. p. 111, 8vo ed. vol. vi. "Though Latin prayers were lawful in English congregations, who do not understand them, yet is it unlawful to pray in English?" Sherlock's Address appended to No. 305, p. 94. See also Willet's Synopsis Papismi, fol. 1634, p. 33; Bingham's Antiquities, B. xiii. ch. iv. The custom of preaching, which constitutes a considerable part of Christian devotion, had not been introduced into the temples of antiquity; see Thomassin, Discipl. de l'Eglise, vol. ii. ch. lxxxiii. "The Council of Trent first transgress the ancient law of Justinian (Novel. 137, p. 225) that public prayers and offerings should be performed with a loud voice, so as to be heard of the people; and then they add sin to sin, and command that they be not made in any tongue but an unknown tongue." (Beveridge on Article XXIV.) Williams, p. 47, refers to Novel. 123. See this vindicated in Bp. Jewel's Reply to Harding's Answer, p. 128, Oxf. ed. vol. vi. p. 320.

265. A Treatise in Confutation of the Latin Service practised &c. by the order of the Council of Trent, continued in the Church of Rome. [By Daniel Whitby, D.D.] **C. L.**

pp. x., 118, 4to Lond. 1687

See Cat. No. 104; Contin. p. 7; Ath. Oxon. vol. ii. col. 1071.

Whitby gives a chronological series of the "testimonies of the Fathers that the publick service was by them celebrated in a tongue understood by the people," pp. 10-16. "This way of arguing negatively we with St. Austin do allow; the Universal Church knows no such doctrine;

ergo, it is no article I am obliged to receive as any part of Christian faith." Treatise of Traditions, part ii. ch. xii. p. 131, by the same author. "Thus far," observes Waterland, "he at that time: and in another treatise which he published in Latin, twenty-five years after, when it is certain he had no friendly disposition towards the Fathers, yet still he thought himself obliged to admit such a negative argument as he had before admitted. A negative argument therefore being allowed it must be allowed also that that the Fathers are of use to us, so far as such an argument can be of use; and that the ancients may be of great use in the Church in this view is very apparent, being that they serve as an outwork (which Daillè takes notice of) for the repelling the presumption of those who could forge a new faith." The Use and value of Ecclesiastical Antiquity. Works vol. v. p. 276. The treatise here referred to is, Dissertatio de Scripturarum Interpretatione, &c. 8vo Lond. 1714. Cf. Waterland ibid. p. 329, Vincentii Lirinensis Commonitorium, and Reeves's Pref. to his translation of that treatise.

266. A Discourse concerning the Celebration of Divine Service in an Unknown Tongue. 4to 1685

[Query, whether the same with No. 264.—J. H. T.]

This controversy arose in the eighth century, when throughout Western Christendom a large part of the population was Roman, or provincials who spoke Latin. In every country converted by the Latin Church the Scripture and the Liturgy had been introduced, not in the vernacular language of the original or conquered population, but in the language of the government or missionaries, the Latin language of the old Empire and the new Church of Rome. Even when new languages were forming in Italy, Spain and Gaul, on a Latin groundwork, the Latin services of the Church ceased, only gradually and partially, to be intelligible to the common ear. *Christianity brought other gifts in her train.* The Slavian dialects were as yet unwritten; their alphabet was the invention of [the missionary] Cyril. This pious man and his colleagues not only so far mastered the language as to preach with success; they translated certain books of the Scripture into the dialect of Moravia, and even ventured to celebrate the services of the Church in that tongue. The use of the Slavian language was permitted by Pope John the Eighth in the ninth century, but two hundred years after it was prohibited by Gregory the Seventh. In Bohemia, John XIII. in founding the bishopric of Prague (A.D. 973), made the use of the Latin ritual a condition. The Slavonic was only maintained here and there, amid constant opposition, in addition to the Latin. In the Eastern Church a contrary method was every where followed. The same principle which had, in his cell at Bethlehem, dictated the original translation of the Bible by Jerome into what was then the one known language of the West, [see Butler's *Horæ Biblicæ*, sect. xiv.], was adopted by the Greek Church with regard to all the nations that came within their sphere. Hence in the remote East sprang up the Coptic, Armenian and Ethiopic Versions; hence Ulfilas immortalised himself by producing the only wide-spread translation of the Scriptures which existed in any Western language till the times of Wycliffe. The rude alphabet invented by Cyril (or Constantine) and his fellow-missionary Methodius, first instructed the Russian nation in letters, and by its quaint Greek characters still testifies in every Russian book the Greek source of the religion and literature of the empire. See Milman's Latin Christianity, vol. ii. p. 351; Stanley's Eastern Church, Lect. ix.; Gieseler, 3rd Period, 2nd Div. § 38; Thomassin, Ancienne et Nouvelle Discipline de l'Eglise, 1725, pp. 1038-9, 1043; Vetus et Nova D. 1688, vol. i. pp. 389-92.

In Ussher's Treatise de Scripturis et Sacris Vernaculis, 1689, Works, vol. xii., a comparison is drawn between the Egyptian mysteries and the βαττολογία of the Latin Church.

"It is unconceivable to me but that so great a number (of ceremonies) must needs employ the mind in the worship of God, as that it is not possible to be intent thereupon, and consequently must prostrate (at least in a great measure) the design of worship. But this is no reason to a Papist, who can not be thoroughly so, and acknowledge the necessity of exercising the mind in divine worship: for his Holy Mother hath taught him this mad and impious doctrine, that the Sacraments confer grace, ex *opere operato*, *from the work done;* and so are differenced from those of the Old Testament, they conferring grace, *ex opere operantis*, *from the work of the Doer;* as also that a mere general attention in saying their prayers and numbering them over, is as much as is necessary. And if we can believe that we need not mind our prayers, we have no reason to blame those of them who do not desire to understand them; nor yet their church for enjoyning the saying them in a language which the generality of her children are ignorant of; as if she designed in so doing to put an affront on S. Paul, who hath taught us in the most express terms the quite contrary doctrine in the 14 chapter of the First to the Corinthians." (Fowler's Discourse of Christian Liberty, pp. 195-6, 1680.)

B. L. The Christian's Birth-right, or a Short Treatise concerning the Holy Scriptures, shewing why and how they ought to be made use of. Reprinted according to the copy printed at Hamburgh. 8vo 1690

"Note," says Fox, "these great reasons of the Catholikes, why the Scriptures should not be in English." "The plowman, when he heareth this in the Gospel, No man that layeth his hand on the plough and looketh back is meet for the kingdom of God, might peradventure when he heareth this cease from his plough. Likewise the baker, when he hears that a little leaven corrupteth a whole lump of dough, may percase leave our bread unleavened, and so our bodies shall be unseasoned. Also the simple man when he heareth in the Gospel, If thine eye offend thee, pluck it out and cast it from thee, may make himself blinde, and so fill the world full of beggers." (Fox's Martyrology; The Frierly Sermon by Dr. Buckneham, vol. iii. p. 455.)

"While Scripture was yet locked up in an unknown tongue and removed from the knowledge of the laity, (who were then generally very ignorant) the clergy were not ashamed to make confident appeals for the truth of their doctrine to the Holy Scriptures....... Before the translation of the Scriptures, lesser artifices (than the plea of tradition) could hide the deformity of their errors, and while ignorant Christians could be securely misled with false and sometimes foolish interpretations of Scripture, while Ecce duos gladios was thought sufficient to evince the coercive power of the Pope over temporal princes, and *Arabant boves, juxta comedebant asini*, could effectually perswade the laity intirely to resign up their judgments to the direction of the clergy, there was no need of any desperate remedy, &c." (Pref. to Peacock's Treatise, p. xiv., No. 242).

See also No. 259 *supra*, and 393 *infra*.

CHAP. XXIV.

Of the Discourses written of the Celibacy of the Clergy.

267. ✠ A Discourse concerning the Celibacy of the Clergy. [By Abraham Woodhead. This is printed with No. 169 *supra.*] C. L.
pp. 39, 4to Oxon. 1687

See Ath. Oxon. vol. ii. col. 616.

"The system of discipline in the Church of Rome as to the marriage of presbyters was very much like that which now prevails in the Greek Church. The evangelical liberty confirmed by the example of the apostles, and that of many illustrious bishops in the second century, had gradually been infringed. There was in conformity with Canons 17-19 [Canones Apostolorum] no vow of celibacy; but it was not thought conformable with St. Paul's saying, "A presbyter should be the husband of one wife," that a presbyter who lost his wife should marry again so long as he kept his office. From this the inference was drawn, that he who had a second or third wife, ought not, strictly speaking, to be made a presbyter. The next step was that he who had been ordained presbyter when unmarried, should not marry during that office. It was on this point more particularly that Hippolytus was at issue with bishop Callistus, who made no difficulty in ordaining, as presbyters, men who had a second or a third wife, or in allowing unmarried presbyters to marry and keep their office. We see that in this respect also the age of Hippolytus was one of transition. There were different ways before the Church. She might have struck out some middle course between the two systems of Callistus and Hippolytus, and then would probably have come to something like the system of the Greek Church in Russia, where a parish priest must be a married man, having his first wife; so much so, that at her death he is expected to retire and go into a convent, the place out of which bishops are generally taken. The majority of the bishops assembled at Nice in 325, first (as Socrates says in his "Ecclesiastical History") introduced a new law, forbidding bishops, priests, and deacons, who were married men, to keep their office, unless they would give up married life. This regulation soon grew into a general custom, notwithstanding the strong Christian and moral opposition of the venerable bishop Paphnutius, and became the basis of still greater encroachments in later times, in spite of the moral reluctance of the Germanic nations." Hippolytus and his Age; or, The Beginnings and Prospects of Christianity. By C. C. J. Bunsen. 1854. Vol. i. p. 470. For the story of Paphnutius see Natalis Alexander, Dissert. Eccl. 1679; Neander, vol. iii. p. 197; Woodhead, p. 25; Tully, pp. 39, 40, 56.

"So Socrates and Sozomen tell the story: to which all that Valesius after Bellarmine has to say is, 'that he suspects the truth of the thing, and desires leave to dissent from his historians.' Which is but a poor evasion, in the judgment of Du Pin himself. . . . . . So that in the judgment of that learned Romanist, there is no question to be made but that the Council of Nice decreed in favour of the married clergy, as the historians relate it did; and that then the practice was different from that of the present Church of Rome, which others are so unwilling to have the world believe. (Bingham's Antiquities, Bk. iv. ch. v. § 7.

C. L. 268. An Answer to a Discourse concerning the Celibacy of the Clergy, printed at Oxford. [By George Tully, Oxon., Rector of Gateside, near Newcastle, and Subdean of York.]
Pref. pp. iv., 98. 4to Oxf. 1688

See Cat. No. 190; Ath. Oxon. vol. ii. col. 925.

"I must ascribe the length of this discourse to the studied brevity and obscurity of my Adversary [Woodhead]: had he been longer and plainer I could have been much shorter. But it is the peculiar character of his works, that the main strength of 'em consists in the deep way, that leads to their meaning, the uncomfortable darkness of the journey, and those asperities of style, wherein he has wrapt up his Conceptions." (Pref. ii.)

C. L. 269. A Treatise of the Celibacy of the Clergy, wherein its Rise and Progress are historically considered. [By Henry Wharton, A.M.] Pref. pp. iv., 168. 4to Lond. 1688

See Cat. No. 101; Contin. p. 7; Ath. Oxon. vol. ii. col. 874. In Gibson's folio ed. vol. i. No vow of celibacy was required of the clergy as a condition of their ordination for the three first centuries of Christianity. pp. 59-65. Cf. Bingham's Antiquities, Bk. iv. ch. v. § 5, &c., where he has entered at length into this controversy. That the clergy were married for some centuries before Gregory VII., and resisted strenuously the yoke of celibacy, see authorities in Chemnitii Exam. Concil. Trident., Part iv. de Cœl. Sacerd. pp. 67-72; Anton. de Dominis, de Rep. Eccles., p. 306 sqq.; Tully *ut infra*, pp. 33-59; Taylor's Ductor Dubit., vol. iii. ch. iv. (Works, Eden's ed., vol. x. pp. 229-30); Bowden's Life of Gregory VII., Bk. iii. ch. v.; Thorndike, Of the Laws of the Church, Bk. iii. ch. xxxii., note f, Oxf. 1844; Hey's Lectures, Art. xxxii. For the marriage of the clergy at Milan see Gieseler, Per. ii. Div. iii. ch. vi. § 34; Milman, vol. ii. p. 485; through the whole of Italy, in Germany, in France, in Normandy and in England, ibid. vol. iii. pp. 15-21. "The best testimony for the whole of Italy, including Rome (even beyond the declamations of Damiani), is the statement of the more sober Pope Victor in his Dialogues . . . [A.D. 1086] Max. Biblioth. Patr. xviii. Compare Bonizo apud Œfel. Rer. Boic. Script. ii. 799." "The famous letter of Ulric, Bishop of Augsburg, to Pope Nicholas, had already boldly asserted the Teutonic freedom in this great question. Ulric had urged with great force the moral and scriptural arguments; and sternly contrasted the vices of the unmarried with the virtues of the married clergy." Milman, ibid.

Non nocuit tibi progenies, non obstitit uxor
Legitimo conjuncta toro; non horruit illa
Tempestate Deus thalamos, cunabula, tædas.

* * * * * *

Prudentia patrum
Non satis advertit, dicunt, quid ferre recuset
Quid valeat natura pati. Cervicibus, aiunt,
Hoc insuave jugum nostris imponere Christus
Noluit; istud onus quod adhuc quam plurima monstra
Fecit, ab audaci, dicunt, pietate repertum.
Tutius esse volunt, qua lex divina sinebat
Isse via, veterumque sequi vestigia patrum:
Quorum vita fuit melior cum conjuge, quam nunc
Nostra sit, exclusis thalamis et conjugis usu.

Baptista Mantuanus, *Vita Hilarii, Ep. Pictav.*

Cf. The Latin Poems attributed to Walter Mapes, collected and edited by Thomas Wright for the Camden Society; Consultatio Sacerdotum.

Ulric's Letter is inserted in Eccard, Hist. Med. Ævi Script. ii. 23-27; Martene et Durand, Collect. i. 449-454; Grynæi Orthodoxographa, t. ii. 481-484; in Brown's Fasciculus, Append. pp. 161-164; and in Flacius Illyricus, who has given the history of this controversy at great length, pp. 973-96. L'Enfant, C. of Constance, tom. ii. p. 359, refers for it to the Casauboniana, p. 302. Bellarmine (Lib. i. de Clericis, ch. xxii. Opp. ii.) *maintains it is a forgery.* The life of St. Ulric will be found in Butler's Lives, July 4, and in Neander, vol. v.,i who seems to think this Letter one of the forgeries of the party opposed to the Hildebrandian plan of reform.

"Mr. Fox," says Wharton, p. 152, "in his English Martyrology hath published two antient Latin Apologies for the Marriage of the Clergy, under the name of Volusianus, Bishop of Carthage, both directed to Pope Nicholas. The first, which is short, is nothing else but the epistle of Hulderieus, before mentioned, which hath been often published. The second is far longer, was never elsewhere published; and seems to have been the Remonstrance or Apology of all the married Clergy of the Western Church, offered to Pope Nicholas the Second, and the other Bishops of the Church who endeavoured to impose celibacy, presently after the Roman Synod in the year 1059, which forbad the Laity to hear Mass from the married Clergy. The author of it writes more elegantly, and argues more strongly than Hulderieus; and indeed, abating some allegorical interpretations of Scripture, the peculiar genius of those ages, it may be accounted a rational and exact Treatise." For authorities see Milman, Gieseler, and Foxe's Martyrology, edited by the Church Historians, vol. v. part i. Wharton shews from Aventinus and the Councils that many of the Clergy retained their wives for some ages after the times of Hildebrand. "I shall only remarque upon the whole what Aventin relates (Annal. Boiorum, Lib. v.) of the thoughts of all sensible men of Hildebrand's days, in relation to his first establishing this iniquity by a law. All good, open, just, ingenious, plain men publickly dated the reign of Antichrist from that time, clearly discovering the completion of those things, which our Saviour had foretold so many years before." Tully, p. 64. The words of Aventinus, when speaking of the interdict, are: *Novum dogma, nova hæresis, quæ unquam Christianorum contus basset regnum, visa est*, p. 460, Basileæ, 1580. Foxe gives us much curious information relating to the marriage of priests in the Church of England, from Henry of Huntingdon, Matthew Paris and William of Malmesbury; and inserts *certain Instruments and Evidences of Ancient Record, declaring the Marriage of Priests to have stood, in times past, both with ancient Custom and public Laws of the Realm.* On the celibacy of the clergy in England, see also Hume (William I.); Collier, Bk. iv. Cent. x. and xi.; and Lingard's remarks on the Six Articles of Henry VIII.; for its developement in the Monastic system and the charges brought against it, Fosbroke's British Monachism; the Act for Suppressing Monasteries in Statutes at Large, 31 Henry VIII. ch. xiii.; Coke's 4th Institute, p. 44; Parliamentary History, vol. iii.; and Suppression of Monasteries, edited by Thomas Wright for the Camden Society, 1843.

"It is no small prejudice to the cause of Celibacy, that all the great patrons and defenders of it could not themselves preserve that Virginity, which they either admitted or imposed. . . . . . This is manifest from the example of all those, who were the main authors of urging and imposing celibacy for the first 1100 years, I mean Tertullian, Eustathius, Heliodorus, Epiphanius, St. Hierom, Dunstan, Hildebrand, Lanfranc and Anselm; to whom we may add the Founders of the four great Monastick Orders in the Church of Rome." Wharton, p. 141. St. Dominic must be excepted, see Sismondi's Crusades against the Albigenses, ch. v. The principal Authorities,—the Councils and Fathers,—inculcating "Singularitas Clericorum," are collected by Birnbeck in his *Tractatus de Clericorum ac præcipue Sacerdotum et Pastorum dignitate et ad vitæ honestatem ac puritatem obligatione.* (Herbipoli, 1676, pp. 395-700.) In the Synod of Winchester, A.D. 1076, for the first time in England a Declaration was made by Priests and Deacons against Matrimony; see Spelman's Concilia, vol. ii. p. 11. This Declaration, remarks Dr. Jelf (Jewel's works, vol iv. p. 560) was gradually discontinued. Cf. Wharton's Specimen of some Errors and Defects in the History of the Reformation of the Church of England, by Gilbert Burnet, D.D., 1693, pp. 130-40; and Polydore Vergil de Rerum Inventoribus, Lib. v. ch. iv.; "Apud Romanos Flamen Dialis ea de causa, mortua uxore sacerdotio se abdicabat, quia vita sacerdotio non modo deberet esse quam castissima, verum etiam omni turpioris intemperantiæ suspicione carere;" p. 347.

Of the Nature of Superstition. A Sermon [on Coloss. ii., 23] preached at St. Dunstans West, March 31, 1682. By Edw. Stillingfleet, D.D. [Works, vol. i.] pp. 46, 4to Lond. 1682

"These Seducers (Judaizing Christians) gave out that the Christian Churches were yet very defective in this matter (abstinence and severity of life), and that there were several Societies of Men both among the Jews and Heathens, which went very far beyond them; as the Essenes, the Pythagoreans, the Gymnosophists and others; who far outstript the Christians in watchings and fastings, in the hard usage of their bodies, and a total abstinence from wine and flesh, and other lawful pleasures of life." Folio edit. p. 325. In determining the question whether celibacy in general was recommended by the writers of the New Testament, it should be borne in mind that it was accounted an absolute crime among the Jews. On ἐθελοθρησκεία, the term which St. Paul here makes use of for superstition, consult Calvin *in loco;* on the subject of this Sermon, Riddle's Bampton Lectures, 1852; and on the origin of the word, Notes and Queries, 2nd Ser. vol. xii., and 3rd Ser. vol. i.

CHAP. XXV.

Of the Discourses written of Auricular Confession.

270. A Discourse concerning Auricular Confession, as it is presented by the Council of Trent and practised in the Church of Rome. With a Postscript on occasion of a book lately printed in France, called Historia confessionis auricularis. [By John Goodman, D.D., Archdeacon of Middlesex.] C. L.

pp. 56, 4to Lond. 1684

See Cat. No. 16; Contin. p. 6.

Dr. Goodman was born 1626, died 1690. He was also rector of Hadham, Herts, and chaplain in ordinary. For his other publications (nine) see Watt. The above tract is in Gibson, folio edit. vol. ii.; 8vo. edit. vol. x.

He relates the famous story of Nectarius, Bishop of Constantinople, which happened something less than 400 years after our Saviour: "In the large cities, especially within the Greek Church, a special presbyter was appointed for the purpose of attending to the duty of confession, and of determining for the penitents their due proportion of church penance. But when the patriarch Nectarius of Constantinople was led by the scandal, created by the crime of an ecclesiastic, thus made publicly known, to rescind this office (about the year 390); the consequence of this was that the whole system of confession and penance, as it had till now existed in the Greek Church, came to an end; and it was left free to each individual according to his conscience to partake in the communion." Neander, vol. iii. p. 243. It is however shewn by Thorndike (Of the Laws of the Church, ch. x. § 23) "that secret confession of sins hath remained in the Eastern Church, and in that of Constantinople particularly, even to this time; so that no man can imagine that it was abrogated by Nectarius. See Morinus de Pœnitentia, 1682, lib. vi. ch. xxiii., pp. 419-20." "The thing which we regret, says Ussher, is that new pick-lock of sacramental confession, obtruded upon men's consciences, as *as a matter necessary to salva-*

tion, by the canons of the conventicle of Trent." Answer to a Challenge &c.; Of Confession. (Works, by Elrington, vol. iii. p. 90.) See Goodman, p. 36, and compare Launoy, Epistolæ, Cantab. 1689, p. 659. Stillingfleet's Council of Trent Examined &c., No. 97 *supra*. "The difference between the two churches is clearly stated by Archbishop Sharpe, one of the ablest opponents of popery in the time of King James II. 'The Papists,' he says, 'do very unjustly traduce and calumniate the Reformation, when they say that the Protestants are against private confession. But it is no such thing. There is no Protestant Church but gives it that due esteem and regard that it ought to have. All that they have done is to regulate it, &c. Sermons, vol. v. p. 122;'" Bishop Blomfield's Letter, published in the *Times* of Nov. 26, 1850, quoted in an excellent theological manual, *A Treatise on the Romish Tenet of Auricular Confession:* wherein the Mind of the Reformed Church of England is fully shown, both in her distinctive teaching and ministerial practice, to be at utter variance with this Romish Dogma. By the Rev. Daniel Ace, B.D. Lond. 1862.

C. L. Historia Confessionis Auricularis, ex antiquis Scripturæ, Patrum, Pontificum et Conciliorum monumentis. Autore Jacobo Boileau. 8vo Lutetiæ Parisiorum 1684

A Doctor of the Sorbonne, born 1635, died 1716. Compare Stillingfleet's account, *ubi supra*, "by what steps and degrees and on what occasions this Auricular Confession came into the Church," pp. 126-47.

Of Confession to a Lawful Priest. By Peter Manby. 4to 1686

In the Pope's bulls the value of confessionals is much extolled. These are forms conveying certain privileges to the purchasers, and containing among other favours the choice of a confessor with full power to absolve both in common and reserved cases. They obviously derive the name of confessional (forma confessionalis) from this principal circumstance. See Banck de Tyrannide Papæ, p. 108.

B. L. A Letter to the Right Hon. A. Earl of Essex from Dublin, declaring the strange obstinacy of Papists in Ireland, who being evidently convict and condemned for criminal cases, yet at their death upon the gallows absolutely deny the fact, and the erroneous and impious motives given by their priests by which they are deluded to do it. folio Lond. 1679

Cf. The Papists bloody Oath of Secrecy, and Litany of Intercession &c. 1680, folio, reprinted in The Harleian Miscellany, vol. vii. pp. 271-9. On the *obligation to secrecy* under the seal of sacramental confession and the limitations required by worldly considerations, the reader is referred to Casaubon, Epistolæ, fol. 1709, p. 419, DCCXXX. Frontoni Ducæo; Taylor's Dissuasive, ch. iii. § 2; Lancelot Andrewes ad Matthæi Torti Librum Responsio, 4to 1609, p. 292, Oxon. 1851, p. 355; Jardine's Criminal Trials, vol. ii. ad finem; Townsend's Accusations of History, 1826, p. 304; and to the authorities by them cited may be added Azpilcuetæ Manuale Confessariorum, 1575, 4to p. 422; and Dens' Theologia, Tract. de Jure et Justitia, No. 103. There is a difference of opinion amongst writers on questions of treason, and whether the detection of heresy is always permissible, notwithstanding the line

Hæresis est crimen quod nec confessio celat,

(quoted by Sanderson de Juramenti promissorii Obligatione). "Azpilcueta was a Spanish canonist whose 'responsa' were received as oracles, not in Rome only, but throughout the Catholic world. Pope Gregory XIII. would sometimes pass hours with Azpilcueta, pausing to talk with him before the door of his house, while at the same time the Spaniard humbly performed the lowest offices in the hospitals." (Ranke's History of the Popes, book iv.)

CHAP. XXVI.

Of the Discourses written of Penance.

C. L. 271. A Discourse concerning Penance; shewing how the doctrine of it makes void true repentance. [By Peter Allix, D.D.] pp. 45, 4to Lond. 1688

See Cat. No. 6; Historical and Critical Dictionary, vol. ii. p. 526. In Gibson, vol. x. folio ed. vol. ii.; tit. viii. ch. ii. Allix shews that in the Church of Rome absolution makes the essence of the sacrament of penance; see also Burnett's Vindication of the Ordinations of the Church of England; Stanley's Devotions of the Church of England; Bishop Hall's Peace of Rome, new ed. Oxford, 1838; Bull's Sermons, S. i.; Marshall's Penitential Discipline of the Primitive Church for the first Four Hundred Years after Christ, 1714; Libr. of Anglo-Catholic Theology. Hooker (book vi. ch. v. 5, 6) quotes St. Cyprian [De Lapsis] on the abuse of martyrs' intercession in behalf of the Lapsi, which grants peace contrary to the vigour of the Gospel, contrary to the law of our Lord and God.

"In the primitive church there were four branches of Ministerial Absolution, that of the two Sacraments, the Declaratory Absolution of the Word and Doctrine, the Precatory Absolution and the Judicial Absolution of Public Discipline." (Bingham's Works, vol. x. p. 317, ed. 1855.) Milman recommends Morini Disciplina Pœnitentiæ on the history of penitential law, and of the different penitentials which prevailed in the western churches. "The intention of the Romish Church being changed [in the midst of the thirteenth century] she hath also altered the sense and meaning of those prayers (pronounced in the name of the Church in behalf of the penitents) which were no longer of any use, since the priests were established judges, and God had invested them with the power of conferring that grace which restores the sinner to the state from whence he was fallen by his sin." (Allix, p. 20.) Compare Ussher's Answer to a Challenge made by a Jesuit, 4to 1686, p. 89 et sqq. edit. by Elrington, vol. iii. p. 135; Forbes's

Instructiones Historico-Theologicæ, lib. xii. In Matthew Poole's Dialogue between a Popish Priest and an English Protestant, there is a passage at pp. 89-90 of the edition 1735, observes Mendham, which refers to the encouragement given to sin by the absolutions of the Romish Church; and contains a *personal testimony* of great value. See also a Defence of Dr. Tenison's Sermon in a Letter by himself subjoined to the Apology (No. 145 *supra*). Soames, in The Latin Church during Anglo-Saxon Times, p. 119, shews how indicative absolutions were gradually introduced. Contrast with these the austerities practised by penitents in the sixth century; vide Climaci Scala Paradisi, Grad. iv. [Bibl. Patrum, 1624, v.] or Dupin, v. 70.

✠ The Roman Doctrine of Repentance and of Indulgences Vindicated from Dr. Stillingfleet's Misrepresentations. By Abraham Woodhead. 4to Lond. 1679

See Stillingfleet on Indulgences; the sixth chapter of his Discourse on Idolatry of the Church of Rome, Works vol. v.; Gibson's Preservative, vol. x. fol. edit. ii. Tit. viii. ch. 4. In the Roman Church there are two distinct classes of theologians, the former declaring that an indulgence is the mere remission of the temporal penance denounced by the canons in certain offenders; the latter that it remits the sin no less than the penalty; that it releases from the torments of purgatory no less than from the ecclesiastical censures of this world. Of the former Bossuet and Gother are the representatives. See likewise Stillingfleet's Doctrines and Practises of the Church of Rome Truly Represented, ch. viii. (Works, vol. vi., Gibson, vol. xiii.)

Foulis, in his Romish Treasons, &c. pref. ed. 1671, quotes from Card. Domini Tuschii Practicæ Conclusiones Juris, tom. iv.. Indulg. § vi.: Quando Papa concedit plenariam Absolutionem, intelligitur quod absolvit tam a culpa quam a pœna quoad omnia peccata quantumque enormia. Mendham subjoins the following references: Amort de Indulg., pp. 233 et sqq., where he gives extracts from one hundred and thirty-five of the most eminent writers of the Roman Church on the subject; Thom. Aquin. Summ. Theol., Suppl. to the Third Book, quæst. xxv.-xxviii. Cajetani Opusc., tom. i. tract xv. and xvi.; Bellarm. Controv. de Indulg., lib. i. throughout.

It is a curious fact that the papal prerogative of granting absolutions was derived from the imperial one of Rome. Suetonius, as Blunt observes (*Vestiges of Ancient Manners in Italy and Sicily*), writes of Vespasian, that among other indecent plans of raising revenue he resorted to that of selling pardons (absolutions) to culprits whether guilty or innocent; nec reis tam innoxiis quam nocentibus, absolutiones venditare cunctatus est. (Vespas. 16.) "Since then the Pope," proceeds our author, "has confessedly adopted some practices of his imperial predecessors, those pontifices maximi whose title he inherits; such for instance as that of his offering his foot for salutation, which was first done by Dioclesian, is it not possible that he may also have followed so tempting an example in his fiscal arrangements, and have thus granted to spiritual offenders, as a spiritual prince, that release from punishment, which it seems was before accorded to temporal offenders by a temporal prince?" pp. 190-1.

"At a Protestant meeting in Liverpool, October 29th 1835, at which William Hulton Esq. of Hulton Park near Manchester, was present, that gentleman in his opening address stated: 'I happen to hold in my hand two indulgences of two Popes, authentic documents delivered to one of my ancestors for the salvation of his soul and mine, if I should not become a heretic. One was given by Pope Eugenius IV. and the other by Pope Boniface IX., granting an indulgence to my ancestors, and extending it to me and my successors, if they remained Catholics.'" (Mendham on the Venal Indulgences and Pardons of the Church of Rome, p. 134.)

The Book of Rates now used in the Sin Custom-house of the Church and Court of Rome, containing the Bulls, Dispensations and Pardons for all manner of Villanies and Wickedness, with the several Sums of Money given and to be payed for them. Published by Ant. Egane. Late Confessor General of the Kingdom of Ireland, and now of the Reformed Religion.

4to 1678

Absolution of crimes on payment of certain fines was prohibited immediately after the Protestants assigned it as a reason for rejecting the Council of Trent.

> Fear not the guilt if you can pay for't well:
> There is no Dives in the Roman Hell:

Gold opens the strait gate, and lets him in;
But want of money is a mortal sin.

Epilogue to Dryden's *Spanish Friar*.

For a full account of the Taxa Pœnitentiaria, or published scale of prices for papal dispensations and indulgences &c., see Marchand's Dictionn. Historique, sub voc. Taxa; Bayle's Dictionary, art. Banck, Pinet, Tuppius; Mendham's Spiritual Venality of Rome, and the Venal Indulgences and Pardons of the Church of Rome, 1839, who mentions, amongst others (the best informed and most conscientious scholars), who protested against these rents or indulgences, Wolfgang Musculus, who was converted from popery by the perusal of some of Luther's writings (see M. Adami Vitæ German. Theol. 8vo. 1653) and whose statement of her Tax-tables is therefore unimpeachable; and Claudius Espencæus, in whose Opera, fol. Paris, 1619, is the following striking passage:

Hinc et ab Italia studiorum noster alumna
Godo parans reditum, quovis melioribus auro
Mille voluminibus Roma ditatus abivit.
Talis Apostolicæ quondam benedictio dextræ
Religionis erat cupidis, atque illius ergo
Clavigeri sedem solitis invisere Petri,
Inde pedem spoliis hospes referebat onustus
Gratuitis, patriamque opibus ditabat inemptis.
Nomen adhuc bullis, diplomatibusque redemptis
Non erat, aut fulvo veniis venalibus auro,
Vilis in hoc plumbi non transitione reperta,
Non qua merce suos pietas expleret alumnos,
Quave Cisalpinas emungeret Itala bulgas.

S. Godonis Vita, p. 1042,

In the fourth part of Hermaunus Von der Hardt's Literaria Reformationis Historia are six articles respecting this matter: 1. *De Indulgentiis, num fuerint origo Reformationis;* 2. Diploma Indulgentiarum Leonis X.; 3. Ex Tezelii Summaria Instructione; 4. Lutheri prima disputatio; and two others by Joannes Chiemensis and Melancthon.

The Pope's Cabinet unlocked, or a Catalogue of all the Pope's Indulgences belonging to the order of St. Mary, together with a List of all the Indulgences daily, yearly and for ever to be had at Rome. S. James of Galatia &c. Written in Italian by Fr. Archangelo Tartello of the said order of St. Mary, and now translated into English by John Sidway, late Seminary Priest, but now of the reformed Religion, and Vicar of Selling in Kent &c. . 4to 1680

"It is said of the Pope, he can never want money while he can hold a pen; his writing of pardons and indulgences filleth his coffers." Swinnock's Christian Man's Calling, p. 104. However proverbial, this is a false impression; see Ranke's History of the Popes, book iv.

"The real state of the case," says Charles Butler, "is as follows: There are some sins so enormous that, in order to raise the greater horror of them, the absolution from them is reserved to the holy See. In these cases the priest, to whom the penitent reveals them in confession, states them, without any mention of person, time or place, to the Roman See; and the Roman See, when it thinks the circumstance of the case renders it proper, grants a faculty to the priest to absolve the penitent from them. All this is attended with expense. An office or tribunal is kept up for the purpose, and to defray the expenses attending these applications a fee is required for the *document* in which the power of absolution is granted." (Book of the Church, Letter x.)

CHAP. XXVII.

Of the Discourses written of Extreme Unction.

272. A Discourse concerning the pretended Sacrament of Extreme Unction: with an account of the occasions and beginnings of it in the Western Church, in Three Parts. With a Letter to the vindicator of the Bishop of Condom [Jos. Johnston, see No. 75 *supra*. By William Clagett, D.D.] **C. L.**

pp. x., 186, 4to Lond. 1687

See Cat. No. 98; Contin. p. 6; Ath. Oxon. vol. ii. col. 327. In Gibson, fol. edit. vol. ii.; 8vo. vol. iii. "The religion of being anointed for health by those that had not the gift of healing was so unknown a thing to Primitive Antiquity that a Bishop of the fifth age wrote to the Pope of Rome about something like it, as men used to do of things that had never been heard of before." Part iii. sect. 5. Cf. Ravanelli Bibliotheca Sacra, s. v. Unctio, &c.

273 ✠ A Letter from the Vindicator of the Bishop of Condom to the author of a late discourse concerning the Sacrament of Extreme Unction.

See Contin. p. 7 (No. 417 *infra.*) Cf. Henry the Eighth's Assertion of the Seven Sacraments. "The Pope has no great cause of being vex'd at his reproaches who charges such enormous crimes upon the Apostle himself (St. James); for seeing 'tis certain this Epistle belongs to the Apostle, what else does he then, but manifestly accuse the Apostle of having (without authority, and against all right) instituted this Sacrament?" p. 120.

274. A Second Letter from the Author of the Discourse concerning Extreme Unction, to the Vindicator of the Bishop of Condom. [By William Clagett, D.D.] pp. 14, 4to Lond. 1688 **C. L.**

See Cat. No. 99; Contin. p. 7. In Gibson, vol. viii. fol. ed. vol. ii.; tit. vii. ch. ii.

"The same policy that kept up the right of anointing the sick, upon the foundation of believing that it was good for their bodies, would, when that could hold no longer, lay another, viz., that at least it was very good for their souls; and that when it did not recover the health of the sick, yet at least it had a wonderful virtue to save the soul of the dying." A Discourse, *ut supra*, p. 78. Cf. Neander, vol. vi. p. 227, and No. 384.

Numerous as are the sacraments of the Romish Church, a sect of Christians sprung up in England early in the eighteenth century who increased their number. The founder of this sect was Dr. Deacon, of Manchester. According to these "Essentialists" every rite and every phrase in the book called Apostolical Constitutions were certainly in use among the Apostles themselves. Still, however, they made a distinction between the greater and lesser sacraments. The lesser are no fewer than ten, viz. five belonging to baptism, exorcism, anointing with oil, the white garment, a taste of milk and honey, and anointing with chrism or ointment. The other five are the sign of the cross, imposition of hands, unction of the sick, holy orders and matrimony. "The mixture of water with the wine considered by them one of the *Essentials* (see Brett's Tradition necessary to explain and interpret the Holy Scriptures, 1718) was defended by Gregory XIII. who said that water ought to be mixed with the wine in the Eucharist, because both flowed from our Saviour's side. Ritteri Diss. *de Aqua Ex Christi Latere profluente*, and that of J. A. Quenstedt, *de Vulneribus Christi* (both printed in the Thesaurus Theologico-Philologicus, appended to the Critici Sacri);" Burton's Bampton Lectures, p. 471. Those Sacraments which are superadded by the Essentialists are described in the following works:—Durandi Rationale Div. Offic.; Gavanti Thesaur. Sacr. Rituum; F. Fortunati Scacchi Sacr. Elæochrismatωn Myrothecium Sacroprophanum. "Clement of Alexandria absolutely enjoins upon Christians the use of the white garment of Pythagoras, on the authority of Plato, Pædag. 2, ch. x. 3, ch. ii. In this doubtless originated the white friars &c. of the Roman Catholics, and probably also the alb or surplice; which now that the habit controversy is as much forgotten as Clement's Gnosticism, few, I think, will be found to deny that it is a harmless custom, and is certainly a decorous and highly becoming one." Osburn's Doctrinal Errors of the Apostolical and Early Fathers, p. 163. Cf. Gavantus, vol. i. p. 168;

Durandus, lib. iii. ch. i. § 10; Heidfeldii Sphinx Theologico-Philosophica, 1608, pp. 701-703. The administration of baptism was succeeded by various rites in the primitive Church, besides that of being clothed in white garments. At this time the newly baptized received a taste of milk and honey. See Bingham, book xii. ch. iv. § 6; Palmer's Origines Liturgicæ, tom. ii. ch. 192. "Those who desire to prosecute their enquiries on the use of the Sign of the Cross are referred to the works of Gretserus, De Sancta Cruce, Ingoldstadt, 1598; Lipsius de Cruce, Antw. 1597 [Opp. tom. ii. pp. 769-802]; Rabanus Maurus, Semita Justorum; and M. Didron's Christian Iconography." An Apology for the Sign of the Cross, by a Priest of the Church of England, published for the Guild of St. Alban, 1857.

In the eleventh century the Western Church celebrated fifteen Sacraments, for in Damiani (Opp. 1783, 4to, Sermo lxix., In Dedicatione Ecclesiæ) we find twelve Sacraments, circa quorum instantiam reflectitur Christianæ religionis auctoritas: I. Baptismus. II. Confirmatio. III. Extrema Unctio. IV. Ordo, *i.e.* consecratio Pontificis. V. Inuncti Regum. VI. Dedicatio Ecclesiæ. VII. Confessio. VIII. S. Canonicorum. IX. Monarchorum. X. Eremitarum. XI. Sanctimonialium. XII. Nuptiarum. Opp. 1783, tom. ii. And in his sixth Opusculum, ch. ix. he treats of tria præcipua Ecclesiæ Sacramenta, Baptismus, Eucharistia, et Ordo, sive ordinatio Clericorum.

CHAP. XXVIII.

Of the Discourses written of Communion in one kind.

C. L. 275. ✠ A Treatise of Communion under both kinds. [By the Reverend Father in God the Lord James Benigne Bossuet, Bishop of Meaux.] Faithfully rendered from the French, and dedicated to Thomas Lord Petre. [By Jo. Davis.] In Two Parts. pp. vi., 116, 4to Lond. 1687

See Contin. p. 21. The authors replied to are Calixtus, Bourdieu and Jurieu. "Our author cites here the *Discourse of Communion in one kind*, which by all appearance is that lately writ by the Bishop of Meaux. This shows that the author and publisher is the same person, though others pretend that the author is dead many years ago. But it seems the publisher thought fit at last to add some new touches, and since he did that he might have thought it worth while to have examined at least the records published by Dr. Burnet; and his history itself might have been considered, as well as Mr. Fuller's and Dr. Heylin's. But since it seems our author thought the Discourse of the Communion in one kind fit to be recommended by him, I will take the liberty to recommend the answer to it in French by Monsieur Larroque, and that lately writ in English [No. 278 *infra*], in which the disingenuity of the discourse mentioned by our author is laid open beyond all possibility of replying." (Burnet's Reflections on the Oxford Theses, p. 81.)

C. L. 276. A Discourse of the Communion in one kind; in answer to a Treatise of the Bishop of Meaux's of Communion under both species, lately translated into English. [By William Payne, M.A., Pastor of St. Mary, White-chapel.] pp. iv., 138. 4to Lond. 1687

See Cat. No. 88; Contin. p. 21; Newcourt's Repertorium Eccl. vol. i. p. 700. In Gibson, vols. viii. and ix., fol. ed. ii. Payne's publications are enumerated by Watt. It has been remarked that none of the peculiar tenets of Rome so taxed the ingenuity of her advocates as the retrenchment of the cup. This perplexity is attested by the records of Constance and Basle; and it deserves particular remark that Gerson, in his very elaborate treatise against the Double Communion, disclosed the source of his difficulty in this simple complaint: "There are many laymen among the heretics who have a version of the Bible in the vulgar tongue, to the great prejudice and offence of the catholic faith," &c. Vide Von Der Hardt, Concil. Constant. vol. ii. p. 770.

277. A Demonstration that the Church of Rome and her Councils have erred; by shewing that the Council of Constance, Basil, and Trent have in all their decrees touching communion in one kind, contradicted the received doctrine of the Church of Christ. With an Appendix, in answer to the XXI. Chapter of the Author of A Papist Misrepresented. [By Daniel Whitby, D.D.] pp. xiv., 110, 4to Lond. 1688 C. L.

See Cat. No. 89; Contin. p. 21; Ath. Oxon. vol. ii. col. 1071.

"The reader that desires to see the authorities produced at large may find them in G. J. Vossius (t. vi. pp. 442 sqq.) and Du Moulin (Novelty of Popery, p. 798 sqq.) and more amply in Chamier (t. iv. pp. 444 sqq.), and a late treatise of a learned writer in our own tongue, shewing that there is no Catholic tradition for communion in one kind." [Dr. Whitby, *ut supra*;] Bingham, book xv. ch. v.

Cardinal Cusanus (or Nicolas de Cusa), who was engaged in the Council of Basle, and was charged by the Pope with an especial mission to the estates of Bohemia, who demanded the restoration of the cup in the Eucharist, replies, Christ is indeed God, but the Pope is his prophet (ὁ προφήτης), his interpreter, who accommodates the Scriptures to the times, and to whom the signification, which is now current in the Church, is divinely dictated. Opp. Basileæ, 1565, p. 833; Epistola de usu Communionis ad Bohemos.

"The Romanists talk of antiquity, while we observe and follow it. For with them both Scripture and Fathers are, as to the sense, under the correction and control of the present Church, &c. Vid. Riveti Tract. de Patr. Authoritate, cap. vii. p. 40 &c.; Patrick on Tradition, p. 41; Stillingfleet's Rational Account, pt. i. ch. v. p. 80 &c. In the fourteenth article of the Creed of Pope Pius IV. are two contradictory things blended together, the sense of their present church and the unanimous consent of Fathers; which are no more to be reconciled than light and darkness; except it be by making antiquity as much a Lesbian rule, as they make the Scripture. I follow the copy of that Creed given in Latin and English at the end of Dr. Hickes's Letters published A.D. 1705." Waterland, vol. v. p. 319.

On this fundamental question of an unvarying tradition of doctrine, or an unlimited explanation of it, there prevails in the Church of Rome the greatest diversity of opinion. See Dupin's Eccl. Hist., Cent. xvii. bk. v. pp. 137-9, in which he gives an analysis of the *Systema Fidei* of Francis Davenport, vulgarly de St. Clara.

278. An Answer to a Treatise of Communion under both kinds. [By Matthias de Larroque. Fr. 1683.]

See Contin. p. 21. "Mons. de Meaux having some years since composed a famous book upon this argument, it was thought fit by those of the Church of Rome to translate that also, as well as the rest of his tracts into our language. Now, however, it might have been sufficient for us to have follow'd their example, in translating that most accurate Answer of the late Mons. Larroque to it."

Matthew de Larroque, an illustrious Protestant minister, born in 1619, died in 1684. The principal of his Works are: L'Histoire de l'Euchariste, 4to 1609, and 8vo 1671; The History of the Eucharist, Transl. into English by Joseph Walker, 4to 1684; An Answer, *ut supra;* An Answer to the Motives of the Minister Martin's Conversion; Conformité des Eglises Reformées de France avec les Anciens. Transl. by Walker, 4to 1691.

"The Primitive Church did excommunicate them that did not receive the holy Sacrament in both kinds, and St. Ambrose says that he who receives the Mystery otherwayes than Christ appointed (that is but in one kind when he hath appointed it in two) is unworthy of the Lord, and he cannot have devotion: Now this thing we ought not to suffer, that our people by so doing should remain unworthy of the Lord . . . . . . or fall by following evil guides into the Sentence of Excommunication." Taylor's Dissuasive to the People of Ireland, p. vii. Cf. Bernardi Ep. lxix.

✠ De Adoratione Eucharistiæ Libri duo. Quibus accedit Disquisitio Theologica de Præcepto Divino Communionis sub utraque specie, a Jacobo Boileau. C. L.

pp. 183-218, 8vo. Lutetiæ Parisiorum 1685

"In his Sermon at the Supper which he had just now celebrated, and which immediately preceded his Passion, Jesus Christ, according to St. John, says expressly to his Apostles, that he was about to leave them, that he should not be long absent, that he would send to them the Comforter; but not one word of his Real Presence in the Eucharist, which he had so lately instituted under the Bread and Wine, to be a Mystery of our Faith for the nourishment of the soul to Life Eternal, as ordinary Bread and Wine are for the nourishment of the body to a temporal Life, and that too for All the faithful, as is clearly signified by those words, 'Drink ye all of this,' whereupon I have elsewhere remarked the custom of *Libations* which were in use time out of mind throughout the whole Roman Empire, and which custom was establish'd *in honour of the gods;* as may be seen in the Version of Athenæus in 1680 [Lib. x.]; and as I had observed long before upon Virgil and Horace, though there was but little notice taken of it. Which makes me think it very probable that our Saviour intended to sanctifie this profane custom, as he did some others which I have remarked in the same place." A Paper by M. de Marolles Abbot of Ville-loyn, "Permission hoped for to speak freely for the Truth." See Tenison's Historical Preface, p. xviii. On the subject of Libations cf. Vaux's Bampton Lect. vi., who refers to Spencer de Leg. Hebr. i. 589 sqq. The classical student may be referred also to Ruhnkenius in Timæi Lexicon, pp. 114, 115; Blomfield's note on Æschyli Persæ, v. 616; and the authorities cited by Farmer on the Worship of Human Spirits, p. 427, sqq.

"The Laity, as well as the Priests, communicate in both Kinds, taking the Bread and wine together in a spoon from the hand of the priest. The wine in the Sacrament before Consecration they mix with water, in representation of the blood and water which issued out of the side of our blessed Saviour, opened by the spear of the Roman Soldier." Ricaut's Present State of the Greek Church, p. 187, 8vo, 1679. "It appears that this rite was at first devised for the purpose of more easily giving the holy things to communicants in the spoon without danger of irreverence, but that a mystical reason was soon devised, namely, that by the separate consecration of the bread and wine the Lord's death was more particularly set forth; by the union of the two the estate of his glorified and incorruptible body." Neal's Hist. of the Holy Eastern Church, vol. i. p. 522. Vossius de Sacræ Cœnæ Symbolis, (Opera, vol. vi. p. 444,) produces an analogous argument for *communio sub utraque specie*: — "Apostolum igitur secuti dicimus, etsi in mysteriis Ecclesiæ dispensandis discrimen occurrat maximum inter quemvis de populo atque Ecclesiæ ministrum; tamen in Christo, ac communione bonorum Ecclesiæ, inter quæ etiam sunt sacramenta, nec clericum nec laicum esse, sed ea bona esse indivisa secundum unitatem corporis, cujus caput est Christus; eoque plane sacrilegium esse, si quis populum fidelem arcere velit a *κοινωνία* sanguinis Christi, quæ in sacramento cœnæ percipitur." Comp. Chrysostom. in epist. ii. ad Cor. Hom. 18, quoted by Gieseler, transl. vol. ii. p. 49; Waterland on the Eucharist, ch. viii. on 1 Cor. x. 16 &c.; Warburton's Serm. on the nature and end of the Lord's Supper.

On the peculiar customs in regard to consecrating the eucharist in the Greek Church; and in the Church of Rome; the argument drawn by Bellarmine from the Greeks' presanctified communion, and on the new device of concomitance, consult Leo Allatius de Missa Præsanctif. p. 1559 (De Eccl. Occid. et Orient. Perpetua Consensione); Thorndike, Of the Laws of the Church, book iii. ch. xxiv. and Bingham, xv. 5, § 1.

CHAP. XXIX.

Of the Discourses written of the Real Presence.

279. ✠ Two discourses concerning the Adoration of our Blessed Saviour in the Holy Eucharist. The first: Animadversions upon the alterations of the rubrick in the Communion Service in the Common Prayer Book of the Church of England. The second: The Catholics defence for their adoration of our Lord, as believed really and substantially present in the Holy Sacrament of the Eucharist. [By Abraham Woodhead.] Part i. pp. 33. Part ii. pp. 38, 4to. [Published by Obadiah Walker, Master of University College.] Oxon. 1687 C. L.

See Contin. p. 19; Ath. Oxon, vol. ii. col. 615.

"Mr. W. doubts not to make it appear, that our divines have asserted the very same presence of Christ, in effect, in the Eucharist, that the Romanists maintain." Contin. p. 19.

"Catholics," says Woodhead, "ground their Adoration not on Transubstantiation, as if Transubstantiation is defeated, Adoration is so too; but on a Real Presence with the Symbols." p. 21.

"In this controversy the two main things that seem worthy to be examined by any Christian who in this point seeks satisfaction, are: 1. Whether the Roman Catholic's grounds of believing Christ's Corporal Presence in the Eucharist, with the Symbols, are solid and true. 2. And next, whether the Church for any one's enjoying her Communion, exacts more of him, than the confessing that Christ as present there is also to be adored; whilst meanwhile such person renounceth and declares against any *adoration of the Species*,—save only such an inferior veneration as is exhibited by us to other Holy Things." p. 38.

On this subject Woodhead also published "The Greeks opinion touching the Eucharist misrepresented by Mr. Claude in his Answer to Mr. Arnald," pp. 34, 4to 1686. This, though printed by itself with this title, is a digression inserted in No. 208. Cf. Note to No. 284, and supplement *infra*.

C. L. 280. A Discourse of the Holy Eucharist in the two great points of the Real Presence and the Adoration of the Host. In answer to the two discourses lately printed at Oxford on this subject. To which is prefixed a large Historical Preface relating to the same argument. [By William Wake, M.A.] First edition. Pref. pp. xxviii., 127, 4to Lond. 1687

See Cat. No. 85; [Present State, p. 33.] Contin. p. 19; Ath. Oxon. vol. ii. col. 615. 1059. In Gibson, vol. x. fol. ed. ii.; Tit. vii. c. iv.

In answer to the two discourses, No. 279. To which is prefixed a large historical preface on the same Argument. On the impossibilities and repugnances to the Christian creed presented by this doctrine compare Cosin's History of Transubstantiation, s. 24, 25;- Wake's Defence of the Exposition, in which he has reprinted Chrysostomi Epistola ad Cæsarium, pp. 146-63. This discourse and that of Tillotson were attacked in a work entitled, Reason and Authority [by Gother.] See Notes and Queries, 3rd ser. vol. i. p. 70. An analysis of Wake will be found in The Young Student's Library, pp. 134, 135. He names several illustrious Persons of the Romish Church, who have been accused of not believing the Real Presence or Transubstantiation, viz: Peter Picherel, Cardinal du Perron, Barnes an English Benedictine, De Marca Archbishop of Paris, F. Sirmond the Jesuit, M. de Marolles, &c. To these may be added those cited by Jeremy Taylor, Tonstal, Erasmus, Durandus, Johannes Ferus, &c.

In reference to the alterations of the Rubric animadverted upon by Woodhead, it may be observed that "as Cranmer kept up a close correspondence with Melancthon and other promoters of the cause in Germany, it will be necessary to study the works of those authors in order to form a right judgment of the opinions which the English Church at that time adopted, and has since preserved; as also to mark the changes which were gradually made, from the time when 'The Necessary Erudition of a Christian Man' was first published, A.D. 1543 (in which some of the obnoxious tenets of the Church of Rome were still retained) until our Church Articles were expunged of every remainder of the Corruptions of the Popish Creed." Bishop Lloyd's List of Books (Theological Studies) in The Christian Remembrancer, vol. xii. 1830. See especially Strype's Life of Cranmer, and No 284 note.

"The Church of England did *not* adopt the opinions of any distinct set or party of the reformers, but chalked out a path for herself, by selecting from each what appeared most agreeable to Scripture. Thus from the Calvinists the doctrine of the Lord's Supper, in opposition to Consubstantiation." Lloyd, ibid. Cf. Lawrence's Bampton Lectures, p. 237.

281. A Reply to two Discourses lately printed at Oxford, concerning the Adoration of our Blessed Saviour in the Holy Eucharist. [By Henry Aldrich, D.D., Canon, and afterwards Dean of Christ Church.] pp. 68, 4to Oxford 1687 C. L. T. C. D.

See Cat. No. 86; Contin. p. 20; Ath. Oxon. vol. ii. col. 615, 1055.

"This Dr. Aldrich is a most ingenious, learned man, and, which is above all, a sincere member of the Church of England, as he has shewed by divers of his late proceedings, whilst prolocutor to the lower house of convocation during the last sessions. He is likewise a most affable complaisant gentleman, and has nothing in him of affectation." (Reliquiæ Hearnianæ, vol. i. p. 79.) Besides his well-known Compendium of Logic, he published The Elements of Civil Architecture, according to Vitruvius and other ancients, &c., which, says Dallaway in his Anecdotes of the Arts in England, "give ample evidence that he was intimately conversant with the science; and two beautiful edifices of their kind are a very honourable proof of his excellence in practice. He built Peckwater Court at Christ Church in a chaste Ionic style, and has made the decoration subordinate to the design. . . . . . . The other building which boasts the design of Dr. Aldrich is the parish church of All Saints in Oxford." Aldrich was author of the epigram:

Si bene quid memini, causæ sunt quinque bibendi,
Hospitis adventus, præsens sitis, atque futura,
Aut vini bonitas, aut quælibet altera causa.

Biographie Universelle.

"One would have expected that a man of the Editor's (Obadiah Walker's) reputation, the famous compiler of an Art of Reason, should neither have writ nor published anything, wherein the author did not reason like a man of art; or at leastwise talk as coherently as ordinary men use to do by the pure strength of natural reason. Yet it pleases the author of the pamphlet to display his great search and quickness, in such illations as these; Gloria in excelsis, is put in the Post Communion, ergo, The Church that puts it there disowns the Real Presence. . . . . This thing is above our reason, ergo, 'Tis contrary to it: with other such deep discoveries; to shew us that his talent in logic is as singular as his judgment in religion." It is alleged against this author that "all his shuffling is only to advance Thorndike's new and singular notion of a presence of Christ's body in, or with, or under the Elements." § 28, p. 32. Cf. Wake, p. 70.

In replying to Woodhead's last question, as above, he remarks: "To worship the true God by an Host, is in effect all as one as to worship him by an image; which is as truly, though not so gross, Idolatry as to worship an image instead of him."

"There is not (says Aldrich) an argument, nor a quotation, nor scarce a sentence, in either of these discourses, but is almost verbatim in the Guide to Controversy. . . . . . . 'Twas but t'other day that a great part of those Discourses was again printed in the Book of Church Government; and for ought I find we must expect the same stuff word for word in every book they (the Fraternity) are to publish." p. 68.

C. L. *T. C. D.* 282. ✠ A Compendious Discourse on the Eucharist. [By Abraham Woodhead.] With two appendixes. The first, The doctrine of the Church of England, concerning the substantial presence, and adoration, of our B. Saviour in the Eucharist asserted; with a vindication of two discourses on that subject, published at Oxon, from the exceptions of a sacramentary answer. [Mr. Wake's, No. 2 *supra.*] Printed at London. [By Francis Nicholson, M.A. of University College.] The second, Animadversions upon the reply to the two discourses concerning the adoration of our B. Saviour in the Holy Eucharist. [By Dr. Aldrich, No. 8 *supra.*] [By Obadiah Walker.] pp. 142. Append. i. pp. 46. Append. ii. pp. 27. 4to Oxon. 1688

See Contin. p. 20; Ath. Oxon. vol. ii. col. 616, 936, 940.

Dodd's Church History, vol. iii. p. 463. Francis Nicolson, son of Thomas Nicolson of Manchester in Lancashire. Abraham Woodhead, whose name occurs so frequently in this controversy, was born in 1608 at Meltham in Yorkshire, died in 1678. "Our Author," says Charles Butler in his Life of Alban Butler, "was a great admirer of the writings of Abraham Woodhead; he purchased his manuscripts, and by his will bequeathed them to the English College at Douay. Mr. Woodhead is one of the writers to whom the celebrated 'Whole Duty of Man' has been attributed." p. 556.

"The Answer (Wake's) seems to have more learning, the Replier (Aldrich) is better at cavilling and mockery, and had it not bin to shew this talent, he needed not to have troubled the world with a new book. He saith indeed it is in defence of their quarters; but for this, who is bonæ, who malæ fidei possessor, we appeal to the judgment of our pious and munificent founders; who will one day declare whether they designed their bounties for them, who hold it not lawful to pray for them, who frustrate their chief intention, count them idolaters, and members of a false Church." Append. ii. p. 192.

283. A Vindication of the Oxford Reply to two Discourses there printed 1687; concerning the adoration of our blessed Saviour in the Eucharist, from the exceptions made to it in the second Appendix to a compendious discourse on the Eucharist, published from the same press. [By Henry Aldrich, D.D.] pp. 91, 4to. C. L. T. C. D.

See Cat. No. 87; Ath. Oxon. vol. ii. col. 1055.

This is inserted in No. 352 *infra*. "I know that Cuthbert Tunstall in his dotage, about an. 1554, imploy'd his notion of a spiritual body to defend the Corporal presence; and for ought I find he was the first that did so ..... But Cuthbert stood alone till the Discourser joyn'd him, and refin'd upon him." p. 88.

284. ✠ A Peaceable Method for the reuniting Protestants and Catholicks in matters of faith; principally in the subject of the Holy Eucharist. Proceeding upon principles agreed on C. L.

and waving points in dispute. Upon occasion of the late contest concerning the perpetuity of faith, touching that great mystery. Written in French by Lewis Maimbourg, S.J. [Translated by G—— W——.] Pref. pp. vi., 87, 4to 1686

See Contin. p. 31. "Some perchance will wonder (observes the translator) what a French writer, what Monsieur Arnaud and Monsieur Claude do upon our stage. But I hope they may be perswaded that it is not the first time a French-man has spoke good sence, though in bad English. As we willingly receive Merchandize, which is for our turn from any place, so need we not be ashamed to admit of Reason from any part. The Reformed Churches of France, which ours here have upon occasion acknowledged a very tender respect and kindness for, do own Monsieur Claude to be their great and learned Champion; and it must be granted, I think, by all that Monsieur Arnaud has in a famous contest behaved himself as a valiant and skilful Souldier of the Catholick Church. The subject of dispute between them is of common concern;" p. 81. . . . . . . "As I must confess myself a Friend of my author's method, particularly in assuming nothing but what his adversary seems to grant; so will I not make it my business to apologize for that Council, which to some may seem to lye open to exceptions. It shall be sufficient for me to give a hint at what has passed within our own dominions, much of the same nature; and to give occasion to those who make any question of it, to search into the several Parliamentary and Synodical proceedings of our own Reformed Church in late dayes: that is, in Queen Elizabeth's, King James's, and King Charles his time; when the 39 Articles, and some other points belonging to religion, have been advanced with as great a claim of legislative and definitive authority as any Council, either of the Catholick or Reformed Church ever challenged to themselves. See, if you please, the very title of the 39 Articles: That these Articles were drawn up for the avoiding diversities of opinions;" p. 82.

So none shall dare to deviate
From the *religion of the state*.
Thus, as we are in story told
Th' Arabian prophet did of old:
And 'twas a politic device,
To fill with *fools* his *paradise*.

England's Reformation, by Thomas Ward, Canto ii.

The method here urged upon the dissentient parties is submission to the juridical declaration of a canonical assembly, according to the Word of God, what is of faith, and the obligation of standing to its decrees, under the penalty of being schismatics. See More, No. 285, p. 71, and No. 249 note.

For the Articles of 1562 and 1571, and reprinted in 1630, as well as the 42 Articles, see Dr. Lamb's History of the 39 Articles; Dr. Cardwell's Synodalia; and Hardwick's History of the 39 Articles, in each of which works the several sets of Articles are given. Bishop Short also in the Appendix to the first volume of his History of the Church of England has some useful matter respecting the original publications. An account of them is given ibid. p. 325; Burnet's Hist. of the Reformation, vol. iii. pp. 210-14. Heylin, in his Hist. of the Reformation, p. 331, shews upon what grounds the revisers in 1562 omitted seven Articles, and qualified the expressions of some others. See also Collier, Hey, and Puller's Moderation of the Church of England.

285. A Brief Discourse of the Real Presence of the Body and Blood of Christ in the celebration of the Holy Eucharist; wherein the witty artifices of the Bp. of Meaux and of Monsieur Maimbourg are obviated, whereby they would draw in the Protestants to imbrace the doctrine of Transubstantiation. [By Henry More, D.D.] pp. 94, 4to Lond. 1686 C. L.

See Cat. No. 78; Contin. p. 74. For an account of this great Platonist, the Angel, as he was styled, of Christ Church, see Ward's Life of him, Lond. 1710, 8vo, the continuation of which has never been printed, and is in Mr. Crossley's possession; the Biogr. Britann. s. voc. More; and Worthington's Diary (Chetham Society), in which many of his letters are given.

Compare Wake's Exposition. No. 24, note, a remark is cited, animadverting on this tract. The passage here referred to is as follows (p. 38): "The Fathers did all eat of the same spiritual meat, &c., 1 Cor. x., where SS. Austin, Anselm, Thomas Aquinas, and others, as you may see in Jacobus Capellus, avouch that the ancient patriarchs ate the same spiritual food that we, which therefore must be the Flesh and Blood of Christ, in that sense Christ understands it in John vi. And that passage of Philo (that Grotius notes on the same place) is worth our taking notice of, and that in two several treatises of his he interprets the manna of the θεῖος λόγος, the Divine Logos, which agrees hereby well with our supposing that the Flesh and Blood of which our Saviour saith, It is meat indeed and drink indeed, he speaks this as he is the eternal God, to whom appertains the universal Divine Body, as being the body of his Ζωή, Life or Spirit, as I have noted in my analytical account of the forepart of the first chapter of St. John's Gospel. See my Scholia at the end of my Enchiridium Ethicum." (Opp. Philosoph. folio, 1679, p. 94.) Cf. pp. 504-5 ib., and The Mystery of Godliness, lib. viii. ch. ix. s. ii. Our author refers to Gratian and Mornæus as making use of the very phrases which he used without consulting them.

A platonic notion has on the other side been represented as the origin of Transubstantiation. "The doctrine of Transubstantiation," remarks Carson, "is in many of its features a copy of the sublime nonsense of Plato's eternal ideas. The platonic philosopher taught that there were eternal models of every thing made by the eternal First Cause; that these ideas were the essences of things even before the things themselves existed; that there was one such idea for every species of things, and but one; yet that one idea of the species existed in every individual of the species, without being either divided or multiplied. Certainly these philosophical mysteries must have been the origin and model of the corresponding absurdities of Transubstantiation." But the physical system of Aristotle, with its theory of Transmutation and notions of Form and Matter, was still more cultivated among schoolmen. "The word elements in the Eucharist was used," observes Archbishop Whately, "agreeably to their language, who framed the doctrine of Transubstantiation, as it now stands, so completely from Aristotle's writings, that it never could have existed in any thing like its present form, had that philosopher not been studied." (Essays on the Errors of Romanism, p. 51.) "It is to be further shewn how the essence or substance of Christ was brought down to the consecrated elements. This was in fact the establishment of the term Transubstantiation as the orthodox language of the Latin Church. Christ had been asserted to be substantially present in the Eucharist during the controversies of the ix[th] and xi[th] centuries. But, as I observed, the term *Substance* was not yet commonly interpreted in its proper metaphysical sense [as the support of accidents]. . . . . . . The accidents of bread and wine,—the taste and colour, and other such qualities,—were not supposed indeed to be in Christ 'as in their subject,' though they evidently remained after the change of the substance, to which they had belonged. In general, however, the accidents are represented, in the mystical phraseology of platonism, as outward veils, under which the real spiritual substance of Christ is latent . . . . the forma substantialis hominis is anima rationalis." (Hampden's Bampton Lectures, p. 334 sqq.) Cf. Bp. Gleig's Directions for the Study of Theology, p. 296 sqq., who remarks: "Had the Apostles understood the words of their Divine Master as they are understood in the Church of Rome, they would have rendered them into Greek, not *τουτο ἐστι τὸ σῶμα μου*, this is my body, but *τουτο ἐστι ἡ ὕλη του σώματος μου*, this is the matter of my body. You will find," he says, "the most perspicuous view of the philosophy of Aristotle in Harris's Philosophical Arrangements."

CHAP. XXX.

Of the Discourses written of Transubstantiation.

C. L. T. C. D. 286. A Full View of the Doctrines and Practices of the Ancient Church relating to the Eucharist. Wholly different from those of the present Roman Church, and inconsistent with the belief of Transubstantiation. Being a sufficient confutation of Consensus Veterum, Nubes Testium, and other late Collections of the Fathers, pretending the contrary. [By John Patrick, Preacher at the Charter-house.]

Pref. and Contents pp. xi., 202, 4to Lond. 1688

See Cat. No. 73; Contin. p. 22. In Gibson, folio ed. i., 8vo ed. ix. "Liber perrarus, summa doctrina scriptus." Chetham MS. See Notes and Queries, vol. iii. p. 214. Cf. No. 66 by the same author. Amongst the late pamphlets he includes "Succession of Church and Sacraments." The contents of the chapters are a summary of (sixteen) differences betwixt the faith and practices of the two churches.

"Montfaucon, in the second tome of his Collectio Nova, p. 18, has out of Athanasius, *οὐχ' αἷμα τοῦ κυρίου ἐστὶν ὁ οἶνος ἀλλα τῆς ἀμπέλου*. This passage is concerning the Eucharistical wine, and is express against Transubstantiation, which he has not observed." Reliquiæ Hearnianæ, vol. i. p. 116. It is not included amongst Patrick's copious quotations.

C. L. T. C. D. 287. ✠ A Seeker's Request to Catholic Priests and Protestant Ministers, for satisfying his conscience in the truth of what he ought to believe of the Lord's Supper.

1 sheet, 4to Lond. 1687

See Contin. p. 23.

288. Transubstantiation Contrary to Scripture: or the Protestant's Answer to the Seeker's Request. [By Robert Nelson, Esq.]

pp. 24, 4to Lond. 1688

See Cat. No. 81; Contin. p. 23. A learned and pious gentleman, born in London in 1656, educated at St. Paul's School and Trinity College, Cambridge; joined the Nonjurors at the Revolution, but in 1709 returned to the communion of the Church of England; died 1715. His Companion to the Festivals and Fasts is still one of the best on the subject. See Lathbury's History of the Nonjurors, ch. vi.

"The secession of his wife (Lady Theophila) to the Romish Church has the further advantage of giving additional prominence to Nelson's own firm and deliberate adhesion to our Reformed religion. The claims of the Church of Rome were thus brought before him in the closest way at an early period of his life, and the effect was only to elicit from him the strongest expression of his dissent from, and his repugnance to, her distinctive errors. He, too, became a pamphleteer in the absorbing controversy of the day, and was the author of an anonymous tract on Transubstantiation, which appeared at the beginning of 1688. A challenge had been thrown down upon the Romanist side in 'A Seeker's Request to Catholic Priests and Protestant Ministers for satisfying his conscience in the truth of what he ought to believe of the Lord's supper:' the writer feigning to be a plain man, who understood neither Greek nor Latin; asking for only one or two express texts of Scripture, for or against the doctrine of the real Presence as taught in the Church of Rome, and declaring himself resolved to be either Catholic or Protestant, as the verdict upon this trial should go. This brought out, as was intended, the Catholic Answer to the Seeker's Request [No. 289] appealing to St. John, ch. vi. 48, and to the words of Institution, St. Matthew, ch. xxvi.; and coarsely threatening to unkennel the fox, and expose the Protestant resort to metaphorical interpretation: 'If they go to figures and parables we know how to handle them.' To this candid and elegant pair of controversialists Nelson thought proper to reply in his 'Transubstantiation contrary to Scripture, or the Protestant's Answer to the Seeker's Request.' He had evidently been brought into personal collision with the writers, and felt himself bound to take notice of their productions for the sake of a friend in whom he was interested. This tract possesses a natural interest as the earliest publication which proceeded from his pen; and this circumstance, with the rarity of its occurrence, will be sufficient apology for somewhat lengthy quotations." Secretan's Life and Times of Robert Nelson, 1860.

"The Seeker offered no rejoinder to this answer of Nelson's, but left it to a friend to interpose in his behalf in A Catholic Letter to the Seeker, or a Reply to the Protestant Answer to the Seeker [No. 291]; while Williams, afterwards Bishop of Chichester, replied on Nelson's side, and closed the debate with The Protestant Answer to the Catholic Letter to the Seeker, or a Vindication of the Protestant's Answer to the Seeker's Request." Ibid.

T. C. D. 289. ✠ The Catholic Answer to the Seeker's Request, in a letter directed to the Seeker, proving the Real Presence by the Scripture only. 4to, 1687

See Contin. p. 24.

290. The Protestant's Answer to the Seeker's Request.

See Contin. p. 24. [Query, whether the same with No. 288.]

T. C. D. 291. ✠ The Catholic Letter to the Seeker, or a Reply to the Protestant Answer, shewing that Catholics have express Scriptures for believing the Real Presence, and that Protestants have none at all for denying it. 4to, 1688

See Contin. p. 24.

T. C. D. 292. The Protestant's Answer to the Catholic Letter to the Seeker, or a Vindication of the Protestant's Answer to the Seeker's Request. [By John Williams, M.A.] 4to, 1688

See Cat. No. 82; Contin. p. 24; Ath. Oxon. vol. ii. col. 1121.

The Seekers are mentioned in Baxter's Church History, *ad finem.* "A second Sheet for the Ministry; justifying our Calling against Quakers, Seekers and Papists, and all that deny us to be the Ministers of Christ."

C. L. 293. A Plain Representation of Transubstantiation as it is received in the Church of Rome: with the sandy foundations it is built upon, and the arguments that do clearly avert and overturn it. [By Henry Pendlebury, M.A.]

pp. 68, 4to Lond. 1687

See Contin. p. 24. A learned and pious Nonconformist, of Christ's College, Cambridge; minister at Holcomb, Lancashire 1651; ejected 1662 for Nonconformity; died 1695. See Calamy's Account of Ejected Ministers, p. 400; Contin. p. 562. He insists upon the blasphemy implied in the multipresence or manifold presence of Christ's body.

"When Jeffrey Hurst of Shakerley in Lancashire, was brought before Justice Leland, he caused a Mass to be sung, and bad Jeffrey first go and see his Maker, and then he would talk with him. Jeffrey answered, 'Sir, my Maker is in Heaven.' p. 9.

"Bellarmine tells us that for five hundred years before his time the truth of Transubstantiation was defined, sub Anathemate, in six Councils one after another. But this is of least weight, for Bellarmine's six Councils were of the Pope's making, and such as decreed more errors than this."

> Una apex verbi ratione valentior omni est,
> Milleque decretis conciliisque prior. (p. 48.)

Cf. Johnson, pp. 16-18, The Historical Preface, *ut infra*, p. vi.; Cosin's History of Transubstantiation; Newcome on Transubstantiation. "Nor did the Church of Rome ever establish this Transubstantiation till the time of Innocent the Third, which was not above five hundred years ago, when the power of Popes was at the highest, and the darkness of the time grown so great as men discerned not the bread that was given them to eat, especially when it was stamped with the figure of Christ upon the Cross, as if they would have men believe it were transubstantiated, not only into the body of Christ, but also into the wood of his Cross, and that they did eat both together in the sacrament." Hobbes's Works, vol. iii. p. 612. "Again, Christ saith not, *This Wine*, but This Cup: and therefore by their conclusion not only the Wine should be turned into bloud, but the Cup too." (H. Smith's Serm., 4to. 1657, p. 56.)

294. The Absolute Impossibility of Transubstantiation demonstrated. [By Samuel Johnson.] pp. xv., 54, 4to Lond. 1688 C. L. T. C. D.

See Cat. No. 83; Contin. p. 24; Works, fol. 1713; pp. 176-200. For an account of Samuel Johnson, see No. 316.

"In short, O my Protestant countrymen, you see what infinite reason there is that you should for ever renounce Transubstantiation;

for otherwise you owe your Saviour but little service, if you will not do Him so much right as to say, that he is not a bit of bread. And there is the same reason that you should renounce that Church, which employs her infallibility in contradicting the plainest Scripture; in defacing those eternal truths which are deeply engraven upon the minds of men; and in doing the utmost dishonour to our Saviour, by making his religion the scorn of mankind. What Averroes said, is recorded by Papists, and is too well known to be repeated upon this occasion [see L'Arroque's History of the Eucharist, ch. ix. p. 302, and No. 286, p. 193]; and for my part, I should take it much more patiently to be forced to believe that I myself am a wafer, than that a wafer is my God. So that the blessed Martyrs were infinitely in the right, to stake down their lives against this doctrine; for they plainly saw that it was not a moot point, or a disputable matter (against which no wise man would lay down a hair of his head), but they saw it was a bottomless pit of falsehood, which swallows up all the natural and theological veritys which ever came from God. And he that dies for so much important truth, most certainly dies for God." Folio edit. p. 199.

"It has been heretofore no small diversion to me to see how the Papists stood on tiptoe, when that great restorer of natural knowledge appeared, expecting whether his new philosophy would favour their old Transubstantiation. But when they found that he was not a man for *substantial accidents* and such kind of contradictious stuff, Dr. Arnault of the Sorbonne, puts it home to him in the Fourth Objection, and tells him that, according to his philosophy, the doctrine of the Church concerning the Sacrament of the Altar could not remain safe and sound; because it is of Faith that the accidents in the Sacrament remain without a subject, whereas Monsieur Cartes seemed to hold (for he had not as yet spoke out, nor expressed himself fully in the matter) that accidents are inseparable from a subject. . . . . A popish physician not satisfied with the apology that the senses may err in accidents only, as colour, figure, &c., declared that the Fathers of Trent ought to have been condemned to feed on the mere accidents of bread all their lives for bringing so great an incumbrance on the Faith." p. 194.

Among the works of Antony le Grand, the first philosopher of the age that reduced the Cartesian system to the method of the schools, and defended it against Samuel Parker's Disputationes de Deo, 1678, in which he had censured certain principles of the Cartesian philosophy as atheistical (see Wood's Athenæ Oxon. vol. ii. col. 819), and who had frequent contests with John Sergeant concerning the nature of Ideas, &c., is *Missæ Sacrificium neomystis succincte expositum*, 12mo Lond. 1695. Dodd gives a list of his works..

Peter Poiret, one of the followers of Madame Bourignon, attacked Descartes in a treatise, De Eruditione Solida Superficiaria et Falsa libri tres in quibus Cartesianismi fundamenta, valor, et errores deteguntur, 1692, 1707, 12mo. Cf. Hampden's Bampton Lectures, p. 537. Though principally famous for his mystical writings Poiret published also a book, De Veritate, Natura et Substantia Corporis Christi in Eucharistia, Lond. 1688. (Voy. Niceron, tt. iv. et x.)

295. An Historical Treatise on Transubstantiation (written by an author of the Communion of the Church of Rome), wherein is made appear that according to the principles of that Church this doctrine cannot be an article of faith. Published by William Wake, D.D. pp. 73, 4to Lond. 1687 C. L.

See Cat. No. 75; Contin. p. 24. This is entirely Peck's description. The tract referred to was published not by Wake, but by Tenison. See No. 105, p. 99, where he says: "He (Pulton) calls for our Catalogue of Witnesses against their Errors. Yet he had heard of the works of Illyricus and others of this nature. And I am not ashamed to own that I published in the English tongue divers months ago the testimonies of writers in the several ages of Christianity against Transubstantiation (A Treatise by an Author of the Roman Communion touching Transubstantiation, 4to Lond. 1687)." p. 99.

"And of this the late author of the Historical Treatise of Transubstantiation (*Traitté d'un Autheur de la Communion Romaine touchant la Transubstantiation*, Lond. 1686), and which is just now set forth in our own language, may be an eminent instance, being a person at this day living in the communion of the Church of Rome, and in no little esteem among all that know him." Historical Pref. prefixed to Wake's Discourse on the Holy Eucharist, p. vi.

"The Bishops of France in their last assembly held at Paris in the year 1682, compos'd a Pastoral Letter addressed to the Protestants, to invite them to return to the Communion of the Church of Rome.

And ...... they laid down several principles which they called methods, as fit to be made use of, whereby to judge what should be received as an article of Faith. In the fourth method they laid down as a maxim that of Vincentius Lirinensis. Transubstantiation is here examined by it. Cf. Albertinus *de Eucharistiæ Sacramento*, where he may find all the arguments against this doctrine proposed, and the testimonies of every Father vindicated against the sophistry of Perron and Bellarmin and all other Romish writers upon this subject." Bingham, xv. ch. v. 4.

C. L. 296. A Brief Declaration of the Lord's Supper written by Dr. Nicholas Ridley, Bishop of London, during his imprisonment. With some other determinations and disputations concerning the same argument, by the same Author. To which is annexed an Extract of several passages to the same purpose out of a book intituled Diallacticon, written by Dr. John Poynet, Bishop of Winchester, in the reigns of Edward VI. and Queen Mary. [By Henry Wharton, M.A.]

pp. xi., 68, 4to Lond. 1688

See Cat. No. 79; Ath. Oxon. vol. ii. col. 875. Compare the Conferences between Dr. Ridley and Master Latimer, in Glocester-Ridley's Life, pp. 445-455, and in Ridley's Works, edit. Parker Soc., p. 97. Printed in 1555.

C. L. 297. Diallacticon Viri boni et literati de veritate, natura, atque substantia corporis et sanguinis Christi in Eucharistia. [Written by Dr. John Poynet, Bp. of Winton. Published by Edward Pelling, Rector of St. Martin's, Ludgate.]

pp. 82, 4to Lond. 1688

See Cat. No. 80; Contin. p. 24.

In this Poynet endeavoured to reconcile the controversy of the Lutherans and Zuinglians. See Bayle, art. Poinet and Harckius; Cosin's History of Transubstantiation, ch. ii. § 4. "The body of Christ, saith Guido Grossus, archbishop of Narbonne, anno 1268, is so called four ways: 1. In respect of similitude, as the species of bread and wine, and that improperly. 2. It is taken for the material flesh of Jesus Christ, which was taken of the Blessed Virgin; and this signification is proper. 3. For the Church, in regard of the mystical union (with Christ). 4. For the spiritual flesh of Jesus Christ, which is meat indeed; and it is said of those who eat this flesh spiritually, that they do receive the truth of the flesh and blood of our Saviour, which as it overthrows the dream of Transubstantiation, so it is the very language of the Ancients, Clemens Alexandrinus, S. Jerome, S. Ambrose, S. Austin and others, who did distinguish Christ's natural body, which was of the Virgin, from that spiritual body which is receiv'd at the Eucharist; as you may see plainly in that excellent little book called the *Diallacticon*, which, God be thanked, is now reprinted at London. A book written, as Bishop Cosin tells us, by Dr. Poinet, bishop of Winchester, a little before Bishop Jewel's Apology came out. Cassander and other divines abroad extolled it deservedly. The late Sa.[muel Parker, bishop of] Oxon (if I may rank him among such company) takes notice of it, but says withal, I have not the book by me; and I verily believe it, for had he ever seen or read that book, I am apt to think he would hardly have wrote his own; at least not that part of it the force whereof is quite destroy'd by that Diallacticon." (Pelling's Fourth Letter, p. 71.)

298. An Account of a Disputation at Oxford, anno Dom. 1554. With a treatise of the Blessed Sacrament. Both written by Bishop Ridley, Martyr. To which is added, A Letter written by Mr. John Bradford, never before printed. All taken out of an original manuscript [and published by Gilbert Ironside, D.D.] Pref. &c., pp. xxii. [no pagination] 40, Bradford 12, 4to Oxford 1688 **C. L.**

See Ath. Oxon. vol. i. col. 95, vol. ii. col. 1184.

This Latin disputation is reprinted from Fox, "Rerum in Ecclesia Gestarum," Basil 1559, in Ridley's Works, Parker Society, Append. i. Cf. Bradford's Hurt of Hearyng Masse.

299. The School of the Eucharist established upon the miraculous respects and acknowledgments which beasts, birds and insects, upon several occasions, have rendred to the Holy Sacrament of the Altar. Whence Catholicks may increase **C. L.**

in devotion towards this divine Mystery, and Hereticks find there their confusion. By F. Toussain Bridoul, of the Society of Jesus. Printed in French at Lille 1672, and now made English, and published with a Preface concerning the Testimony of Miracles. [By William Claget, D.D.]

Editor's Pref. pp. xxiv., Pref. ii., 45, 4to Lond. 1687

See Cat. No. 84.

"By all means therefore let every one go to this school; and that no man who is come thus far may be altogether ignorant of the lessons he is to learn, I do not care if I give him a sample or two out of the Liber Festivalis." (Editor's Pref. p. 21.) For an account of the Liber Festivalis, compiled from the Legenda Aurea, and first printed by Caxton 1483, folio, see Blades's Life of Caxton, vol. ii. pp. 134-6, 237-9; and Bibl. Spenceriana, vol. iv. pp, 359-65. There was a second edition by Caxton without date, and of which it is a curious fact that no perfect copy is known to exist.

300. Transubstantiation examined and confuted in two Sermons on the Lord's Supper, preached in the reign of Q. Elizabeth by Henry Smith, Preacher at St. Clement's Danes. 4to, 1688

See Antiquities of Leicestershire by W. Burton, p. 313; Ath. Oxon. vol. i. col. 263; Fuller's Worthies, 2nd alphabet, p. 134; Strype's Life of Aylmer, p. 154. Consult also Athenæ Cantabrigienses, vol. ii., and Notes and Queries, 2nd ser., pp. 8-9. No copy of this edition appears in the Catalogues of the British Museum, the Bodleian, Sion's College, Queen's College, Cambridge; nor is it mentioned in Athenæ Cantabrigienses. The two Sermons are included in
C. L. the collection published by Fuller, with a Life and Portrait of Smith in 1657, 4to.

C. L. 301. A Discourse concerning the Adoration of the Host, as it is
T.C.D. taught and practised in the Church of Rome. Wherein an Answer is given to T.[homas] G.[odden] on that subject, and to Monsieur Boileau's late book De Adoratione Eucharistiæ, Paris 1685. [By William Payne, M.A.]

pp. 66, Lond. 1685

See Cat. No. 14; [State, p. 8;] Contin. p. 6. In Gibson, fol. edit. vol. ii. tit. vii. ch. ii. 8vo edit. vol. x. For Boileau's book see supplement.

302. A Discourse concerning the Sacrifice of the Mass. [By William Payne, M.A.] pp. 96, 4to Lond. 1688. **C. L.**

See Cat. No. 74; Contin. p. 76.

In Gibson, folio ed. vol. ii. tit. vi. ch. ii., 8vo ed. vol. vi. "The word [Mincha] here (Malachi, i. 11) from which some of our adversaries are so foolish as to derive the Latin word Missa, that signifies only a dismission of the catechumens and penitents before the office of the Eucharist, does not signify a propitiatory sacrifice, but only a meat-offering, which was merely Eucharistic." (p. 23.) Cf. Waterland's Review of the Doctrine of the Eucharist as laid down in Scripture and Antiquity, ch. i., who for the ancient names of the Sacrament with their proper authorities refers to Hospinian, Casaubon, Suicer (Exercit., p. 418 alias 582), Turretin and Cangius. See also Forbesii Irenicon, lib. ii. ch. xi.; Clagett's Discourse (No. 326) p. 28; Outram on Sacrifices, Diss. ii.; Larroque's History of the Eucharist, ch. viii. "Without intending or, in fact, really giving any countenance to the sacrifice of the Mass, some divines have considered the Eucharist as the Christian sacrifice, corresponding in nature to the sacrifices of the Law. This theory however endangers a depreciation of the sacrifice of the Cross itself, as is admitted by its most strenuous advocates. See Johnson's Unbloody Sacrifice, pt. i. ch. ii. § i., and pt. ii. Introduction; and Brett's True Scripture Account of the Nature and Benefits of the Holy Eucharist, in answer to Hoadley, 1736, pp. 59-76." Vaux's Bampton Lectures, p. 214, &c. An account of the writings of the Nonjurors on this subject will be found in Lathbury, pp. 378-80. "The most eminent of our divines who have taught this doctrine are the Archbishops Laud and Wake, the Bishops Andrews, Bull, and Patrick; Messrs. Mede, Bingham, Wheatly, and Johnson." (Bishop Gleig.)

CHAP. XXXI.

Of the Discourses written of the Roman assertion that Transubstantiation is as evident as a Trinity.

C. L. 303. ✠ The Protestant's Plea for a Socinian: justifying his doctrine from being opposite to Scripture or Church authority, and him from being guilty of heresie or schism. In five conferences. [By Abraham Woodhead.] pp. 45, 4to Lond. 1686

See Contin. p. 38.

This is the fourth discourse in the author's Rational Account of the Doctrine of Roman Catholicks (*ut supra*) pt. i. No. 192. "The design," observes Clagett, in The Present State, p. 33, "was to prove that in interpreting Scripture by reason, and not submitting to the infallible interpretation of what they call the Church, we make an apology for Socinians and all other hereticks whatsoever. The falseness of this pretence has been at large shewn in the Answer which an eminent person of our Church has lately put out to it, called,"

C. L. 304. The Difference betwixt the Protestant and Socinian Method: in answer to a book written by a Romanist, and intituled, The Protestant's Plea for a Socinian. [By Thomas Tenison, D.D.] pp. 64, 4to Lond. 1687

See Cat. No. 33; [State, pp. 33, 34;] Fasti Oxon. col. 159; Lives of the Protestant Archbishops, by John Le Neve, p. 236.

Cf. No. 249, note. "It may be noted that the author of this book [Woodhead] is not the inventor but the borrower of this argument call'd, The Protestant's Plea for a Socinian. It has been used by Valerianus Magnus; by the author of the Brief Disquisition; by Sir Kenelm Digby, in his discourse concerning the Infallibility of Religion (if he be the genuine author); by the Jesuite who cavill'd against Dr. Potter's book call'd Want of Charity; which argument of the Jesuite was long ago answer'd by Mr. Chillingworth. . . . . Since that time Louis Maimbourg, then a Jesuite, wrote a book intituled Traité &c. (a Treatise concerning the True Word of God), à Paris 1671. Four chapters of that little book are spent in the managing of this Method," p. 13.

305. ✠ A Discourse concerning a Judge of Controversies in Matters of Religion; shewing the necessity of such a Judge.
4to Lond. 1686

See Cat. No. 34. This is printed with the Answer, No. 306.

"Lady Theophila Nelson is said to have been the author of this Discourse. (See Birch's Life of Tillotson, p. 120.) It was thought deserving of an elaborate reply on the Protestant side by so eminent a writer as Sherlock (No. 306), and it is written with a vivacity and clearness which yield no mean impression of the intellectual capacity of the lady whom Nelson had espoused." (Secretan's Memoirs of the Life and Times of the pious Robert Nelson, p. 26.)

In the words of Tennemann (Hist. of Philosophy, p. 343), "Peter Huet, Bishop of Avranches, employed Scepticism as a means of converting Protestants." "In his book on the Imbecility of the Human Understanding, and in his Evangelical Demonstration he commends the process of reasoning, which invalidates all philosophical principles previous to or independent of Revelation. Thus he prepared the way for the reception of a living infallible guide. For how should Revelation be understood since Reason is hopelessly incapable, unless some unerring Judge is always at hand. Thus Rome rises on the ruins of Reason. His Supremacy of Faith is the Supremacy of the Pope. See Mosheim's Eccl. cent. xvii. s. i. part i. note." Wordsworth's Letters on the Church of Rome, p. 61. Cf. Swift, 1755, vol. ii. part i. p. 93. Scott's edit. viii. p. 75, and Bentley on Freethinking, p. 111. Birch states that it was in the indignation Tillotson felt at the design to make men first Atheists that they might be more easily made Papists, the foundation was laid of his great zeal against Popery.

306. A Discourse concerning a Judge of Controversies in Matters of Religion; being an Answer to some Papers asserting the necessity of such a Judge. Written for the private satisfaction of some scrupulous persons, and now published for common use. With a Prefacc concerning the Nature of Certainty C. L. T. C. D.

and Infallibility. [By William Sherlock, DD.]
Pref. pp. xiii. 100, 4to Lond. 1686

See Cat. No. 34; Contin. p. 30. In Gibson, folio edit. vol. i. tit. i., 8vo edit. vol. iv.

Compare the controversy between Stillingfleet and Serjeant, concerning whom there is a note in the recent edition of Bramhall's Works, vol. ii. p. 358. It was on Lady Theophila Nelson's account, the author of the "Papers" referred to (No. 305), that Hickes published Letters between Dr. G. Hickes and a Popish Priest on a young gentlewoman's departing from the Church of England. 8vo 1705. See Nichols's Literary Anecdotes, vol. i. p. 17.

T.C.D. 307. ✠ A Dialogue between a New Catholic Convert and a Protestant, shewing the doctrine of Transubstantiation to be as reasonable to be believed as the great mystery of the Trinity by all good Catholics. 1 sheet, 4to Lond. 1686

See Cat. No. 35; Contin. p. 23. Compare Godden's *Catholics no Idolators.*

C. L. *T.C.D.* 308. An Answer to a late Dialogue between a New Catholic Convert and a Protestant, to prove the mystery of the Trinity to be as absurd as Transubstantiation: by way of short notes on the said Dialogue. [By William Sherlock, D.D.]
pp. 14, 4to Lond. 1687

Compare Aldrich's Oxford Reply, p. 21, and Vindication, p. 84.

C. L. *T.C.D.* 309. A second Dialogue between a new Catholic Convert and a Protestant, shewing why he cannot believe the doctrine of Transubstantiation though he do firmly believe the doctrine of the Trinity. [By Richard Kidder, M.A.]
1 sheet, 4to Lond. 1687

See Cat. No. 36; Contin. p. 23; Fasti Oxon. vol. ii. col. 123.

C. L. 310. The Doctrine of the Trinity and Transubstantiation compared as to Scripture, Reason and Tradition: in a New Dialogue between a Protestant and a Papist. Part. I. Wherein an answer is given to the late proofs of the antiquity of Transubstantiation in the books called Consensus Veterum and Nubes Testium. [By Edward Stillingfleet, D.D.]

pp. 47, 4to Lond. 1687

See Cat. No. 37; Contin. p. 23. In Gibson, folio edit. vol. ii. tit. vii. ch. iv., 8vo. ed. vol. ix. p. 299. Works, vol. vi. p. 591. "In the year 787 the second Council of Nice began with a rash determination, that the sacred symbols are not figures or images at all, but the very body and blood. About 831 Paschasius Radbertus carried it further, even to Transubstantiation, or somewhat very like to it. The *name of Transubstantiation* is supposed to have come in about A.D. 1100, first mentioned by Hildebertus Cenomanensis of that time, p. 689, edit. Benedict. A.D. 1215 the doctrine was made an article of faith by the Lateran Council under Innocent the Third. Afterwards it was re-established in the Trent Council A.D. 1551, and at length in Pope Pius's Creed A.D. 1564." (Waterland, vii. 182.) Jeremy Taylor states in his Real Presence and Spiritual Presence of Christ, proved against the doctrine of Transubstantiation, that the word was first invented by Stephen, bishop of Augustodunum in the year 1100. (vol. vi. § xii.) The words of the Bishop are: "Oramus ut cibus hominum fiat cibus Angelorum, scilicet ut oblatio panis et vini *Transubstantietur* in corpus et sanguinem Christi;" (vide Bibl. Patr. 1618, vol. x. p. 418; Bibl. Patr. 1624, vol. vi. p. 982; Bibl. Maxima, vol. xx. p. 1878). Cf. Albertinus de Eucharistiæ Sacramento, 1655, folio, p. 969; Bingham, bk. xv. 5, § 4.

311. The Doctrine of the Trinity and Transubstantiation compared as to Scripture, Reason and Tradition; in a new Dialogue between a Protestant and a Papist. Part II. Wherein the doctrine of the Trinity is shewed to be agreeable to Scripture and Reason; and Transubstantiation repugnant to both. [By Edward Stillingfleet, D.D.] C. L. T. C. D.

pp. 43, 4to Lond. 1687

See Cat. No. 38; Contin. p. 23.

In the homely language of Bradford (No. 298, p. 6): "If God be God [infinite, incomprehensible] then follow Him; if Baal and a piece of Bread be God then follow it." Cf. Pearson on the Creed, art. vi., Of God the Father Almighty, pp. 216-218, folio, Lond. 1692; Vogan's Bampton Lectures, 1837, and his Lectures on the Lord's Supper, Lec. vi.; and the versified epitome of Transubstantiation by Louis de Leon, quoted in "Lambeth and the Vatican," 12mo, 1825,

If this we see be bread, how can it last,
So constantly consumed, yet always here?
If this be God, then how can it appear
Bread to the eye, and seem bread to the taste?
If bread, why is it worshipped by the baker?
If God, can such a space a God comprise?
If bread, how is it it confounds the wise?
If God, how is it that we eat our Maker?
If bread, what good can such a morsel do?
If God, how is it we divide it so?
If bread, such saving virtue could it give?
If God, how can I see and touch it thus?
If bread, how could it come from heaven to us?
If God, how can I look at it and live? Vol. ii. p. 53.

C. L. *T. C. D.* 312. A Paraphrase, with Notes and Preface, upon the sixth Chapter of St. John, shewing that there is neither good reason nor sufficient authority to suppose that the Eucharist is discoursed of in the Chapter, much less to infer the doctrine of Transubstantiation from it. By William Clagett, D.D.

pp. 52, 4to Lond. 1686

See Cat. No. 76; Contin. p. 24. In Gibson, folio ed. vol. ii. tit. vii. ch. iv., 8vo edit. vol. ix. In a postscript he notices Godden's sermon on St. Peter's day, in which he infers the doctrine of Transubstantiation from the same chapter. Du Moulin, on the other hand, argues from verse 53 against a corporal and oral manducation, seeing that without it so many are saved; see his Anatomy of the Mass, ch. xxxvii.

C. L. *T. C. D.* 313. An Historical Discourse Concerning the Necessity of the Minister's Intention in administering the Sacrament. [By Peter Allix.] pp. 68, 4to Lond. 1688

See Cat. No. 118; Contin. p. 7; Critical Dictionary, vol. ii. p. 526. In Gibson, folio ed. vol. ii. tit. vii. ch. i. 8vo ed. vol. viii. "This error entered the Church of Rome (*it is found in no other Church*) at a time when the Priests were so ignorant of the Latin tongue that they scarce could read it without making them laugh that heard them, and when the corruption was so ordinary and the profanation so public that they celebrated Mass the day of the Feast of Fools with actions and gestures more proper to raise laughter than to excite any respect for the Sacrament," p. 61. See Clemangis de corrupto Ecclesiæ statu (Brown's Fasciculus, vol. ii. p. 555). This is one of the first works published by a Catholic against the corruptions of the Romish Church, more particularly the tribute which she exacted from the Christian world. In Neander's Church History there is an ample review of this remarkable work.

"Whilst they anathematise those who oppose the belief of the necessity of the minister's intention . . . . . they have not clearly determined wherein they make that intention to consist, whether it be an intention actual, virtual or habitual that is required. . . . . . To say the truth, these good fathers did not trouble themselves to explain their meanings. Cæteri homines, said the Ambassador of France, writing to the Chancellor of the Hospital, loquuntur ut intelligi possint, isti nihil minus volunt quam ut intelligantur." p. 60.

On the supposed uncertainty in the Sacraments &c. of the Roman Catholic Church, see also No. 188, Gavanti Thesaurus Sacr. Rituum, tom. i. pt. iii. p. 14 seqq., who enumerates the authors who had taught that *internal intention* is necessary, and adds, "recentissime, non solum dignitate, sed etiam sapientia et pietate eminentissimus, Cardin. Gotti, tom. xiii. suæ Theologiæ quæst. vii. dub. 4." Cf Palmer's Origines Liturgicæ, vol. ii., and Biogr. Univers., *v.* Catharin. From the uncertainty of the minister's intention Taylor argues that it were fit to omit the giving God's due to that which they do not know to be anything but a piece of bread. Dissuasive from Popery, pt. ii. ch. ii. § 12. Cf. Du Moulin's Anatomy of the Mass, ch. xvii.

Missale Romanum, or the Depth and Mystery of the Romish Mass, laid open and explained for the use of both reformed and unreformed Christians. By Daniel Brevint, D.D. 8vo Oxf. 1672 *T. C. D.* *B. L.*

Ibid. 1673 and 1847. Born in the Isle of Jersey in the reign of James I.; studied at Saumur, of which university he took his degree of M.A. 1634; constituted the first Fellow of the French Fellowship founded in Jesus College by King Charles I.; ejected for refusing the covenant, he went to France, where he became Chaplain to the Prince of Turenne; Prebendary of Durham 1661; Dean of Lincoln 1681; died 1695.

C. L. ✠ Missale Romanum Vindicatum; or, the Mass Vindicated from Dr. Daniel Brevint's calumnious and scandalous Tract. 8vo 1674

See Wood's Ath. Oxon. vol. ii. col. 705.

C. L. The Christian Sacrament and Sacrifice &c. By D. Brevint. 8vo Oxf. 1673

C. L. *T. C. D.* Saul and Samuel at Endor; or the New Ways of Salvation and Service ...... as also, A Brief Account of R. F. his Missale Vindicatum, or Vindication of the Romish Mass. By D. Brevint, D.D. 8vo Oxf. 1674

He wrote other tracts in Latin bearing on the same subject. See Wood and Watt.

Anti-Goliah; or an Epistle to Mr. Brevint, containing some reflexions upon his Saul and Samuel at Endor. By Edward Worsley. pp. 59, 8vo 1678

See De Backer's Bibliothèque, Ser. vii., Southwell, Oliver, and Dodd.

B. L. A Famous Conference between Pope Clement X. and Cardinal de Monte Altocone. The discovery of the Mass in H. Scripture made by the worthy Father Patrick, an excellent engineer of the Church of Rome in England. 4to Lond. 1674

T. C. D. The Funerall of the Masse; or, the Masse dead and buried without hope of resurrection, transl. out of the French [of David De Rodon]. By S. A. 8vo Lond. 1673

Seventh edition, 8vo Lond. 1685. The best English edition of this work, which contains learned notes referring to all the writers in the controversy, and is very scarce, is entitled, The Funeral of the Mass, with an Answer to what Mr. W. C. has since publish'd by way of reply in a discourse intitled, Missa Triumphans, *ut infra*. Wherein the Adoration of the Host .... Mr. W. C.'s pretended Oath relating to Transubstantiation &c. are incidentally touch'd upon. A distinct Answer is also given to the chief arguments used by the Bp. of Meaux in his Exposition to prove our Saviour's Corporeal Presence in the Eucharist; and to the Primitive Authorities cited in the Nubes Testium. By Robert Hill. 8vo Lond. 1716.

"How little reason the Romish Doctors have to applaud their present Romish Mass-Book has been sufficiently proved by Dr. Hickes, in his first volume of Controversial Letters, 1705, pp. 294-305; Icon Libellorum, 1715, p. 227 &c.; Peter du Moulin's short Discourse, intituled, The Mass, in Latin and English. Printed at London in 1641. Books ii. iii. [New translation. To which is prefixed, A Concise History of the Eucharist. By the Rev. Robert Shanks, A.M. Edinburgh, 1833, 12mo.] Four Books by my Lord Mornay in 1600, folio, pp. 1-109 [viz. de Eucharistia]. The Romish Mass-Book translated into English, with Notes and Observations thereupon, 1683. And in a Discourse of the Sacrifice of the Mass. [No. 302.] 1688, p. 41, &c." Hill's Notes, p. 266.

Missa Triumphans, or, The Triumph of the Mass, wherein all the sophistical and wily arguments of Mr. De Rodon against that Venerable Sacrifice, in his funestuous Tract, by him called, The Funeral of the Mass, are fully, formally and clearly answered. Together with an Appendix by way of Answer to the Translator's Preface. By F. P., M. O. P. Hib. Permissu Superiorum. 12mo 1675 — C. L. *T. C. D.*

In "The Epistle Dedicatory to Her Royal Highness the Dutchess of York," the author subscribes himself C. W. The author's name was William Collins, Ord. Prædicatorum; see Notes and Queries, 2nd ser. vol. iv. pp. 8 and 57.

Historia Transubstantiationis Papalis; cui præmittitur, atque opponitur, tum S. Scripturæ, tum veterum patrum et reformatarum ecclesiarum doctrina Catholica, de sacris symbolis, et præsentia Christi in Sacramento Eucharistiæ. pp. 165, 8vo 1675 — C. L. *T. C. D.*

The History of Popish Transubstantiation &c. was written by Dr. John Cosin at Paris in the year 1656 for the use of some of his countrymen, who were frequently attacked upon that point by the Papists.

C. L. It was published by Dr. Durell at London 1675, 8vo, and translated into English in 1676 by Luke de Beaulieu, 8vo pp. 160. The preface by Durell gives an account of the occasion of writing and publishing this discourse (in the fourth volume of Cosin's works, Oxford 1851.) In the first volume is reprinted the Life of Cosin, which appeared in the Biographia Britannica. See also Smith's Vitæ quorumdam eruditissimorum virorum, 4to Lond. 1707.

Cosin's "History &c.; to which is premised and opposed The Catholick Doctrine of the Holy Scripture, the Ancient Fathers and the Reformed Churches, about the Sacred Elements, and Presence of Christ in the Blessed Sacrament of the Eucharist" was answered in

✠ The Catholick Doctrine of Transubstantiation proved to be ancient and orthodoxal against the slanderous tongue of Dr. John Couzens. Small 8vo printed at Paris 1657

B. L. ✠ A Rational Discourse concerning Transubstantiation. In a Letter to a Person of Honour, from a Master of Arts of the University of Cambridge. pp. 46, 4to 1676

T. C. D. Reflections on that Discourse which a Master of Arts once of the University of Cambridge calls Rational, presented in print to a person of honor, 1676, concerning Transubstantiation. By one of no arts but downright honesty. [Arthur Annesley, Earl of Anglesey.] 4to Lond. 1676

This, which was published with another tract by the same author, entitled, The Truth Unveiled, was answered in a tract called, Roman Tradition Examined. See Ath. Oxon. vol. ii. col. 790.

C. L. Roman Tradition Examined as it is urged infallible against all men's senses, reason, the Holy Scripture, the tradition and present judgment of the Universal Church, in point of Transubstantiation, in answer to A Rational Discourse &c. 4to 1676

Mensa Mystica; or a Discourse concerning the Sacrament of the Lord's Supper. In which the ends of its institution are manifested &c. [By Simon Patrick, D.D.] 8vo Lond. 1676

Fifth edition, 1684, pp. 500. In his Works, vol. i. Oxf. 1858. "A valuable companion (observes the editor) to its predecessor upon the other sacrament" (Baptism); Pref. lix. He quotes (ch. i.) the arguments of a divine in the Council of Trent, proving that this sacrament is only a memorial of a sacrifice, and not a propitiatory sacrifice. [Hist. Conc. Trent. Sarpi, by Brent, lib. vi. p. 520.] Ch. ii.: "It is a remembrance of Christ with thanksgiving, for it is a feast. The Jewish feasts upon their sacrifice a pattern of it, especially the paschal supper, in which they sung an hymn, &c. The better sort of heathens did in their feasts sing the praises of famous men; which good critics make the true original of the word encomium. [Vid. Etymol. Magn. in voce ἐγκώμιον et Aphthon. Progymn. p. 48. Ed.] Ch. iii.: By feasting at the same table covenants were anciently made &c. As a feast upon a sacrifice (in which notion it is most rarely explained by an excellent doctor of our own), from which it will evidently appear to be intended as a solemn profession of Christ's religion, and a renewal of our covenant with God." Dr. Cudworth is here intended in his discourse concerning the true notion of the Lord's Supper. Compare Warburton's Sermon above cited. "Now from the Gospel-history of the institution of the Lord's Supper, and from St. Paul's reasoning upon it (1 Cor. x. 16), a celebrated person hath long since shewn with great compass of learning, and force of argument, that Jesus, about to offer himself a sacrifice upon the cross for our redemption, did in conformity to a general practice, institute the last supper, under the idea of *a feast after the Sacrifice*. So far that learned writer." The same opinion was asserted by Bishop Cleaver and Waterland, who refers to Pelling on the Sacrament, ch. iii. vol. iv.; Abp. Potter on Church Government, p. 266; Vitringa, Observ. Sacræ, tom. iii. p. 113; Dodwell, One Altar, ch. vii. p. 165; Mede's Christian Sacrifice, p. 370; Bishop Patrick's Christian Sacrifice, p. 31 &c.; Payne's Disc. of the Sacrifice of the Mass, pp. 42-54; and Archbishop Sharpe, vol. vii. Serm. ii.

The Christian Sacrifice; shewing the necessity, end and manner *S. C.*

of receiving the Holy Communion &c. By S. Patrick. Eighth edition. [In his Works, vol. i.] 8vo Lond. 1687

A plain Confutation of the Doctrine of Transubstantiation, with a Reply to what R. H. hath offered on that subject. By D. Whitby. 8vo Lond. 1677

In his Works, vol. i.

The absurdity and idolatry of Host Worship proved, with an Appendix against Transubstantiation, and some Reflections on a late Popish book, called The Guide in Controversies. By D. Whitby, D.D. 8vo Lond. 1679

" There are most certain demonstrations that there could be no such thing as host-worship in the ancient Church, not only from their not believing transubstantiation and the corporeal presence, but from many other topics solidly deduced and substantially proved by two learned writers, Mr. Daillé and Dr. Whitby, in two excellent discourses upon this very subject, to which I will commend the reader, contenting myself to mention the heads of the principal arguments, which they have more fully drawn out and proved." (Bingham, bk. xv. 5, § v.

Animadversions upon the Doctrine of Transubstantiation; a Sermon preached before the Lord Mayor and Court of Aldermen, Oct. 19, 1679, at the Guildhall Chapel, London, by John Turner, Fellow of Christ's College, Cambridge, and Hospitaller of St. Thomas, Southwark. pp. 31, 4to Lond. 1679

C. L. The Anatomy of Transubstantiation. pp. 22, 4to Lond. 1680

The Great Idol of the Mass Overthrown in six arguments, wherein the doctrine of Transubstantiation is fully refuted. 4to Lond. 1680

T. C. D. An Argument drawn from the Evidence and Certainty of Sense against the Doctrine of Transubstantiation. By George
C. L. Morley, Bishop of Winchester. (In his several Treatises.) pp. 22, 4to Lond. 1683

A Vindication of the Argument drawn from Sense against Transubstantiation from a pretended Answer to it, by the Author of a Pamphlet, called, A Treatise of the Nature of Catholic Faith and Heresie. Ch. xi. pp. 54, 55, 58. By G. Morley. pp. 27, 4to Lond. 1683

The History of the Eucharist done into English by Jos. Walker. 4to Dublin 1684

See No. 278 note.

✠ The Great Sacrifice of the New Law expounded by the Figures in the Old, by J. D.. To which is added, The Mass for the Dead, with divers alterations and additions. 18mo Antwerp 1685

The Catholick Doctrine of the Eucharist in all Ages, in answer to what Arnaud alledges touching the belief of the Greek, Muscovite and other Eastern Churches, &c. By John Claude. Translated from the French by J. R. R. Folio Lond. 1684 *T. C. D.*

The Greeks' Opinion touching the Eucharist mis-represented by Monsieur Claude in his Answer to Mr. Arnald. [By Abraham Woodhead.] pp. 34, 4to Lond. 1686 C. L.

"This controversy required authorities and testimonies. Hence the French envoys at Constantinople with the Jesuits on the one part, and the English and Dutch ministers on the other, laboured indefatigably to collect opinions of the Greeks in favour of their respective sides. ..... The names and works of the principal writers on this controversy may be learned from Fabricius, Bibl. Gr. x. 444 sqq. .... Here should be consulted above all others John Covel, who was resident at Constantinople when this drama was acted, and who saw by what artifices the Greeks were induced to give testimony in favour of the Latins. See his Account of the Present Greek Church, Pref. p. ii. and Book i. ch. v. p. 136," &c. 1722, folio; Mosheim's Ecclesiastical History. vol. v. p. 221. Cf. Wake's Preface to his Exposition.

The fifth chapter of Covel's very learned work contains "Some

Observations concerning the first rise of that new doctrine of Transubstantiation, and the endeavours used to propagate it all over the whole Christian world." pp. 106-81. After having traced the ***Eucharist considered in a Sacrificial View*** through four centuries, and part of the fifth, Waterland adds: "If any one is disposed to trace this matter down, even to the dark ages, he will find that most of the Greek and Latin Liturgies contain the same notion with the Fathers, of the spiritual sacrifice of the Eucharist. See Covel, preface, p. 47, bk. p. 36, 41, 46, 53, 67, 68, 175; Deyling, Observat. Miscellan. p. 310 &c." (Works, vol. vii. p. 389.)

C. L. T. C. D. A Discourse of the Sacrament of the Lord's Supper. Wherein the faith of the Catholick Church concerning that Mystery is explained, proved and vindicated, after an intelligible, catechetical and easie manner. By Edward Pelling, Chaplain to His Grace the Duke of Somerset.

Dedic. and Contents pp. xiv., 328, 8vo Lond. 1685

"A little above four hundred years after our Saviour, Nestorius the heretick taught that the divinity and humanity of our Lord was not united in one person. Upon this a general council met at Ephesus, and unanimously condemned this heresie. St. Cyril of Alexandria was a great man at the council, and had a great hand in the condemnation of Nestorius; and one reason he gave to justifie their proceedings was this, because Nestorius by that his doctrine made void the virtue of the Sacrament. And how did they conclude so? Why this was the principle of St. Cyril and the rest of them, that the body of Christ is vivific and that the souls of communicants live by receiving vital virtue from it. Now if (as Nestorius said) the divinity and humanity of Christ be not united, it is impossible for his flesh to yield any life; because no flesh quickeneth of itself, neither can Christ's flesh quicken but by the power of the word. Seeing, therefore, that heretick denied the union between the word and the flesh of Christ, it would follow of necessity that the body of Christ is not vivific, and consequently that we receive no vital virtue from it at the sacrament," p. 263. Cf. the argument of Theodoret (Dial. vol. i. p. 8, and Dial. vol. ii. edit. Hal. 1772, vol. iv. pp. 26, 126-7); and of Pope Gelasius against the Eutychians. (Max. Biblioth. Patr. vol. viii. p. 703, quoted in Stratford's

Discourse concerning the Necessity of a Reformation; by Patrick, No. 66; by Gardiner, No. 212; and by Bingham, bk. xv. p. 5, § 4.)

"I have noted all this to shew how grossly the Romanists are deceived in that which many poor wretches among them take to be a main part of religion, though I am afraid their crafty guides tell them so for their own interest and advantage. For do but take away the doctrine of Christ being *really sacrificed under the species of bread and wine*" [or Transubstantiation which went to the elevation of the priesthood by supposing a resident power in them of working a perpetual miracle] "and their masses for quick and dead must go away next, then the doctrine of purgatory must down also" [the state where penitential deficiencies are made up by the devotions and bought masses of survivors] "and then the conceit of absolutions and indulgences" [which arose out of the strict discipline of the early Church, by which were imposed ecclesiastical censures and punishments upon delinquents, for which long acts of penance &c. were made necessary], "and divers other lucrative arts" [as auricular confession] "whereby the knavish priests cheat ignorant and easie people out of their money; till in the end by taking away first one shore" [shore-post, a buttress, Halliwell] "then another, the old rotten house drops down upon their heads, which hath been held up hitherto by this artificial drop among others" [as works of supererogation] "that our blessed Saviour is really and truly offered up a sacrifice for all men in this mystery, whereas it is not a sacrificing of him but a representation and memorial of the great sacrifice of the cross." p. 47.

The Faith of the Catholick Church concerning the Eucharist, translated from the books of Anthony Arnauld, of the Perpetuity of the Faith. [By Bruzeau.] 12mo Lond. 1687

Anthony Arnauld (Arnaldus) was celebrated especially as a controversialist writer, and carried on a perpetual pen and ink warfare against the Jesuits (Maimbourg, Annat), the Protestants (Jurieu, Aubertin), and the philosophers (Descartes, Malebranche). "This book (La Perpétuité) has given occasion to the most famous dispute that ever was raised between Roman Catholics and Protestants. M. Claude, who was advocate for the latter, has gained the greatest honour by it that ever minister gained; and M. Arnauld, who was principal advocate for the former, perhaps never exerted the whole force of his genius with more application than on this occasion." (Bayle.) "With all his great qualities, all that he did was to repeat over and over that Transubstantiation being now the common doctrine of the Church, it followed that there never was any other Belief, because it cannot be comprehended how all Christians should have agreed to change their opinion, which, had it happened, the certain time should be marked wherein the universal Church had varied in this point; and when and how each particular Church came to corrupt the ancient doctrine..... There wanted no great strength to ruin these imaginary trophies. The Protestants had no harder task than to shew .... that the beginning of idolatry is disputed upon, and nothing yet decided." (Wake's Preface to his Exposition abridged in the Young Student's Library.)

B.L. Determinatio Fratris Johannis Parisiensis, seu de Parisiis, al. de Poliaco, de modo existendi Corporis Christi in Sacramento altaris, cui præfixa est historica Præfatio de dogmate Transubstantiationis à Petro Allix. 8vo Lond. 1686

"There is no question in Popery (except Purgatory, the Popes publican and tasker) about which the Papists are at such civil wars among themselves as about this Transubstantiation. They cannot tell when the change beginneth, nor what manner of change it is, nor how long the change continueth: some hang one way, and some another, like the Midianites, which fought one against another." (H. Smith's first Sermon upon the Lord's Supper, 1657, p. 67.) Archbishop Bramhall gives a catalogue of the "questions and debates" which arose from Transubstantiation. Answer to M. de la Millitiere. (Works. Oxf. 1842, vol. i. pp. 14-19.)

An Historical Treatise written by an Author of the Communion of the Church of Rome touching Transubstantiation. *Ut supra,* No. 295.

[The author of this treatise was Louis Dufour, Abbe de Longuerue, born at Charleville in France in 1652, died at Paris in 1733. Ce traité a été publié par Allix, à qui on l'attribue ordinairement; mais M. Barbier l'a rendu à son auteur, dans le Diction. des Anonymes, No. 7114. T. Fisher.]

A Sermon of the true Spiritual Transubstantiation opposed to the gross, carnal and imaginary Transubstantiation on Matthew xxvi. 26. By Thomas Beverley. 4to 1687 *B. L.* *S. C.*

Cf. Smith's First Sermon.

Of Transubstantiation; or a Reply to a late Paper called A Full Answer to Dr. Tenison's Conferences concerning the Eucharist (No. 110). 1 sheet, 1687

Defence of the most Holy Sacrament of the Mass to the Sectaries of his times. By John Barclay. Englished by a Person of Quality. 4to 1688

This is book ii. ch. ii. of his Paræenesis ad Sectarios, Colon. 8vo 1617. John Barclay, the celebrated author of "Argenis," was born at Pont-à-Mousson, 1582; died at Rome, 1621. He lived about ten years in England, together with his wife and family; all the while enjoying a place of profit which the King (James I.) had bestowed upon him. [The best Life of John Barclay is that given by Dr. Irving in his Lives of Scottish Writers: Edinburgh, 1850, vol. i. p. 371. Lord Hales had previously written and privately printed a careful and exact summary of his life, in 4to. J. Crossley.]

✠ Transubstantiation defended and prov'd from Scripture, in answer to the first part of a Treatise, intitled, A Discourse against Transubstantiation. [By John Gother.] Printed by Henry Wills. pp. xxii., 64, 4to Lond. 1687

See No. 132. The Discourse against Transubstantiation [No. 125] is here reprinted section by section, and a reply made to the sections in their order.

"Luther indeed tells us of about ten opinions of the Sacramentarians in his time; and a book was publish't in the year 1527, in which were reckon'd no less than two hundred several expositions of the sense of these words: Hoc est Corpus meum; This is my Body. What we would gladly know of our adversaries with whom we have now to deal, is, which of these (now two hundred and one) opinions it is that they maintain, or whether they have any other yet in store (for error hath no end) different from all these. For surely after all, they must be forc'd to allow that there is but one true sense of our Saviour's words, viz., either that it is his true substantial Body, which is taken and received, or a figure only, whatsoever they please to assign to it. If the former, they fall in with the Catholics, or Dr. Moor's tenet [the author of The Brief Discourse &c.]; if the latter, what vertue soever they assign to a figure, it is not the real Body, nor the Body really present. Let them speak plain, that the world may understand them. The faithful are not to be deluded with ambiguities in a point of so great concern to their immortal souls." See No. 132 *supra*; Hospiniani Historia Sacramentaria, 1598, folio; Von der Hardt, Hist. Literar. Reformat. p. 74 &c.; Weismanni Hist. Eccles. et unà Pfaffii Acta et Scripta Eccles. Wirtemberg, 2 voll. 4to 1718, and Ranke's Hist. of the Reform. vol. iii. p. 88 &c.

A Reply to the Popish doctrine of Transubstantiation, shewing that it is not agreeable to the opinion of the Primitive Fathers. 24mo 1687

Queen Elizabeth's Opinion concerning Transubstantiation, or the Real Presence of Christ in the Blessed Sacrament; with some Prayers and Thanksgivings composed by her in imminent danger. [A broadside, with woodcut Portrait of Queen Elizabeth at top.] Lond. 1688

"Dryden insists upon a supposed inconsistency in this doctrine (of the Church of England, the 28th Article), but his argument recoils upon the creed of his own Church.. The words of our Saviour are to be interpreted as they must have been meant when spoken; a circumstance which excludes the literal interpretation contended for by the Romanists; for by the words "Hoc est Corpus meum" our Saviour cannot then be supposed to have meant that the morsel which he gave to his disciples was to be transferred into his body, which then stood before their eyes, and which all but heretics allow to have been a real, natural, human body, incapable of course of being divided into as many bodies as there were persons to partake of the communion, and of retaining its original and identical form at the same time. But unless such a multiplied transformation actually took place, our Saviour's words to his Apostles must have been emblematical only.

Queen Elizabeth's homely lines are, after all, an excellent comment on this point of divinity:

> His was the word that spake it;
> He took the bread and brake it;
> And what that word did make it
> That I believe, and take it.
>
> Notes on *The Hind and the Panther*,
> Scott's Dryden, vol. x.

Compare Fuller's Holy State, bk. iv. ch. xv. "In her time of persecution, when a Popish Priest pressed her very hardly to declare her opinion concerning the presence of Christ in the Sacrament, she truly and warily presented her judgement in these verses. . . . . . . And though perchance some may say, this was but the best of shifts, and the worst of answers, because the distinct manner of the Presence must be believed, yet none can deny it to have been a wise return to an adversary who lay at wait for all advantages."

Transubstantiation a Peculiar Article of the Roman Catholick Faith. By Mr. Goodwin. *Ut supra*, No. 21. 1688 **C. L.** *T. C. D.*

A Testimonie of Antiquity, shewing the Ancient Faith in the Church of England, touching the Sacrament of the Body and Bloude of the Lord here publicly preached and also receaved in the Saxons time, above 600 years agoe. Translated from the Saxon Tongue and printed from a very ancient copy. pp. xiv., 24, 4to Lond. 1687 **C. L.**

"This is a very considerable Testimony of Antiquity, as being an Evidence not only of the Doctrine of the ancient English Church, but also of that of the Church of Rome, by whom the Saxon English were converted to the belief of the Christian Faith." (A Defence of the Communion Office and Catechism of the Church of England &c., by John Lewis, 8vo 1742, p. 20.)

The "very ancient copy" above mentioned was imprinted at London by John Daye, no date; but by the name of the subscribing Bishops it appears to have been first published this year (1567). See Ames's Typographical Antiquities, published by Herbert, art. Day, vol. i. p. 642. Reprinted by William L'Isle in 4to in 1623, in his "Divers An- **C. L.** **C. L.**

cient Monuments," being "A Sermon of the Paschal Lambe;" next follow Two Epistles of Elfrike, Abbot of St. Albons, to Wulffine byshop of Scyrburne. Then a certificate of the agreement of this printed copy with the original MS. signed by the two Archbishops and thirteen Bishops &c. Annexed are, "The Lordes Prayer, the Creede and the X Commaundments," in Anglo-Saxon and English.

The life of Ælfric, Archbishop of Canterbury, who died in 1005, will be found in Wright's Biographia Britannica. To Ælfric we are indebted for much of the Anglo-Saxon literature which we possess. His works are as follow: Paschal Homily (Saxon and English) see L'Isle's Divers Ancient Monuments, 4to 1633; Foxe, vol. ii. pp. 450-56; Soames's Bampton Lectures, pp. 428-43; Homilies of the Anglo-Saxon Church by the Ælfric Society, vol. ii. pp. 263-82. Epistolæ duæ de Canonibus et quando dividitur Crisma. Parts of them with a Latin version in Whelock's Bede, 1644, folio; with an English version in Thorpe's Laws, 1840, 8vo; and the greatest part also in Foxe, L'Isle, Whelock, Thorpe, Spelman's Concilia, vol. i. pp. 578-84, folio, 1639; and Wilkins' Conc. vol. i. p. 250, folio, 1737. The MS. at Cambridge, from which Spelman and Wilkins printed a portion of this Epistle, is mutilated. The matter which will be found in L'Isle's Ancient Monuments ad calc. supplies a sufficient explanation of the mutilation; see also Soames's B. L. pp. 424-5. "The doctrine of Transubstantiation was so far from being planted here by Augustine that Elfric, his successor in the see of Canterbury four hundred years after, wrote many things inconsistent with this absurd notion, which had been indeed published and defended in France by Paschasius Radbertus, above an hundred years before Elfric, but was not yet established either in France or any other part of Christendom; and no man in this age can say anything more irreconcileable to it than he has done in his Homilies [the Paschal Homily and the two Epistles, see Soames]. And his Homilies were received as the doctrine of the Church of England in the tenth and eleventh centuries; for they were publicly read by the priests instead of sermons. And I am fully persuaded that the Homilies of Elfric are more positive against Transubstantiation than the Homilies of the Church of England compiled in the reigns of Edward the Sixth and Queen Elizabeth." Johnson's Ecclesiastical Laws, vol. i. pref. p. xx. His other works, being irrelevant to this subject, I shall not notice. See Cave, Tanner, and Wright.

Transubstantiation never own'd by the Ancient Church.
4to Lond. 1688

No Antiquity for Transubstantiation plainly proved from the judgment of the most learned men that lived in that time of the Saxons. [With a Preface by John Joscelin.] Lond. 1688 *B. L.*

Bertram or Ratram, Concerning the Body and Blood of the Lord, in Latin; with a new English Translation [by Mr. Hopkins]. To which is prefix'd, An Historical Dissertation touching the Author and this Work [by Dr. Peter Allix]. The second edition enlarged, with an Appendix, wherein M. Boileau's French Version and Notes upon Bertram are considered, and his unfair dealings in both detected. **C. L.**
pp. 504, 8vo Lond. 1688

This is the best of Dr. Allix's two editions. His Historical Dissertation was first published in 1672 in Latin and in French. He endeavours to prove that Bertram's (or Ratram's) opinion on the sacrament of the Eucharist was totally different from that of the Romish Church. Cf. Pelling's Fourth Letter, p. 24 sqq. B. Ratramus or Be Ratramus, *i.e.* Beatus Ratramnus, was corrupted in the MSS. into Bertramus.

Cf. Ælfric's Canons, Epistles and Pascal Homily; Soames's Bampton Lectures, vol. vii. "Some writers naturally anxious to extenuate the opposition encountered anciently by asserters of that doctrine, have contended that Erigena's piece upon the Eucharist is in fact that which we have under the name of Ratramn, or Bertram." Proofs and Illustrations, p. 418. Cf. Birkbeck's Protestant's Evidence, fol. 1657, p. 268. In the supplement to Gibson, vol. ii. L'Arroque's History translated, p. 403. That it was not written by Scotus Erigena is admitted by Mabillon (Act. Ben. Sect. iv. Pref.) "The style of Bertram and Scotus are not at all alike: Scotus is full of Greek words and notions and citations out of the Greek fathers, which Bertram is free from. His way of arguing is not syllogistical as Bertram's, so far as I can observe by his book 'De Naturis.' And his notion that Christ's glorified body is absorpt in the divine nature, and is not local, nor visible, nor had the same members after its resurrection which it had before, will quite overthrow many of Bertram's arguments." (Allix, p. 58.) Respecting this notion of Scotus, Ranke observes that it nearly coincides with Luther's doctrine, that the identity of the divine and human natures is set forth in the mystery of the Sacrament. (History of the Reformation, vol. iii. p. 94.) "The discovery of the famous Treatise of Berengar by Lessing, and its recent publication at Berlin, furnishes us with Berengar's own distinct, deliberate statement of his views. . . . . . Much of the Treatise de Sacra Cœna is devoted to the proof that his own doctrines and those of Erigena were the same as those of Ambrose and Augustine." (Milman, vol. iii. pp. 23, 25.) Cf. Cosin, ch. vii.; Gieseler, vol. ii. pp. 396-411; Neander, vol. viii.

The Latin text of Bertram is printed in the Catalogus Testium, pp. 1057-75. Respecting the author see Cave's Historia Literaria, 1743, vol. ii. pp. 27, 28; Mabillonii Acta, sæc. iv. pt. ii., Præfat. xlviii.–lxii.; Ittigius de Biblioth. et Catenis Patr. pp. 167-70. "He asserts our doctrines as expressly as we (Protestants) ourselves can do; delivering it in the same words, and proving it by many of the same arguments and authorities which we bring. See Bishop Burnet on the Twenty-eighth Article. He was a monk of the Abbey of Corbey in the ninth century. . . . . . . In the London edition of the Catalogus Testium Veritatis all the objections of the Romanists against this writer are learnedly and acutely refuted." Todd's Vindication of Cranmer. Cf. Lewis, *ut supra.*

Bertram's Fourth chapter is entitled, "Of the true sense of the author in some *controverted expressions.* He first explains Figure and Truth. Secondly, Manifestation. Another controverted term is Species, which hath two senses in this book. It is most commonly used to signify the kind and specific nature of anything, and is always so taken where it is set in opposition to a Figure or Sacrament, or where the author is declaring the nature of the consecrated elements. Sometimes it signifies the appearance or likeness of a thing; so it is taken when it is opposed to truth, as in the Post-Communion Prayer cited by Ratramn, and in his inferences from it. Besides these, the Romanists have another acceptation of the word, making it to signify the sensible qualities of the consecrated elements subsisting without their substance, in which sense I positively affirm that Species is no where used in this Treatise." In pp. 428-62 he shews "how gross an error Boileau is guilty of in expounding the word Species, and cites passages from several authors, in which it signifies the kind or sort of creatures in conformity to the use of the word in the Roman Laws, or the Natural Substance." Cf. Patrick, No. 286.

A Friendly Debate between a Roman Catholick and a Protestant concerning the Doctrine of Transubstantiation, wherein the said Doctrine is utterly confuted; and Antichrist is clearly and fully described, and his inevitable destruction predicted, with a challenge to all Romish Doctors that preach the same and teach the said Doctrine to answer it. pp. 44, 4to 1688

Extract of the First Liturgy of King Edward VI. (Title-page lost.) pp. viii. 40, 4to 1687 C. L.

On the alterations in the Review or Second Liturgy, with which Stephens, Whiston, Collier, Brett &c. were dissatisfied, see Downes's Lives of the Compilers of the Liturgy, and for the reasons for restoring the first see the *Tracts of the Essentialists*, and pp. 17 to the end of this Tract.

A Discourse on Transubstantiation. By Bishop Burnett. *Ut supra*, No. 23. 1688 C. L.

The Papists Doctrine of Transubstantiation not agreeable to the Primitive Fathers quoted by J. Patrick as "the Dublin Letter."

In No. 66 are copious extracts from it.

Six Conferences concerning the Eucharist. *Ut supra*, No. 110.

A Fourth Letter to a Person of Quality. [By Edward Pelling, D.D.] *Ut infra*, No. 345. C. L. *T. C. D.*

Three Sermons upon the Sacrament in which Transubstantiation is impartially considered as to Reason, Scripture and Tradition. 12mo 1688

T. C. D. The Sum of a Controversy on February 21, 1686, between Dr. Clagett and Father Godden rectius Gooden about the point of Transubstantiation. By W. Clagett.

pp. xi., 20, 4to Lond. 1689

C. L. And at the end of his Seventeen Sermons preached upon several occasions. 8vo 1689.

"Peter Gooden, born near Manchester, in Lancashire, educated in the English College at Lisboe, where he improved his bright parts in all kinds of literature. Being ordained priest he was sent back into England upon the mission, and resided for the most part at Audcliff, [Aldcliffe] near Lancaster. In King James Second's reign he was made chaplain to the Duke of Berwick's regiment; and during that time had frequent conferences with several learned divines of the Church of England, especially with Doctor Stillingfleet, Doctor Claget, &c. [See ch. vii.] No man was better qualified to come off with reputation, in a personal conference, than Mr. Gooden. . . . . . The revolution in 1688 obliged him to retire to his old place of abode in Lancashire, where he died December 29th, 1695. He published, 1. Controversial Letters, against Mr. Birch, parson of Preston. 2. An Account of a Conference with Dr. Stillingfleet." (Dodd.)

Q.C.C. Contra nefandum Transubstantiationis dogma Dissertatio ad xi. Kal. Maii An. 1681 in publico Cantabrigiensium Gymnasio recitata a Joan. Turner, Eccl. Angl. Presbytero sacerdote.

Lond. 1690

This is the Hospitaller of St. Thomas, Southwark, who wrote the "Animadversions on Transubstantiation," see p. 384. A list of his works, but by no means complete, will be found in Watt. They are most of them on very curious subjects, and are as curiously treated. In his Discourse on the Messias, 1685, 8vo, he attacked Cudworth for his opinions on the Trinity, for which he has been pilloried by Warburton in one of the prefaces to his "Divine Legation." Turner was a man of learning, but lamentably deficient in logic and judgment. His name has not been included in any general biography that I am aware of. (J. Crossley.)

Q.C.C. Transubstantiation Discussed in two parts. The first, considering the Pleas for it. The second, the Arguments against it. In several papers that have passed between T. B., a Popish Priest, and Henry Newcome, Rector of Middleton in the County Palatine of Lancaster.

Pref. pp. iv., Introd. pp. xxi., 232, 4to Lond. 1705

"Finding myself charged by T. B. with false citations, I demanded that we might proceed according to our first agreement, and proposed a meeting in Manchester Library, where books might be produced, and that our papers might be read, and mutually subscribed and delivered as at the first. The first of these proposals was declined, but after much tergiversation another meeting was consented to, where should be a review of all our papers before two Protestant and two Popish Gentlemen; which with some occasional verbal debates took up four days, December 15, 16, 27 and 28. And there we agreed to read our papers in that order, wherein I now publish them." Preface. In the Collection of James Crossley, Esq. Henry Newcome was the son of Henry Newcome of Manchester, the Nonconformist. See the interesting account of the family of Newcome in the Introduction to the "Autobiography of Henry Newcome," CHETHAM SOCIETY, 1852.

See also pt. i. Nos. 20, 21, 23, 28, *infra* 345 and 385-6.

CHAP. XXXII.

On Purgatory.

C. L. T. C. D. 314. A Discourse against Purgatory. [By John Hartcliffe, a Dissenter, Master of Merchant Taylors School.]

pp. 37, 4to Lond. 1685

See Ath. Oxon. vol. ii. col. 1130; Wilson's Hist. of Merchant Taylors School, 4to, 1814; Nichols's Literary Anecdotes, vol. i. p. 64.

"Bellarmine would persuade us that by this washing or baptism for the dead [1 Cor. xv.] they intended to afford their friends some relief in Purgatory, and he might with as much reason have told us that the Sea burns," p. 7. An explanation of this text will be found in Bingham's Antiq. bk. xi. ch iv.; Patrick's Aqua Genitalis (Works, 1858, vol. i. p. 27); Hammond or Bloomfield (Recensio Synopt.) in loco. *Baptizing for the dead* is an elliptical expression for being baptized into the faith or belief of the resurrection of the dead. (Bingham, vol. iv. p. 50.)

Gee, in The Primitive Fathers no Papists, shews that the Purgatory of the Church of Rome is inconsistent with the belief of the ancients about the state of the dead, from the belief of its being a place of torments. pp. 93-113. Cf. Ussher, Of Purgatory, and Prayer for the Dead.

The writer of the article on Universalism, referred to under the next title, does not appear to have been aware of the merciful opinions here cited by Gee, p. 112: "That they prayed also even for the damned is plain from S. Chrysostom, who in his Third Homily upon the Philippians, did advise such prayers upon this persuasion, that though they could not obtain a release for them from Hell, yet they would procure for them some alleviation of torments, some small relief: and St. Austin himself seems to be for the same thing, when he speaks of the prayers of the living profiting so much, as either to procure a compleat and full remission, or that their damnation should be made more tolerable." I find indeed that Gerhard, in his Loci Theologici, tom. viii. p. 287, considers this interpretation irreconcileable with that Father's other writings. At quomodo potest Bellarminus illis gaudium et requiem tribuere, quibus damnationem tribuit? Serm. x. de verbo Apostol. Duæ habitationes sunt, una in regno æterno, altera in igne æterno. Serm. ccxxiii. de Temp. Nemo se decipiat, fratres, duo loca sunt et tertius non est ullus. Qui cum Christo regnare non meruerit, cum Diabolo absque dubitatione ulla peribit. Lib. de vanit. seculi ch. i. Scitote vero &c. (In margine ad hunc Augustini locum in ipsa Parisiensi editione annotatur: *Ubi nunc purgatorium?*) Compare the avowal of the Benedictine Editor of St. Ambrose's Works in his Preface to the De Bono Mortis, vol. i.

Alban Butler, commenting on the visions of St. Perpetua, March 7, says: "By the conclusions which St. Perpetua was led to make from her two visions, it evidently appears that the Church, in that early age, believed the doctrine of the expiation of certain sins after death, and prayed for the faithful departed. This must be allowed, even though it should be pretended that her visions were not from God. But neither St. Austin nor any other ancient father ever entertained the least suspicion on that head. Nor can we presume that the goodness of God would permit one full of such ardent love of him to be imposed upon in a point of this nature. The Oxonian Editor of these acts knew not what other answer to make to this ancient testimony than that St. Perpetua seems to have been a Montanist (p. 14). But this unjust censure Dodwell (Diss. Cypr. A. n. 8, p. 15) and others have confuted. And could St. Austin, with the whole Catholic Church, have ranked a Montanist among the most illustrious martyrs? That Father himself, in many of his works, clearly explains the same doctrine of the Catholic faith concerning a state of temporary sufferings in the other world, and conformably to it speaks of these visions." (L. de Orig. Animæ, lib. i. ch. x. p. 343, and lib. iv. ch. xviii. p. 401, tom. x. &c.) Cf. Notes and Queries, third ser. vol. vi.; and Stillingfleet's Doctrines and Practices of the Church of Rome, ch. xxiii.; and Maria Maddalena de Pazzi's vision in Smith's translation of her Life, No. 331, *infra*.

315. Two Discourses of Purgatory and Prayers for the Dead. By William Wake, M.A. pp. 71, 4to Lond. 1687 C. L. *T. C. D.*

See Cat. No. 100; Contin. p. 6; Ath. Oxon. vol. ii. col. 1059.

In Gibson, fol. edit. vol. ii. tit. viii. c. 6, 8vo. vol. xi. "The doctrine of Purgatory as well as many other things in the religion of the Church of

Rome (derived) from her worthy ancestors the Heathen Poets and Philosophers." Cf. Gerhardi Loci Theolog; Gale's Court of the Gentiles, pt. iii. pp. 218-22. The opinions of Origen, Jerome and Augustine, the tendency of which may be comprehended in these few words, Heaven, Hell or Purgatory, are commented upon by Bishop Newton in his Dissertation on the final state and condition of Men; and he refers to Huet's Origeniana, lib. ii. Quæst ii. for passages not very dissimilar from Justin Martyr, Irenæus, Gregory Nazianzen and Gregory Nyssen. He mentions, among other modern works on a universal restoration, a treatise published in 1761, entitled *Universal Restitution a Scripture Doctrine.* "In this treatise a memorable quotation is made from Sophocles, but without any reference to the place from whence it is taken; which as my memory hath not served me to recollect, so neither hath the most diligent search enabled me to find out. Authors should in justice to themselves as well as to their readers be more careful and correct in their quotations, especially when they allege them in proof of any particular point in question. The sense of the passage is to this effect: For we think that in Hades or the invisible state there are two paths, one the way of the just, and the other of the unjust. And afterwards God will save all things which before he had destroyed." (Works, vol. vi.) For the passage referred to by Newton, but which according to the context implies not the restitution of mankind, but, after the conflagration, the renovation of the earth, see Sophoclis quæ extant omnia, à Brunck, Argentorati, 1786, 4to, vol. ii. ad calcem, p. 41. For a defence of these two dogmata of Origen, that after long periods of time the damned shall be delivered from their torments and try their fortunes again in such regions of the world as their nature fits them for, and that the earth, after her conflagration, shall become habitable again, and be the mansion of men and other animals; and this in eternal vicissitudes, see A Letter of Resolution concerning Origen and the chief of his Opinions, in the Phœnix (and of which Rust, Bishop of Dromore, was the author), vol. i. pp. 52-60. "Scotus Erigena perhaps alone dared to question the locality of Hell, and the material tortures of the damned. . . . . Erigena boldly cites Origen, and extorts from other authorities an opinion to the same effect, of the final salvation, the return unto the Deity, of the devil himself." Milman's Latin Christianity, vol. vi. p. 251. On Universalism and

Eternal Punishment see an able article in the Christian Remembrancer, April, 1863; and Neander's Church Hist., "Doctrine concerning the Last Things," vol. iv. p. 453 &c. Origen's *Purgatory*, or the purging fire at the burning of the world, by which not only the wicked shall be tormented, but the saints themselves shall be scorched, in order that the worldly dross they died with might be purged away, and which was admitted by many of the fathers (see Notes and Queries, vol. ii. p. 366) is shewn by Thorndike to be wholly inconsistent with the Roman Purgatory. (Of the Laws of the Church, bk. iii. ch. xxix.) Cf. Gallæus de Sibyllis, 1688, 4to, p. 564 sqq.

816. **Purgatory proved by Miracles collected out of Roman Catholic Authors, with some remarkable histories relating to British, English and Irish Saints. With a Preface concerning the miracles. [By Samuel Johnson.]** C. L.

"No article was ever with more force of spirit, or more grave authority set forth since the beginning of Christian Religion than this one of Purgatory; never nation was converted to the faith but had this truth not only taught by word, but by miracles also confirmed." W. [Cardinal] Allen's *Defence of the Catholick Doctrine of Purgatory*, [ann. 1565, 8vo.] p. 112.

Pref. pp. iv. 44, 4to Lond. 1688

See Cat. No. 179; Contin. p. 6. Peck and Gee, in the Catalogue, attribute this Tract to Samuel Johnson, but query, as it is not in his works, printed in 1713, folio. In pp. 42-44 is the history of St. Patrick and his miracles. Cf. Milman's Latin Christianity. "Purgatory possible with St. Augustine (who though a strenuous advocate for the eternity of punishments denominates those of the contrary opinion merciful doctors, see Newton *ut supra*), probable with Gregory the Great, grew up I am persuaded (its growth is singularly indistinct and untraceable) out of the mercy and modesty of the priesthood. . . . The keys of Heaven and Hell were a fearful trust, a terrible responsibility; the key of Purgatory might be used with far less presumption, with less trembling confidence." Vol. vi. p. 254. In William of Malmesbury's relation of the vision of Charles the Fat is the following: "We descended into a valley, which was in one part dark and burning like a fiery furnace, but in another so extremely enchanting and glorious that I cannot describe it. . . . . . When guided by the thread of light I proceeded thither (to the light somewhat brightening), I looked into the vessel containing boiling water, and saw my father Louis standing therein up to his thighs. He was dreadfully oppressed with pain and agony, and said to me, Fear not, my lord Charles; I know that your spirit will again return into your body, and that God hath permitted you to come hither that you might see for what crimes myself and all whom you have beheld undergo these torments. One day I am bathed in the boiling cask; next I pass into that other delightful water, which is effected by the prayers of St. Peter and St. Remigius, under whose patronage our royal race has hitherto reigned. But if you and my faithful bishops and abbots, and the whole ecclesiastical order will quickly assist me with masses, prayers and psalms, and alms and vigils, I shall shortly be released from the punishment of the boiling water." Bohn's Engl. ed. bk. ii. ch. ii. "Matthew Paris," continues Milman, "relates two or three journeys of the monk of Evesham, of Thurkill, an Essex peasant, very wild and fantastic. [No. 316, pp. vii.–xi.] The Purgatory of St. Patrick, the Purgatory of Owen Miles, the vision of Alberic of Monte Casino, were amongst the most popular and wide-spread legends of the ages preceding Dante; and as in Hell, so in Purgatory, Dante sums up in his noble verses the whole theory, the whole popular belief as to this intermediate sphere. — On Patrick's Purgatory, in all its forms as sanctioned by Popes and by the Bollandist writers, as it appears in Calderon's poetry, and as it is kept up by Irish popular superstition and priestcraft, Mr. Wright has collected many wild details." Ibid. note. "It should be borne in mind that this Purgatory had nothing to do with the Purgatory of a future life, a mistake into which Harris seems to have fallen. *Bishops*, p. 25. It was a cave, or series of caves, in which living pilgrims were made to do penance, to atone for the sins of their previous life." Dr. Todd's St. Patrick Apostle of Ireland, 1864. "Bollandus shews the falsehood of many things related concerning it. Upon complaint of certain superstitious and false notions of the vulgar in 1497 it was stopped up by an order of the Pope. See Bollandus [pp. 587-91]; Tillemont, p. 787 [tom. xvi]; Alemand, in his Monastic History of Ireland; and Thiers, Hist. des Superst., tom. iv., ed. nov." Alban Butler, March 17. Cf. Ferraris Bibliotheca, s. v. Purgatorium, who refers to Petrus Le Brun nella Storia Critica delle Pratiche superstiziose, tomo terzo.

"Near the end of the tenth century in the year 998, by the influence of Odilo, abbot of Cluny, the number of festal days among the Latins was augmented by the addition of the annual celebration in memory of all departed souls. [Cf. Possevini Apparatus Sacer, vol. ii. p. 166.] . . . . . The author of this suggestion was a Sicilian recluse or hermit, who caused it to be stated to Odilo that he had learned from a divine revelation that the souls in Purgatory might be released by the prayers of the monks of Cluny." Mosheim. "The story of the hermit is differently related. One says the hermit stated that wandering near Mount Etna he overheard the souls burning in that volcano relate the benefits they received from the prayers of Odilo." Murdock's note ibid.; Narrant idem Sigebertus [Pertz, Monum. Germ. vol. vi. p. 353]; Vincentius [Speculum Historiale, lib. xxiv. p. 102]; Joannes Parisiensis, Bernardus Guidonis, et alii. Vide Petri Damiani Opp. i. p. 409. Cf. No. 316, "The occasion of the Institution of a set and solemn day for the *Praying for Souls out of Purgatory*," extracted from The Flowers of the Lives of the Saints, p. 828, and Ussher on Prayer for the Dead. (Works. vol. iii. and in Tracts for the Times, vol. iii. No. 72.) Cf. Baronius ad Martyrolog. Nov. 2, and Beyerlinckius, Magnum Vitæ Humanæ Theatrum, fol. 1631, tom. vi. p. 844, who cite a similar service for the dead from Amalarius Fortunatus [Hittorp, de Div. Offic.], vol. i. p. 443, who preceded Odilo nearly two hundred years. "Neither is it to be forgotten that the invention of All-soules day (of which you may reade, if you please, Polydore Vergil in his sixth book of the Inventers of Things, the ninth chapter) that solemn day, I say, wherein our Romanists most devoutly perform all their superstitious observances for the dead, was occasioned at the first by the apprehension of this same erroneous conceit, that the soules of the damned might not only be eased, but fully also delivered by the almes and praiers of the living." Ussher, p. 251.

Compare the extract from Allen with Sir H. Lynde's Via Devia § viii.; Sguropuli Vera Historia Unionis Ecclesiarum, § v., p. 13; and Ussher, Of Purgatory, Of Prayer for the Dead, 4to edit. 1631, p. 238 sqq., who frames this syllogism: "They who are of the judgement that prayers and oblations should not be made for such as are beleeved to be in blisse; do reject that kinde of praying and offering for the dead, which was practised by the ancient Church (and by the Greek Church at present.) But the Romanists are of this judgement.

Therefore they reject that kind of praying and offering for the dead, which was practised by the ancient Church." (p. 268.) He adduces the testimony of Petrus Cluniacensis, Epist. contra Petrobrusianos [Bibl. Patr. 1618, tom. xii. pt. ii.], of Pope Gregory II. ad Bonifac. [Labbe, Concil. vi.], and Hugo Etherianus de Animarum regressu [Bibl. Max. Patr. tom. xxii. et Grynæus], that the lawfulness of offering oblations for the dead was in the twelfth century called into question. Many divines of the English Church have shewn that the belief in Purgatory has rendered it inexpedient to continue prayers for the departed. See Palmer's Origines Liturgicæ. On the other side consult Campbell, *The Doctrine of a Middle State between Death and the Resurrection*, folio, 1721, pp. 157-197; "The Judgment of several Great and Learned Protestant Divines, since the Reformation, concerning a Middle State, and (advocating) Prayers for the Dead."

C. L. The Tragical History of Jetzer, or a Faithful Narrative of the feigned Visions, counterfeit Revelations and false Miracles of the Dominican Fathers of the Convent of Berne in Switzerland, to propagate their Superstitions &c.

Pref. and Contents, pp. xlv., 201, 16mo Lond. 1680

There is an account of this imposture, which originated in the contest between the Dominicans and Franciscans on the subject of the Immaculate Conception of the Virgin Mary, in Lavaterus de Spectris &c., 16mo, 1687. An engraving represents the Prædicatores placing their "cheirographa proprio sanguine descripta" in the hand of the conspiring cacodæmon, who appears "specie Æthiopis." "Tandem Bernam Helvetiorum, quod gens simplex ibi esset et bellicosa, sibi delegerunt," p. 40. On the prevalence of witchcraft in Switzerland compare Addison's Travels in Italy. "It is certain there have been many executions on this account, as in the Canton of Berne there were some put to death during my stay at Geneva;" Works, edit. 1701, 4to, vol. ii. p. 175; and the sixth volume of the Foreign Quarterly Review, Art. v. Witchcraft, p. 22.

Lavaterus concludes this account with the following remark: "Ad hæc non immerito dubitari cœpit de transubstantiatione panis in corpus *Christi*, quam toties hostiam veneno infecerint. Item de illis quæ de indulgentiis, vigiliis, ordinibus, purgatorio, aqua lustrali, satisfactionibus pleno ore declamitarunt," p. 50. This second part of Lavaterus contains several histories and speculations relative to Purgatory. Cap. i. Gentilium, Judæorum, et Turcarum doctrina vel fides de animabus separatis a corporibus. Capp. ii. et iii. Papistarum doctrina de animabus, earumque apparitione. "It will not be improper to observe here that the famous pagan doctrine concerning the purification of departed souls, by means of a certain kind of fire, was now (in the fifth century) more amply explained and established than it had formerly been. See particularly concerning this matter, Augustin's book de viii. Quæstionibus ad Dulcitium, N. xiii. tom. vi. Opp. p. 128; de fide et operibus, cap. xvi. p. 182; de fide spe et charitate. § 118, p. 222; Enarrat. Psalm xxxv. § iii. &c.;" Mosheim's Eccl. Hist. fifth cent. pt. ii. ch. iii. Cf. Lavaterus, who in pp. 178-196, maintains verum Samuelem Pythonissæ in Endor non apparuisse; and Zuingeri Theatrum Vitæ Humanæ, folio, 1586; "Purgatorii Pœnarum Revelatio. Inferni Pœnarum Revelatio i. Christianorum ii. Ethnicorum," vol. iv. pp. 1392-97. Marulus is here referred to, who appears to be an inexhaustible source Dictorum Factorumque Memorabilium. (Antw. 1577, 8vo; Paris, 1586, 8vo. Watt.)

Visions of Purgatory anno 1680, in which the errors and practices of the Church of Rome are discovered. [By Edward Petit.] 8vo 1685

With a frontispiece. In the Vision of Purgatory Milton is introduced in conversation with a Provincial of the Jesuits.

The Rev. Wm. Thornber, in his History of Blackpool, mentions a curious practice in the Fylde district of Lancashire of kindling fires on the vigil of All Souls for the object of succouring their friends in Purgatory. See Notes and Queries, first series, vol. iii. p. 241. Such was not the design of the "funeral ordinances related by St. Chrysostom, which were appointed to admonish the living that the parties deceased were in a state of joy, and not of griefe. For tell me (saith he) what do the bright lampes meane? do we not accompanie them therewith as champions?" Ussher, Of Prayer for the Dead, p. 197, ed. Elrington, vol. iii. p. 301.

The Belief of Praying for the Dead. 4to 1688

For the doctrine of the Church concerning Purgatory and Prayer for the Dead, Cressy (Roman Catholick Doctrines No Novelties, p. iii.) refers to Concil. Trident. Sess. 25. [See Brent's Translation of Sarpi, p. 798.] In Bingham's Antiquities, bk. xv. ch. iii. p. 17, are enumerated all the reasons we meet with in the ancients for praying for souls departed, none of which have any relation to their being tormented in the fire of Purgatory, but most of them tend directly to overthrow it. Cf. Du Moulin's Novelty of Popery, and Ussher's Answer to the Jesuit's Challenge — Of Purgatory; Of Prayer for the Dead; Of Limbus Patrum. "Lazarus, lying in Abraham's bosom, enjoyed everlasting life." Ambrose, quoted by Ussher, vol. iii. p. 287. See also Sixtus Senensis, Bibl. Sanct. lib. vi. annot. 345.

No farther seek their merits to disclose,
Or draw their frailties from their dread abode,
(There they alike in trembling hope repose),
The bosom of their Father and their God.

Peck has no tract by a Romanist within the chronological limits assigned to this series, which is reducible to this head, Purgatory; but in the year 1660 was published,

C. L. ✠ A Remembrance for the Living to Pray for the Dead. The second Edition, augmented and altered by the Author, as the Preface declares. The first and fundamental Part, proving that there is a Purgatory. That Souls are thence deliverable before the day of Judgment. The second Part recommending Prayer for the Dead. By J[ames] M[umford].

How doth any one of us know, whether he shall be passing through that Purging fire, dayes, or moneths, or perhaps years? St. Austin's Sermon xli de Sanctis.

pp. 480, 12mo, Printed at Paris, 1660.

See Oliver, who refers to Southwell, and De Backer, Series iii. "Mumford was distinguished for his charitable compassion for the suffering souls in Purgatory." Oliver, p. 146. "A Remembrance" concludes with the following summary of what he considered he had proved in his book:

"And having thus (dear Reader) faithfully put down and answered all that I could as yet hear, or read objected against our opinion, I hope, that I leave all the proofes of it standing in their full force, so that the grounds thereof are solidly settled, by the Authority of the Scriptures; of the Greek Fathers; of the Latine Fathers before St. Austin; of St. Austin himself; of the Latine Fathers after him; by undeniable History; by testimony of the Church in her Liturgies; by her Decrees and practice in point of Indulgences; by her Decrees in Council, and definitions of the Sea Apostolique; by the verdict of the Catholique world; by Reason itself; by the several ill sequels of the contrary Opinions, and the ill grounded Principles from which these sequels follow; Lastly, by the satisfactory Answers to all contrary Objections. Wherefore, seeing nothing else can appeare to be exacted, I shall passe to my Second part, wholy tending, and attending to recommend the devotion of Prayer for the Dead. For whatsoever hath been here so largely treated, is entirely ordained to the firm settling of such solid foundations of that most pious Exercise, that hereafter we shall have no need to disquiet the Devotion of the Reader with the distractive jangling of Arguments."

Mumford's Book was answered by a writer of his own communion, the famous Thomas White, in his "Devotion and Reason; wherein modern Devotion to the dead is brought to solid principles and made rational. 12mo, Paris." See Dodd, vol. iii. p. 288.

Cf. Caussin's Holy Court, folio 1650, part iii. Maxim xvii. Gregory the Great, "the author, if we may so speak, of Rome's popular religion, and the third great founder of the Papal authority not only over the minds but the hearts of men," was the first who spoke of the doctrine of Purgatory. See Middleton's Enquiry into the Miraculous Powers &c., pp. lxvii.-lxxi., and No. 316, pp. 4, 5. "Whence came the custom of saying, Thirty Masses for the Dead, which are called the Masses of St. Gregory."

CHAP. XXXIII.

The Invocation and Intercession of Saints.

T. C. D. 317. ✠ A Sermon preached the 28th of August, before the King at Chester. By Lewis Sabran, S. J.

See an account of it in Contin. p. 45. "And here (No. 237) it was thought this controversie would have ended, till the other day the Representer peept out with his Defence of one Chapter of his Nubes Testium, which I have already mentioned under this title, The Popes Supremacy asserted [No. 238]. . . . . And here this debate might have ended, had not a short Postscript at the close of the first Answer to the Nubes Testium, engaged our worthy author in a new quarrel with Father Sabran a jesuit." . . . . .

"In his Sermon before the king at Chester this Jesuit told his majesty and the auditory that he followed the advice of St. Austin when he recommended himself to the Blessed Virgin's intercession, and advised them to do the same; and for this quotes his Thirty-fifth *Sermon de Sanctis*. Upon this there began a hot debate in letters betwixt Sabran and the Answerer, concerning this authority of St. Austin; and at last from a particular passage rose up to a general point of the practise of the Primitive Church as to the *Invocation of Saints*."

For the Life and Writings of Father Sabran I have referred in Part i. p. 146 to Oliver's Memoirs. The latter are enumerated in De Backer, 2nd Series, pp. 541-43.

C. L. *T. C. D.* 318. ✠ A Letter to a Peer of the Church of England, clearing a Point touched in a Sermon preached at Chester before the King on the 28th of August. In answer to a Postscript joyned unto the Answer to Nubes Testium. By the Preacher, Father Lewis Sabran, of the Society of Jesus. Printed by Henry Hills. pp. 10, 4to Lond. 1687

See Contin. p. 46.

"I cannot but remember that you appeared with the same confident blustering in the defence of the forged Thirty-fifth Sermon of St. Austin; that you made as much noise and talked to the Protestant Peer with as much assurance as if it had been the certainest thing in the world that the Sermon was St. Austin's, and that I was an impudent, ignorant fellow for offering to deny it: but after all that storm the world remembers, and I hope the Lord was satisfied too, that it was the most impudent controversy that ever was attempted by any man to defend that Sermon; and that it was defended with arguments and authorities that every scholar would have been ashamed of. What ado had we with St. Hierom, Hephonsus, Mallion's Sermon, with Nicephorus's Juvenal, every one of which were the most wretched forgeries that could have been pickt up. What a pass were things brought to in the reply, when you were for denying your own words about S. Bernard, for eating up those about the Assumption signifying the day of the saint's death; and for asserting that the Louvain divines had not left the Eighteenth Sermon de Sanctis as doubtful. Never was cause managed with more impudence and more forgeries, and yet after all your confidence at first, and blustering throughout, it was dropt as quietly as if no such thing had ever been, and in your new defence not a syllable of it, or in Answer to my Second Letter, which it seems now must never have one." (A Third Letter to F. Lewis Sabran, p. 2.) Vid. August. Opp. v. pp. 198, 210; Hospin. de Fest. p. 89.

319. A Letter to Father Lewis Sabran, Jesuit, in answer to a Peer of the Church of England. Wherein the Postscript to the Answer to Nubes Testium is vindicated, and F. Sabran's mistakes further discovered. [By Edward Gee, M.A.] C. L. T. C. D.

pp. 8, 4to Lond. 1688

See Cat. No. 150; Contin. p. 46.

"*Advertisement:* The same day that F. Sabran's Reply to my last Letter was published there came out a pretended Letter from a Dissenter to the Divines of the Church of England &c., wherein I am accused of being a Papist. I am sufficiently certain that it came out of the same Printer's hands that F. Sabran's Reply did, and that it is from a Popish hand. I do here promise the world a speedy vindication of myself from that calumny, wherein I will shew that the

Authour of that Letter is as good at Misrepresentations as at stealing a Nubes Testium out of Natalis Alexandre."

C. L. 320. ✠ The Reply of Lewis Sabrau of the Society of Jesus to the Answer given to his Letter written to a Peer of the Church of England, by a nameless Member of the Same. Printed by Henry Hills. pp. 8, 4to Lond. 1687

See Contin. p. 46.

C. L. 321. A Second Letter to Father Lewis Sabran, Jesuit, in answer
T. C. D. to his Reply. [By Edward Gee, M.A.]
pp. 16, 4to Lond. 1688

See Cat. No. 151; Contin. p. 46.

"And here the Controversie about St. Austin's Sermon was either ended or dropt, the Jesuit being now ferretted by the Second Letter out of all his starting holes. But Mr. G. in his Primitive Fathers no Papists [No. 237 *supra*] taking into consideration a Challenge which the Jesuit had made in one of his Letters about Invocation, published an Historical Discourse to prove that *Invocation of Saints* was neither the doctrine nor the practise of the *Primitive Fathers*. Upon this the Jesuit begun again, after having taken a little breath, and in a whole sheet undertakes to answer that large Historical Account with this Title:"

C. L. 322. ✠ The Challenge of R. F. Lewis Sabran, of the Society of
T. C. D. Jesus, made out against the Historical Discourse concerning Invocation of Saints. The First Part.
pp. 8, 4to Lond. 1688

See Contin. p. 46.

"The more distinguished Christians were dismissed if not to absolute deification, to immortality, to a state in which they retained profound interest in, and some influence over, the condition of men. During the perilous and gloomy days of persecution, the reverence for those who endured martyrdom for the religion of Christ had grown up out of the best feelings of man's improved nature. Reverence gradually grew into veneration, worship, adoration. Although the more rigid theology maintained a marked distinction between the honours shown to the martyrs and that addressed to the Redeemer and the Supreme Being, the line was too fine and invisible not to be transgressed by excited popular feeling." (Milman's Hist. of Christianity, vol. iii. p. 434.) Cf. p. 540 sq.

323. A Third Letter to F. Lewis Sabran, Jesuit: wherein the Defence of his Challenge concerning Invocation of Saints is examined and confuted. [By Edward Gee, M.A.] pp. 14, 4to Lond. 1688 C. L. T. C. D.

See Cat. No. 153; Contin. p. 47.

"In this Letter Mr. G. made such discoveries of the strange disingenuity and confident ignorance of the Jesuit that he was resolved to rid his hands of such an adversary as had neither learning nor good manners, and therefore told him in the conclusion of his Letter that he would trouble himself no more with answering such an adversary. Upon this the Jesuit, whose only stock is confidence, being turned off by his learned adversary, was forced to address his next reply to a third person, and pitcht upon Mr. Needham, because he had licensed Mr. G.'s Third Letter to him; and directed a letter to him with this title:"

324. ✠ A Letter to Dr. William Needham, in answer to the Third Letter by him licensed, written to Father Lewis Sabran of the Society of Jesus, wherein the said Letter is examined and confuted. [By Lewis Sabran.] pp. 23, 4to Lond. 1688 C. L. T. C. D.

See Contin. p. 47.

325. A Letter to the Superiours (whether Bishops or Priests) which approve or license the Popish Books in England, particularly to those of the Jesuits Order, concerning Lewis Sabran, a Jesuit. [By Edward Gee.] pp. 14, 4to Lond. 1688 C. L. T. C. D.

See Cat. No. 154; Contin. p. 47.

"All these engagements the first answer to the Nubes Testium produced." "I do here offer and undertake (says Gee) to refer the determination of that Controversie (about the Thirty-fifth Sermon de Sanctis) to any learned persons or societies beyond the seas. I will refer it if you please to the Benedictines (Congregationis Sti Mauri) at Paris, concerning whom you, Gentlemen of the Jesuits Order, must pardon me that I think them to be as far before your order in learning and knowledge in antiquity as their order was before you in standing. But if exceptions be made against them as parties on my side that have already determined against Mr. Sabran and those that allowed his papers to the press, I am as willing to refer it to those learnedest men now in France, Father Mabillon, Monsieur Baluze and Monsieur Bigot, or any two of them," p. 3. "Rome combated her Protestant antagonists by the aid of the Jesuits in the world, and of the Benedictines in the closet. Yet to those alliances she owes much of the silent revolt against her authority which has characterised the last hundred years, and of which the progress is daily becoming more apparent. The Jesuits involved her in their own too well merited disesteem. The Benedictines have armed the philosophy both of France and Germany with some of the keenest weapons by which she has been assailed." (Edinburgh Review, January, 1849.)

C. L. *T. C. D.* 326. A Discourse concerning the Worship of the Blessed Virgin and the Saints, with an Account of the beginnings and rise of it amongst Christians, in answer to M. de Meaux's appeal to the Fourth Age, in his Exposition and Pastoral Letter. [By William Clagett, D.D.] pp. 114, 4to Lond. 1686

See Cat. No. 144; Contin. p. 52; Ath. Oxon. col. 326.

In Gibson, folio ed. vol. ii. tit. vi. ch. iv., 8vo ed. vol. vii. "Let us hear what St. Austin says: 'The Gentiles,' saith he, (De Civit. Dei lib. xxii. ch. x.) 'have built Temples, raised Altars, and ordained Priests, and offered Sacrifices to their Gods. But we do not erect Temples to our Martyrs as if they were Gods, but Memories as to dead men, whose Spirits live with God. Nor do we erect Altars upon which to sacrifice to Martyrs, but to one God onely do we offer, the God of Martyrs, and our God; at which Sacrifice as men of God who in confessing him have overcome the world, they are named in their place and order, but they are not invocated by the priest who sacrifices,'" p. 91. "St. Austin, it seems (though it was a singular opinion of his) thought it an injury (De Verb. Apost. Serm. 17) to a martyr to pray for him, by whose prayers we ourselves are to be commended; and therefore the martyrs were not mentioned in that place of the service, where other dead persons were commemorated; viz. those for whom prayer was made. And says he (Tractat. in Job. 84) at the Holy Table we do not so commemorate them as we do others that rest in peace, viz. as those for whom we pray; but rather as those that pray for us, that we may tread in their steps. Now though St. Austin was one of those who doubted whether the petitions of the faithful arrived to the knowledge of the martyrs, yet he doubted not that the martyrs prayed for the faithful, which is all that can be proved from these places. But what is this to the invocation of them which St. Austin also expressly denies in saying that they are not invocated by the priest who sacrifices?" p. 92. That Augustine's opinion that it is an injury to a martyr to pray for him is "singular" is evident from Bingham's Antiquities, bk. xv. ch. iii. § xvi., and Ussher, Of Prayers for the Dead.

327. Speculum Beatæ Virginis. A Discourse of the due Praise and Honour of the Virgin Mary. By a true Catholick of the Church of England [George Hickes, Dean of Worcester.] pp. 39, 4to Lond. 1686 C. L. T. C. D.

Second edition. pp. 42, 4to Lond. 1686. (More full and correct than the former.) It is also included in his Collection of Sermons, 2nd vol. 1713, 8vo. C. L. T. C. D.

"I was the first time," says Hickes (Preface to his Letters to a Popish Priest) "forced to write by the insolence of a Popish Physician who had the confidence to tell one of my parishioners in company, that whereas I had in a sermon lately delivered some things concerning the Popish Worship of Saints, I was a lyar, and could not prove what I asserted, and bid him tell me what he said. Now whosoever shall consider the Litanies of the Blessed Virgin and her Rosaries and the Prayers and Hymns of her Saturday's Office and her Psalters, and the vast number of Books of Devotion to her, and the worship that is accordingly given to her in pretended Catholic countries; whosoever shall consider what they say to her in those Prayers and Hymns &c., which the Speculum Beatæ Virginis, just now published, has put together, may perhaps find there are causes of horror which Monsieur de Meaux is not so much concerned at as he ought to be; he may justly fear that if the Reformation did not give some little check neither would these excesses stop here, though in many places nothing now remains to be done, but without any farther reservedness, to erect altars proper to the Blessed Virgin in every Church, as the Jesuites began to do in China." See Trigautii Exp. ad Sinas, lib. v. ch. xv., xx.; Clagett's Discourse, *ut supra*, p. 112. Cf. Heylin's Commentary on the Creed, art. Born of the Virgin Mary. "The conformity is so great between the Pagan and the Pagano-Christians in the worship of one Supreme Deity and many subordinate Tutelar Spirits that Trigautius conceiveth hope of the ancient Chinese (Sinic. lib. i. ch. x. p. 104) that not a few of them found Salvation in the Law of Nature." (Brocklesby's Explication of Gospel Theism, ch. iv. § i. p. 49.)

C. L. *T. C. D.* 328. ✠ Contemplations on the Life and Glory of Holy Mary, the Mother of Jesus, with a Daily Office agreeing to each mystery thereof. By J. C., D.D. pp. xiv. 103, 12mo, Paris 1685

See Contin. p. 53.

Dedicated to Her Most Excellent Majesty Catherine, of England, Scotland, France and Ireland, Queen Dowager.

T. C. D. 329. ✠ An Apology for the Contemplations on the Life and Glory of the Holy Mother of Jesus, shewing the innocency, equity and antiquity of the honour and veneration given to her by the Holy Catholic Church. By J. C., D.D. 1687

See Contin. p. 53.

C. L. *T. C. D.* 330. An Account of the Life and Death of the Blessed Virgin, according to Romish writers. With the grounds of the Worship paid to Her. And a Preface in answer to the Apology for the Contemplations, &c. By a Lay Hand. [William Fleetwood, Fellow of King's College, Cambridge.]

pp. xliii., 39, 4to Lond. 1687

See Cat. No. 147; Contin. p. 52.

Reprinted in Gibson, folio ed. vol. iii. tit. xii., 8vo ed. vol. xv. William Fleetwood, D.D., born 1656, died 1723; Bishop of St. Asaph 1706; translated to Ely 1714. "'Tis not my business to confute this story of the Assumption, here; let it suffice at present that I advertise you it was unknown to all the ancients for the first four centuries. That passage in the Chronicle of Eusebius is acknowledged by men of understanding to be false and spurious; as likewise are the pieces attributed to St. Austin and St. Jerom; together with the false Dionysius, who wrote between four and five hundred, at the soonest. [See the Preface, pp. xxviii.-xxxiii.] In a word the men of sense and honesty, even among the Romanists, do at this day look upon the Assumption as an idle business, but I must not tell the people so. . . . . . . Claudius Joly, Canon of the Church, and one of the Commissaries deputed to examine this affair, hath made a Dissertation thereupon [de verbis Usuardi Martyrologii]. And the learned Monsieur de Launoi has given his judgment on the same subject, in whose works one may find enough to confound this story of the Assumption, and answer Baronius and the rest, who look upon it as a point of faith, or at least a Sacred History, that nobody must touch, or offer once to disbelieve," pp. 20, 21; see J. Launoii Opp. vol. i. de controversia super exscribendo Martyrologio. The fables relating to our Lady of Mount Serrat, our lady of Liessi, our Lady of Loretto, "such as the Pagans would blush to own," pp. 24-30; Cf. Notes and Queries, 3rd ser. vol. vi. p. 17.

This is the work of a learned and renowned Frenchman, drawn up in English with some little alterations of the style; Pref. xlii.

331. A Discourse about discerning and trying the Spirits, wherein are laid down Rules, shewing what are the essential and necessary Doctrines and Practices of Christianity. To which is prefixed, The Life of St. Mary Magdalen de Pazzi, a Carmelite Nunn. With a Preface concerning the nature, causes, concomitants and consequences of Ecstacy and Rapture. [By Thomas Smith, D.D., Fellow of Magdalen College, Oxon.] The second edition. pp. Introduction, xxxiii.; Life, 37-84; A brief discourse, 85-134. 4to Lond. 1688 C. L.

See Cat. No, 148; Contin. p. 52; Ath. Oxon. vol. 1021.

Dr. Smith was also the author of No. 437. "Love hath two singular properties: the first is to delight itself in singing the praises of its well-beloved, when he is absent. . . . . The second propriety of love is to suffer for the lover, and to sympathise with his pains. . . . The devise of St. Theresa was, either to suffer or to die: that of our Saint not to die, but to live to suffer: and indeed she repeated very often, I am not forward and in haste to go to Paradise, for that is not a place of suffering but delight. This, in my opinion, is what is wanting to the state of the blessed." The Life [by Vincentio Paccini] pp. 65-66. "F. Ferdinandi Salvi, sub-prior of the Carmelites at Bologna, in Italy, made a collection of twelve letters of St. Mary Magdalen of Pazzi, with several other monuments. They were reprinted at Venice in 1739, at the end of the spiritual works of this holy virgin. F. Salvi published in Italian several relations of miracles performed at Bologna through the intercession of this holy virgin, printed at Milan in the years 1724, 1730, 1731." Butler's Lives of the Saints, May 25.

C. L.
T. C. D.

In the title-page of the first edition, 1687, this life is said to be "newly translated out of Italian by the Reverend Father Lezin de Sainte Scholastique, Provincial of the Reformed Carmelites of Touraine. At Paris, for Sebast. Cramoisy in St. James's Street, at the Sign of Fame. 1670."

"What horrid doctrine, corruptive of honesty and morality, was vented in the last age by several vile and ungodly men, under the pretense of being divinely inspired, such as David George, Muncer, John of Leyden, Matthews, and Knipperdoling, may be seen in Sleidan and the other historians of that time. [Robertson's Charles V. bk. v.] They seemed to be above the ordinary rules of life, by which the civilized part of mankind is governed, and under no obligation of the laws of Christ, observed in all Christian governments throughout the world, gratifying their wild and lustful inclinations with the multiplicity of wives. This consideration certainly ought to have awakened another poor deluded man (Dr. Dee) out of his dreams of folly, into which his own credulity and most unlawful curiosity had cast him, that those spirits, with which he had so long conversed, and who pretended to discover to him the will of God in fuller measures than it had yet been known, and the mysteries of nature, to gratify his mathematical genius, and the great events and revolutions that should soon after be brought about, were not good angels sent from God, as by other manifest signs and indications, so by this especially, when they commanded him and his companion to have their wives in common, but that he was under a strong and fatal infatuation, and out of an immoderate desire of knowledge had lost all sober and right use of his reason, and was besotted in his imagination." Discourse &c., p. 102.

Cf. A True Relation of Dr. Dee's Actions with Spirits &c., with a Preface by Meric Casaubon, 1659, ad calc. p. 11. There is a Life of Dr. Dee in Dr. Thomas Smith's Vitæ Quorundam Eruditissimorum Virorum, 1707, 4to.

332. The Virgin Mary Misrepresented by the Roman Church in the Traditions of that Church concerning her Life and Glory; and in the Devotions paid to her as the Mother of God. Both shewed out of the Offices of that Church, the Lessons on her Festivals, and from their allowed Authors. Part I. Wherein Two of her Feasts, her Conception and Nativity, are considered. [By John Patrick, D.D., Preacher of the Charter-house, London.] pp. 155, 4to Lond. 1688 C. L. T. C. D.

See Cat. No. 149; Contin. p. 53. In Gibson, folio ed. vol. iii. tit. xii.; 8vo ed. vol. xv.-xvi., where it is erroneously ascribed to Simon Patrick, in which mistake he is followed in Cumming's reprint. Vide Cæremoniale Episcoporum, folio, Parisiis, 1633; Hospinianus de Festis Christianorum, folio, Genevæ, 1674. Cf. Patrick's Reflections &c., *infra*.

"The Immaculate Conception of the Virgin became the subject of contention and controversy, from which the calmer Christian shrinks with intuitive repugnance. It divided the Dominicans and Franciscans into hostile camps, and was agitated with all the wrath and fury of a question in which was involved the whole moral and religious welfare of mankind." Milman's Latin Christianity, vol. vi. p. 239 sqq. Patrick's fourth section is entitled "The History of the Embassie from Two Kings of Spain to Rome to obtain a decision of the Controversy about the Immaculate Conception." Cf. The Tragical History of Jetzer, *ut supra*, p. 404. The same discrepancy of opinion on the Immaculate Conception existed between St. Bridget and St. Catharine of Sienna in the fourteenth century. See Gallæus de Sibyllis, p. 213 sq.

333. The Virgin Mary Misrepresented by the Roman Church. Part II. By John Patrick, D.D.

Promised, but quære if ever printed? See Contin. p. 53. "We are in hopes that the excellent author of this most ingenious and diverting discourse will ere long oblige the world with a second part, and teach the Papists at length to grow ashamed of their intolerable superstitions towards the Virgin Mary." The quære is Peck's, but there appears to be no doubt that this second part was never published.

T. C. D. 334. Miracles of the Blessed Virgin; or an Historical Account of the original and stupendous performances of the image entitled, our Blessed Lady of Halle; viz. restoring the dead to life; healing the sick; delivering of captives, &c. Written originally in Latin by Justus Lipsius; afterwards translated into French, then into Dutch, and now rendered into English, with a Preface. pp. 36, 4to Lond. 1688

"Let him (the mere scholar) meditate upon the degradation of the eminently erudite Lipsius, who sullied the laurels of his literary fame by such drivelling effusions of superstition as the Diva Virgo Hallensis, and the Diva Sichemiensis, sive Aspricollis,—effusions, in the penning of which it is impossible, however desirable, to admit the low apology of sincerity." Mendham on the Venal Indulgences and Pardons of the Church of Rome, pp. xxxviii.-ix. The same remarks are applicable to the Lyrica of the elegant Casimir, Odes xxii., xxiv., xxxiii. of lib. iv. Erycius Puteanus, a very learned Professor at Louvain, was the author of Aspricollis diva Virgo, beneficia ejus et miracula novissima, 4to 1622; and Pietatis thaumata in Protheum Parthenicum, unius verbi librum et unius versus librum, stellarum numeris sive formis 1022 variatum. Antw. 1617, 4to. Being a repetition of the verse, "Tot tibi sunt dotes, Virgo, quot sidera cœlo," in 1022 different shapes. Cf. Tenison, Of Idolatry, ch. xii.

C. L. 335. An Abridgment of the Prerogatives of St. Ann, Mother of
T. C. D. the Mother of God. With the Approbation of the Doctors at Paris: and thence done into English to accompany the Contemplations on the Life and Glory of Holy Mary; and the Defence of the same; with some Pieces of the like nature. To which a Preface is added concerning the Original of the Story. [Published by William Clagett, D.D.]

Pref. pp. xv., Dedic. v., 20, 4to Lond. 1688

See Cat. No. 153; Contin. p. 58; Ath. Oxon. vol. i. col. 326. "The

Epistle to Chromatius concerning the nativity of the Virgin, which is at the end of S. Hierom's Works [edit. Paris, 1706, tom. v. p. 446] is no less than that other of the same stamp concerning her Assumption [ibid. p. 95] spurious. Yet this and the Proto-Evangelium [S. Jacobi] are the incomparable Pieces that have had so many copiers. [See Fabricii Codex Apocryphus N. Test. and Grynæi Orthodoxographa, pp. 71-84.] Nor shall I be too forward to give any more credit to so many other fabulous narrations as have crept into the world . . . . under the banners of such insinuating and specious titles as those of De Infantia Salvatoris, the Conformity of St. Francis, the Golden Legend, the Proto-Evangelium, the Nine or Ten Gospels, and a many such like, which having been at first printed in the Micropresbyticon, have been since prudently left out of the Orthodoxographa and the Library of the Fathers." Naudæus, History of Magic, Englished by J. Davies, 1657. Cf. Toland's Cat. of Books ascribed to the Apostles, vol. i. of the Collection of Pieces, 8vo 1726, and the Preface to this tract, an analysis of which will be found in the Young Student's Library, p. 121. According to S. Basil, S. Hilary, S. Hierome and Lactantius, all men, Christ only excepted, shall be burned with the world's conflagration at the day of judgment; even the Blessed Virgin herself is to pass through this fire; see Sixtus Senensis, Bibl. Sanct. lib. vi. annot. 345, tom. ii. p. 962 sq.; and Taylor's Dissuasive from Popery, pt. i. ch. i., who describes some of the purgatorial histories referred to *supra*, p. 405.

336. The Enthusiasm of the Church of Rome demonstrated in some observations upon the life of Ignatius Loyola, founder of the Jesuits. By Henry Wharton, M.A. C. L. T. C. D.

pp. 139, 4to Lond. 1688

See Cat. No. 173; Contin. p. 53; Ath. Oxon. col. 875. "In the life of Ignatius Loyola, written by a very eloquent man (whether as faithful as eloquent I know not) we are told that he was seen at his devotions . . . . four cubits almost above the earth, the weight of his bodily lump being elevated by the strength of the spirit. . . . Now if the Jesuit had read Apollonius [Philostratus' Life of Apollonius, who was carried up two cubits] there was all the reason in the world that he should double the measure" &c. M. Casaubon's Treatise concerning Enthusiasme, 12mo 1655, pp. 215-17. Cf. The Life of S.

Teresa and Wharton, p. 101, who notices another common character of enthusiasm, the pretence of an infused knowledge, and refers to Philostratus, lib. i. ch. xiii., lib. ii. ch. x., lib. iii. ch. vii. (p. 51). Philostratus (vide lib. i. ch. v., lib. v. ch. x. &c.) ascribes the actions of Apollonius, and Bonaventure (vol. vii.) those of St. Francis, to Divine Impulse, p. 62. He notices also Xavier and St. Philip Neri. "A Mary Magdalen of Pazzi, in an extasie, saw the soul of Ignatius in a glorious seat in Heaven," p. 33. Cf. Bonaventuræ Legenda S. Francisci, cap. xiv. (Opp. vol. vii. pt. iv.); S. Gregorii Dialogi, lib. ii. cap. xxxiv. and Stillingfleet and Cressy, *ut infra.* For an account of the enthusiasm, the visions and the ecstacies of Ignatius see Owen's Speculum Jesuiticum, 4to 1629, p. 38; Imago primi Sæculi Societatis Jesu, folio, 1640; Bouhours, Vie de St. Ignace, p. 49-52, ed. Paris, 1680; Stillingfleet's Discourse concerning the Idolatry practised in the Church of Rome (Works, vol. v.); Pasquier, Cat. des Jesuites, p. 17; Geddes's View of all the Orders of Monks and Fryars in the Roman Church, with an Account of their Founders, &c. (Works, vol. iii.)

C. L. 337. A Discourse Concerning the Object of Religious Worship; Or, A Scripture Proof of the Unlawfulness of giving any religious worship to any other Being besides the One Supreme God. Part I. [By William Sherlock, D.D.]

pp. ii. 75, 4to Lond. 1685

See Cat. No. 12; [State, p. 7]; Contin. p. 5. In Gibson, fol. edit. vol. ii. tit. vi. ch. i. 8vo ed. vol. vi. Compare Bingham's Antiquities, bk. xiii. ch. iii.

C. L. *T. C. D.* 338. A Discourse Concerning the Object of Religious Worship. Part II. By W. Sherlock, D.D. Quære, if ever printed?

The quære is Peck's, but there seems to be no doubt that no second part was ever published. The first part appeared with two dates, 1685, 1686. Watt altogether omits this work; in the Biogr. Brit. the title of the tract is given in the list of Sherlock's works without date or mention of its being a part only.

C. L. *T. C. D.* 339. A Discourse Concerning Invocation of Saints. [By Samuel Freeman, D.D., Rector of S. Anne, Aldersgate.]

pp. 72, 4to Lond. 1684

See Cat. No. 15; [State, p. 8]; Contin. p. 6. In Gibson, folio edit. vol. i. tit. vi. ch. iv.; 8vo ed. vol. viii.

340. Wholesome Advice from the Blessed Virgin to her indiscreet Worshippers. Written by one of the Roman Communion, and done out of French into English by a Gentleman of the Church of England. With a Preface shewing the motives to the translation. [By James Taylor.] C. L. T. C. D.

pp. 20, 4to Lond. 1687

See No. 67, which is the same as this. The original author was Adam Widenfeldt, a lawyer, born in 1617, in the diocese of Cologne.

One of the tracts in the collection, Avis Salutaires *ut supra* (No. 67*n*.), was La Véritable Dévotion envers la Sainte Vierge, établie et défendue par J. Crasset de la Compagnie de Jesus, 1679. Cf. Wake's Defence of the Exposition, Appendix No. ii. pp. 109-14. No. iii. ibid. is Cardinal Bona's Doctrine and Practice of this Worship. "Father Crasset gave the Bishop of Meaux a sensible stroke in his Book of the true Devotion to the Blessed Virgin, printed at Paris in 4to in the year 1679. The Dauphin's Tutor was too powerful an adversary to be opposed directly. But a writer of lesser authority that adopted the opinion of this prelate, touching the Invocation of Saints and Worship of Images, felt the weight of Father Crasset's anger. This author was a German gentleman called M. Widenfelt," &c. . . . . . "The Jesuit assures us that that writing scandalized the good Catholicks; that the Learned of all Nations refuted it, that the Holy See condemned it, and that in Spain it was prohibited to be printed or read, as containing propositions suspected of heresie and impiety, tending to destroy the particular devotion to the Mother of God, and in general the Invocation of Saints and the Worship of Images." The Young Student's Library, p. 125. See also the third volume of Tracts for the Times, No. 71.

A Discourse Concerning the Idolatry practised in the Church of Rome, and the hazard of salvation in it; wherein a particular account is given of the fanaticisms and divisions of that Church. By Edward Stillingfleet, D.D. 8vo Lond. 1671 T. C. D.

Works, vol. v. pp. 1–219. Extract from this Work in Gibson, see p. 343, *supra*.

T. C. D. An Answer to Several Treatises occasioned by a book entitled, A Discourse &c. By Edward Stillingfleet, D.D. 1673

In his Works, vol. v. pp. 138.

T. C. D. A Defence of the Discourse of the Idolatry practised in the Church of Rome in answer to a book [by Dr. Tho. Godden] entituled Catholicks no Idolaters. The two first parts. By Edward Stillingfleet, D.D. 8vo Lond. 1676

Works, vol. v., paged irregularly, 1–54 and 333–576.

C. L. ✠ Some Generall Observations upon Dr. Stillingfleet's Book and way of Writing. With a Vindication of St. Ignatius Loyola and his followers the Jesuits from the foul aspersions he has lately cast upon them, in his discourse concerning the Idolatry, &c. In Four Letters written to A. B. pp. iii., 69, 4to 1672

✠ Account of Dr. Stillingfleet's late book against the Church of Rome. By Thomas Candish. 8vo 1672

This Work is attributed by Dodd to John Vincent Canes, with the title, *Τω καθολικῷ* Stillingfleeto: being an Account, &c. Bruges, 8vo. 1672. "A frier of the order of St. Francis; a person of singular parts and learning. He lived sometimes in Lancashire." He was author also of Diaphanta, against Stillingfleet. Besides J. V. C. was John Keynes, a Jesuit born at Compton Painsford in Somersetshire, author of Dr. Stillingfleet against Dr. Stillingfleet. See Wood's Ath. Oxon. vol. ii. p. 744, and Part i. p. 222.

C. L. ✠ Fanaticism Fanatically Imputed to the Catholic Church by Dr. Stillingfleet &c. pp. 182, 8vo 1672

C. L. ✠ The Roman Church's Devotions Vindicated from Dr. Stillingfleet's Mis-representation. By O. N., a Catholick. pp. 114, 8vo 1672

✠ Answer to part of Dr. Stillingfleet's book entitled, Idolatry practised in the Church of Rome. 8vo 1674

The last three by Serenus Cressy. See pt. i. pp. 223-4.

Animadversions upon a Book, intituled, Fanaticism Fanatically Imputed to the Catholick Church, by Dr. Stillingfleet, and the Imputation refuted and retorted by S. C. The Second Edition. By a Person of Honour [Edward Earl of Clarendon.] 8vo 1674 C. L. T. C. D.

Catholicks no Idolaters, *ut infra*, No. 446. By T[homas] G[odden.] 8vo Lond. 1672

A Discourse Concerning the Idolatry of the Church of Rome; wherein that charge is justified, and the pretended Refutation of Dr. Stillingfleet's Discourse is answered. By Daniel Whitby, D.D. 8vo Lond. 1674 *T. C. D.*

A Just Discharge to Dr. Stillingfleet's Unjust Charge of Idolatry against the Church of Rome, with a discovery of the vanity of his late Defence in his pretended Answer to "Catholicks no Idolaters." By Thomas Godden. 1677 *T. C. D.*

The author's real name was Tilden. See Dodd's Church History, vol. iii. p. 471; Ath. Oxon. vol. ii. col. 1070, and Biogr. Brit. *s. v.* Patrick, Symon.

Reflections upon the Devotions of the Roman Church. With the Prayers, Hymns and Lessons themselves, taken out of their Authentic Books. In three Parts, this first part containing their devotions to Saints and Angels; with two digressions concerning the reliques and miracles in Mr. Cressy's late History. [Anon.] By John Patrick, D.D. 8vo Lond. 1674

The Second Edition. With an Appendix. [Anon.] pp. x., 434, Appendix &c. 20, 8vo Lond. 1686 C. L. *T. C. D.*

C. 1. The Third Edition. pp. x., 434, Index &c. 20, 8vo Lond. 1696

In Notes and Queries (third ser. vol. i. pp. 250, 320, 379) the question is discussed whether this book was written by Bishop Patrick or John his Brother; but this third edition settles it conclusively, as John Patrick is given on the titlepage.

"I might wonder indeed, and so I did, when I read the late Book called Reflections on the Romish Devotions; and I wondered again and again that rational men in any age much less in this age and in this climate (where learning and knowledge is so much refined, improved and sublimed) should so night-mare their vitalities with a rudis indigestaque moles of ridiculous trash, and suffer themselves to be blind-folded, waving their proper conduct of reason, and following they know not whom, they know not how, they know not whither, especially in their devotions. And therefore, Sir, you may forbear your Hermitical Dispensatory." A Journey into the Country, p. 27. Cf. Riveti Apologia pro Sanct. Virgine Maria. Opp. vol. iii. In No. 316 are copious quotations from Cressy's History.

Barlow, in his Directions to a Young Divine, has enumerated the Offices of the Church, or Romish Liturgical books. Of these, but more especially the Breviaries, both before and since the time of the Tridentine Council, the reader will find much information in the "Reflections" *ut supra*. The recent introduction into the Church Services of the Invocations to the Blessed Virgin and the Saints is distinctly confessed by Roman Ritualists. See Tracts for the Times, No. 75. The authorities here used are Gavanti Thesaurus Rituum, Zaccaria's Bibliotheca Ritualis, and Palmer's Origines Liturgicæ. For the differences between the Breviary of Cardinal Quignon, sanctioned by Clement VIII. and Paul III., and that of the Doctors of Trent, see Mendham's Life and Pontificate of St. Pius V. p. 98.

"Most of the stories are still retained in the present Roman Breviary, and seem to be taken out of Usuardus, or Ado's Martyrologies, who lived in the ninth century, the proper age for rappers;" p. 265.

Décrets portans la Suppression d'un Office de la Conception Immaculate par Innocent XI. 1678, 1679. In English, 1680

This contains a translation of the Hymn Te Deum to the Blessed Virgin. Cf. Bonaventuræ Opera, 1609, vol. vi. p. 480. Notes and

Queries, 2nd ser. vols. ii. and iii.; Patrick's Virgin Mary Misrepresented, § iii.

"Maria Agreda, a religious visionary, wrote the Life of the Virgin, which, like a circulating novel, delighted the female devotees of the seventeenth century. See Amort, Controversia de Revelationibus Agredanis explicata cum Epicrisi &c., 1749. But one of the most extravagant works projected on the subject of the Virgin Mary was the Summa Deiparæ, by a Monk in Paris, who, according to Varillas (in his Histoire des Révolutions arrivées dans l'Europe en matiere de Religion, Paris, 1686), laboured in this work full thirty years, and boasted he had treated three thousand questions concerning the Virgin." See D'Israeli's Curiosities of Literature, vol i.; "Religious Nouvelettes." In the third volume of Geddes's Miscellaneous Tracts is The Life of Maria de Jesus of Agreda, a late famous Spanish (Franciscan) Nun.

Answer to a Challenge made by a Jesuit in Ireland (Malone), wherein the judgement of antiquity in the points questioned is truly delivered &c. By Archbishop Ussher. The Fourth Edition. 4to 1686 C. L.

First printed 1625. In edit. Elrington, vol. iii. Prayer to Saints, pp. 420-496.

✠ A Sermon Preached in the Chapel of his Excellency the Spanish Ambassador on the second Sunday in Advent, December 4, 1687, on which was solemnized the Feast of St. Francis Xaverius, of the Society of Jesus, Apostle of the Indies and Kingdom of Japan. pp. 39, 4to Lond. 1687 C. L.

See Dryden's Translation of the Life of Xavier, by Bouhours, in the sixteenth volume of his Works, ed. Scott.

A Letter concerning Invocation of Saints and Adoration of the Cross, writ ten years since to John Evelyn of Depthford Esq. By Dr. Barlow, then Provost of Queen's Colledge, and now Bishop of Lincoln. pp. 39, 4to Lond. 1689 *T. C. D.*

A Sermon preached on the 8th of January at S. Nicholas Church in Newcastle-upon-Tyne: shewing that Jesus Christ is our only Mediator of Redemption and of Intercession, in exclusion of justification by the works of the Law, or of such as are called meritorious; and also of the necessity of invocating or of praying to Saints and Angels, &c. By Thomas Davison, M.A., Presbyter of the Church of England at Balmbrough in Northumberland. 4to 1688

Cf. Penrose's Bampt. Lect. App. 17, who refers, on the similarity between Pagan idolatry and Papal superstition, to the Third Part of the Homily against Perils of Idolatry, fol. Lond. 1815, p. 151, &c.; Augustini Tractat. contra Faustum, lib. xx. (Opp. 1694, tom. ii. pp. viii. 334); Jortin's Remarks on Ecclesiastical History, vol. iii. pp. 9-18; M. de Beausobre, Hist. Critique du Manichéisme, tom. ii. p. 628-700; Warburton's Div. Leg. book iv. § vi.; the two last pages with the Note against Middleton, and Middleton's Postscript to the Letter from Rome (Miscell. Works, vol. v.), and Gibbon at the close of ch. xxviii. See also Field of the Church, book iii. ch. xx.; and Gale's Court of the Gentiles, vol. i. pp. 149-238. For the character of several works of Hagiology see Milman's L. C. vol. vi. p. 244. See also Nos. 57, 80, 83, 237, 323.

CHAP. XXXIV.

Of the Discourses written of Images.

341. The Antiquity of the Protestant Religion, with an Answer to Mr. Sclater's Reasons and the Collections made by the author of the pamphlet entitled Nubes Testium. In a Letter to a Person of Quality. The First Part. [By Edward Pelling, Rector of St. Martin's, Ludgate, London.] pp. 59, 4to Lond. 1687 — C. L. *T. C. D.*

See Contin. p. 48.

This part is merely introductory, prefacing the controversy concerning Images and Image-worship with remarks on the design of the first Six General Councils, the Common or Apostles Creed, the controversy about Primacy (pp. 14-58), Dr. Stillingfleet's account of the Florentine Council out of Sguropulus in his defence of the Greek Church. "Vera Historia Unionis non Veræ inter Græcos et Latinos, &c. Græce scripta per Sylv. Sguropulum, Latine et cum Notis per Robertum Creyghton." Hagæ-Comitum, 1660, fol.

342. The Antiquity of the Protestant Religion concerning Images, with an Answer to the Collections made by the author of the pamphlet entitled Nubes Testium. In a Letter to a Person of Quality. The Second Part. [By Edward Pelling.] pp. 78, 4to Lond. 1687 — C. L. *T. C. D.*

See Cat. No. 156; Contin. p. 48.

The Disputations of the Council of Frankfort, anno 794, which go under the name of Charles the Great, were probably put together by more than one counsellor, although it is difficult not to attribute these books to Alcuin. They allowed the setting up of Images as a thing not evil in itself. See Milman, vol. ii. p. 237.

In favour of Alcuin's authorship of the Caroline Books see Soames's Bampton Lectures, p. 148; Neander's General Church History,

Edinburgh ed. vol. v. p. 303; against it Lingard's Anglo-Saxon Church. That the Caroline Books contain the acts of the Frankfort Council was acknowledged by Baronius, Tilius, Hincmarus and Bellarmine. See Pelling's Postscript. His Capitulare de non adorandis imaginibus will be found in Goldasti Constitut. Imper. Cf. Histoire Littéraire de la France, t. iv. and Clement, Biblioth. Curieuse, t. vi.

T. C. D. 343. ✠ A Discourse of the use of Images in relation to the Church of England, and the Church of Rome. In vindication of Nubes Testium against a pamphlet entitled, The Antiquity of the Protestant Religion concerning Images, directed against some leaves of that Collection. [By John Gother. See Dodd's Church History.] (Printed by Henry Hill.)

pp. 39, 4to Lond. 1687

See Contin. p. 48.

"If a Christian has a greater reverence in his soul for the Book of the Holy Scriptures than for any other book whatsoever, may he not lawfully express this reverence by kissing it?" p. 22. "Dr. Field affirms that the Nicene Fathers mean nothing else by adoration of images but reverently using of them, like to the honour we do the Books of Holy Scripture," p. 29. (Of The Church, lib. iii. ch. xxxvi.) Cf. Bellarmine, vol. ii. p. 763 sq. cited by Bishop Phillpotts in his Letters to Charles Butler, 1826, p. 74,

T. C. D. 344. A Third Letter to a Person of Quality, being a Vindication of the former in answer to a late pamphlet intitled, A Discourse of the use of Images. [By Edward Pelling, D.D.]

pp. 34, 4to Lond. 1687

See Cat. No. 157; Contin. p. 48.

The same subject is introduced in another tract by the same author, 𝕮. 𝕷. Ancient and Modern Delusions discoursed of in Three Sermons upon *T. C. D.* 2 Thes. ch. ii. v. 4; Concerning some Errors now prevailing in the Church of Rome, pp. 58, 4to Lond. 1679. For the benediction and consecration of Images see Pontificale Romanum, folio, Antverpiæ 1627, pp. 364-368; and "Liber Pontificalis" of Edmund Lacy, Bishop of Exeter, a manuscript of the fourteenth century, edited by Ralph Barnes, Esq., Exeter, 1847, quoted by Tyler, p. 33. For pictures and "storied glass," "the laymen's books," see Aringhi, Roma Subterran. 1651; Mamachii Orig. et Antiq. Christianæ, 1749, t. iii; Gorii Thesaurus Vet. Diptychorum, 1759; Lord Lindsay's Sketches of Christian Art, and the authorities cited in Perret's Catacombes de Rome, t. vi. 1851-56; and in Gieseler's Eccles. Hist. vol. ii. ch. 5.

345. A Fourth Letter to a Person of Quality; being an Historical Account of the Doctrine of the Sacrament from the Primitive Times to the Council of Trent; shewing the Novelty of Transubstantiation. [By Edward Pelling, D.D.] C. L. T. C. D.

pp. 77, 4to Lond. 1688

See Contin. p. 48.

This Tract has been annexed to Chap. xxxi. p. 386, and the reader is referred to the note subjoined. It may further be observed that the argument employed by the writers there mentioned against the Eutychians and Nestorians was used against the Apollinarians by Chrysostom in his Epistola ad Cæsarium. Cf. Wake's Defence of the Exposition &c., App. p. 127, No. 78 *supra*, and by Ephrem (in Photii Bibl. cod. 229, and Kohlii Introd. in Hist. et Rem Literariam Slavorum: accedunt duo Sermones Ephremi Syri de Sacra Cœna. Altonaviæ, 1729, p. 369 sqq.) The passages in Theodoret here referred to I find in ed. 1642, vol. iv.; Dial. ii. p. 84. The extraordinary opinions of Amalarius on Christ's Tripartite Body will be found in Hittorpius and in Bibl. Patr. 1618, tom. ix. ch. ix. The work in which Paschasius promulgated his dogma on the Eucharist is printed in Martene et Durand, Collectio ix. pp. 367-470. It was opposed by Joannes Scotus Erigena, the author of De Divisione Naturæ, Rabanus Maurus, Ratramn or Bertram, Hincmarus, Walafridus Strabo, and others. The Berengarian controversy here occupies pp. 43-60. The confession of Engelbert, Archbishop of Treves (p. 57) that Gregory VII. doubted about the Corporal Presence will be found in Eccardi Corpus Historicum Medii Ævi, vol. ii. p. 170; see Bowden's Life and Pontificate of Gregory VII. vol. ii. p. 246, and Notes and Queries, 1st ser. vol. iii. p. 379.

346. The Fallibility of the Roman Church demonstrated from the manifest error of the second Nicene and Trent Councils, which C. L. T. C. D.

assert that the veneration and honorary worship of Images is a Tradition primitive and apostolical. [By Daniel Whitby, D.D.] pp. xii. 79, 4to Lond. 1687

See Cat. No. 155; Contin. p. 51; Ath. Oxon. vol. ii. col. 1071. In Gibson, folio ed. vol. ii. tit. vi. ch. v. 8vo ed. vol. vii.

In some copies the title begins, The Errors of &c. Cf. Wake's Discourse on the Nature of Idolatry; Stillingfleet's Doctrines of the Church of Rome, p. 25, Of the Second Commandment; Scott's Christian Life, pt. ii. vol. ii. p. 246; and Notes and Queries, 1st ser. vol. iii. p. 413. "It is as much beyond my design to pursue this history any further, as it is needless, there being so many excellent discourses on this particular subject, especially those of Mr. Daillé, Bishop Stillingfleet (Defence of the Discourse of Idolatry &c., Works, vol. v.), and Spanheim (Hist. Imag. Lugd. Bat. 1686, 8vo, Opp. ii. p. 707) who have omitted nothing on this head that was necessary to answer the cavils of their Romish antagonists" &c. Bingham, bk. viii. ch. viii. It would be inexcusable in me if I here omitted to notice *The Image-Worship of the Church of Rome proved to be contrary to Holy Scripture, and the Faith and Discipline of the Primitive Church, and to involve contradictory and irreconcilable Doctrines within the Church of Rome itself.* By J. Endell Tyler, B.D. Lond. 1847. For other works by the same learned and accomplished Divine, which relate to the subject of the preceding chapter, see Darling's Cyclopædia Bibliographica.

C. L. *T. C. D.* 347. A Discourse concerning the second Council of Nice which first introduced and established Image-worship in the Christian Church, anno Domini 787. [By Thomas Comber, D.D.] pp. xi., 59, 4to Lond. 1688

See Cat. No. 158; Contin. p. 51. In Gibson's Preservative, folio ed. vol. ii. tit vi. ch. v., 8vo ed. vols. vii. and viii. "This book solely applies itself to the Second Council of Nice; and after an historical narration of the occasion, and the character of the Persons chiefly concerned in it, doth further from the Acts of it discover the mistakes, impostures and falsifications; and how at last it was of no authority, and though received as a General Council by the Church of Rome, doth in many instances notoriously contradict it." Pref. Cf. Hickes's

Letters, p. 64; Thorndike, vol. iv. p. 790-799 sq. For Definit. Synodi see Labbe, Conc. t. vii. For a description of images by Prudentius and others see Estius, In iii. Sentent. distinct. ix. p. 32; Baronius, t. ix. (v. Index). See also Maimbourg's Hist. des Iconoclastes, 4to 1686.

348. A Discourse concerning the worship of Images, preached before the University of Oxford, on Exod. xx. 4, 5. 24 May, 1686. By George Tully. pp. xi. 59, 4to Lond. 1689 C. L.

See Ath. Oxon. vol. ii. col. 925. In a Dedicatory Epistle to the Lord Bishop of London he states that he was "the first clergyman in England who suffered in those days in defence of our religion against Popish superstition and idolatry."

349. ✠ A true and perfect Narrative of the strange and unexpected finding of the Crucifix and Gold Chain of that pious Prince S. Edward, the King and Confessor, after 620 years interment. By Charles Taylour, Gent. [or more truly, by Henry Keepe.] 4to, Lond. 1688 C. L.

See Ath. Oxon. vol. ii. col. 822. The several instances of the respect paid by the Ancient Church to relics are embodied in Thorndike's Epilogue, Works, vol. iii. 30, p. 354. Muratori in his Antiq. Ital. vol. v. p. 7 gives numerous examples of the passionate fondness for relics in the ninth century. In Notes and Queries, third ser. vol. vi. p. 401, Lalanne's Curiosités des Traditions is referred to as containing a list of reliques and reliquaries.

A Just Discharge of Dr. Stillingfleet's Unjust Charge of Idolatry, *ut supra.* *T. C. D.*

An Impartial and Exact Account of the divers Popish books, beads, crucifixes and images taken at the Savoy, and burnt in the New Palace Yard, Westminster, February 11th. By Sir William Waller. 4to Lond. 1678 *B. L.*

Of Idolatry, a Discourse in which is endeavoured a declaration of C. L. *T. C. D.*

its distinction from superstition; its notion, cause, commencement and progress &c. By Thomas Tenison, D.D.
pp. x., 430, 4to Lond. 1678

"'That the professing one only true God does not necessarily quit a people from the guilt or capacity of being idolaters,' is the first thesis of bk. i. ch. xiii. of More's Mystery of Iniquity, pt. i. (Works, p. 417). Cf. More's Antidote against Idolatry;" Thorndike, Reformation of the Church of England better than that of the Council of Trent (Works, vol. v. p. 521). Cf. Tenison, p. 203. This *Treatise of Idolatry* is the great work of this excellent Prelate, learned himself and the ardent and liberal encourager of learning.

A Letter to an Honourable Member of the House of Commons in vindication of the Protestant and Reformed Church as established by Law, in opposition to the superstitious and idolatrous Church of Rome. pp. 13, 4to Lond. 1679

A Letter written to a Friend concerning Popish Idolatry, by the Right Rev. Father in God Herbert [Croft] Lord Bishop of Hereford. Lond. 1679

B. L. A Letter wherein is shewed, First, What worship is due to images according to the Second Council of Nice. Secondly, that the Papists are very unjust in charging Schism on the Church of England. As also that the Church of Rome is most notoriously guilty of that Sin. B. S. pp. vi., 24, 4to 1680

B. L. ✠ Concerning Images and Idolatry. [Anon. By Abraham Woodhead.] 4to Oxf. 1689

"Quære, whether compleated." Wood, Ath. Oxon. vol. ii. p. 617. See also Pt. i. pp. 221-2.

Two Letters to the Most Learned Janus Ulitius, wherein by way of vindication it is abundantly proved that neither St. Augustine nor any one of the Fathers who flourished in the ages before him did either by their doctrine or practice in any way countenance the Invocation of Saints, written by the Rev. George Morley, D.D., in the year 1659, while he remained in exile at Breda, and, when he published the treatise, the Lord Bishop of Winchester, now made English by a Divine of the Church of England, with a Letter to the Translator by G. Hickes, D.D. Lond. 1707

The original in Latin is in his "Several Treatises," 1683, 4to, and commences with "de Oratione pro Mortuis," pp. 67.

"Tum demum (sexto sæculo) a Gregorio Magno Pont. Rom. Invocatio Sanctorum publicis Ecclesiæ Litaniis addita et inserta: sed non adhuc talis, qualem nunc videmus. Nam quantumvis inter disputandum dicant Pontificii se Sanctos invocando nihil aliud intelligere, quam ut Sancti pro illis Deum orarent: tamen ex usu communi, ex publicarum privatarumque precum formulis typis excusis, et ex picturis et imaginibus quas Laicorum libros appellant, passim et palam est videre, quod aliam in sinu fovent opinionem, aut saltem quod aliter a vulgo credi volunt; Sanctos scilicet invocandos esse, non ut Intercessores tantum, sed ut datores et largitores bonorum omnium; quæ quidem a Sanctis, et præcipue a B. Virgine sæpius et fidentius peti solent, quam ab ipso Deo vel Christo." (p. 65.)

CHAP. XXXV

Of the Discourses written of Good Works.

C. L. T. C. D. 350. ✠ Pietas Romana et Parisiensis: or a faithful relation of the several sorts of charitable and pious works eminent in the Cities of Rome and Paris. The one taken out of the book written by Theodore Amydenus. The other out of that by Mr. Carre. [By Abraham Woodhead.]

4to Oxon. [in Obadiah Walker's lodgings] 1687

See Ath. Oxon. vol. ii. col. 616.

"Thomas Carr, alias Miles Pinkney, educated at Doway. He undertook the project of founding a monastery of nuns at Paris of St. Augustine's order, where he resided as their confessor till he died. . . . He was much respected by the Court of France, especially by Cardinal Richelieu, who was a singular benefactor to the English abroad, through his mediation." Dodd.

C. L. T. C. D. 351. Some Reflexions upon a Treatise called Pietas Romana et Parisiensis, lately printed at Oxford. To which are added, I. A Vindication of Protestant Charity in answer to some passages in Mr. E[dward] M[eredith's] Remarks on a late Conference [No. 102 *supra*]. II. A Defence of the Oxford Reply to two Discourses there printed A.D. 1687. [By James Harrington. See No. 102 and 106 *supra*.]

pp. xi., 31. Vindication 32, Defence 44.

See Cat. No. 203; Ath. Oxon. vol. ii. col. 1059. On Harrington's Vindication, cf. Part i. p. 140.

"I am sensible this gentleman is not much acquainted with the learned languages, but being of the Latin Church and University College [Wood and Dodd say of Christ College] I presume he may understand four verses which are there gratefully preserved, and I recommend 'em to his consideration."

Vana suum jactet *Benedictum* Roma; *Benettum*
Ordo *Reformatæ* Religionis habet.
Ergo Domum qui fronte octoque ornavit alumnis
Æternum nobis hic *Benedictus* erit. (p. 21.)

Cf. in Willet's Synopsis Papismi, pp. 1210-43, *A Catalogue of such Charitable Workes* as have beene done in the times of the Gospell within the space of sixty yeeres under the happy raignes of K. Edward, Q. Elizabeth, K. James, our Gracious Soueraigne. In the "Reflexions," pp. 21, 22, a comparison is drawn between the libraries founded by the Romanists and Protestants.

352. A Discourse concerning the Merit of Good Works. [By Peter Allix, D.D.] pp. 32, 4to Lond. 1688 **C. L.** *T. C. D.*

See Cat. No. 102.

In Gibson's Preservative, fol. ed. vol. i. tit. viii. ch. v. 8vo. ed. vol. x. The Popish clergy of 1534 taught that all good works of their own nature are so completely perfect that they truly merit the reward of eternal life. Conc. Trid. Sess. vi. ch. xvi. and can. 32. Cf. Gentileti Examen C. T. in quo demonstratur in multis articulis hoc Concilium antiquis Conciliis et Canonibus Regiæque authoritati contrarium esse. Gorinchemi, 1678. Upon this principle Bellarmine and all the best writers of his church rest the right of the saints in heaven to interest themselves with God for their fellow-creatures upon earth. Bellarmine de Indulgentiis, lib. i. ch. ii. (Opp. t. iii. ch. ii. p. 48); The Roman Doctrine of Repentance and of Indulgences vindicated from Dr. Stillingfleet's Misrepresentations, by S. Cressy, p. 67 &c. 12mo. 1672.

Some Queries to Protestants Answered. And an Explanation of the Roman Catholick's Belief in Four Great Points considered. I. Concerning their Church. II. Their Worship. III. Justification. IV. Civil Government. 4to Lond. 1686

"That the reader may see what credit is to be given to the Romanists in this point, I shall give an account of the Doctrine of the several Reformed Churches about the necessity of good works; and then shew with what confidence these gentlemen affirm that the Protestants teach that good works are not necessary." The Missionaries Arts, No.

107, pp. 85-90. Cf. Davenant de Justitia habituali et actuali, translated by Allport, ch. xxxi.; Bishop Bull's Harmonia Apostolica, cap. xviii. (Works, vol. iii.); Daubeny's Vindication of the Character of the Pious and Learned Bishop Bull, 1827, in which (pp. 145-152) is an extract of "sterling good sense" from Bishop Patrick's Pilgrim on the doctrine of *imputed righteousness;* (cf. Whitby, at the end of his Commentary on the New Testament;) Homilies, v. Good Works; Articles, xii. Good Works.

A Sermon preached on the 8th of January at St. Nicholas Church, in Newcastle-upon-Tyne, shewing that Jesus Christ is our only Mediator of Redemption and of Intercession in Exclusion of Justification by the Works of the Law, or of such as are called Meritorious; and also of the necessity of Invocating of, or Praying to, Saints and Angels, made evident &c. By Thomas Davison, M.A. pp. 30, 4to Lond. 1688

This has been inserted before, but it ought not to be omitted here. The author, a member of St. John's Coll. Cambr. published also The Fall of Angels; a Sermon on 2 Pet. ch. ii. 4. That works of penance are not Satisfactions to Divine Justice is shewn in No. 389 *infra*, in Willet's Synopsis, bk. iv. pp. 1000-2, ed. Smith, 1634; Ames's Bellarminus Enerv. lib. vii.; Stillingfleet's work, The Council of Trent examined and disproved, § iv.; and Thorndike's Laws of the Church, bk. iii. ch. xxix. See also A Funeral Sermon on Bishop Patrick Forbes, by Dr. Baron (Spottiswoode Soc.); Field, Of the Church, bk. iii. ch. xvi.; the Romanist Gerson's Tractat. contra Sectam Flagellantium (Opp. t. ii. p. 660-4); and on Satisfactory Works, see Dens's Theologia, tom. vi. No. 175.

CHAP. XXXVI.

Of the Discourses written of the Notes of the Church.

353. A Brief Discourse concerning the Notes of the Church, with some reflections on Cardinal Bellarmine's Notes. By William Sherlock, D.D. pp. 24, 4to Lond. 1687 C. L. T.C.D.

See Cat. No. 55; Contin. p. 27.

In Gibson, fol. edit. vol. i. tit. iii. 8vo. ed. vol. iii. Compare the Anatomy of Popery, *ut infra*, pp. 71-93; Whitakeri Controversia ii. Quæstio v. pp. 492-557; Ames's Bellarminus Enervatus, vol. ii.; and Field, Of the Church, vol. i. bk. ii. and iii. "Because Bellarmine and Stapleton have taken most pains with this argument, I will therefore propose the objections I find in them, assuring myself that there are not any other of moment to be found in the writings of any other of that side;" ch. ii. On what have been assigned as notes of the True Church at various periods, consult Palmer's Treatise on the Church, where other authors are cited, Jer. Taylor, &c.

354. Bellarmine's First Note of the Church, concerning the name of Catholick examined. By Samuel Freeman, D.D. pp. 16, 4to Lond. 1687 C. L. T. C. D.

See Cat. No. 56; Contin. p. 26.

355. The Second Note of the Church examined, viz. Antiquity. By Simon Patrick, D.D. pp. 16, 4to Lond. 1687 C. L. T. C. D.

See Cat. No. 57; Fasti Oxon. vol. ii. col. 166; Works, vol. iii.

356. The Third Note of the Church examined, viz. Duration. By John Williams, M.A. pp. 16, 4to Lond. 1687 C. L. T. C. D.

See Cat. No. 58; Ath. Oxon. vol. ii. col. 1121.

C. L. T. C. D. 357. The Fourth Note of the Church examined, viz. Amplitude, or Multitude and Variety of Believers. By Edward Fowler, D.D. pp. 20, 4to Lond. 1687

See Cat. No. 59. The author of Athenæ Oxon. vol. ii. col. 1031, forgets to mention this piece among the works of Dr. Fowler. Peck.

C. L. T. C. D. 358. The Fifth Note of the Church examined, viz. The Succession of Bishops. By George Thorpe, D.D. pp. 20, 4to Lond. 1687

See Cat. No. 60.

C. L. T. C. D. 359. An Examination of Bellarmine's Sixth Note, of agreement in doctrine with the primitive Church. By William Payne, M.A. pp. 24, 4to Lond. 1687

See Cat. No. 61.

C. L. T. C. D. 360. An Examination of Bellarmine's Seventh Note, of Union of the Members among themselves and with the Head. By William Clagett, D.D. pp. 36, 4to Lond. 1687

See Cat. No. 62; Ath. Oxon. vol. ii. col. 327.

C. L. T. C. D. 361. The Eighth Note of the Church examined, viz. Sanctity of Doctrine. [By John Scot, D.D.] pp. 35, 4to Lond. 1687

See Cat. No. 63; Ath. Oxon. vol. ii. col. 922.

C. L. T. C. D. 362. The Ninth Note of the Church examined, viz. The Efficacy of Doctrine. [By Thomas Lynford, M.A.] pp. 35, 4to Lond. 1687

See Cat. No. 64; Fasti Oxon. vol. ii. col. 202.

C. L. T. C. D. 363. The Tenth Note of the Church examined, viz. Holiness of Life. [By Thomas Tenison, D.D.] pp. 16, 4to Lond. 1687

See Cat. No. 65; Fasti Oxon. vol. ii. col. 159.

C. L. T. C. D. 364. The Eleventh Note of the Church examined, viz. The Glory

of Miracles. [By Nathanael Resbury, D.D., Minister of Putney.] pp. 35, 4to Lond. 1687
See Cat. No. 66; Ath. Oxon. vol. ii. col. 191.

365. The Twelfth Note of the Church examined, viz. The Light of Prophecy. [By William Clagett, D.D.] pp. 23, 4to Lond. 1687 C. L. T. C. D.
See Cat. No. 67; Fasti Oxon. vol. ii. col. 327.

366. The Thirteenth Note of the Church examined, viz. The Confession of Adversaries. [By Richard Kidder, M.A.] C. L. T. C. D.
See Cat. No. 68; Fasti Oxon. vol. ii. col. 123.

367. The Fourteenth Note of the Church examined, viz. The Unhappy End of the Church's Enemies. [By Nicholas Stratford, D.D.] pp. 31, 4to Lond. 1687 C. L. T. C. D.
See Cat. No. 69; Ath. Oxon. vol. ii. col. 1067.

368. The Fifteenth Note of the Church examined, viz. Temporal Felicity. [By Robert Grove, D.D.] pp. 35, 4to Lond. 1687 C. L. T. C. D.
See Cat. No. 70; Ath Oxon. vol. ii. col. 877.

369. ✠ The Use and Great Moment of the Notes of the Church, as delivered by C. Bellarmine De Notis Eccl. justified, in answer to a late discourse concerning the Notes of the Church. pp. 46, 4to Lond. 1687 C. L. T. C. D.
This is an answer to Sherlock's Brief Discourse concerning the Notes of the Church; with some reflections on Cardinal Bellarmine's Notes. Lond. 1687, 4to pp. 400.

370. A Vindication of the Brief Discourse concerning the Notes of the Church. In answer to a late Pamphlet entitled, The Use and Great Moment of the Notes of the Church, as delivered by Cardinal Bellarmine, de Notis Ecclesia, Justified. [By William Sherlock, D.D.] pp. 69, 4to Lond. 1687 C. L. T. C. D.
See Cat. No. 71; Contin. p. 27.

C. L. T. C. D. 371. Advice to the Confuter of Bellarmine, with some Considerations upon the Antiquity of the Church of England.
pp. 12, 4to Lond. 1687

C. L. T. C. D. 372. A Defence of the Confuter of Bellarmine's Second Note of the Church, Antiquity, against the Cavils of the Adviser. [By George Tully, M.A., preacher at St. Nicholas, Newcastle.] pp. 22, 4to Lond. 1687

See Cat. No. 72; Contin. p. 27; Ath. Oxon. vol. ii. col. 925.

C. L. T. C. D. 373. The Notes of the Church, as laid down by Cardinal Bellarmine, examined and Confuted. A general Title, Table, and Contents. pp. 30, 4to Lond. 1688

The above is the title prefixed to a volume containing the following tracts bound together, without any preface: A Brief Discourse &c, *ut supra*, No. 353; The Fifteen Notes, Nos. 354-368, followed by Nos. 369, 370, 371, 372, all of which are contained in Gibson, folio ed. vol. i., 8vo ed. vols. iii., iv. A reprint appeared Lond. 1840, 8vo.

"He must be very little acquainted with the late methods made use of by those of the Church of Rome, in propagating their religion among us, who knows not this to have been all along their great endeavour to fly, as much as possible, all particular disputes, and keep themselves within the general notions of the Church. One of the first controversies to be remarked in this point is that of the Notes of the Church; and upon which they undertake theirs, exclusive of all others, to be the Catholic Church of Christ Militant upon Earth.

"The former part of the State of the Controversie [p. 36] gave an account of the beginning of these; how our divines engaged themselves to a weekly consideration of them till they had past through the largest catalogue we have yet had of these notes, viz. that of Cardinal Bellarmine. They were then advanced to the third only, but now the whole is finished; and those little exceptions which our adversaries thought fit to make to them are fully answered, and they altogether compose a just volume; and plainly shew that were the Church indeed endued with all those prerogatives they pretend it is, yet would it stand them in no stead, seeing that according to their own notes the Church of Rome cannot possibly be the Catholic or Universal Church." Continuation of State of Controversy, pp. 25, 26.

CHAP. XXXVII.

Of the Discourses written of those particular Texts of Scripture which the Papists cite to prove their several Doctrines.

374. Popery not Founded on Scripture, or the Texts which Papists cite out of the Bible for the Proof of the Points of their Religion, examined and shewed to be alledged without ground. The Introduction. [By Thomas Tenison, D.D.] C. L. T. C. D.

pp. 16, 4to Lond. 1688

See Cat. No. 204; Contin. p. 76.

"I have before recounted how by a joint labour they (our divines) run through the consideration of the pretended *Notes of the Church*, on which the Romanists establish their usurped authority. No sooner were those ended but they presently resolved upon another and a more useful project, which was to search into our adversaries books, and collect all those passages of Scripture which are usually alledged by them to maintain their errors. And by giving the true explication of them, at once to secure their flock from their false glosses, and let them into a better understanding of those sacred books."

Proofs of Popery from Scripture were set out by Father Coton in a distinct work in Greek, and in two little tracts, the Touchstone of the Reformed Gospel and the Catholic Scripturist [by Joseph Mumford]. The most complete treatise on the other side against Popery are Whitaker's Disputatio de Sacra Scriptura contra hujus Temporis Papistas, imprimis Bellarminum et Stapletonum, folio, Genevæ, 1610, pp. 253-417 (translated and edited for the Parker Society by the Rev. W. Fitzgerald, 1849), and Fulke on the Rhemes N. Testament, 1617.

375. The Texts which Papists cite out of the Bible for the proof of their Doctrine concerning the obscurity of the Holy Scriptures examined. By Edward Fowler, D.D. C. L. T. C. D.

pp. 35, 4to Lond. 1688

See Cat. No. 205; Contin. p. 76.

In Gibson, folio ed. vol. i. tit. v. ch. iii., 8vo ed. vol. vi. The author of Athenæ Oxonienses, vol. ii. col. 1031 forgets to mention this piece among the works of Dr. Fowler, and there charges No. 376 *infra* to Dr. Fowler, which was in truth written by Dr. Williams. Peck. In the fifth volume of "Morning Exercises" there are Sermons on the same subject by Christopher Fowler and Thomas Manton.

C. L. *T. C. D.* 376. The Texts examined which the Papists cite out of the Bible, for the proof of their Doctrine concerning the Insufficiency of Scripture, and Necessity of Tradition. By John Williams, D.D. pp. 24, 4to Lond. 1688

See Cat. No. 206; Contin. p. 76; Ath. Oxon. vol. ii. col. 1121.

In Gibson, folio ed. vol. i. tit. iv. ch. iii., 8vo ed. vol. v.

C. L. *T. C. D.* 377. The Texts examined which Papists cite out of the Bible to prove the Supremacy of St. Peter and of the Pope over the whole Church. Part I. pp. 28, 4to Lond. 1688

See Cat. No. 207; Contin. p. 76.

In Gibson, folio ed. vol. i. 8vo ed. vol. iii.

The author of Ath. Oxon. vol. ii. col. 1021 charges this to Dr. John Williams, which was in truth written by Dr. Simon Patrick. Peck.

C. L. *T. C. D.* 378. The Texts examined which Papists cite out of the Bible to prove the Supremacy of St. Peter and of the Pope over the whole Church. Part II. By Simon Patrick, D.D. pp. 35, 4to Lond. 1688

See Cat. No. 208; Contin. p. 76.

In Gibson, folio ed. vol. i. tit. ii., 8vo ed. vol. iii.

C. L. *T. C. D.* 379. The Texts examined which Papists cite out of the Bible for the proof of their Doctrine of Infallibility. By George Tully, M.A. pp. 47, 4to Lond. 1688

See Cat. No. 209; Contin. p. 706; Ath. Oxon. vol. ii. col. 925.

In Gibson, folio ed. vol. i. tit. iv. ch. i., 8vo ed. vol. v.

380. The Texts examined which Papists cite out of the Bible for the proof of their Doctrine concerning the Worship of Angels, and Saints departed. By Samuel Freeman, D.D. Part I. pp. 43, 4to Lond. 1688 C. L. T. C. D.

See Cat. No. 210; Contin. p. 76.
Both parts in Gibson, folio ed. vol. ii. tit. vi. ch. iv., 8vo ed. vol. vii.

381. The Texts examined which Papists cite out of the Bible for the proof of their Doctrine concerning the Worship of Angels, and Saints departed. By Samuel Freeman, D.D. Part II. pp. 43, 4to Lond. 1688 C. L. T. C. D.

See Cat. No. 211; Contin. p. 76.

382. The Texts examined which Papists cite out of the Bible for the proof of their Doctrine concerning the Worship of Images and Reliques. By Edward Gee, M.A. pp. 27, 4to Lond. 1688 C. L. T. C. D.

See Cat. No. 212; Contin. p. 76; Fasti Oxon. vol. ii. col. 222.
In Gibson, folio ed. vol. ii. tit. vi. ch. v., 8vo ed. vol. viii.

383. The Texts examined which Papists cite out of the Bible for the proof of their Doctrine concerning Seven Sacraments, and the efficacy of them. By Edward Gee, M.A. Part I. Concerning the Sacraments of Confirmation and Penance. pp. 27, 4to Lond. 1688 C. L. T. C. D.

See Cat. No. 213; Contin. p. 76; Fasti Oxon. vol. ii. col. 222.
Both parts in Gibson, folio ed. vol. ii. tit. vii. ch. i., 8vo ed. vol. viii.

384. The Texts examined which Papists cite out of the Bible for the proof of their Doctrine of Seven Sacraments and the efficacy of them. Part II. Concerning the Sacraments of Orders, Matrimony and Extreme Unction. By Edward Gee, M.A. pp. 24, 4to Lond. 1688 C. L. T. C. D.

See Cat. No. 214; Contin. p. 76; Fasti Oxon. vol. ii. col. 222.

385. The Texts examined which Papists cite out of the Bible for C. L. T. C. D.

the proof of their Doctrine of the Sacrifice of the Mass. Part I. By Richard Kidder, D.D. pp. 39, 4to Lond. 1688

See Cat. No. 215; Contin. p. 76.

Both parts in Gibson, folio ed. vol. i. 8vo ed. vol. vi.

C. L. T. C. D. 386. The Texts examined which Papists cite out of the Bible for the proof of their Doctrine of the Sacrifice of the Mass. Part II. By Richard Kidder, D.D. pp. 36, 4to Lond. 1688

See Cat. No. 216; Contin. p. 76.

C. L. T. C. D. 387. The Texts examined which Papists cite out of the Bible for the proof of their Doctrine of Transubstantiation. By John Williams, D.D. pp. 24, 4to Lond. 1688

See Cat. No. 207; Ath. Oxon. vol. ii. col. 1121.

In Gibson, folio ed. vol. ii. 8vo ed. vol. ix.

C. L. T. C. D. 388. The Texts examined which Papists cite out of the Bible for the proof of their Doctrine of Auricular Confession. By Thos. Linford, D.D. pp. 35, 4to Lond. 1688

See Cat. No. 218.

In Gibson, folio ed. vol. ii. 8vo ed. vol. x.

C. L. T. C. D. 389. The Texts examined which Papists cite out of the Bible for the proof of their Doctrine of Satisfaction. By John Gaskarth, M.A., Rector of All Saints, Barking. Part I. pp. 44, 4to Lond. 1688

See Cat. No. 219.

Both parts in Gibson, folio ed. vol. ii. 8vo ed. vol. x.

C. L. T. C. D. 390. The Texts examined which Papists cite out of the Bible for the proof of their Doctrine of Satisfaction. By John Gaskarth, M.A., Rector of all Saints, Barking. Part II. pp. 43, 4to Lond. 1688

See Cat. No. 220.

C. L. T. C. D. 391. The Texts Examined which Papists cite out of the Bible for the proof of their Doctrine concerning Purgatory. Part I. [By John Bramston, Lecturer of St. Martin's, Ludgate.] pp. 28, 4to Lond. 1688

See Cat. No. 221.

In Gibson, folio ed. vol. ii. 8vo ed. vol. xi.

392. The Texts examined which Papists cite out of the Bible for the proof of their Doctrine concerning Purgatory. Part II. [By John Bramston, Lecturer of St. Martin's, Ludgate.] pp. 36, 4to Lond. 1688 C. L. *T. C. D.*

See Cat. No. 222.

In the copy of Gibson's Preservative in the library of Trinity College, Dublin, the authorship of this tract is ascribed in MS. in an old hand to Mr. Brampston, Prebendary of Worcester. Now the Prebendary of Worcester was William Bramston who died August 1735, and was the father of John, Rector of Theydon Germon, Essex. I have taken pains to ascertain which of the two men was the author, but cannot find decisive evidence on either side. T. Fisher.

393. The Texts examined which Papists cite out of the Bible for the proof of their Doctrine for Prayers in an unknown Tongue. By John Scot, D.D. Part I. pp. 44, 4to Lond. 1688 C. L. *T. C. D.*

See Cat. No. 23; Ath. Oxon. vol. ii. col. 922.

Both parts in Gibson, folio ed. vol. ii. 8vo ed. vol. vii.

394. The Texts examined which Papists cite out of the Bible for the proof of their Doctrine for Prayers in an unknown Tongue. By John Scot, D.D. Part II. pp. 56, 4to Lond. 1688 C. L. *T. C. D.*

See Cat. No. 224; Ath. Oxon. vol. ii. col. 922.

395. The Texts examined which Papists cite out of the Bible for the proof of their Doctrine concerning the Celibacy of Priests and Vows of Continence. By William Payne, M.A. Part I. pp. 36, 4to Lond. 1688 C. L. *T. C. D.*

See Cat. No. 225.

Both parts in Gibson, folio ed. vol. i. 8vo ed. vol. ii.

C. L. 396. The Texts examined which Papists cite out of the Bible for
T. C. D. the proof of their Doctrine concerning the Celibacy of Priests and Vows of Continence. By William Payne, M.A. Part II. pp. 35, 4to Lond. 1688

See Cat. No. 226.

C. L. 397. The Texts examined which Papists cite out of the Bible for
T. C. D. the proof of their Doctrine concerning the Visibility of the Church. By Nathaniel Resbury. pp. 35, 4to Lond. 1688

See Cat. No. 227; Fasti Oxon. vol. ii. col. 191.
In Gibson, folio ed. vol. i. 8vo ed. vol. iii.

C. L. 398. The Texts examined which Papists cite out of the Bible for
T. C. D. the proof of their Doctrine of Merits. By Thomas Linford. pp. 31, 4to Lond. 1689

See Cat. No. 228.
In Gibson, folio ed. vol. ii. 8vo ed. vol. x.

C. L. 399. Two Tables to the whole set. Of the several Texts which are
T. C. D. made use of by the Romanists for the proof of their several Doctrines. Of the principal Matters. By Mr. Pulleyn. pp. 9, 47, 4to 1689

The whole of these Treatises on the Texts were collected in two vols. 4to, 1688-9, containing 879 pages.

T. C. D. A Table briefly pointing out such places of Scripture as either plainly or by good consequences condemn the principal points of Popery. Folio half-sheet divided into six columns, 1688

Discourses on Select Texts, wherein several weighty Truths are handled and applied against the Papists and Socinians. By Henry Bagshaw. 8vo 1680

An Answer to a Book spread abroad by the Romish Priests,

entitled The Touchstone of the Reformed Gospel, wherein the true Doctrine of the Church of England and many Texts of the Holy Scriptures are faithfully explained. By Symon Patrick, D.D. 8vo 1692

See for an account of the circumstances under which this was written the Editor's Preface to Patrick's Works, vol. i. p. cxv. The tract itself is inserted in vol. vii. of his Works.

✠ Abridgment of Christian Doctrine, with Proof of Scripture for points controverted. By Henry Turbervil. 12mo Douay 1624, Lond. 1687

✠ A Manual of Controversy, clearly demonstrating the Truth of the Roman Catholic Religion by Texts of Holy Scripture &c., and fully answering the Objections of Protestants and all other Sectaries. By H[enry] T[urbervile]. Douay 1654, Lond. 1686 C. L.

"The Clergy," says Dodd, "had a great esteem for the author, and consulted him on all matters of moment."

✠ Scripture Mistaken, the ground of Protestants and common plea of all new Reformers against the ancient Catholike Religion of England. By John Spencer. 8vo Antwerp 1655

"An able controvertist." Dodd.

Answer to Spencer's Scripture mistaken, with Survey of Antiquity. By Henry Ferne, D.D., Bishop of Chester. 12mo Lond. 1660

"Fulke's work [The Text of the New Testament translated at Rhemes] may be said to embody the whole Popish controversy respecting the Scriptures. Fulke was a very able man, and his work is entitled to a place in every library. Mr. Butler very candidly recommends it as very curious, and deserving of attention." Orme's Bibliotheca Biblica. A succinct account of the tenets of the Roman Catholics, *with texts cited as authorities*, will be found in The Book of Churches and Sects &c., by the Rev. Charles Boone, B.A., Lond. 1826. See also Chaps. XX., XXI., XXII.

CHAP. XXXVIII.

Of Certain Popish Sermons preached before King James II., Queen Mary, Catherine the Queen Dowager, and other persons of high rank, and afterwards published, most of them by His Majesty's command.

C. L. T. C. D. 400. ✠ The First Sermon preached before their Majesties in English, at Windsor, on the first Sunday of October, 1685. By the Reverend Father Dom: P. E[llis], Monk of the Holy Order of St. Benedict, and of the English Congregation. [After the Revolution Bishop of Segne in the Pontifical States.] pp. 31, 4to Lond. 1686

See Ath. Oxon. vol. ii. col. 362; Notes and Queries, 1st ser. vol. vi. pp. 125, 298, 400; vol. vii. p. 242; 2nd ser. vol. iii. pp. 406, 432, 518; and Gent. Mag. for July, 1769, p. 328.

C. L. T. C. D. 401. ✠ The Second Sermon preached before the King and Queen, and Queen Dowager, in their Majesties Chappel at St. James's, upon All Saints Day, November 1, 1685. By the Reverend Father Dom: Ph. Ellis. Monk of the Holy Order of St. Benedict, and of the English Congregation. Published by His Majesties command. pp. 32, 4to Lond. 1686

Reprinted in *Cath. Sermons*, vol. i. pp. 1-31.

C. L. T. C. D. 402. ✠ The Third Sermon preached before the King and Queen, in their Majesties Chappel at St. James's, on the third Sunday in Advent, December 18, 1685. By the Reverend Father Dom: Ph. Ellis, Monk of the Holy Order of St. Benedict, and of the English Congregation; Chaplain in Ordinary to His Majesty. Published by His Majesties command. pp, 29, 4to Lond. 1686

In *Cath. Sermons*, vol. i. pp. 65-92.

403. ✠ The Fourth Sermon preached before the King and Queen in their Majesties Chappel at St. James's, on New Year's Day, 1685-6. By the Reverend Father Dom. Ph. Ellis, Monk of the Holy Order of St. Benedict and of the English Congregation, Chaplain in Ordinary to His Majesty. Published by His Majesties command. pp. 29, 4to Lond. 1686 C. L. *T. C. D.*

In *Cath. Sermons*, vol. i. pp. 161-186.

404. ✠ The Fifth Sermon preached before the King and Queen in their Majesties Chappel at St. James's, upon the Feast of St. Francis de Sales, January 29, 1685-6. By the Reverend Father Dom. Ph. Ellis, Monk of the Holy Order of St. Benedict and of the English Congregation, Chaplain in Ordinary to His Majesty. Published by His Majesties command. pp. 28, 4to Lond. 1686 C. L. *T. C. D.*

See Marsollier's Life of S. Francis de Sales, translated by W. H. Coombes, D.D., 8vo, 1812.

405. ✠ The Sixth Sermon preached before the King and Queen in their Majesties Chappel at St. James's, upon the first Wednesday in Lent, February 24, 1685. By the Reverend Father Dom. Ph. Ellis, Monk of the Holy Order of St. Benedict and of the English Congregation. Published by His Majesties command. pp. 31, 4to Lond. 1686 C. L. *T. C. D.*

406. ✠ A Sermon preached before the King and Queen in their Majesties Chappel at St. James's, upon the Annunciation of our Blessed Lady, March 25, 1686. By Jo. Betham, Doctor of Sorbon. Published by His Majesties command. pp. 32. 4to, Lond. 1686 C. L. *T. C. D.*

In *Cath. Sermons*, vol. ii. pp. 1-30.

407. ✠ A Sermon preached before the King and Queen in their Majesties Chappel at St. James's, on Sunday October 24, 1686 (on Matth. xxii. 21). By the Reverend Father Dom. C. L. *T. C. D.*

W. Marsh, Monk of the Holy Order of St. Benedict and of the English Congregation, Chaplain in Ordinary to His Majesty. Published by His Majesties command.

pp. 48, 4to Lond. 1687

In *Cath. Sermons*, vol. i. pp. 291-318.

C. L. 408. ✠ A Sermon preached before their Majesties in their Chappel at St. James's, the 25th Sunday after Pentecost, November 17, 1686. By John Dormer, of the Society of Jesus. Published by His Majesties command.

pp. 30, 4to Lond. 1687

C. L. 409. ✠ A Sermon of Judgment, preached before the Queen Dowager in Her Majesties Chappel at Somerset House, on the first Sunday in Advent, being the 27 November, 1686. By John Dormer, of the Society of Jesus. Published by Her Majesties order. pp. 32, 4to Lond. 1687

C. L. 410. ✠ The Whys and the Hows, or a Good Enquiry: a Sermon preached before their Majesties in their Chappel at St. James's, the second Sunday in Advent, December 6th, 1685. By John Dormer, of the Society of Jesus. Published by His Majesties command. pp. 34, 4to Lond. 1687

T. C. D. 411. ✠ A Sermon preached in the Chappel of His Excellency the Spanish Ambassador, on the second Sunday in Advent, December 4, 1687, on which was solemnized the Feast of St. Francis Xaverius, Apostle of the Indies and Kingdom of Japan. By the Reverend Father Lewis Sabran, of the Society of Jesus. pp. 39, 4to Lond. 1687

C. L. 412. ✠ A Sermon of the Nativity of our Lord, preached before the King and Queen at Whitehall, 1687. By Bonaventure Giffard, Doctor of Sorbon, Chaplain in Ordinary and Preacher to their Majesties. Published by His Majesties command. pp. 33, 4to Lond. 1688

See Ath. Oxon. vol. ii. col. 820; Dodd, vol. iii. p. 469; Macaulay vol. ii. p. 149; Gent. Mag. vol. iv. p. 164.

413. ✠ A Sermon preached before their Sacred Majesties the King and Queen, and Queen Dowager, in their Majesties Chappel at St. James's, on the feast of the Holy Patriarch St. Benet, anno 1685. By Father John Cross, D.D., of the Holy Order of St. Francis. Published by His Majesties command. pp. 34, 4to Lond. 1687 C. L.

The volume now before me, which contains the preceding Sermons and some of the following, came from "William Boothby's" library.

Besides Geddes's curious little work on the Romish Orders of Monks and Friars, already referred to, the reader may consult Mrs. Jameson's highly interesting and valuable book on the Monastic Orders. 1852.

✠ Two Sermons preached before the Queen Dowager, in her Majesties Chappel at Somerset House, by the Rev. Father Dom. Phil. Ellis, Monk of the Holy Order of St. Benedict, and of the English Congregation, Preacher and Chaplain in Ordinary to their Majesties. pp. 42, 4to Lond. 1686

✠ A Sermon preached before the Queen Dowager, in her Majesties Chappel at Somerset House, on Whitsunday, 1686. By the Rev. Dom. Father Ph. Ellis, Preacher and Chaplain in Ordinary to their Majesties. pp. 18, 4to Lond. 1686

✠ A Sermon preached before the King and Queen upon the second Sunday in Advent, December 5, 1686. By the Rev. Father Dom. Philip Ellis, Chaplain in Ordinary and Chaplain to their Majesties. pp. 33, 4to Lond. 1686

✠ A Sermon preached at the Funeral of a person of the highest C. L.

quality in France. By James Benigne Bossuet, Councellour to the King, Bishop of Meaux, formerly of Condom, Preceptor to the Dauphin, first Almoner to the Dauphiness. Printed at Paris by the King's special command. pp. 31, 4to Lond. 1686

C. L. T. C. D. ✠ A Sermon preached at Worcester April 18th, 1686, being the second Sunday after Easter, by H. H., of the Society of Jesus. pp. 22, 4to Lond. 1686

T. C. D. ✠ A Sermon preached on the Feast of the Annunciation of the B. Virgin, at St. Martin in the Fields, Westminster. By John Hill, M.A., Fellow of Queen's Colledge, Oxon. In the Savoy, Printed by Thomas Newcomb.
pp. 31, 4to Imprimatur and title pp. 4, Lond. 1686
See Wood's Ath. Oxon. vol. ii. p. 977.

C. L. T. C. D. ✠ A Sermon preached before the King, November 13, 1686, being the Feast of all the Saints of the Holy Order of St. Benedict. By the Rev. Father Dom. Phil. Ellis, Monk of that Order, and Chaplain in Ordinary and Preacher to their Majesties. pp. 34, 4to Lond. 1686

T. C. D. ✠ A Sermon preached before the Queen Dowager, in her Majesties Chappel at Somerset House, upon St. Stephen's Day. By the Rev. Father Dom. Philip Ellis, Monk of the Order of St. Benedict, and of the English Congregation, Chaplain and Preacher in Ordinary to their Majesties command. pp. 32, 4to Lond. 1687

T. C. D. ✠ A Sermon preached before the King and Queen upon Ephes. v. 16, Redeeming the Time, because the days are evil. By the Rev. Father Philip Ellis, Monk of the Order of St. Benedict, and of the English Congregation, Chaplain and Preacher in Ordinary to their Majesties. Published by His Majesties commands. pp. 36, 4to Lond. 1687

✠ A Sermon of the Blessed Sacrament, preached in the Chappel of His Excellency the Spanish Ambassador, on Corpus Christi Day, June 8, 1686. By the Rev. Father James Blake, of the Society of Jesus. pp. 38, 4to Lond. 1686 C. L.

✠ A Sermon preach'd before the King and Queen, in their Majesties Chappel at St. James's, on the twentieth Sunday after Pentecost, October 25, 1685. By the Rev. Father John Persall, of the Society of Jesus, Professor of Divinity. Published by His Majesties command. pp. 25, 4to Lond. 1686 C. L. *T. C. D.*

✠ A Sermon preached before the King and Queen, in their Majesties Chappel at Windsor, on Trinity Sunday, May 30, 1686. By the Rev. Father Persall, of the Society of Jesus, Professor of Divinity. Published by His Majesties command. pp. 29, 4to Lond. 1686 C. L. *T. C. D.*

✠ A Sermon preached before the Queen Dowager, in Her Majesties Chappel at Somerset House, on Quinquagesima Sunday, February 6th, 1686-7, being also the anniversary day of His late Majesty King Charles II. of Blessed Memory. By Thomas Codrington, Preacher in Ordinary to His Majesty. Published by Her Majesties command. pp. 32, 4to Lond. 1687 C. L.

✠ A Sermon of the Passion of our Blessed Saviour Jesus Christ, preached on Good Friday, in His Excellencies the Spanish Ambassador's Chappel. By J. G., D.D. pp. 34, 4to Lond. 1686 C. L.

✠ A Sermon of St. Peter, preached before Her Majesty the Queen Dowager, in her Chapell at Somerset House, 29th June, 1686. By Thomas Godden, D.D. [Same as No. 223.] pp. 42, 4to Lond. 1686 C. L.

C. L. ✠ A Sermon of the B. Sacrament, preached in the Chappel of His Excellency the Spanish Ambassador, on Corpus Christi day, June 3, 1686, by the R. F. James Blake, of the Society of Jesus. pp. 38, 4to Lond. 1686

C. L. ✠ A Sermon preach'd before Her Majesty the Queen Dowager, in her Chapel at Somerset House, upon the Fifth Sunday after Easter (Rogation Sunday), May 9, 1686. By William Hall, Preacher in Ordinary to His Majesty. Published by Her Majesty's command. pp. 38, 4to Lond. 1686

In p. 21 there is a passage evidently based on the historical facts in which originated the Rogations, described in the Quarterly Review, vol. lxxiv. p. 295. See Notes and Queries, 3rd ser. vol. v. 131.

C. L. ✠ A Sermon preached by William Darrell, Priest of the Society of Jesus; The Vanity of Human Respects. pp. 25, 4to 1688

✠ A Sermon preached upon the Feast of St. George. By N. N., Preacher in Ordinary to their Majesties. 12mo, Lond. 1688

Printed, with other Sermons, as follows: Three Sermons upon the Sacrament in which Transubstantiation is impartially considered, as to Reason, Scripture, and Tradition. To which is added a Sermon upon the Feast of St. George. By N. N., Preacher in Ordinary to their Majesties. London, MDCLXXXIII. 12mo pp. 264. A postscript is inserted, inscribed around, Silvester Jenks, Philosophiæ Professor; A.D. 1689; no doubt the author. These are four Sermons before the King, and a Letter concerning the Council of Trent.

M. L. ✠ Catholick Loyalty: A Sermon before the King and Queen, in His Majesties Chappel-Royal, White Hall, January 30, 1687, by yᵉ Rev. Edward Scarisbrike. 4to Lond. 1688

A Select Collection of Catholick Sermons, preached before their Majesties King James II., Mary Queen Consort, Catherine Queen Dowager, &c., now published in 1741, two vols. 8vo Lond. The authors of the Sermons in the Collection are:

James Ayray, Franciscan: Sermon in Spanish Ambassador's Chapel, December 12, 1686; Sermon preached before Queen Dowager, in her Chapel at Somerset House, April 10, 1687.

John Betham, Doctor of Sorbon: Sermon in Queen Dowager's Chapel, January 6, 1686; Sermon before King and Queen, in Chapel at St. James's, March 25, 1686. [No. 406]. See Dodd, vol. iii. p. 485.

Angel Bix, Franciscan: Sermon before Queen Dowager, in her Chapel, Good Friday, April 13, 1688. See Dodd, vol. iii. p. 491.

James Blake, Soc. Jesus: Sermon in Spanish Ambassador's Chapel, on Corpus Christi Day, June 3, 1686.

Thomas Codrington: Sermon in St. James's, November 28, 1686; Sermon in Chapel at Somerset House, February 6, 1686-7. See Dodd.

Nicholas Cross, Franciscan: Sermon before the Queen, in her Chapel at Windsor, 21st April, 1686.

Philip Ellis: Besides the Six Sermons mentioned by Peck, there is another preached before the Queen Dowager, in her Chapel at Somerset House, on Whitsunday, 1686. See Dodd.

Bonaventure Giffard: Sermon (Peck, p. 412); Sermon before the King and Queen, at Whitehall, on the Fourth Sunday after Easter, 1687. See Dodd.

Thomas Godden, D.D.: Sermon before the Queen Dowager, in her Chapel at Somerset House, Christmas, 1686.

William Hall: Sermon before Queen Dowager, Fifth Sunday after Easter, May 9, 1686. "Preacher to K. James II.; became a Carthusian." Dodd.

Henry Humberstone, Soc. Jesu: Sermon at Worcester, 18th April, 1686.

Sylvester Jenks: Sermon before the King at Whitehall, June 14, 1688; Sermon before their Majesties at Windsor, August 26, 1688; Sermon before the King at Windsor, August 24, 1687. All on the Eucharist and Transubstantiation. See Noble's Continuation of Granger (vol. iii. p. 168, Lond. 1806), where he is designated "A Roman Catholic Divine, as is supposed." "Professor of Douay Coll." Dodd.

Richard Levison, Soc. Jesu: Sermon before Lord Petre, in his Chapel at Ingatestone Hall, April 1, 1688.

John Persall, Soc. Jesu: Sermon before King and Queen at Windsor, Trinity Sunday, May 30, 1686; Sermon before their Majesties at St. James's, October 25, 1685.

Edward Scarisbrike, Soc. Jesu: Catholick Loyalty, a Sermon before the King and Queen, in Chapel Royal at Whitehall, 30th January, 1687; Sermon before the Queen Dowager, Thirteenth Sunday after Pentecost, 1686. See Dodd.

This description of the "Select Collection" was kindly communicated by Dr. Travers.

Lord Macaulay observes of the Roman Catholic divines of this period: — "When they preached, their outlandish accent moved the derision of the audience. They spelt like washerwomen. Their diction was disfigured by foreign idioms; and when they meant to be eloquent they imitated, as well as they could, what was considered as fine writing in those Italian academies where rhetoric had then reached the last stage of corruption. Disputants labouring under these disadvantages would scarcely, even with truth on their side, have been able to make head against men whose style is eminently distinguished by simple purity and grace." Vol. ii. p. 110.

CHAP. XXXIX.

Of certain Miscellaneous Discourses not reducible to any of the former heads, or not coming to hand time enough to be so disposed.

414 ✠ Roman Catholic Principles in reference to God and the King. [By James Corker.] One sheet 4to [1680? Reprinted in 1684 and in 1686.] C. L. T. C. D.

See pt. i. p. 6; Notes and Queries, 1st ser. vol. x. p. 253; in Somers' Tracts (Scott's edit.) vol. ix. p. 58; and in vol. xiii. p. 85 of the Pamphleteer, 1818. T. Fisher.

"A Benedictine monk, educated at Lambspring in Germany, a monastery of that order; whereof Mr. Corker was some time abbot." Dodd. He was one of those against whom Oates, Bedloe and Prance appeared as witnesses.

In the Protestant Family-Piece; or, A Picture of Popery: drawn from their own Principles, exprest in the very words of their Popes, Councils, Canons, and celebrated Writers, &c. [by Solomon Lowe], Lond. 1716, 12mo, there are references to 132 authors who endeavour to prove that the Regal Authority is given, and taken away, at the Pope's pleasure.

415 ✠ Dr. Sherlock sifted from his Bran and Chaff; or a certain way of finding out the true sense of the Scriptures, and discovering who are the true living members of Christ. In a Dialogue between the Master of the Temple and a Student there. 4to Lond. 1687 T. C. D.

See Contin. p. 56, in which Wake says: "Having thus reduced the principal treatises that have been set forth to their particular heads, as far as in so great a confusion of matter I could do it, it remains only to add such treatises on both as I have before passed by, or which could not be so readily brought to any special consideration," [viz. Nos. 415-16-17-18-20-32-33-34.]

Probably by Lewis Sabran. See Oliver, De Backer.

T. C. D. 416. ✠ The Pharisee Unmasked, in a new discovery of the artifices used by Roman Catholic Priests to convert prisoners both at and before the time of execution. 4to Lond. 1687

See Contin. p. 56.

C. L. *T. C. D.* 417. ✠ Assertio Septimorum Sacramentorum, [or an Assertion of the Seven Sacraments against Martin Luther by Henry VIII. of England, France and Ireland, King. To which is adjoined his Epistle to the Pope; Mr. John Clark's Oration, and the Pope's Answer thereunto; as also the Pope's Bull, by which his Holiness was pleased to bestow upon K. Henry VIII. (for composing this book) that most illustrious, splendid and most Christian-like title of Defender of the Faith. Translated with additions by T[homas] W[ebster.]

pp. xxviii., 133, 4to Lond. 1687]

See Contin. p. 56.

"The original, in an elegant MS., is still preserved in the library of the Vatican, and is usually shewn to Englishmen on their visits to Rome, vide Dr. Smith's Tour to the Continent, vol. ii. p. 200. From this copy it was printed at Rome, in ædibus Francisci Priscianensis Florentini, 1543, as appears by the colophon, Descriptus liber ex eo est quem ad Leonem X. Pont. Max. rex ipse misit, but it had before been published in London, in ædibus Pynsonianis 1521, and at Antwerp, in ædibus Michaelis Hillenii in the year 1522." Roscoe's Leo X. vol. iv. p. 41. The Chetham Library has a copy of Pynson's edition 4to, 1521. Accedit Ejusdem Epistola Regia ad illustrissimos Saxoniæ Duces pie admonitoria. The former is inserted in Bishop Fisher's Works, folio, 1597, pp. 6-79. For a particular account of this book and its contents see Collier's Eccl. Hist., vol. ii. pp. 11-17. For its bibliography see Ames's Typogr. Antiq., Herbert's and Dibdin's editions. In 1845 was published, The Papal Jewel in the Protestant Crown, an historical note, illustrative of the Fac-Simile Bull of Leo X.

conferring on Henry VIII. the title of Defender of the Faith, 8vo. Cf. Historia Operis à Reginaldo Polo adv. Henricum VIII. scripti, ap. Schelhornii Amœnitates Literariæ &c. 1, 12, et Poli Epist. 1, 24. The Bull is in Rymer Fœdera, vol. vi. pt. i. p. 199, and is inserted in the Appendix of Roscoe's Life of Leo X., No. cxcii.

418. ✠ A Reformed Catechism, by Peter Manby. *T. C. D.*
4to Dublin 1687

See Pt. i. p. 151.

419. A Sermon by the Bishop of Bath and Wells (Dr. Thomas Ken) on Ascension Day, May 5, 1687.
See Ath. Oxon. vol. ii. col. 990.

420. ✠ Animadversions on the Bishop of Bath's Sermon on Ascension Day, 5th May, 1687. By F. J. R. C. J. *T. C. D.*
4to Lond. 1687

See Contin. p. 57; Ath. Oxon. vol. ii. col. 990.

421. A Request to Roman Catholicks to answer the Queries upon these their following Tracts: 1. Their Divine Service in an Unknown Tongue. 2. Their taking away the Cup from the people. 3. Their withholding the Scriptures from the Laicks. 4. The Adoration of Images. 5. The Invocation of Saints and Angels. 6. The Doctrine of Merit. 7. Purgatory. 8. Their Seven Sacraments. 9. Their Priests intention in Baptism. 10. The Limbo of unbaptised Infants. 11. Transubstantiation. 12. The Propitiatory Sacrifice of the Mass. 13. Private Masses. 14. The Sacrament of Penance. 15. The Sacrament of Marriage, with the Clergies restraint therefrom. 16. Their Sacrament of Extreme Unction. 17. Tradition. 18. That threadbare question, Where was your Church before Luther? 19. The Infallibility of the Pope with his Councils. 20. The Pope's deposing power. 21. Their Uncharitableness to all other Christians. By a Moderate Son of the Church of *C. L.* *T. C. D.*

England [— Gourdon of Scotland]. pp. 43, 4to Lond. 1687
See Contin. p. 58; Catal. No. 191.

T. C. D. 422. The Judgment of Private Discretion, in matters of Religion, defended; in a Sermon at St. Paul's, Covent Garden. By Richard Kidder, D.D. 4to Lond. 1687
See Cat. No. 59; Contin. p. 192; Ath. Oxon. vol. ii. col. 123. Part i. p. 247. He published in 1697 Twelve Sermons preached upon several occasions; amongst which is reprinted "The Judgment of Private Discretion . . . . . a Sermon on 1 Thess. v. 21, with a Preface." Biogr. Brit. See also Birch's Life of Tillotson.

C. L. 423. ✠ A Net for the Fishers of Men, and the same which Christ gave to his Apostles. Wherein the points controverted between Catholiques and Sectaries are briefly vindicated by way of dilemma. By C. J. and J. McC., two Gentlemen, late Converts. And by them dedicated to the Queen. [Reprinted, Dublin, 1812.] pp. xv., 113, 24mo Lond. 1686
Dedicated to The Holy Wisdom of The Glorious Trinity. For books dedicated to the Deity see Notes and Queries, 2nd ser. vols. ix., x., xi. and xii.

424. A Plain Defence of the Protestant Religion, fitted to the meanest capacity; being a full Answer to *The Popish Net for the Fishers of Men* that was writ by two Converts; wherein is evidently made appear that their departure from the Protestant Religion was without cause or reason. Fit to be read by all Protestants. By H[icks] the Author of *The Missionaries Arts* (No. 107 *supra*). 8vo Lond. 1687
See Contin. p. 59; Cat. No. 193.

T. C. D. 425. Some Queries to Protestants answered; and an explanation of the Roman Catholics Belief in four great points considered, viz. Concerning their Church. 2. Worship. 3. Justification. 4. Civil Government. By Michael Altham, M.A. pp. 39, 4to Lond. 1686

See Cat. No. 193; Contin. p. 59. Second Edition, 1687, pp. 41. C. L. T. C. D.

426. Two short Discourses against the Romanists. 1. An Account of the Fundamental Principle of Popery, and of the Insufficiency of the Proofs which they have for it. 2. An Answer to Six Queries proposed to a Gentlewoman of the Church of England, by an Emissary of the Church of Rome. With a new Preface particularly relating to the Bishop of Meaux, and other Modern Complainers of misrepresentation. By Henry Dodwell, M.A., late of Trinity College near Dublin, now Camden Professor of Oxford. pp. 56, 4to Lond. 1688 C. L.

See Cat. No. 198; Contin. p. 59; Ath. Oxon. vol. ii. col. 232; see pt. i. p. 118.

427. ✠ The Triple Cord.

Dodd mentions a book with this title by Lawrence Anderton, St. Omer, 1634, 4to, but query, whether the book referred to?

428 A Letter of Enquiry to the Reverend Fathers of the Society of Jesus. Written in the Person of a dissatisfied Catholick, by James Taylor, Gent. pp. 44, 4to Lond. 1689 C. L. T. C. D.

See Cat. No. 202.

429. A Discourse wherein is held forth the opposition of the Doctrine, Worship and Practices of the Roman Church to the Nature, Designs and Characters of the Christian Faith. By Gilbert Burnet, D.D. pp. 71, 4to Lond. 1688 C. L. T. C. D.

See Contin. p. 59; Cat. No. 182.

In Gibson, vol i. p. 145, 8vo ed. vol. i. This is the second edition in which the first part of the title, "The Mystery of Iniquity Unveiled," is omitted. J. H. T.

430. ✠ A Short Catechism against all Sectaries [said to be translated by C. M.] 8vo, Lond. 1662 T. C. D.

431. A Dialogue betwixt two Protestants (in answer to a Popish C. L. T. C. D.

Catechism, called a Short Catechism against all Sectaries), plainly showing that the members of the Church of England are no Sectaries but true Catholicks; and that our Church is a sound part of Christ's Holy Catholick Church, in which Communion therefore the people of this Nation are most strictly bound in conscience to remain. In two Parts. By [John] Rawlet, late Preacher at Newcastle-upon-Tyne.
pp. xviii, 262, 8vo Lond. 1685

See Contin. p. 58; Cat. No. 186.
In Gibson, folio edit. vol. iii. ad finem, 8vo ed. vol. xvii.

C. L. T. C. D. 432. ✠ First Question: Why are you a Catholic? The Answer follows. Second Question: But why are you a Protestant? An Answer attempted in vain. Written by the Rev. Father S[erenus] C[ressy], Monk of the Holy Order of St. Benedict, and of the English Congregation. First printed in 1673 8vo.
pp. iii., 72, 4to Lond. 1686

See Contin. p. 56; Ath. Oxon. vol. ii. col. 531.

C. L. T. C. D. 433. ✠ The Question of Questions, which rightly resolved, resolves all our Questions in Religion. This Question is, Who ought to be our Judge in all these Differences? By James Mumford, Priest of the Society of Jesus. Second edition. Permissu Superiorum. Lond. 1686-7

"The Roman Church having been proved to be our infallible Judge, all under pain of damnation are bound to submit to her judgement." See Table of Contents, § 25.

C. L. T. C. D. 434. ✠ Popery Anatomized, or the Papists cleared from the False Imputation of Idolatry and Rebellion. pp. 16, 4to 1686

See Contin. p. 56.

435. A seasonable Collection of plain Texts of Scripture (in words at length, against several points in the Romish Religion) for the use of English Protestants.

436. A Plain Representation of Transubstantiation as it is received in the Church of Rome; with the sandy foundations it is built upon, and the arguments that do clearly evert and overturn it. By Mr. H[enry] Pendlebury. Same as No. 293. C. L. T.C.D.

See Cat. p. 33.

In the year 1768 was published another work of the same author: Sacrificium Missaticum, mysterium iniquitatis; or, a Treatise concerning the sacrifice of the Mass, with a short account of the author's life. 8vo Lond.

437. A pacific Discourse of the Causes and Remedies of the differences about Religion which distract the peace of Christendom. By Thomas Smith, D.D. pp. 34, 4to Lond. 1688 C. L. T. C. D.

See Cat. No. 189; Contin. p. 58; Ath. Oxon. vol. ii. col. 1021.

"This is a translation for the most part from his book De Causis et Remediis Dissidiorum quæ Orbem Christianum hodie affligunt, Exercitatio Theologica in Rom. iv. 19, Oxon. 1675, qu."

438. A Continuation of the present State of the Controversy between the Church of England and the Church of Rome, being a full account of the Books that have been of late written on both sides. By William Wake, M.A. pp. 76, 4to Lond. 1688 C. L. T. C. D.

See Ath. Oxon. vol. ii. col. 1059. A second edition was published in the same year. The Present State, of which this is a Continuation, is by Clagett, No. 71.

439. The Catalogue of all the Discourses published against Popery during the reign of King James II. By the Members of the Church of England and by the Nonconformists. With the names of the authors of them. By Edward Gee, M.A. pp. 34, 4to Lond. 1689 C. L. T. C. D.

See also Dodd's Certamen Utriusque Ecclesiæ.

Addenda.

C. L. 440. A Treatise of the Corruption of Scripture, Councils and
T. C. D. Fathers, by the Prelats, Pastors and Pillars of the Church of Rome, for the maintenance of Popery. By Thomas James, Library Keeper at Oxford. Together with a sufficient answer unto James Gretser and Anthony Possevine, Jesuits, and the unknown author of The Grounds of the Old Religion and the New. Lond. 1611, 4to. Ib. 1688, 8vo pp. xxvii., 560.

See Ath. Oxon. vol. i. cols. 537-38-39-40.

Dr. James was a Wykehamist, and one of the most eminent bibliographers of the seventeenth century, as well as one of the greatest polemical writers of his day. See Biblioth. Chetham. Index. This treatise was reprinted in 1843, edited by the Rev. J. E. Cox.

T. C. D. 441. Mr. William Chillingworth's Book [called The Religion of Protestants a Safe Way to Salvation] made more generally useful, not only by omitting personal contests, but inserting whatsoever concerns the common cause of Protestants, or defends the Church of England. With an addition of an useful table, and also of some genuine pieces of the same author never before printed; viz. 1. A Conference between him and Mr. Lewgar, whether the Roman Church be the Catholick Church, and all out of her communion heretics or schismatics. 2. A Discourse against the Infallibility of the Roman Church, with an answer to all those texts of Scripture which are alledged to prove it. 3. A Conference concerning the Infallibility of the Roman Church, proving that the present Church of Rome either errs in the worshipping of the B. Virgin, or that the ancient Church did err in condemning the Collyridian heretics. 4. An Argument drawn from the Communicating Infants (as without which they could not be saved) against the Church's Infallibility. 5. Several Arguments against Infallibility, drawn from the doctrine of the Millenaries. 6. A Letter relating to the same subject. 7.

An Argument against Infallibility, taken from the contradiction in the doctrine of Transubstantiation. 8. An account of the arguments which moved the author to turn Papist; with his Confutation of the same. 4to, Lond. 1687

See Ath. Oxon. vol ii. col. 43; pt. i. p. 242-3.

On Chillingworth's controversy with writers of the Roman Communion see Dodd, Des Maizeaux, Barlow's Remains, and the Preface to Smith's Translation of Daillé's Apology for the Reformed Churches, 1653, 12mo. The misrepresentations to which his opinions on Primitive Tradition have long been subjected have been exposed by Manning on the Rule of Faith, an analysis of which will be found in the British Magazine, vol. xv. p. 65, where the reader is referred to Chillingworth, vol. i. p. 218, ed. Oxford.

442. A Dissuasive from Popery, to the People of Ireland. By Jeremy [Taylor] Lord Bishop of Down. (Works, Eden, vol. vi.) pp. xi., 173, 4to Dublin 1664 C. L. *T. C. D.*

See Ath. Oxon. vol. ii. col. 405. On the merits of this composition see Mant's History of the Church of Ireland, and Heber's Life, p. 122.

In answer to this "Dissuasive" appeared A Letter to a Friend touching Jeremy Taylor's Dissuasive from Popery, discovering above one hundred and fifty false or wrested quotations in it; 4to, 1665.

443. ✠ Truth Will Out: or, A Discovery of some Untruths smoothly told by Dr. Jeremy Taylor in his Dissuasive from Popery; with an Answer to such Arguments as deserve answer. By his Friendly Adversary E[dward] W[orsley]. pp. xi., 217, 4to, 1665 C. L.

See Athen. Oxon. vol. ii. col. 403; Dodd, vol. iii. p. 314. First printed in one of the Appendices to Sargeant's Sure Footing to Christianity. See also Pt. i. p. 220.

444. A Dissuasive from Popery. The Second Part, in vindication of the First Part [No. 442], and further reproof aud conviction of the Roman Errors. In two Books. By Jeremy Tay- C. L.

lor, late Bishop of Down and Connor. The Introduction in answer to J[ohn] S[argeant].

Pref xvi., Introd. 75, pp. 295, 4to Lond. 1667

This I conceive is the same with No. 442 *supra*. Peck. The reader will see from the fuller title which I have given that it is not so. See Heber's Life, p. 205.

C. L. 445. A Dissuasive from Popery. Book II. By Jeremy Taylor, late Bishop of Down and Connor. pp. 158, 4to Lond. 1667

See Heber's Life, p. 209. This, with 442 and 444, comprises the whole work by Jer. Taylor, generally known as The Dissuasive from Popery.

C. L. 446. ✠ Catholics no Idolaters; or a Full Refutation of Dr. Stil-
T. C. D. lingfleet's unjust charge of Idolatry against the Church of Rome. By T[homas] G[odden]. pp. 448, 8vo Lond. 1672

In pp. 283-286 he quotes Dr. Beaumont's Psyche, or Love's Mystery, stanzas 74, 81-86, 88-91, 99, 100, on the contradictions which have been objected against the Mysteries of the Trinity and Incarnation. A notice of this singular poem, which has some fine passages, with copious extracts, will be found in the Retrosp. Review, vol. xi., pp. 288-307, vol. xii., pp. 229-48.

447. The Tryal of Religions, with cautions to the Members of the Reformed Church against defection to the Roman. By Francis Gregory, D.D. Lond. 1674-75

See Fasti Oxon. vol. ii. col. 147.

"This Dr. Gregory had a younger brother named John Gregory, born at Woodstock, educated at Cambridge...... He hath written Greek Scholia on the New Testament, but whether yet printed I know not." They were published by his son, John Gregory, of Magdalen Hall in 1703.

T. C. D. 448. The Grand Presumption of the Roman Church in equalling their Traditions to the written Word; and their jealousies in refusing to admit the Holy Scriptures as the rule for the trial of their religion. In two discourses. By Francis Gregory, D.D. 4to Lond. 1675

See Fasti Oxon. vol. ii. col. 147.

449. The Unreasonableness of the Romanists requiring our Communion with the present Romish Church; or, a Discourse drawn from the perplexity and uncertainty of the principles; and from the contradictions betwixt the prayers and doctrines of the present Romish Church to prove that it is unreasonable to require us to joyn in Communion with it. By William Squire, M.A., Rector of Rolleston in Derbyshire. 8vo Lond. 1672 *S. C.*

See Ath. Oxon. vol. ii. col. 588.

450. Some more Considerations proving the Unreasonableness of the Romanists in requiring us to return to the Communion of the present Romish Church. By William Squire, M.A. 8vo Lond. 1674 *S. C.*

451. The Several Ways of Resolving Faith in the Roman and Reformed Churches, with the Author's impartial thoughts upon each; and his own opinion at length shown wherein the rule of Faith doth consist. Which clears, upon rational grounds, the Church of England from criminal schism, and lays the cause of the separation upon the Roman. [By Matthew Banckes. *Liber accurate, ingeniose et solide scriptus*. J. K.] 12mo York 1677 *S. C.*

This was reprinted with the following title: The Several Ways &c. The second edition, enlarged in several of its sections; with the addition also of an appendix of divers objections and their answers, and an explanation of the different acceptations of the word Tradition, as it is used in the book. By a Layman. 8vo 1682.

452. The Funeral of the Mass; or the Mass dead and buried without hope of resurrection. Translated from the French of

Monsieur de Rodon, Professor of Philosophy at Mismes in Languedoc. By S. A., and by him dedicated to the Lord Chancellor Shaftsbury. The Fourth Edition.

12mo Lond. 1680

Another translation was published by Robert Hill, M.A., which is far superior; see p. 381. See the Supplement to Chap. XXXI.

"There is a great difference between the Sacrifice of Melchizedeck and that of the Mass; what was offered in one was Bread and Wine, the other is the Body and Blood of Christ; the substance of Bread and Wine is in one (therefore it is an *unbloody sacrifice*), the accidents only in the other (therefore it is a *bloody sacrifice*)." Kidder, No. 385. The doctrine of the Sacrifice cannot be the same, where Transubstantiation is held and where it is not. For a Catena Patrum or Testimony of the later Writers of the English Church to the Doctrine of the Eucharistic, not Propitiatory, Sacrifice, with an historical account of the changes made in the Liturgy as to the expression of that doctrine, see Tracts for the Times, vol. iv. No. 81. For the Confessions of the Martyrs of the Reformation see Todd's edition of Cranmer's Defence of the True and Catholic Doctrine of the Sacrament.

C. L. 453. ✠ A Manual of Controversies, clearly demonstrating the truth of the Catholic Religion by texts of Holy Scripture, Councils in all ages, Fathers of the first five hundred years, and common sense and reason, And fully answering the principal objections of Protestants and all other sectaries. By H[enry T[urbervil], a clergyman. The Fourth Edition, corrected. pp. x., 364, 12mo Lond. 1686

Two editions were before published at Douay, pp. 414, 1654, 1671. The edition of 1686 now before me has appended a poem on the Real Presence and the Rule of Faith. This was answered in Roman Oracles Silenced; or, The Prime Testimonies of Antiquity produced by Henry Turbervil in his Manual of Controversies Examined and Refuted. By William Thomas, Bishop of Worcester. pp. xi., 70, 4to Lond. 1691. He was one of the Bishops who refused to take the oath; see Lathbury's History of the Nonjurors, pp. 51-2.

B. L. 454. Fides Ecclesiæ Anglicanæ vindicata ab incertitudine; sive concio coram academia Oxoniensi habita. 9 Oct. 1688. A Johanne Cudworth, S. T. B. et Coll. Trin. Socio. *B. L.*

4to Oxon. 1688

See Fasti Oxon. vol. ii. col. 225. He was Rector of Kiddington, in Oxfordshire; see Warton's Hist. and Antiq. of Kiddington, 4to, 1815, pp. 18, 19.

455. De Ecclesia Romana Dissertatio. Pars Operis multo Majoris de Judice Controversiarum et Catholicæ veritatis Regula. A Georgio Ashwello. S.T.B. pp. 116, 4to Oxon. 1688 C. L. *T. C. D.*

See Ath. Oxon. vol. ii. col. 911. Of a preceding part Wood observes: "De Socino et Socinianismo dissertatio. This is but a piece, and that too the least of a far greater work quite finished, and lying by the author in MS."

456. Seasonable Advice to Protestants, shewing the necessity of maintaining the Protestant Religion in opposition to Popery. By John Fell (late Lord Bishop of Oxon.) 4to 1688

Anthony à Wood says in his usual carping way (Ath. Oxon. vol. ii. col. 1170): "He left behind him the character among some men of a *Valde vult* person, who by his grasping at and undertaking too many affairs relating to the public (few of which he thoroughly effected), brought him untimely to his end to the loss of learning, &c."

457. The Salvation of Protestants Asserted and Defended in opposition to the rash and uncharitable sentence of their eternal damnation pronounced against them by the Romish Church. By J[ohn] H[erman] Dalhusius, Inspector of the Churches in the County of Weeden upon the Rhine. Newly done into English. pp. 64, 4to Lond. 1689 C. L.

Reprinted at Edinburgh, 4to 1691. See pt. i. p. 237.

It will be seen that the additional list, which follows, does not extend beyond the reign of James II., that being the period mentioned in Peck's title-page. To have included all the

Tracts not before noticed, published in the reign of Charles II., and which are very numerous, would have exceeded the limits prescribed for the present work.

The Apology of the Church of England, Engl. from the Latin of John Jewel, Bp. of Sarum, with his life, and his Letter to Seignor Scipio concerning the Council of Trent. Translated by Deg. Wheare. [Works, Parker Soc. vols. iii. and iv.; edit. by Jelf, vol. viii.] 8vo. Lond. 1685

See the art. "Church of England," in the 69th vol. of the Quarterly Review, p. 476, containing testimonies to the virtues and learning of the recognised defender of the Church of England.

C. L. Dr. John Cosin, late Bishop of Durham, his Opinion (when Dean of Peterborough and in exile) for communicating rather with Geneva than Rome. 8vo London, 1684. Reissued with the title, Two Letters of Dr. John Cosin, with Annotations by Richard Watson, D.D. [Works, Oxf. 1851, vol. iv.] 8vo Lond. 1685

In "A Collection of Controversial Discourses wrote by the learned Dr. George Hickes and a Popish Priest," &c., 1727, originally published in 1705, under the title of "Several Letters which passed between Dr. Hickes and a Popish Priest," is another tract by Bishop Cosin, entitled, "The differences and arguments in the chief points of religion betwixt the Church of Rome and the Church of England."

C. L. A Dialogue between a Popish Priest and an English Protestant, wherein the principal points and arguments of both Religions are truly proposed and fully examined. By Matthew Poole. [First published in 1667.] pp. xi., 178, 12mo 1685

C. L. A Dialogue betwixt two Protestants, in answer to a Popish Catechism called A Short Catechism against the Sectaries, plainly shewing that the Members of the Church of England are no Sectaries, but true Catholics; and that our Church is a sound part of Christ's Holy Catholick Church, in which Communion therefore the people of this Nation are most strictly bound in conscience to remain. In two Parts. pp. 262, 1685

In Gibson, folio ed. vol. iii., App. 8vo ed. vol. xvii.

A Short Account of the Violent Proceedings and Unheard of Cruelties which have been exercised upon the Protestants of Montauban, to make them renounce their Religion. 1685

Cf. The Student's Library, pp. 94-5. "Reflections on the Cruel Persecutions that the Reformed Church suffered in France, through the Conduct and Acts of the last Assembly of the Clergy of that Kingdom, with an examination of the pretended Calumnies whereof the Clergy complain to the King in the Profession of Faith." See Pt. i. p. 121; cf. Mosheim's Eccl. Hist. vol. ii. pp. 237-8; Buckle's Hist. of Civilization, vol. i. ch. viii.; Hickes's Serm. vol. i. p. 199.

The Old Religion; or the True State of the Difference between the Reformed and the Romanists, wherein the Schism is charged upon the latter. By Joseph Hall, Exon. [Works, Oxf. 1837, vol. ix. In Cumming's edit. of Gibson, vol. xvii.] 8vo Lond. 1686 *S. C.*

Answer to a Challenge made by a Jesuit [Malone] in Ireland &c. With the Discourse of the Religion anciently professed by the Irish. By Archbishop Ussher. 4to Lond. 1686 **C. L.**

The best edition before his Works were collected.

A Sermon preached at Whitehall, before his late Majesty, April 4th 1679, on 1 John iv. 1. By John Tillotson, D.D. [Works, 1696, p. 225.] pp. 30, 4to Lond. 1686

An Edict of the French King, prohibiting all publick exercise of the pretended reformed religion in his kingdom; wherein he recalls and totally annuls the perpetual and irrevocable edict of K. Henry IV., his grandfather, full of most gracious concessions to Protestants: to which is added the French King's Letter to the Elector of Brandenburg, containing several pas- **C. L.**

sages relating to the foregoing edict: as also a brief and true account of the persecution carried on against those of the foresaid religion, for to make them abjure and apostatize: together with the form of abjuration the revolting Protestants are to subscribe and swear to; and a declaration of his Electoral Highness of Brandenburg in favour of those of the reformed religion who shall think fit to settle themselves in any of his dominions. pp. vi., 82, 4to 1686

See Part I. p. 124, and Gent. Mag. 1854, vol. xli. p. 92.

B. L. Account of the Complaints and Cruel Persecutions of the Protestants of France. By John Claude, Minister of the Reformed Church at Charenton. pp. 48, 4to Lond. 1686

Redmayne's edit., 8vo 1707, see Townsend's Life of Claude, pp. lx., lxi. Niceron, Mémoires pour servir à l'Histoire des Hommes Illustres, tom. x. pt. ii. p. 310, and Pt. i. pp. 95 and 101. For Answers to the "Complaints" see pt. i. pp. 120.

S. C. History of Monastical Conventions and Military Institutions, with a Survey of the Court of Rome. 18mo Lond. 1686

✠ Dialogue between two Church of England men concerning Matters of Religion, as set forth in the Pulpit. 18mo Lond. 1687

S. C. Reasons why a Protestant should not turn Papist. By a Person of Quality. 1687

A Copy of a Letter written to a Gentlewoman newly seduced to the Church of Rome. By the Rev. J[eremy] T[aylor], late Bishop of Down and Connor. [Works, edit. Eden, vol. vi.] 8vo 1687

Cf. Bull's Sermon on the Necessity of Works of Righteousness, vol. i. p. 9 sq.

Europæ Speculum, or a Survey of the State of Religion in the

Westerne Parts of the Worlde; wherein the Romane Religion and the pregnant Policies of the Church of Rome to support the same are notably displayed. By Sir Edwin Sandys. 8vo 1687

This very interesting and ably written book was published in 1605, reprinted 1629. "The masterly Survey of the Popish System by Sir Edwin Sandys, Hooker's pupil, an account which is as accurate at this day as ever, and well deserves to be reprinted." Quarterly Review, 1842, vol. lxix. p. 478.

There are several other tracts representing "Popish Policies and Practices," and against the Court of Rome: Ways and Means whereby the Pope and his Agents have endeavoured to propagate their doctrines, by Joshua Stopford, B.D., 8vo 1675; The Roman Horseleech, concerning the intolerable charge of Popery to this Nation, by William Staveley, 8vo 1674; The New Politick Lights of Modern Rome's Church Government; or, The New Gospel according to Cardinal Pallavicini, revealed by him in his History of the Council of Trent. 8vo Lond. 1678, &c.

✠ The Catechism of the Curats, compos'd by the Decree of the Council of Trent, and publish'd by Command of Pope Pius the Fifth. Faithfully translated into English. Printed by Henry Hills. 8vo Lond. 1687 C. L.

It was also translated, with notes, by T. A. Buckley. Post 8vo. Lond. 1852.

"The Catechism of the Council of Trent was drawn up for the express purpose of providing preachers with subjects for their sermons; and as my whole work has been a defence of myself, I may here say that I rarely preach a sermon but I go to this beautiful and complete Catechism to get both my matter and my doctrine." Newman's Apologia, p. 425.

In 1686 was published a "Letter concerning the Council of Trent," signed with the initials N.N., which were used by Sylvester Jenks, Peter Talbot Abp. of Dublin, Nicholas French Bp. of Ferns, and John Leyburn.

B. L. ✠ Carier's Missive to James I., containing the Motives of his Conversion to the Catholic Religion.

Liége, 1614. Reprinted 8vo Lond. 1649, 1687

See Pt. i. p. 62, and Wood's Fasti Oxon. vol. i. col. 154.

✠ Advice from a Catholic to his Protestant Friend, touching the doctrine of Purgatory. 18mo 1687

B. L. ✠ The Hind and the Panther, a Poem. Holy-Rood House.

Lond. 4to 1687

"Dryden," says Sir Walter Scott, "left to English literature a name second only to Milton and Shakspeare." His controversial pieces, The Religio Laici and The Hind and the Panther, are copiously illustrated by Scott; see also p. 82. He makes the same complaint as the tract above described, No. 414:

> An hideous figure of their foes they drew,
> Nor lines, nor looks, nor shades, nor colours true;
> And this grotesque design exposed to public view.
>
> *The Hind and the Panther*, Works, vol. x. pp. 231.

Here may be mentioned "A Remonstrance of Piety and Innocence, containing the last Devotions and Protestations of several Roman Catholics, condemned and executed on account of the Plot; to which is added, A Summary of Roman Catholic Principles," 8vo Lond. 1683; and Peter Walsh's Four Letters on several subjects to Persons of Quality, the fourth being an Answer to the Lord Bp. of Lincoln's Book, entitled Popery, &c. (see p. 5.) 8vo 1686.

This celebrated poem was answered by Lord Halifax and Prior in "The Hind and Panther transversed, or the City and Country Mouse." For some of the satirical pieces on the same occasion mentioned by Macaulay, vol. ii. p. 200, see "A Collection of the Newest and most Ingenious Poems &c. against Popery," 4to 1689. "Most of the early editions of Dryden's works are in the British Museum and the Bodleian Library." Lowndes, by Bohn. "A superb edition of this poem was printed in Scotland at the Roman Catholic press established in Holyrood House." Macaulay.

Rules of the Schools of the Savoy. 1 folio half-sheet, 1687

See Clarke's Life of James II., vol. ii. pp. 79, 80; Lingard's History, vol. x. p. 220; Macaulay, vol. ii. p. 98; Bacon's Advancement of Learning, bk. i., Works (Philosophical), ed. by Ellis and Spedding, vol. iii. p. 300; and Chateaubriand's Beauties of Christianity, translated by Kett, vol. iii. pp. 208-9. But Mariana, the Spanish historian, denies their merits in the government of the schools. See the History of the Jesuits [by John Poynder], vol. ii. pp. 282. Martelière denounced their education in The Argument for the University of Paris against the Jesuits. 4to Lond. 1689. It is stated in the History of King William the Third (by David Jones) 1702, p. 95, that these schools gave occasion to Dr. Tenison's "erecting his Free School at St. Martin's, adorn'd with a choice library." Cf. Scott's Notes on "The Hind and the Panther," p. 256, and Reresby's Memoirs, pp. 245-6.

✠ Institutions of the Congregation of the Oratory at St. Marie's, in Vallicella, within the City of Rome, founded by St. Philip Nerius, with memorable sayings and advices of St. Philip. Sm. 8vo Oxford 1687.

At the end is added, "Concerning the Institution of the Society of Jesus." On the Oratory, see Baronius, Annal. Eccles. tom. i. p. 555.

A Letter containing Reflections on "Good Advice to the Church of England. [No. 37.] 4to Lond. 1687

Catherine Lamb's Dr. Tenison's Invisible Evidence Unclouded. 4to Lond. 1688

The Great Necessity of Unity and Peace among all Protestants, and the bloody principles of the Papists made manifest. By the most eminently pious and learned Bishop Ussher, sometime Lord Primate of Ireland. 4to 1688

Not in the new edition of his Works. Cf. Stillingfleet, Sermon xiii. Works, vol. i. p. 192.

T. C. D. The History of the Inquisition as it is exercised at Goa. Written in French by the ingenious Monsieur Dellon, who laboured five years under those severities. With an account of his Deliverance. Translated into English. Printed for James Knapton. pp. 70, and Contents 1 page. Prefatory Matter pp. 6. 4to Lond. 1688

This is not mentioned by Gee or Peck. It was translated by Henry Dodwell. See his curious account of it and of the Preface which the publisher was compelled to prefix to it, in the Appendix to D'Oyley's Life of Sancroft, vol. ii. pp. 123-125, 130, 131.

S. Dellon was a physician, born 1649; who travelled as a medical man in several commercial voyages. In 1674 he was seized by the Inquisition, and condemned to five years' slavery in the Portuguese gallies. In 1709 were published in three vols. 12mo his "Voyages aux Indes Orientales, avec sa relation de l'Inquisition de Goa, augmentés de diverses pièces curieuses, et de l'histoire des dieux qu' adorent les gentiles des Indes." But there was an earlier edition of this work, from which the present tract was translated, 2 vols. 8vo, Paris [1685]. Reprinted at Hull, 1812. New edition, with an appendix, containing an account of the escape of Archibald Bower, one of the Inquisitors from the Inquisition at Macerata in Italy. 8vo Lond. 1815. Wharton received five guineas from the bookseller (Knapton) for this translation. Life of Sancroft, ibid. p. 132. J. H. T. With regard to Bower's Letters see Chalmers' Biogr. Dictionary, and Bp. Douglas's Select Works, 4to 1820.

✠ A Defence of the Doctrine and Holy Rites of the Roman Catholic Church, from the calumnies and cavils of Dr. Burnet's Mystery of Iniquity Unveiled. By John Warner, Soc. Jesu. The second edition. 8vo Lond. 1688.

See also Anti-Haman &c. *ut supra*, p. 252.

Important Considerations which ought to move all true and sound Catholics who are not wholly Jesuited. 4to Lond. 1688

Compare The Epistle Congratulatory of Lysimachus Nicanor of the Society of Jesus to the Covenanters of Scotland, 4to Oxf. 1684; and the Letters of Bishop Bramhall to Archbishop Ussher, and of Sir William Boswell to Archbishop Laud in Archbishop Ussher's Life by Parr, folio Lond. 1686, p. 611, and Appendix p. 27. These Letters are annexed to *The Prophecy* of Archbishop Ussher &c., 4to 1687. "From these and other documents it is clear that the Church of Rome has had its hidden adherents, and even missionaries, not only among the Puritans and Independents of former days, but also in our very churches; as was the case with Heth in Elizabeth's reign, with Goodman, Bishop of Gloucester, whom the honest zeal of Archbishop Laud discovered, to say nothing of the notorious case of Parker, Bishop of Oxford, in James the Second's time." Christian Remembrancer.

In pt. i. p. 63, it should have been stated that the first part of Foxes and Firebrands was written by Dr. John Nalson, who is also said to have been the author of a Letter from a Jesuit, *ut supra*, pt. i. p. 5, and to have been imprisoned by the House of Commons for writing it. See an Address to the Freemen and Freeholders of the Nation [by Edmund Bohun], pt. ii. pp. 12 and 26, and also the Commons' Journals.

Three Letters from a Jesuit at Liége to a Jesuit at Fribourg, giving an Account of the Happy Progress of Religion in England. 4to 1688

In Somers Tracts, vol. i. pp. 248-51. Cf. A Short and True Account of the Several Advances &c., Pt. i. p. 181. Fribourg is well known as the stronghold of the Jesuits in Switzerland.

In the first letter it is said that at an interview one of the society had with his Majesty (James II.) he declared, "that he would either convert England or die a martyr; and that he would rather die to-morrow, that conversion wrought, than reign fifty years without that, in happiness and prosperity." "Bishop Burnet's account [Hist. of his Own Time, vol. i. p. 711] of the 'famous letter of the Jesuits of Liége to the Jesuits of Fribourg,' which Dycvelt showed the King, is no longer worth notice, that 'letter' being a recognised and branded fabrication." Mackintosh's Hist. of Engl. vol. viii. p. 113. Cf. Scott's Notes on The Hind and the Panther, p. 256.

For other tracts relating to the Jesuits see Pt. i. pp. 4-9, and Chap. III. Also Biogr. Brit. s.v. Morton, and Bibliographical Notices of

Church Libraries at Turton and Gorton, bequeathed by Humphrey Chetham, p. 194 sqq.; Reliquiæ Hearnianæ, note by Bliss, vol. i. pp. 26, 27; Southey's Common Place Book, 4th ser. p. 671. For their general history see Hospiniani Hist. Jesuitica, &c.; Item de eorum dolis, fraudibus, imposturis, &c., folio, Tiguri, 1670; and Lucii Hist. Jesuitica, 4to 1627. I have already given a list of tracts relating to the Powder Plot, to which may be added the rare publications of Edward Stephens, of which Bliss has given as perfect a catalogue as possible; (Reliquiæ Hearnianæ, vol. i. p. 59;) Great Brittaine's Great Deliverance from the great danger of the Popish Powder, by William Leigh, B.D., 1606, 12mo, an eloquent Sermon dedicated to Sir Peter Leigh, Knight, of Lyme, Cheshire; and Defensio Ecclesiæ Anglicanæ contra M. Anton. de Dominis, Archiep. Spalat. Injurias, Auctore Ric. Crakanthorp, Lond. 1625 (Libr. of Anglo-Catholic Theology, 1847). Here are subjoined some references to writers on the Popish Plot in the reign of Charles II., with the origination of which the Jesuits were charged by Titus Oates, viz.: North's Examen, Fox's Hist. of James II., Dryden's Absalom and Achitophel, with Scott's notes, vol. ix. p. 259 sq.; his Notes to Peveril of the Peak; Macaulay, vol. i. p. 238; State Trials reviewed by Phillips, 8vo 1826. But the fullest account of the Plot is found in an Historical Narrative &c., by William Eusebius Andrews, 1818, 8vo; nor can we omit Florus Anglo-Bavaricus, seu Historia Fundationis Collegii Anglorum Soc. Jesu Leodii quæ sub Maximiliano et Maria Bavariæ Ducibus ad hæc tempora gesta sunt complectens, et in nupera procella contra Catholicos et præsertim Patres Soc. Jesu in Anglia a Tito Oate excitata, paucis exponens. Leodii 1685. Among the satirical pieces of the time is, A Narrative of the Old Plot, No. 81 of the Halliwell Collection.

Popish Errors exposed in a Selection of Texts of Scripture, with notes and comments. 1688

Reprinted by Rev. T. Young, 12mo Lond. 1823. Francis Veron, who had a conference with the learned Bochart and other Huguenots, was of opinion that the Protestants should be obliged to prove their tenets by plain passages of Scripture, without being allowed the liberty of illustrating these passages. See Mosheim, Cent. xvii. § ii. ch. i.

✠ Errata to the Protestant Bible, or the Truth of the English Translations examined by T[homas] W[ard]. 4to Lond. 1688 *B. L.*

✠ Speech in the Upper House of Parliament, 1555, by N. Heath, Abp. of York, on occasion of the Supremacy, with proofs from Scripture and the Fathers that there is no Salvation out of the Catholic Church. [Somers Tracts, col. iii. vol. i.] 12mo Lond. 1688 *B. L.*

Cf. p. 237, and Lord Castlemain's Apology, p. 345 sqq.

The accomplishment of the Scripture Prophecies; or the approaching deliverance of the Church: proving that the Papacy is the Antichristian Kingdom; and that that Kingdom is not far from its ruin. Engl. from the French of Peter Jurieu. 8vo Lond. 1687 *B. L.*

The Continuation of the Accomplishment of Scripture Prophecies, in a large deduction of historical Evidences. By P. J. 8vo Lond. 1688

"Meliora nunc," says Muratori, "Deo juvante, sapimus, et ejusmodi ridendas Prophetias dimisimus phantasticis quibusdam hominibus extra Ecclesiæ castra militantibus, qualis ævo nostro fuit Calvinista Jurieu." Antiquit. Ital. Medii Ævi. Dissert. xliv. Cf. Bayle's Dictionary, s.v. Leo the Great.

"A special evidence," says Hammond, "which most men have used, to conclude the papacy to be ὁ 'Αντίχριστος, the Antichrist, is this, that the Pope exalteth himself above all that is called God, *i.e.*, the kings of the earth." *Of Resisting the Lawful Magistrate.* Works, vol. i. tom. ii. p. 68.

✠ The Life of St. Francis Xavier, of the Society of Jesus, Apostle of the Indies and of Japan. Written in French by Father Dominick Bohours, of the same Society. Translated into English by Mr. Dryden. 8vo Lond. 1688 C. L.

Reprinted, Dublin, 1812. "The creed and the character of Catholic faith are now so much forgotten among us (popularly speaking) that in reading the 'Life of Xavier,' the Protestant finds himself in a new and enchanted land. The motives, and the incidents and the doctrines, are alike new to him, and, indeed, occasionally form a strange contrast among themselves. There are few who can read, without a sentiment of admiration, the heroic devotion with which, from the highest principle of duty, Xavier exposes himself to hardship, to danger, to death itself, that he may win souls to the Christian faith." Scott's Life of Dryden, p. 337.

"But now," observes Bp. Hall; (*No peace with Rome*, 1634, fol. sec. 18.) "this multipresence doth not belong to Christ only. St. Xavier, in our age, one of Loyola's brood, was seen, at once, both in the ship and in the boat. Tursellian reports it. Unto this fabulous saint, and his fellow-fabuler the reporter, I cannot devise to set a better match, than that Plautine Amphitrio: 'Darest thou say, thou fond slave, that which never man yet saw, nor indeed can be done, that one man should, at the same time, be in two places at once?'" Plaut. Amphit. Act ii.

For other authorities besides Bouhours and Torsellini see Œttinger, Bibliographie Biographique. Before Xavier's reputed miracles had co-operated with "efficacy of doctrine," or the conciliation of the prejudices of idolaters, it is supposed that this illustrious missionary and negotiator, some of whose enterprizes were directed not less immediately to promote the temporal power of Portugal than the ecclesiastical sovereignty of Rome, owed his first success to the exhibition of a beautiful picture of the Virgin, "imago tristium lætorumque"! Cf. Southey's Vindiciæ Ecclesiæ Anglicanæ, p. 467.

CHAP. XL.

A List of the Popish Writers.

Several persons mentioned in this and the following list were dead before the time of King James II. But their works being then reprinted, they were thereby, as it were, raised from the dead and brought upon the stage again. I have marked the most of them dead with an *Asterisk*. And by turning to the several numbers in this Catalogue (as directed by the figures set after their names) the reader may quickly see what share each person had in the contest. *Peck*. The names without a number before them are those of the authors of the additional Tracts enumerated at the end of each chapter and not contained in Peck's original List, and the references regarding those names are to the pages of this work. — Ed.

Ayray, James (*a Franciscan*), p. 455. [Dodd, edit. 1742, vol. iii. p. 490.]

Barclay, John, p. 389 n. [Dodd, vol. ii. p. 423. Biogr. Brit.. Chalmers.]

Bassett, Joshua, *master of* Sydney C. C., 126 n.

Bastide, Marc Antoine de la, 73 n, 84.

1. Betham, John, *doctor of* Sorbon [chaplain to James II. Dodd, vol. iii. p. 485.]

Bix, Angel (*a Franciscan*), p. 455 n.

Blake, James (*a Jesuit*), p. 455.

Bohours., Father Dominick, pp. 420, 479. [Biographie Universelle.]

Boileau, James, 131, 353, 393, pp. 340 n, 358. [Niceron, voll. 10-20.]

2. Bossuet, James Benigne (*Bishop first of* Condom, *then of* Meaux), 73 n, 76 n, 79 n, 203 n, 275 n, pp. 244, 255. [Chalmers, B.D.

On the conversions effected by him see The Christian Observer, March, 1823. "Memoir of Bossuet, Bishop of Meaux."]

3. C.... J.... 328, 329, 423. [The same as the author named in No. 9.]

4. C.... R.... 219. [Written by T. K., and now publ. by R. C.]

Candish, Thomas, p. 422 n.

Carier, Dr. Benjamin, p. 474 n. [Wood's Fasti Oxon. vol. i. col. 154.]

5. Carre, Thomas (*confessor of* Sion), 350 n.

*Champ or Champney, Anthony, p. 212. [Dodd, vol. iii. p. 81.]

6.*Charles II., 12 n, 13 n, pp. 251, 252.

7. Clenche [Will.], 229. [Macaulay, vol. ii. p. 110.]

Codrington, Thomas, p. 455. [Dodd, vol. iii. p. 484.]

Collins, William, p. 381 n.

Constable, John, p. 215.

Corker, James (*a Benedictine*), p. 457 n. [Dodd, vol. iii. p. 488. Lingard, vol. x. p. 294.]

8. Cressy, Serenus (*a Benedictine, sometime Bishop of* Laughlin.) 432. [Hugh Paulin de Cressy. Serenus was the name taken at his monastic profession. See pt. i. pp. 132, 157-8 n, 222-24, 422, 423, and Chalmers.]

9. Crosse, J. (*a Grey Friar*), 413. [Dodd, vol. iii. p. 490. Chaplain to K. James II.]

D.... J.... p. 385.

10. Darrel, William (*a Jesuit*), 46, 114? 258 n, pp. 77, 454. [De Bacquer, vol. iii. p. 266.]

11. Deane, Thomas, 170, 171 n. [Dodd, vol. iii. p. 462.]

Dimock, James, p. 385, 3rd title, printed also London, 12mo, 1687.

12. Dormer, John (*a Jesuit*), 408, 409, 410, p. 385, 3rd title. [Oliver's Biography of the Society of Jesus, 1845, 8vo. De Bacquer, vol. iv. p. 183.]

13. Dryden, John, *Esq.*, 15. See p. 474 n, and Dodd, vol. iii. p. 459. [On his conversion see also Johnson's, Malone's and Scott's Lives, Macaulay, vol. ii. p. 197, and Bodleian Library Catalogue, s.v. Bays, and R. (J.) a convert of Mr. Bays.]

Dufour, Louis, 295, p. 385 n.

14. Ellis, Philip (*a Benedictine*), 400, 405. [Dodd, vol. iii. p. 467. One of the chaplains to the Chapel Royal. "Episcopus Aureliopolis."

After the Revolution Bishop of Segni in Italy. See also Lingard, vol. x. p. 296.]

15. G. . . . E. . . . 253.

16. G. . . . T. . . . 446.

17. G. . . . W. . . . 284.

18. Giffard, Bonaventure, D.D. (*a secular priest*), 412. [Dodd, vol. iii. p. 469. "Episcopus Madaurensis" in 1687. Obtained a Bull of Confirmation for a Community of English Nuns founded in Germany, who were brought into England by Catherine of Braganza, and still exist in York, in Hulme, Manchester, and in Ireland. Communicated by the Rev. Canon Toole.]

19. Godden, Thomas. See Chap. VII. 223 n, 446, and pp. 423 n, 453.

20. Goodall, Edward (*Vicar of* Prescot in Lancashire), 188. [Dodd, vol. iii. p. 460.]

Gother. See L. . . . J. . . .

H. . . . H. . . . (*a Jesuit*), p. 452.

Hall, William (*a Carthusian*), p. 454, 455 n.

Heath, Nicholas (*Archbishop of York*), p. 479. [Collier's Eccles. Hist.]

21.*Henry VIII, 417 n.

22. Huddlestone, John and Richard (*Benedictines*), 12 n. [Dodd, vol. iii. p. 490.]

Humberstone, Henry (*a Jesuit*), p. 455. [Oliver. De Bacquer, vol. iv. p. 308.]

J. . . . C. . . . 423.

23. J. . . . F. . . . 420.

Jenks, Sylvester, p. 455 n. [Dodd, vol. iii. p. 486.]

Johnston, Joseph (*a Benedictine*), 76, 79, 81.

24. K. . . . T. . . . 219.

25. Keepe, Henry, M.D., 349. [Dodd, vol. iii. p. 463. Author of Monumenta Westmonasteriensia.]

26. L. . . . J. . . . 51 n, 53, 56, 58, 60, 63, 72, 126 n, 132, 144 n, 146 n, 209 n. 238 n, 343, p. 389. [Joannes Lisboensis, or John Gother. Dodd, vol. iii. p. 482. "Gother, whom, on account of the purity and harmony of his language, Dryden pronounced a perfect master of English style." Lingard, vol. x. p. 226.]

Levison, Richard (*a Jesuit*), p. 455. [De Bacquer, vol. iii. p. 451.]

Lewgar, John, pp. 213, 242. [Athen. Oxon. vol. ii. col. 354. Dodd, vol. iii. p. 264.]

Leyburn, John (*Bishop*), p. 250. [Dodd, vol. iii. pp. 466, 467.]
27.*Lipsius, Justus, 334. [General Dict. Hist. and Crit. Chalmers.]
28. M'C. . . . J. . . . 423.
29. Maimbourg, Lewis (*a Jesuit*), p. 284 n, No. 284. [General Dict. Chalmers. De Bacquer, vol. iv. p. 371. In 1682 he had to leave the Society in consequence of having written in favour of the propositions of the Assembly of the French Clergy. At the time of his death he was engaged in writing a treatise on the "English Schism."]
30. Manby, Peter (*sometime Dean of* Derry), 128 n, 418. [Oliver, p. 258.]
31. Marsh, W. (*a Benedictine*), 407. [Dodd, vol. iii. p. 318.]
32. Meredith, Edward, 90 n, 102, 351. [Dodd, vol. iii. p. 465. He wrote Some Remarks upon Johnson's Julian the Apostate, &c.]
33. Mumford [James], 256 n, 433, pp. 306, 406. [Dodd, vol. iii. p. 321.]
34. N. . . . N. . . . 2, 3, p. 454. The writers who adopted this signature are mentioned in p. 473.
Nelson, Lady Theophila, 305 n.
35. Nicholson Francis (*M.A. of* University College, Oxon), 282 n.
Persall, John (*a Jesuit*), p. 455. [Dodd, vol. iii. p. 494.]
36. Pulton, Andrew (*a Jesuit, one of the masters in the Jesuits' School in the* Savoy), 99, 100, 104, 106 n, pp. 140, 321. See also Athen. Oxon. vol. ii. col. 934. [Dodd, vol. iii. p. 493. Jones's Hist. of K.William III, p. 96, where an abstract is given of this Account, No. 100.]
37. Sabran, Lewis (*a Jesuit*), 120 n., 123, 317 n., 318, 320, 322, 324, 411, 415 n, p. 147.
38. Sergeant, John (*a secular priest*), 86 n, 88, 91 n, 93, 94 n, pp. 62, 176, 326, 438 containing S's Letter to the Continuator, 443.
Scarisbrike, Edward (*a Jesuit*), p. 456 n. [De Bacquer. He was of a Lancashire family.]
39. Schelstrate, Emmanuel (*a Prefect of the* Vatican Library), 175 n. [Rose's Biogr. Dict.]
40. Sclater, Edward (*sometime minister of* Putney, 130 n. ["It will perhaps interest you to know that Sclater's Recantation is printed in the volume of the Christian Observer for 1843, pp. 781 &c., with some appropriate observations by the then editor and proprietor of that journal, whose attention I called to it, and pointed

out Horneck's very rare account of Sclater's abjuration of Popery to him." Tho. Hartwell Horne to the Editor of this Catalogue.]

Spencer, John (*a Jesuit*), pp. 173, 447. [Dodd, vol. iii. p. 312.]

Talbot, Peter (*Roman Catholic Abp. of Dublin*), pp. 212 n, 241.

Touchet, George (*a Benedictine*), p. 271. [Dodd, vol. iii. p. 493.]

41.*Turbervil, Henry (*a priest*), 453 n, p. 447. [Dodd, vol. iii. p. 302.]

42. W. . . . J. . . . 98.

43. W. . . . T. . . . 173.

44. Walker, Obadiah (*Master of* University College, Oxon), 163 n, 163 n, 167, 189, 190, 191, 192, 193, 267, 279, 282, p. 327. [Dodd, vol. iii. p. 454.]

Walsh, Peter (*a learned Irish Franciscan*), pp. 4, 193, 261, 289, 290, 474. [Dodd, vol. iii. p. 323.]

45. Ward T[homas] (a Roman *Catholic soldier*), 109 n, 116, 118 n, 173 n, 174 n, 214 n, p. 247, 360. [Dodd, vol. iii. p. 459. Lingard, vol. x. p. 226. Life prefixed to his Controversy with Mr. Ritschel, Manchester, 1819, 8vo.]

Warner, John (*a Jesuit*), p. 476. [Dodd, vol. iii. p. 491.]

46. Webster . . . . . (of Lynne), 184 n.

47. Woodhead, Abraham (of University College, Oxon), 162, 163 n, 167, 189, 190, 191 n, 192, 193, 208 n, 267, 279, 282 n, 303, 350, pp. 385, 432. [Dodd, vol. iii. p. 266. Chalmers. The Life prefixed to the third part of his Ancient Church Government, and to the Paraphrase and Annot. upon all the Epistles of St. Paul, in which he was jointly concerned with Dr. Allestree and Ob. Walker.]

48. Worsley, Edward (*a Jesuit*), pp. 219, 220, 251, 380 n, 443 n. [Oliver. "Born in Lancashire."]

49. York, *Duchess of*, 13. [p. 253, Lingard, vol. ix. p. 195.]

With many others whose names (not being set to their works) I am not yet able to recover. *Peck.*

CHAP. XLI.

A List of the Protestant Writers.

1. Aldrich, Henry, D.D. (*Canon of* Christ's Church, Oxon.), 281 n. 283. [Biogr. Brit. Hawkins's Hist. of Music. Burnet's Own Times. Birch's Tillotson. Nichols's Atterbury's Letters, vol. i. pp. 29, 35, 96, 114, 123, 189, 481. Ath. Oxon., vol. ii. p. 1055.]
2. Allix, Peter [D.D., Minister of Charenton in France, and father of Peter Allix, Dean of Ely], 271 n, 313, 352, pp. 388, 393. [Biogr. Brit. Biogr. Universelle.]
3. Altham, Michael, M.A. (*Vicar of* Latton in Essex). [Fasti Oxon., vol. ii. p. 384.] He appears to have been of a Lancashire family. See Morant's Essex, vol. ii. pp. 488, 489; 148 n, 211 n, 212, 425.

Annesley, Arthur, Earl of Anglesey, p. 382 n. [Biogr. Brit. Chalmers.]

4. Ashwell, George, B.D. [Rector of Hanwell, near Banbury, 455. [Biogr. Brit. Chalmers.]
5. Assheton, Will., D.D. (*Rector of* Beckenham in Kent, son of Will. Assheton, Rector of Middleton, Lanc.), 136 n, 137, 139, 140, 141. [Life of Dr. Assheton, by Watts, 8vo 1714. Biogr. Brit. Chalmers.]
6. Atterbury Fr., (*Student of* Christ's Church) [Bp. of Rochester], 168. [Chalmers. Cattermole's Literature of the Church of England.]

Bacon, Nathaniel, p. 159.

7. Bambridge, Tho., D.D. (*Fellow of* T. C. C.), 127 n.
8. Banckes, Matthew, 451.
9. Barlow, Tho. (*Bp. of* Lincoln), descended from the ancient family of Barlow-Moore in Lancashire, 201 n, and p. 425. [Biogr. Brit. Chalmers.]

Barrow, Isaac, D.D., pp. 28 n, 245. Life prefixed to his Works, edited by the Rev. Alexander Napier, Cambridge, 1859.

Bastide, Marc Antoine de la, 84, p. 112.

Beverley, Thomas, p. 389.

Blackerly, Samuel, p. 72.

Bolde, Samuel, 220 n.

10. Bolieu, rather Beaulieu, Luke (*Chaplain to* the Lord Chancellor Jefferies) [Prebendary of Gloucester], 216 n.
Boyle, Hon. Robert, 202 n.
11. Bradford (John) (*sometime Minister of* St. Sepulchre's), 298. [Biogr. Brit. Life and Letters by Stephenson. Life prefixed to his Writings, ed. for the Parker Society. A native of Manchester.]
12. Brampton, John (*Lecturer of* St. Martin's, Ludgate), 391, 392 n.
Brevint, Daniel, D.D., pp. 379 n, 380.
13. Browne, Tho. D.D. (*Fellow of* St. John's C. C.) 183 n, p. 217. [Republic of Letters, vol. vi.]
Bruzeau, p. 387.
Bull, George, *Bp. of* St. David's, p. 246. [Cattermole.]
14. Burnet, Gilbert D.D. [*Bp. of* Salisbury], 23, 172 n, 182 n, 429, pp. 8 (13th title), 19, 65, 80, 81, 82, 92, 120, 158 (Bedell and Cohan), 242, 253. [Biogr. Brit. and Life by Flexman, prefixed to his History of his Own Times. Chalmers. Sir W. Scott's Notes on Dryden's Hind and Panther, vol. x. p. 267 sq.]
Cade, William, p. 272.
15. Case (Henry), 24, 41 n, 226 n.
16. Cave, Will. (*Canon of* Windsor), 9, 161, p. 274. [Biogr. Brit. Chalmers.]
Cawley, William, p. 69.
17.*Chillingworth (Will.), M.A., 441 n, pp. 242 n, 243, 248, 306. [Life by Birch, prefixed to his Works, tenth edition, folio 1742, and repr. Oxford 1838. Cattermole.]
18. Claget, Nich. M.A., 682 n. [Biogr. Brit. Chalmers.]
19. Claget, Will. D.D. (*late preacher to the Society of* Gray's Inn), 7, 61, 71, 161 n, 164, 174, 272, 274, 299, 312, 326, 335, 360, 365, p. 172 (fourth title reprinted in Cardwell's Enchirid. Anti-Romanum), 253, 396. [Biogr. Brit. Chalmers. Life prefixed to his Sermons.]
Clarendon, Edward Earl of, p. 157, 423.
20. Claude, John (*minister of* Charenton in France), 204, 205 n, 206, 472 n, p. 123. [Chalmers. General Dict. Hist. and Crit.]
21. Coles, Gilbert D.D. (*fellow of* Winchester College), 1 n.
22. Comber, Tho. D.D. (*precentor of* York), 143, 347 n, pp. 164, 233, 286 n, 326 n. [Memoirs by T. Comber, 1800, 8vo. Chalmers.]

Cosin, John (*Bp. of* Durham), 381 n, 470 n.

23.*Cranmer, Tho. D.D. (*sometime Abp. of* Canterbury), 259. [Strype's Memorials. Fox reprinted in Wordsworth's E. B., in Richmond's Fathers, and in Parker Soc. ed. of Cranmer on the Lord's Supper; Lives by Todd and Gilpin; Jenkyns's Preface; and Biogr. Notice prefixed to his Remains and Letters, Parker Soc.]

24. Cressner, A. . . . (*schoolmaster in* Long-acre), 108.

Croft, Herbert (*Lord Bp. of* Hereford), p. 97, 321 n, 432.

25. Cudworth (John), B.D. (*Fellow of* Trinity Coll. Oxon.), 454 n.

26. Dalhusius (J. H.) (*inspector of the Churches in the County of* Weedon on the Rhine), 457.

Davison, Thomas, M.A. (*Presbyter at* Balmbrough), p. 426, 436.

Derby, Charles [Seventh] Earl of, pp. 3 n, 320.

Dillingham, William, D.D. (*Rector of* Woodhill, Bedfordshire), p. 135.

27. Dodwell, Henry, M.A. (Camden *Professor of History in* Oxon.), 426. [Biogr. Brit. Chalmers. Life by Brokesby.]

Earbery, Matthew (*a Nonjuror*, see Lathbury, ch. vii.), p. 216.

Edward VI., p. 277. "When three swords were delivered at his Coronation unto him, as King of England, France and Ireland, he said, There was yet another sword to be delivered unto him. Whereat when the Lords marvelled, he said, I mean the sacred Bible, which is the sword of the Spirit, without which we are nothing, neither can doe anything." [Balæus in Centuriis. Camden's Remaines. Wise Speeches.]

Egane, Antony (*late Confessor General of the Kingdom of* Ireland), p. 344.

28. Ellis, Clement, M.A. (*Rector of* Kirkby in Nottinghamshire), 87 n, 89, 221. [Chalmers. Veneer's Account of his Life and Writings prefixed to "The Scripture Catechism." Cattermole. Neither he nor Watt mentions these controversial tracts.]

Episcopius, Simon, p. 241. [Life by Calder. Chalmers.]

Falkland. Lucius, Lord, p. 157. In Hammond's Works, vol. ii. pp. 561-566, 648-696, 704-708. See Warburton's Julian, Introd. vii. Lady Theresa Lewis's Lives from the Clarendon Gallery, vol. i.

Felgate, S., p. 245, (*Rector of* Mytton, Yorkshire.)

29. Fell, John (*Bp. of* Oxon.), 456 n. [Biogr. Brit. Chalmers.]

30. Fleetwood, Will., M.A. (*Fellow of* King's Coll. Cambridge), 330 n. [Life prefixed to his Works. Biogr. Brit. Chalmers.]

31. Fowler, Edward, D.D. (*Rector of* St. Giles's, Cripplegate, *Bp. of* Gloucester), 238, 357, 375, p. 332. [Biogr. Brit. Chalmers. Macaulay's History, vol. ii. p. 344. Author of "The Design of Christianity."]

32. Freeman, Samuel, D.D. (*Rector of* St. Anne, Aldersgate), 200 n, 339, 354, 380, 381.

Fuller, Samuel, *S. T. P.* of Cambridge (one of K. William's *Chaplains*), p. 214.

Fullwood, Francis, D.D., p. 273 n.

Gardiner, Samuel, 212 n.

33. Gascarth, John, M.A. *S. T. P.* of Cambridge (*Rector of* All Hallows, Barking), 389, 390.

34. Gee, Edward, M.A. (*Rector of* S. Benedict, Paul's Wharf), 131 n, 235, 259 n, 319, 321, 323 n, 325, 382, 383, 384, 439, p. 63. [He was one of K. William's *Chaplains*. See Mackintosh's History of England, continued by Wallace, vol. viii. p. 280.]

Gilbert, Claudius (*Minister of* Belfast), p. 119.

35. Gilbert, John, M.A. (*Vicar of* S. John Baptist's, Peterborough), 77 n.

36. Giles, William (a Protestant footman), 121 n.

37. Goodman, John (*Archdeacon of* Middlesex), 270 n.

•38. Goodwin [Thomas] (*a Dissenter*), 21, p. 253.

39. Gourdon of Scotland, 421.

Grascome, Samuel, p. 19. [Author also of "Certamen Religiosum", 1704, 8vo. A Nonjuror, see Lathbury, p. 127.]

40. Gregory, Francis, D.D., p. 326, 447 n, 448 n.

41. Grove, Robert, D.D. (*Rector of* S. Andrew's, Undershaft, afterwards *Bp. of* Chichester), 255 n, 368 n.

*Gunning, Peter, p. 172 n. [Wood's Athen. Oxon. col. 766. Chalmers. Cf. No. 156.]

42. H. . . . 107 n, 108, 424.

Halifax, George Savile, Marquis of, 39 n, p. 85 n. [Walpole's Royal and Noble Authors.]

*Hall, J. (*Bp. of* Norwich), p. 471. [Jones's Life and Times.]

43. Harrington, Mr. James, of Oxon., 351 n, p. 140 n.

44. Hartcliffe, John (*a Dissenter, master of* Merchant-Taylors *School*), 314 n. [Wilson's Hist. of Merchant-Taylors School.]

45. Hascard, Gregory, D.D. (*Dean of* Windsor and *Chaplain in Ordinary*), 180.
46. Hickes, George, D.D. (*Dean of* Worcester), 153 n, 327 n, pp. 26, 29, 260, 306, 376, 413. [Biogr. Brit. Chalmers.]
47. Hill, Samuel, M.A. (*Rector of* Kilmington in Somersetshire), 225 n, 231.
48. Hooper, George (*Dean of* Canterbury, *Bp. of* Bath and Wells), 195. [Chalmers. Nichols's Literary Anecdotes, iv. 567-74.]
49. Hutchinson, ... *Esq.*, 164 n.
James, Eleanor, p. 66. [Author of political broadsides (Nos. 984, 985, 987, 988, 989, 996, 997, in the Halliwell Collection), and the wife of a Bookseller and Publisher who was prosecuted.]
50.*James, Thomas (*first library keeper of* the Bodleian *library*), 440, p. 232. [Biogr. Brit. Chalmers. Oldys's British Librarian.]
51. Jenkin, Robert (*Fellow of* S. John's College C.), 207. [Chalmers. Nichols's Literary Anecdotes, vol. iv. pp. 241-248.]
Jenkins, *Sir* Leoline, 19, pp. 20, 253. [The letter referred to in p. 17 is in Somers Tracts, vol. i. Life by Wynne. Biogr. Brit. Williams's Eminent Welshmen. A great benefactor of Jesus College, Oxford, and Biographer of the Principal, Dr. Mansel.]
*Jewel, J. (*Bp. of* Sarum), p. 470 n. [Wordsworth. Life by Le Bas.]
52. Johnson, Mr. Samuel, 294, 316 n, p. 66. [Biogr. Brit. Chalmers. Life prefixed to his Works. "S. Johnson the whig . . . . . was a sort of Cobbett-Burke." Coleridge's Table Talk, 1851, p. 248.]
*Joscelin, John, p. 393. Archbishop Parker's chaplain.
53. Ironside, Gilbert, D.D. (*Bp. of* Bristol), 298 n.
Jurieu, Peter (*a Calvinist minister*), p. 119, 479. [Chalmers]
54. Ken, Thomas (*Bp. of* Bath and Wells), 419. [Biogr. Brit. Chalmers. Lives by Hawkins (repr. in his Prose Works ed. by Round, 1838, of which there is a review in Brit. Crit. vol. xxiv.), by Bowles, reviewed in Ed. Rev. 55; and by a Layman, J. L. Anderdon. See also Lathbury's Hist. of the Nonjurors, ch. vii.]
55. Kidder, Richard, M.A. (*Rector of* S. Martin's, Outwich), 309 n, 366, 385, 386, 422. [Biogr. Brit. Chalmers.]
56. King, William (*Chancellor of* S. Patrick's, *Abp. of* Dublin), 129 n, p. 245. [Harris's Ware. Biogr. Brit. Chalmers. Mason's Cathedral of St. Patrick.]

57. Larroque [Matthias de], 278 n. [Niceron, vol. xxi. Chalmers.]
Lindsay, John, 216, 217. [Lathbury, ch. ix.]
58. Linford, Thomas, M.A. (*Rector of* S. Edmund the King in Lombard-street), 254 n, 362, 388, 398.
Littleton, Adam, D.D., p. 283 n.
59. Lloyd, William, 4, pp. 62, 66, 181, 250, 254. [Chalmers. Lathbury, ch. vi. Died "Bishop of Worcester."]
Locke, John, p. 72 n. [See Fabricii Salut. Lux Evangelii, p. 504.]
60. Marsden, Thomas, M.A. (*Vicar of* Walton *in* Lancashire), 188 n.
Marvell, Andrew, p. 247. [Life by Capt. Thompson prefixed to his Works. Life in Coleridge's Biographia Borealis.]
*Mason, Francis, pp. 216 n, 217.
61. Maurice, Henry, D.D., 214 n. [Williams's Eminent Welshmen.]
Menzies, John, p. 241.
62. Milburne, Luke (*Minister of* Yarmouth), 184. [Chalmers.]
*Milton, John, p. 68 n. [See Johnson's Life.]
63. More, Henry, D.D. (*late Fellow of* Christ's *College*, Cambridge), 285 n, p. 432. [Biogr. Brit. Chalmers.]
Morley, George (*Bp. of* Winchester), pp. 18 n, 384, 385, 432 n.
Moulin, Peter du, 3, pp. 5, 181 n, 250. [Chalmers.]
64. N.... T.... 44.
65. Nelson, *Esq.*, Robert, 288 n. [Biogr. Brit. Chalmers. Nichols's L.A.]
Newcome, Henry, p. 396, 397 n.
O. T., p. 322. [In the Bodleian.]
Oates, Titus, p. 478. The Memoirs of Titus Oates. Lond. 1685, 4to.
Owen, John, p. 241. [Memoirs of his Life and Writings by W. Orme, prefixed to his Works ed. by T. Russell, 1826. This tract is in vol. xviii. Williams's Biogr. Dict. of Eminent Welshmen.]
66. Owen, Thankful (*a dissenter*). See No. 11 and p. 251.
67. Parker, Samuel, D.D. (*Bp. of* Oxon.), 19, 20 n, pp. 7, 275, 294. [Biogr. Brit. Chalmers. The Nonjuror of the same name, author of various learned works, Bibliotheca Biblica &c., was his son.]
68. Patrick, Mr. John (*preacher to the* Charterhouse), 66 n, 286, 332 n, p. 423, 424 n.
69. Patrick, Simon, D.D. (*Dean of* Peterborough), 198 n, 213, 262, 232, 255, 377, 378, p. 383 n. [Biogr. Brit. Chalmers. Works, 1858, Editor's Preface &c.]

70. Payne, William, M.A. (*Rector of* S. Mary, Matfallon, *alias* Whitechapel), 276 n, 301, 302, 359, 395, 396, p. 66, 3rd title.

71.*Peacock, Reginald (*sometime Bp. of* Chichester), 242 n. [Rose. Chalmers. Williams's E. W. Southey's Com.-Place Bk., 3rd s. 464-5.]

Pearson, John, D.D. (*Bp. of* Chester), p. 172. ("In 1657 he was associated with the learned Dr. Gunning in a public discussion with two popish divines; of this conference a garbled report was published at Paris;" Cattermole) p. 286 n.

72. Pelling, Edward (*Rector of* S. Martin's, Ludgate), 240 n, 297, 341, 342, 344, 345, p. 386.

73. Pendlebury, . . . (*a dissenter of* Lancashire), 293 n, 436.

74. Penn, William (*the Quaker*), 37, 38. [Biogr. Brit. and Life prefixed to his Works, 1726. Clarkson's Life. Chalmers.]

Petit, Edward, p. 405.

Pettus, Sir John, p. 205 (1st title). [Rose.]

75. Phillips, John (*nephew to* John Milton), 28. [Le Neve's Fasti, p. 13. Chalmers. Lives of Edward and John Philips, by Godwin.]

76. Placette, de la, 110, 111 n. [Niceron, vol. xi. Moreri. Chalmers.]

77.*Poynet, John (*sometime Bp. of* Winton), 296, 297 n. [Tanner. Chalmers.]

78. Prideaux, Humphrey, D.D. (*Prebendary of* Norwich), 187 n. [Biogr. Brit. Chalmers.]

R. J. R., p. 385. [Translator of Claude's Catholic Doctrine.]

79. Rawlet, John (*late preacher at* Newcastle-*upon*-Tyne), 431. [Rose.]

80. Resbury, Nathaniel (*minister of* Putney), 364, 397.

81.*Ridley, Nicholas (*sometime Bp. of* London), 296, 298. [Life by Gloucester Ridley. Fox. Wordsworth's Eccles. Biogr.]

Rodon, David de, p. 380. [Chalmers. Rose.]

Salgado, James, (*a convert from* Popery), p. 155. [Notes and Queries, 1st ser. 111, 284.]

Sall, Andrew (*a convert from* Popery), p. 176 n.

*Sanderson, Robert (*Bp. of* Lincoln), pp. 27, 205. [Life by Walton. Biogr. Dict. Chalmers. Cattermole. Life pref. to his Works, 1854.]

82. Saywell, William, D.D. (*master of* Jesus College, Cambridge), 156 n.

83. Scott, John, D.D. (*Rector of* S. Peter's Poor), 361, 393, 394. [Biogr. Brit. Chalmers.]

84. Seller, Abednego (*minister of* Plymouth), 55 n, 185 n. [Rose.]

85. Shaw, John (*Rector of* Whalton *in* Northumberland, and *preacher at* S. John's, Newcastle-upon-Tyne), 2, p. 249.

86. Sherlock, William, D.D. (*master of the* Temple), 54 n, 57, 59, 119, 122, 124, 152, 158, 166 n, 196 n, 197, 222, 244, 246, 306 n, 308, 337, 338, 353, 370, pp. 28, 29, 40. [Biogr. Brit. Chalmers. Lathbury, p. 115 sqq. Wallis on the Trinity, ed. by Flintoff, 1840, note 1, p. 255, by J. Crossley, Esq. This voluminous writer, author of "The Case of Resistance of the Supreme Powers" &c. (p. 29), and whose "conversion from Jacobitism" required in self-justification the publication of "The Case of Allegiance to Sovereign Powers stated" (p. 29) does not appear to have been of the same family as Richard Sherlock of Oxton, Cheshire, and Rector of Winwick. "I should be disposed to agree with you that there was no very near connection between the families of Sherlock of Oxton and of Southwark. The Rector of Winwick was, according to Keble, of humble parentage like his nephew Wilson, and as the poor and the Wilsons were his heirs, it may be inferred that any of his own name were remote relatives. He does not appear to have had issue, and probably was never married." F. R. Raines.]

Sidway, John, p. 346. [Translator of Tartello, The Pope's Cabinet.]

87. Smalridge, George, B.A. (*student of* Christ's Church), 165, 166 n. [Biogr. Brit. Chalmers. Campbell's Doctrine of a Future State, p. 175. Lathbury, p. 299.]

88.*Smith, Henry (*sometime lecturer of* S. Clement's Danes), 300 n. [Chalmers. Southey, *ut supra*.]

89. Smith, Thomas, D.D. (*Fellow of* Magdalen College, Oxon.), 331, 437 n. [Biogr. Brit. Chalmers. Letters in Ken's Prose Works.]

90. Squire, William, M.A., 449, 450.

91. Stanley, William, D.D., 8, p. 327 n. [Rose.]

Steward, Richard, D.D. (*Dean of* Westminster), p. 172.

92. Stillingfleet, Edward, D.D. (*Dean of* S. Paul's, *Bp. of* Worcester), 14, 17, 52 n, 85, 90, 92, 95, 97, 98, 155 n, 176 n, 310, 311, pp. 134, 174 n (2nd edit.), 296, 326, 421, 422. [Biogr. Brit. Chalmers. Life prefixed to his Works.]

93. Strange, *Sir* Roger le, 42 n, p. 5.

94. Stratford, Nicholas, D.D. (*Dean of* S. Asaph, *Bp. of* Chester), 70 n, 177 n, 178, 179, 230 n, 239, 247 n. [Ormerod. Hibbert-Ware.]

Sudbury, John, D.D.. p. 245. [Zouch's Works, vol. ii.]

95. Taylor, James, *gent.*, 67 n, 68, 340, 428.

96.*Taylor, Jeremy (*late Bp. of* Down *and* Connor), 442 n, 444, 445 n. [Harris's Ware. Biogr. Brit. Chalmers. Life by Bonney. Aris Wilmott's Biography.]

97. Tenison, Thomas, D.D. (*Vicar of* S. Martin's *in the field*), 101, 107, 110 n, 111, 117 n, 194, 304 n, 363, 374, p. 432. [Biogr. Brit. Chalmers. Memoirs of his Life and Times, 8vo, 1716.]

98. Thorpe, George, D.D. (*Canon of* Canterbury), 358.

99. Tillotson, John, D.D. (*Dean of* Canterbury), 125, pp. 205, 304, 305, 321. [Life by Birch. Chalmers. Wordsworth. Burnet's Funeral Sermon, 1694. Macaulay's History. Cattermole's Literature of the Church of England. "The Archbishop's Discourses against Popery were attacked, after his death, by a Romanist named Colson. This writer was answered by Lewis Atterbury, the brother of the famous Bishop of Rochester." In the anonymous Life in the 4th vol. of Wordsworth's E. B. mention is made of a pamphlet entituled, "Some Discourses upon Dr. Burnet and Dr. Tillotson," charging them with apostacy from their once avowed principle of non-resistance and passive obedience; and of "Reflections" upon the pamphlet by Burnet himself.]

Tong or Tongue, Dr. Esrael, p. 6 (2nd title). [Tong or Tongue, "Of Dr. Esráel, one of the most extraordinary persons of a very eventful time, the only biography that I am aware of is that contained in Wood's Athenæ, vol. ii. p. 671." Worthington's Diary, p. 196.]

100. Tully, George, M.A. (*preacher at* S. Nicholas in Newcastle), 268, 348 n, 372, 379. [Chalmers.]

Turner, John (*Fellow of* Christ's Coll. Cambridge), pp. 384, 396 n.

Twysden, *Sir* Roger, p. 205. [Chalmers. Rose.]

*Ussher, James (*Abp. of* Armagh), pp. 403, 406, 425. [Life prefixed to his Works by Elrington. Biogr. Brit. Cattermole. Chalmers. Rose.]

Veil, C. M. du, p. 305. ["He was born a Jew, but afterwards embraced the Popish religion, which he at last renounced for the Protestant, and entered into the communion of the Church of England, whither he retired about 1679." Chalmers.]

Wadsworth, James (*a Jesuit that recanted*), pp. 158, 63, 64 n. [Bibliographiana, Manchester, 1817, 8vo.]

101. Wake, William, M.A. (*preacher to the society of* Gray's Inn, *Archbishop of* Canterbury), 22, 74, 78, 80, 83, 227 n, 280 n, 295 n, 315, 438, p. 294. [Biogr. Brit. Mosheim's Church History. Chalmers.]

102. Walker, Joseph, 84, 278 n, p. 385. [Translator of Bastide.]

Waller, Sir William, pp. 404 (Jetzer), 431. [Chalmers. Rose. Life prefixed to his "Divine Meditations," 1793, 1839.]

103.* Walsingham, *Sir* Francis, 36. [Biogr. Brit. Chalmers.]

104. Wharton, Henry, M.A. (*Chaplain to Abp.* Sancroft), 115 n, 242, 269, 296, 336. [Life prefixed to his Sermons. Biogr. Brit. Chalmers. D'Oyly's Life of Sancroft. Ducarel's Hist. and Antiq. of Lambeth Palace, (Nichols's Bibl. Top. Brit. No. 27, pp. 63-67).]

105. Whitby, Daniel, D.D. (*præcentor of* Sarum), 260, 261, 265, 277, 346 n, pp. 69, 240, 384 n, 423. [Biogr. Brit. Chalmers.]

106. Whitfield, ... (*Fellow of* King's College, Cambridge), 186.

Williams, Daniel, pp. 214, 216. [Chalmers. Rose. Life by Defoe. Williams's Eminent Welshmen. He was the founder of the second Public Library in London.]

107. Williams, John, M.A. (*Rector of* S. Mildred's, Poultry). 5 n, 62, 64, 65, 69, 96, 145, 147, 150 n, 159, 199 n, 249 n, 251, 263, 364, 292, 356, 376, 387. [Chalmers. He died Bishop of Chichester.]

Woodroffe, Benjamin, 241 n.

With many others, whose names (not being set to their Works) I am not yet able to recover. Peck.

SUPPLEMENT.

It will have been seen that a considerable part of the Treatises here enumerated was collected and republished by Bishop Gibson, in three volumes in folio, 1738, with the appropriate title of *A Preservative against Popery*; and that this collection has recently been revised and edited by the Rev. John Cumming, D.D., in eighteen vols. 8vo, 1848-9. The first and second volumes folio (eleven volumes 8vo edit.) relate chiefly to doctrines; the design of the third is to prove from facts that the errors charged against the Papists are really held and maintained by them. To the second volume are appended four and to the third volume two general Discourses against Popery by Lloyd, Sherlock, Stillingfleet, &c.

The editor of the reprint states that "the references in the old and scarce edition of Gibson are so loose and often so inaccurate as to be almost useless. In this edition the Protestant reader will find references he may safely rely on, or very easily verify, and those alone who, like the editor, have taken a part in the Romish controversy, can appreciate the importance of such references." The eighteenth, or last volume, besides a table of the general contents of this collection of treatises, comprises a list, with biographical notices of [most of] the authors of the several treatises, as well as of the writers therein quoted or referred to; a list of the names of councils also quoted or referred to, and an alphabetical list of the principal councils, with the years when they were severally held. Both editions are accompanied by a copious general index to the principal matters contained in this most valuable *Bibliotheca Protestantium*.

GENERAL CONTENTS.

TIT. I. OF THE ENGLISH REFORMATION.

CHAP. I. *The Reformation vindicated on account of the necessity of it.*

Author.	*Title.*	*Folio.*	*Octavo.*	*Catal. No.*
1 Dr. Stratford	The necessity of reformation...........	vol. i. pp. 75	vol. i. pp. 164	177, 178
2 Dr. Clagett	Ch. of Rome before the Reformation	76-90	165-95	161
3 ———	Several captious queries	91-104	196-225	200
4 Dr. Burnet	(Antichristian) opposition of the Roman Church	105-32	226-89	429

CHAP. II. *The Reformation vindicated from the charge of Schism.*

5 Dr. Thorp	Unity of the Catholic Church	133-51	290-332	9
6 M. Altham	Vindication of the Church of England	152-79	333-89	148
7 Dr. Hickes	Apologet. vindic. of the Ch. of Engl.	180-214	vol. ii. pp. 1-81	153

CHAP. III. *The Reformation vindicated from the charge of Novelty.*

8 Dr. Hascard.........	Charge of Novelty upon the Church of England	215-26	82-108	180

CHAP. IV. *The Reformation vindicated from the charge of wanting a regular Ordination and Ministry.*

9 Dr. Burnet	Vindication of the ordinations of the Church of England	227-77	109-225	182

CHAP. V. *The Reformation vindicated from the charge of allowing the Marriage of the Clergy.*

10 H. Wharton	Treatise on celibacy of the clergy......	278-339	226-381	269
11 W. Payne	Texts examined, priests' celibacy.. ...	340-59	382-428	396

TIT. II. AGAINST THE DOCTRINE OF THE PAPAL SUPREMACY.

1 Dr. Lloyd	Papal supremacy; a novel doctrine...	2nd pt. pp. 5	vol. iii. pp. 3	4
2 Dr. Patrick	The texts examined, &c..............	6-25	8-52	377, 8
3 —— Resbury	The texts &c.; visibility of the Church	26-36	53-76	397

TIT. III. OF THE CATHOLICK CHURCH.

CHAP. I. *The True Notion of the Catholick Church.*

1 Dr. Freeman.........	A plain and familiar discourse	3rd pt. pp. 25	77-127	200
2 Dr. Sherlock.........	Nature, unity &c. of Catholick Church	26-43	128-65	196

CHAP. II. *Notes of the Church Examined and Confuted.*

3 Dr. Sherlock.........	A brief discourse conc. the notes &c.	44-71	166-226	353, 370
4 Dr. Freeman.........	Examination of Bellarmine's first note, catholicity	72-77	227-39	354

Author.	Title.	Folio.	Octavo.	Cata. No.
5 Dr. Patrick	Examination of Bellarmine's second note, antiquity	vol. i. pp. 78-83	vol. iii. pp. 240-51	355
6 Dr. Williams.........	—— third note, duration	84-89	252-63	356
7 Dr. Fowler	—— fourth note, amplitude...........	90-96	264-77	357
8 Dr. Thorp............	—— fifth note, succession of bishops	97-103	278-91	358
9 W. Payne	—— sixth note, agreement with the primitive Church	104-11	292-310	359
10 Dr. Clagett	—— seventh note, union of members	112-23	311-36	360
11 Dr. Scott	—— eighth note, sanctity of doctrine	124-33	337-59	361
12 T. Linford	—— ninth note, efficacy of doctrine .	133-40	360-77	362
13 Dr. Tenison	—— tenth note, holiness of life	141-46	vol. iv. pp. 13	363
14 N. Resbury	—— eleventh note, glory of miracles	146-59	14-38	364
15 Dr. Clagett	—— twelfth note, light of prophecy.	157-63	39-54	365
16 Dr. Kidder	—— thirteenth note, confession of adversaries	164-71	55-72	366
17 Dr. Stratford.........	—— fourteenth note, unhappy end of the Church's enemies	171-80	73-95	367
18 Dr. Grove	—— fifteenth note, temporal felicity	181-90	96-119	368

CHAP. III. *Safety of Salvation in the Protestant Church.*

Author.	Title.	Folio.	Octavo.	Cata. No.
19 C. Ellis	The Protestant resolved	191-217	120-84	221
20 L. Beaulieu	Protestants are on the safer side	218-29	185-213	216

CHAP. IV. *Danger of Salvation in the Church of Rome.*

Author.	Title.	Folio.	Octavo.	Cata. No.
21 Dr. Tillotson.........	Sermon on 1 Cor. iii. 15	230-36	214-30	

TIT. IV. THE POPISH RULE OF FAITH EXAMINED AND DISPROVED.

CHAP. I. *As resting upon the Doctrine of Infallibility.*

Author.	Title.	Folio.	Octavo.	Cata. No.
1 Dr. Tenison	Of a guide in matters of faith	4th pt. pp. 21	231-70	194
2 Dr. Maurice	Doubts concerning Roman infallibility	22-34	271-308	214
3 Dr. Sherlock.........	Discourse conc. a judge of controversy	35-74	309-81	306
4 Dr. Patrick	The pillar and ground of truth.........	75-122	vol. v. pp. 102	225
5 G. Tully	The texts &c. of infallibility	123-38	103-36	379

CHAP. II. *As resting upon the Authority of General Councils.*

Author.	Title.	Folio.	Octavo.	Cata. No.
6 Hutchinson and Dr. Clagett	Authority of councils and rule of faith	139-77	137-218	164

CHAP. III. *As resting upon Tradition.*

Author.	Title.	Folio.	Octavo.	Cata. No.
7 Dr. Stillingfleet......	Scripture and tradition compared......	178-89	219-44	92
8 Dr. Patrick	A discourse about tradition	190-205	245-80	324
9 Dr. Williams.........	Texts conc. insufficiency of Scripture	206-13	281-98	376

TIT. V. THE PROTESTANT RULE OF FAITH EXPLAINED AND VINDICATED.

CHAP. I. *By way of General Defence.*

Author.	Title.	Folio.	Octavo.	Cata. No.
1 Dr. Sherlock	Protestant resolution of faith	5th pt. pp. 15	299-326	164

Author.	*Title.*	*Folio.*	*Octavo.*	*Catal. No.*
Chap. II. *Upon the Head of Private Judgment.*				
2 Dr. Kidder	Judgment of private discretion.........	vol. i. pp. 16-24	vol v. pp. 327-45	422
Chap. III. *As resting upon the Authority of Scripture.*				
3 Dr. Stratford	People's right to read the H. Scripture	25-53	346-413	70
4 Dr. Grove	Protestant and Popish way of interpreting Scripture	54-79	vol. vi. pp. 62	255
5 Dr. Fowler	Texts conc. obscurity of the H. Scrip.	80-90	63-89	375
Tit. VI. The Worship of the Church of Rome justly Condemned.				
Chap. I. *As an Idolatrous Worship.*				
1 Dr. Sherlock	Discourse conc. the object of religious worship	vol. ii. pp. 26	90-147	337
2 Dr. Wake	Discourse conc. the nature of idolatry	27-54	148-214	22
Chap. II. *As to the Sacrifice of the Mass.*				
3 W. Payne	Discourse of the sacrifice of the mass	55-86	215-92	302
4 E. Gee & Dr. Kidder	Texts examined &c.	87-110	293-346	
Chap. III. *As in an Unknown Tongue.*				
5 Dr. Williams.........	Discourse conc. the celebration of divine service &c......................	111-28	347-87	266
6 Dr. Scott	Texts examined for prayers &c.........	129-56	vol. vii. pp. 70	394
Chap. IV. *As directing Prayers to Saints and Angels.*				
7 Dr. Freeman.........	Discourse conc. invocation of saints...	157-79	71-124	339
8 Dr. Clagett	Discourse conc. the worship of B. V. &c.	180-216	125-217	326
9 Dr. Freeman.........	Texts conc. the worship of angels &c.	217-43	218-80	381
Chap. V. *As directing the Worship of Images and Relics.*				
10 Dr. Whitby	Fallibility of the Church of Rome ...	244-80	281-372	346
11 Dr. Comber	Discourse conc. second council of Nice	281-304	373-400	347
12 E. Gee	Texts examined	305-12	vol. viii. pp. 30	382
Chap. VI. *As not answering the True Ends of Devotion.*				
13 Dr. Stanley	Discourse conc. the devotions of the Church of Rome......................	313-23	31-48	8
Tit. VII. The Popish Doctrine concerning the Sacraments Confuted.				
1 Dr. Stillingfleet......	No catholic tradition for the seven sacraments	2nd pt. pp. 18	98-133	97

Chap. I. *As to the number and nature of them.*

Author.	*Title.*	*Folio.*	*Octavo.*	*Catal. No.*
2 E. Gee	Texts examined conc. seven sacraments	vol. ii. 19-33	vol. viii. pp. 134-67	383, 384
3 P. Allix	Historical discourse conc. the minister's intention	34-53	168-213	313

Chap. II. *As to the pretended Sacrament of Extreme Unction.*

4 Dr. Clagett	Discourse conc. the pretended sacrament &c.	54-101	214-319	312

Chap. III. *As to Communion in One Kind.*

5 W. Payne	Discourse of communion in one kind	102-51	320-404 and vol. ix. pp. 35	276

Chap. IV. *As to Transubstantiation.*

6 Dr. Clagett	Paraphrase upon the sixth chapter of St. John	125-75	36-88	312
7 Dr. Patrick	Full view of the doctrines &c. of the ancient church	176-252	89-298	286
8 Dr. Stillingfleet	Doctrine of the Trinity and transubstantiation compared	253-82	299-366	
9 Dr. Williams	Texts examined	283-90	367-85	387

Chap. V. *As to the Adoration of the Host.*

10 Dr. Wake	Discourse of the holy Eucharist &c.	291-338	vol. x. pp. 115	280
11 W. Payne	Discourse conc. adoration of the Host	339-57	116-60	301

Tit. VIII. The Popish Methods for the Pardon of Sin groundless.

Chap. I. *Upon the Head of Auricular Confession.*

1 Dr. Goodman	Discourse conc. auricular confession	3rd pt. pp. 21	161-201	270
2 T. Linford	Texts examined &c.	22-32	202-24	388

Chap. II. *Upon the Head of Penances.*

3 P. Allix	Discourse concerning penance	33-50	225-63	271

Chap. III. *Upon the Head of Satisfaction.*

4 Dr. Gascarth	Texts examined	51-78	264-324	389, 390

Chap. IV. *Upon the Head of Indulgences.*

5 Dr. Stillingfleet	Treatise against indulgences	79-90	325-49	pp. 343, 421

Chap. V. *Upon the Head of Merit of Good Works.*

6 P. Allix	Discourse conc. merit of good works	91-101	350-71	352
7 T. Linford	Texts examined &c.	102-12	372-94	398

Chap. VI. *Upon the Head of Purgatory.*

Author.	*Title.*	*Folio.*	*Octavo.*	*Catal. No.*
8 Dr. Wake	Discourse of purgatory	vol. ii. pp. 113-46	vol. xi. pp. 35	315

Chap. VII. *Upon the Head of Prayer for the Dead.*

Author.	*Title.*	*Folio.*	*Octavo.*	*Catal. No.*
9 Dr. Wake	Discourse of prayers for the dead......	147-56	36-81	315

An Appendix containing (four) General Discourses against Popery.

Author.	*Title.*	*Folio.*	*Octavo.*	*Catal. No.*
1 Dr. Sherlock	Preservative against Popery............	pp. 63	104-246	119, 122
2 Dr. Sherlock	Summary of the principal controversies	64-102	247-338	246
3 Dr. Stillingfleet......	Council of Trent examined &c..........	103-33	339-414	97
4 Dr. Lloyd	Confutation of the chief doctrines of Popery....................................	134-51	vol. xii. pp. 46	

Tit. IX. The Doctrines in Dispute between the Church of England and the Church of Rome, truly represented.

Author.	*Title.*	*Folio.*	*Octavo.*	*Catal. No.*
1 Dr. Wake	Exposition of the doctrine of the Ch. of England....................................	vol. iii. pp. 48	47-143	74
2 Dr. Wake	Defence of the foregoing	49-111	144-279	78
3 Dr. Wake	Second defence of the exposition	112-240	280-413 and vol. xiii. pp. 14	80
4 Dr. Williams.........	Difference between the Ch. of England and the Ch. of Rome..................	241-64	15-207	159
5 Dr. Stillingfleet......	Doctrines and practises of Ch. of Rome	265-318	208-322	52
6 Dr. Clagett	View of whole controv. betw. the repres.	319-31	323-50	61
7 Dr. Clagett	Answer to the representer's last reply	332-97	350-406 and vol. xiv. pp. 93	82
8 Dr. Sherlock	Vindication of Protestant principles .	398-437	94-182	158
9 Dr. Clagett	Difference of the case &c.	438-60	183-233	7

Tit. X. Examination of the Doctrines contained in the New Creed of Pope Pius IV.

Author.	*Title.*	*Folio.*	*Octavo.*	*Catal. No.*
1 M. Altham	Creed of pope Pius IV..................	2nd pt. pp. 6	234-421	210
2 S. Gardiner	Examination of the present Roman Catholic faith............................	7-59	242-368	212

Tit. XI. The Authority of General Councils examined, and Roman Forgeries therein detected.

Author.	*Title.*	*Folio.*	*Octavo.*	*Catal. No.*
1 R. Jenkin	Histor. examination of the authority &c.	3rd pt. pp. 40	vol. xv. pp. 88	207
2 Dr. Comber	Roman forgeries in the councils &c....	41-106	89-243	p. 233

Tit. XII. The Virgin Mary truly represented against the Inventions and Misrepresentations of Papists.

Author.	*Title.*	*Folio.*	*Octavo.*	*Catal. No.*
1 Dr. Fleetwood	Account of the life and death of B.V.	4th pt. pp. 24	244-91	330
2 Dr. Patrick [Jno. P.]	The Virgin Mary misrepresented......	25-92	292-389 and vol. xvi. pp. 56	332

Tit. XIII. Arts and Practices of Missionaries and Papists discovered and laid open.

Author.	Title.	Folio.	Octavo.	Catal. No.
1 Anonymous	The missionaries arts discovered	vol. iii. pp. 54	vol. xvi. pp. 57-175	107
2 Dr. Tenison	Incurable scepticism of the Ch. of Rome	55-125	176-342	111
3 N. Clagett	Persuasive to an ingenuous tryal	126-44	343-83	6
4 W. Watson	Brief histor. account of the Jesuits &c.	145-65	vol. xvii. pp. 47	p. 55
5 By direction of Lord Burleigh	Execution of justice in England	166-78	48-78	p. 45

Appendix: General Discourses against Popery.

Author.	Title.	Folio.	Octavo.	Catal. No.
1 J. Rawlett	A dialogue between two Protestants..	pp. 85	79-267	431
2 Anonymous	The Protestant's companion...........	86-103	268-306	p. 326
3 J. Hall	The old religion		307-94	p. 471

SUPPLEMENT to Gibson's Preservative from Popery; being important Treatises on the Romish Controversy. 8 vols. 8vo Lond. 1849. *To each work have been subjoined Indexes of Subjects and generally of Authors.*

Vol. I. Barrow Isaac, D.D. A treatise of the Pope's Supremacy. Edited by the Rev. J. Cumming, D.D See Catalogue, p. 28.

Vol. II. Birckbek, The Rev. Simon. The Protestants Evidence, being the Succession of Protestant Doctrine in all ages. Edited [from the edition of 1657] by the Rev. John Cumming, DD.

Vol. III. The same continued.

Vol. IV. Lynde, Sir Humphrey. Via Tuta, the Safe Way: Via Devia, the Bye-Way. Edited by the Rev. R. P. Blakeney, M.A.

Vol. V. —— and Featley, D. A Case for the Spectacles; or a Defence of Via Tuta, in answer to a book by J. R., called a Pair of Spectacles; together with a Treatise entitled, Stricturæ in Lyndomastigem, by way of Supplement to the Knight's Answer, by Daniel Featley, D.D. Edited by the Rev. R. P. Blakeney, M.A.

Vol. VI. Edwards, the Rev. John, D.D. The Doctrines Controverted between Papists and Protestants, particularly and distinctly considered; with an Introduction, giving an account of the Rise and gradual Progress of Popery. Edited by the Rev. J. Cumming, D.D.

Vol. VII. Foye, The Rev. M. W. Romish rites, offices, and legends; or authorised superstitions and idolatries of the Church of Rome, containing the greater portion of the Roman Pontifical; the Ordinary of the Mass; the principal festivals and offices of the Virgin Mary; the ceremonies at most of the season masses; the offices at the Roman Anglican Ritual; copious selections from the services, hymns and legends of the Roman Breviary and the legends of the last saints canonized; the office of electing and crowning a Pope; and the beatification and canonization of saints. Literally translated and compiled from the authorized editions, with the Latin text, for the most part in opposite columns, and with copious notes. Edited by the late Rev. R. P. Blakeney.

Vol. VIII. Serces, The Rev. James. Popery an enemy to Scripture; or an account of the several methods pursued by the Church of Rome to sink the authority of the Holy Scriptures, and of the various falsifications introduced in some versions of the New Testament.

—— Mussard, P. Roma antiqua et recens; or the conformity of ancient and modern ceremonies, shewing from indisputable testimonies that the ceremonies of the Church of Rome are borrowed from the Pagans. Translated from the French by James Du Pré.

—— Barrow, Isaac, D.D. A Discourse concerning the Unity of the Church.

The British Society for promoting the Religious Principles of the Reformation have also republished in the same form and as a further Supplement to Gibson:

Willet, Andrew. Synopsis Papismi, that is, a General View of the Papistrie. Edited by the Rev. John Cumming.
10 vols. 8vo, 1852

They have also published:

The Sketch of the Roman Controversy. Part the first, containing the persecuting principles of the Church of Rome and the corruptions of the Nicene Church in the fourth century, and of the Church of Rome from the fourth century until the middle of the sixteenth century. Part the second, containing extracts from the Fathers, extracts from the Roman Breviary, the Council of Trent, &c., explanatory of Romish Doctrines, &c. By G. Finch.
2 vols. 8vo, 1850

The Editor of the second edition of the *Preservative* observes, in the Advertisement to Vol. II.:

"The Editor is aware that a second edition of the first treatise in this volume, viz. Dr. Hickes' able Vindication of the Church of England, was published in 1706, with many alterations and additions, a fact which Bishop Gibson must have overlooked. The Editor has not adopted the second edition with its alterations and additions, being bound as he conceives to publish the 'Preservative' as the Compiler left it. The second edition too is much more bulky, and it would puzzle the most ingenious Editor to correct the numerous errata in it."

Whether Dr. Cumming's determination to adhere to Hickes's first edition was a judicious one will admit of a question.

It should also be noticed that in the second edition the Preface to the third volume, folio, is omitted; and that *Pagano-Papismus*, by Joshua Stopford, rector of All Saints, York, 1675, 8vo, originally announced as intended to be included in the Supplement, has not been inserted. See also Dr. Todd's remark, p. 133, as to Gibson's reprint in the *Preservative* of Stillingfleet's *Council of Trent examined.*

It is to be regretted that Clagett's *Present State of the Controversy*, 4to Lond. 1687, Wake's *Continuation*, 4to Lond. 1688, and Gee's *Catalogue of the Discourses published against Popery*, 4to Lond. 1689, referred to in the note to Peck's Preface, were not added to the republication of Gibson's *Preservative*, to which they would have formed so appropriate an Introduction.

INDEX TO TITLES.

The articles a, an, the, *when commencing a title, are omitted.*

ADDENDA ET CORRIGENDA.

PREFACE, Part I. p. v. — The Editor made the statement that the MS. annotations in the copy which was in the possession of the late Rev. J. T. Allen, were in the handwriting of Bp. White Kennett, on the authority of that gentleman and Mr. William Ford, of Manchester, of whom he purchased it; but as that bishop died some years before the publication of the Catalogue, it is in all probability a mistake.

PAGE 2 — *Browne's Concio. For* 1628 *read* 1688. The order &c. is given also in Ducarel's Antiquities of Lambeth.

PAGE 3 — *No.* 3 contains pp. 26.

PAGE 4 — The Person of Honour to whom Du Moulin replied was the Earl of Castlemain, author of The Catholique Apology with a Reply to the Answer, together with a clear Refutation of the Seasonable Discourse, its reasonable Defence &c. [by Bp. Lloyd], and Dr. Du Moulin's Answer to Philanax; as also Dr. Stillingfleet's last Gun-powder Treason Sermon, his Attaque about the Treaty of Munster, and all matter of Fact charg'd on the English Catholiques by their Enemies. 1674, 12mo. Bp. Lloyd's *Defence* was an answer to A full answer and confutation of a scandalous pamphlet &c. 4to, 1673. There is another tract by Peter Du Moulin, Anti-Coton, or a Refutation of Coton's Letter Declaratory, lately directed to the Q. Regent of France, and apologizing for the Jesuits touching the doctrine of Killing Kings; 4to, 1689. An account of this Letter will be found in Foulis's History of Popish Treasons, p. 6. In Bayle's Dict. s.v. Prierias there is a quotation from the Anti-Coton, tracing the doctrine of equivocation to the Summa Sylvestrina, 2 voll. 4to, 1515, and folio, 1581, s.v. Accusatus. An account of the *Casuistical Summæ* is given in Whewell's Hist. of Moral Philosophy in England, p. xxx.

The Jesuits Loyalty. *Add*, [with a Preface by Bishop Stillingfleet]. J. H. T.

PAGE 5 — *The eighth title*, the author was Ch. Blount; see Biogr. Brit. *Add*, An Answer to the Appeal &c. by Sir Roger L'Estrange, 4to Lond. 1679; 4to Lond. 1681.

PAGE 13 — *No.* 12. Repr. in the English Catholic Library, vol. i. 8vo 1844. The name Huddlestone is said to be derived or corrupted from Athelstane.

PAGE 27 — Fisher's real name was John Perse or Piercy; see Dodd, vol. iii. p. 294, and De Bacquer, vol. i. p. 309.

PAGE 28 — "The places" &c. to follow at the end of the paragraph.

PAGE 31 — *No.* 30. By Thomas Long.

PAGE 34 — Fourth line. Overall's Convocation Book, 4to 1690. Written in opposition to Parsons' Conference. See Winwood's Mem. vol. i. p. 51; Gen. Dict. art. Hayward; and Cardwell's Synodalia, vol. i. p. 331.

PAGE 35 — In favour of the Divine Right of Kings may also be mentioned The Prerogative of Primogeniture; showing that the right of succession to our Hereditary Crown depends not upon Grace, Religion &c. but only upon Birth-right and Primogeniture. By David Jenner, 1685, 8vo. The Rebels' Catechism, *add*, by Peter Heylin. Sacrosancta &c. by John Maxwell, Bp. of Killala and Achonry, see p. 33 *supra*.

PAGE 43 — Second paragraph, third and fourth lines. *For* invention *read* intention; *for* truthes *read* frutes.

PAGE 45 — First paragraph, see Notes and Queries, 2nd Ser. vol. iv. p. 130 on Oliver Carter.

Fourth paragraph. Cf. Reliquiæ Hearnianæ, ii. by Bliss, p. 26.

PAGE 53 — Fifth line. *Declaration* &c. In the Catalogue of the Library of the late Very Rev. Canon Tierney, 1862, No. 314, is as follows: "Elizabeth (Queen), A Declaration of the Sentence and Deposition of Elizabeth the usurper and pretended Quene of Englande. Broadside, excessively rare. 1588. This scurrilous broadside excommunication issued with the name of Sixtus V. was intended to have been posted on the walls throughout England if the Armada had been successful. . . . . . On the failure of the expedition this broadside was so studiously suppressed and destroyed that its very existence has been doubted and denied." It was bought by Mr. Toovey for £31.

"The Pseudo-Martyr of the celebrated John Donne is a work containing passages of sound argument and research on an important subject, with flashes of sustained eloquence to be met with only in productions of the highest order." J[oseph] M[endham] in the twelfth volume of the British Magazine, p. 4. This may be considered an unanswerable confutation of Papal Supremacy.

PAGE 66 — *Answer to Vox Cleri, add*, by William Payne, D.D., who in the same year, 1690, published An Answer to a Printed Letter to Dr. W. P. concerning Non-Resistance, and other Reasons for not taking the Oathes &c, pp. 38. The Letter contains pp. 4.

PAGE 78 — *No.* 49. *For* Sir Robert *read* Sir Roger L'Estrange.

PAGE 82 — To the first title C. L. should have been prefixed.

PAGE 86 — To the first note *add*, The Papacy of Paul 4th, or the Restitution of Abby-Lands and Impropriations an indispensable condition of reconciliation to the Infallible See, 4to Lond. 1673.

PAGE 88 — *A Vindication* &c. *add*, by Thomas Cartwright, D.D., Bp. of Chester. And also, An Impartial Relation of the whole Proceedings against St. Mary Magdalen College. [By Dr. C. Aldworth]. 4to 1688. Cf. Dodd's Church History, vol. iii. p. 530 sqq. and Jones's Reign of K. James II., vol. ii. p. 105 sqq.

PAGE 99. — *The Dissenters Jubilee, add*, The Humble Address of the Presbyterians presented to the King, pp. 8, 4to 1687.

PAGE 101 — *Parliamentum Pacificum, add*, by John Northleigh, M.D. Burnet answered it; see the Catalogue of his Works at the end of the Oxford edition of his History of his own Time.

PAGE 102 — *No.* 51 contains pp. 120.

PAGE 104 — *No.* 53 *add*, by J. Gother.

PAGE 110 — *No.* 71. It is rather singular that Peck should have been mistaken as to the Author of this Tract, which in the advertisement prefixed to the Catalogue, and also in this place he attributes to Dr. William Clagett, but it was in fact written by the same writer as the Continuation, namely, Dr. William Wake. See advertisement at the end of Wake's Sermons, 1690, 8vo. James Crossley.

PAGES 112, 113 — I have been favoured with the following communication by Thompson Cooper Esq., Cambridge: The English translation of Bossuet, 12mo Brussels, 1672, has the initials W. M. on the title, but at the end of the preface the name of the translator, Walter Montagu (not the Abbé Montague) appears at length. He was of a noble family, and abbot successively of Nanteuil and Pontois. His death took place in 1670. I write from memory, as the work has been misplaced in the University Library There never was an Irish translation of Bossuet by Father Porter. But the second part of Molloy's Lucerna Fidelium, printed Romæ Typis Sacræ Congregationis de Propaganda Fide M.D.CLXXVI consists of a translation into Irish of the Exposition of the Doctrine of the Catholic Church. It commences at p. 181. T. C.

On the question whether Dryden translated "the Exposition" see Scott's Life, p. 339, and Reliquiæ Hearnianæ, vol. i. p. 53.

PAGE 119 — *Préservatif* &c. Jurieu's Pastoral Letters contain an account of the Hungarian Persecution. In the first volume of An Antidote against Popery, delivered in a Morning Lecture in Southwark, 1779, is added, A Picture of Popery, from the *Pastoral Letters* of the famous Mr. Peter Jurieu. Compare The Secret History of the Austrian Government and of its systematic Persecutions of Protestants, by Alfred Michiels, 1859, 8vo. In the same year, 1689, was published The History of the Persecutions of the Protestants by the French King in the Principality of Orange, from 1660 to 1687, by James Pineton de Chambrun, of which an extremely clever and interesting review appeared in the Journal des Débats of the 30th November, 1853. (See Notes and Queries, 1st Ser. viii. p. 639, ix. p. 67, and p. 471 sqq. of this Catalogue.) Also, Popish Treachery, or a short and new account of the horrid cruelties exercised on the Protestants in France, being a true prospect of what is to be expected from the most solemn promises of R. Catholic Princes. 4to.

Bayle's Commentaire &c., *add*, in the second volume of his Œuvres diverses. There is an English translation in two vols. 8vo Lond. 1708.

PAGE 129 — Peck's suggestion referred to in the first and second paragraph is not groundless, for *No.* 93 is the fourth Catholic Letter. In Dolman's Catalogue is advertised An Account of Dr. Stillingfleet's late Book against the Church of Rome, together with a short Postil upon his Text, 12mo 1672. (Supplementary List, No. xix.)

PAGE 133 — "The collected edition of Stillingfleet's Works is far from complete. It does not include the concluding portion of the Origines Sacræ, nor his Miscellaneous Discourses, which his son the Dean of Worcester edited long after his father's death. His MSS. notes on books in his Library should also be collected. Those on the Common Prayer I transcribed some years ago for the Rev. T. P. Pantin, who intended to publish them." (R. Travers.) See also Notes and Queries, 1st Ser. viii. p. 389.

PAGE 134—Second paragraph. The first two Parts of Chemnitii Exam. Concilii Tridentini were published in 1566.

Sergeant's Letter to the Continuator, which is probably that styled by Dodd, vol. iii. p. 477, the sixth Controversial Letter against D[r.] W[ake], contains pp. 16. To the second edition of the Continuation is appended a Postscript of pp. 3 in answer to the Letter, which in the copy before me is subjoined.

PAGE 138—*No.* 105. *For* date 1667 *read* 1687:

PAGE 139—Second paragraph. *For* Bird *read* Birch.

PAGE 141—*No.* 109. This is a mistake. The name Thomas Ward is printed at the end of the sheet. T. Fisher.

PAGE 145—First note. This name is printed on the title-page. T. F.

PAGE 149—Archbishop Parker, De Antiq. Brit. Eccl. 1572, in the Chetham Library; see Martin's Cat. of Privately Printed Books, who has inserted a collation I furnished of this copy in the second edition of that work. Cf. Ames's Typographical Antiquities by Dibdin, vol. iv. p. 126, and Bibliotheca Grenvilliana. The following is a MS. note in this copy of Parker, probably by Thyer.

"Parker is generally supposed to be the author of this book, though there have always been some who gave it to Josseline his chaplain. Bramhall is clear in his opinion that it is the Bishop's. See his Consecration of Protestant Bishops vindicated. Selden expressly says that Josseline was the author, and seems to take it for granted as a matter out of dispute. See his History of Tythes, chap. ix. Nicolson is of the same opinion as Selden; see his Historical Library. "L'Auteur de la premiere partie de cette Histoire qui contient les antiquitez est D. Arkworth, comme nous l'apprend le docte Ussérius dans son Traité de la Succession des Eglises Chrést. p. 34, de l'édit in folio. L'Auteur de la seconde partie qui comprend les vies des Archevesques c'est Jean Jousselin, secrétaire de Matthieu Parker. Voyez Colomesii Opera, Bibl. Choisie, p. 491, de l'édit. Fabricienne, Hamburg, 1709, 4to. Voyez aussi Selden dans son Uxor Hebraica, p. 374." (Placcii Theatrum Anon. et Pseudon. vol. i. p. 269.)

The Editor of Bramhall's Works, Oxf. 1844, gives authorities for both sides of the question, vol. iii. p. 12.

PAGE 168—To *Nos.* 148 and 150 𝕮. 𝕷. should have been prefixed.

PAGES 212, 213—Mr. Tierney thinks "Erastus Senior" was written by John Lewgar, but assigns it to Archbp. Talbot, on the authority of

William Talbot, Lady Shrewsbury's father; see his Sale Cat., in which also appears "Politician's Catechisme for his Instruction in Divine Faith and Morall Honesty, written by N. N." [Peter Talbot]. Sold for £6 10s.

PAGE 235 — *No.* 213. *For* St. Mark's *read* St. Peter's.

PAGE 237 — *No.* 216. Beaulieu on the Inquisition, cf. Milman's L. C. vol. iv. p. 379. Another work has been ascribed to this author iu Notes and Queries, 3rd Ser. vii. 37., "The Reformed Monastery," 1677. He also translated Cosin's Hist. of Transubstantiation, *ut supra*, p. 382.

PAGE 238 — *No.* 218. This is a very interesting volume, full of biographical and historical matter. I can only enumerate those converts here noticed who were themselves authors, or whose lives have been written by contemporaries: *Galeazzo Caracciolo*, see Watt, s.v. Crashaw, William. *John Valdes*, see Watt, Lowndes by Bohn, Biogr. Universelle. *Wolfgang, Prince of Anhalt*, one of the Princes of Germany, by whom the Centum Gravamina were presented to the Pope, see Brit. Mag. vol. xiv. p. 41 sqq. *Nicholas Radzevil*, see Watt. *Andrew Dudithius*, see Chalmers. *Constantine Pontius*, see Chalmers. *George Buchanan*, see Irving's Memoirs of G. B. *Jerome Zanchius*, see Melch. Adami Vitæ Germanor. Theolog. t. ii. pp. 148-152. *Petrus Paulus Vergerius*, see Adamus, pp. 116-120. *Peter Martyr Vermilius*, see Adamus, pp. 24-63, t. ii.; anecdotes of him in D'Israeli's Amenities of Literature. *Œcolampadius*, see Adamus, pp. 45-59. He is one of Cardinal Bellarmine's instances of the unhappy end of the Church's enemies. In the evening he went well to bed, and in the morning was found dead! *Sebastian Munster*, see Chalmers, Saxius, t. iii. p. 142. *Andrew Sall* see p. 176. "Formerly of the Order of Jesus and Professor of Divinity in the Colleges of Pamplona, Polència and Tudela in Spain, Rector and Professor of Controversies in the Irish College of the University of Salamanca . . . . . I omit his Sermon in justification of the change he had made, as being too prolix for this place. However it shews him to have read much, and to have seriously studied the point of his conversion." A Historical Relation &c. p. 24. Of the publications of James Salgado, a convert mentioned in Chap. XI., an account will be found in Notes and Queries, 1st Ser. vols. ii. and iii.

PAGE 253 — Thomas Goodwin is referred to in Salter's Hall Lectures.

PAGE 258 — Second paragraph, *equivocation*. A remarkable instance of the lawfulness of this principle maintained on both sides will be found in Notes and Queries, 3rd Ser. vol. i. p. 292. Cf. Brerely's Protestants' Apology for the Roman Church, p. 703, where reference is made to Osiander "reporting for a receyved principle with the Calvinistes hanc maximam seu regulam" &c. See authorities for the same objection against Lutherans and Calvinists in Wood's Antiq. Univ. Oxon. pp. 380-81, and Grey's Examin. of Neal, vol. ii. p. 169. This principle is discussed at large in Newman's Apologia pro Vita Sua.

PAGE 271 — Papal Supremacy. It ought to have been stated that the pamphlet from which this extract was taken (No. 4) "Considerations touching the true way to suppress Popery" was in part the composition of Peter Walsh as far as page 80, the remainder being written by Bp. Lloyd. James Crossley.

PAGE 316 — *No.* 253 is said to have been written by Robert Brown, a Scotchman; see Dodd's Certamen.

PAGE 318 — Kidder's *Reflections on the Bourdeaux Version.* See also Popery an Enemy to Scripture by James Serces (in the Supplement to Gibson, vol. viii.)

PAGE 320 — Mr. Dolman advertises, 1843, Bibles translated from the Latin Vulgate in 8vo at reasonable prices; and a new version of the Four Gospels, with Notes Critical and Explanatory by a Catholic, is advertised, which was designed "to refute the false and unfounded assertion that Catholics forbid or impede the reading of the Holy Scriptures." Cf. The Church of Rome: her present Moral Theology, Scriptural Instruction, and Canon Law; A Report on the Books and Documents on the Papacy, deposited in the University Library, Cambridge, the Bodl. Library, Oxford, and the Library of Trinity College, Dublin, 1853.

PAGE 335 — An analysis of the arguments of Helvidius and Jovinian, against whom St. Jerome wrote (*Wharton*, p. 95 sq.) will be found in Clinton's Epitome of Chronology of Rome and Constantinople, pp. 401-404. On celibacy see also pp. 459, 460, and his Fasti Rom. vol. ii. p. 524 n. w.

PAGE 337 — *No.* 270. *For* presented *read* prescribed.

PAGE 342 — *No.* 271. Doctrine of it, *add*, in the Church of Rome.

PAGE 344 — Egan published a Recantation Sermon, 4to 1673; and in Thorpe's Catalogue, 1836, is advertised a work by him, as follows: The Romanist Designs detected, and the Jesuits' subtil Practices discovered and laid open, collected by Anthony Egan. 4to 1674;

scarce, £1 1s. "Some interesting particulars of Peter Walsh's Formulary &c., and two Letters of Pope Urban VIII. for the encouragement of the Irish Rebellion; the first to O'Neale, and the second to the nobility and people of Ireland." In the Tierney Sale Catalogue is inserted — Wilson (R.) The Friar Disciplin'd; or Animadversions on Friar Peter Walsh, his new Remonstrant Religion (this Answer to the Loyal Formulary is very rare), Gant, 1674. It sold for £6 10s. Mr. Crossley has a copy.

PAGE 348 — The quotation from Burton commences in line 21, "was defended."

PAGE 351 — *No.* 277. Cf. Newman's *Essay on the Development of Christian Doctrine*, p. 161 sqq.

PAGE 459 — *No.* 420. C. L. should have been prefixed.

PAGE 465 — *No.* 443 n. The title is as follows: A Discovery of the groundlessness and insincerity of my Lord of Down's Dissuasive, being the fourth Appendix to Sure Footing, with a Letter to Dr. Casaubon, and another to his Answerer. By J[ohn] S[ergeant], 8vo, 1665.

PAGE 487 — Clarendon, p. 263. Claude, pp. 123, n. 385, in the Chetham Library. *For* Case *read* Care. His tergiversation has already been noticed (p. 76); see also A Collection of the Newest and most Ingenious Poems &c. against Popery, 1689. His translation of Cornelius Agrippa's Female Preeminence was accompanied by a fulsome dedication to Q. Catherine.

PAGE 488 — Derby, Charles, *eighth* Earl. In p. 4 should have been mentioned also, Religion of the Church of England, the surest establishment of the Royal Throne &c, 4to 1673.

PAGE 498 — Tit. iii. ch. iv. Tillotson's Sermon on 1 Cor. iii. 15 is S. xi. in Works, fol. 1696.

PAGE 501 — Appendix 4 to vol. ii. Dr. Lloyd's Confutation &c., 1679, pp. 72, 4to, in the Chetham Library.

CPSIA information can be obtained
at www.ICGtesting.com
Printed in the USA
LVHW112141080422
715402LV00007B/55

9 783752 589450